Not Just Another
WAR STORY
A True To Life Account of WWII

Wayne G MacDowell

DOCUMEANT PUBLISHING

NOT JUST ANOTHER WAR STORY
Wayne G. MacDowell

Published by
DocUmeant Publishing
244 5th Avenue, Suite G-200
NY, NY 10001

646-233-4366

Library of Congress Control Number: 2014944038

MacDowell, Wayne G.
Not Just Another War Story / by Wayne G. MacDowell. -- 1st ed.
p. cm.

1. World War, 1939-1945--Fiction. 2. Air pilots, Military--Historical Fiction.
3. Bildungsromans.
4. War stories. I. Title.

Copy edits by Philip S Marks

Cover design and Layout by Ginger Marks, DocUmeant Designs

Printed in the United States of America.
ISBN13: 978-1-937801-46-5 (pbk.)
ISBN10: 1-937801-46-2

Other books by this author:
Not Just Another Love Story, CasAnada Publishing ©1999

To First Lieutenant Wright Ellis Gerke,
World War II B-17 bomber pilot with the 366th Squadron,
305th Bombardment Group (H), Eighth Air Force

Very best Wishes,
Wayne WooDruckll

CHAPTER ONE

Steve Carmichael woke up much later than usual on this beautiful, high-sky spring morning. It was well past 11:00 a.m. as Steve rolled out of bed in his dormitory room in Sledd Hall. He and some fellow teammates had been out quite late the night before, celebrating the University of Florida's victory in the final game of their 1942 baseball season. While the team had a successful season, winning 27 of their 32 games, this particular victory was extra sweet because they overcame a four-run deficit in the bottom of the ninth inning to defeat their arch rival, the University of Georgia. Steve was the catcher on the team and co-captain of the squad. He contributed a key double down the left field line during the dramatic ninth inning rally, driving in two runs to help cap the victory.

Graduation was now only a little more than a week away. Many of Steve's fellow teammates had already committed to enlisting in one of the branches of the service.

After the surprise attack and defeat at Pearl Harbor in Honolulu, Hawaii, the United States of America was now fighting desperately to bounce back. There had been an initial setback with the fighting in the Pacific and North Africa. World War II was underway in earnest.

Steve had not signed up yet. He wanted to have a final discussion with his dad before making this all-important decision. Like most of the graduates, Steve had options open to him, professional baseball being one. He had been heavily scouted by the Detroit Tigers of the American League. Although no contract had been offered yet, Tigers scouts told him that one would be coming and that Steve would start playing with the Tigers AAA team, the Buffalo Bisons of the International League. Ranching was another option. Steve and his father, Ray, owned a good-sized cattle ranch in Central Florida, just outside of the town of Kissimmee. His dad had

1

planned that at some point Steve would carry on the family business. Working with his dad on the ranch could qualify him for an exemption from the service, at least for the present. Steve, though, had plans of his own and the discussion with his dad was key before a final decision.

The days before graduation presented many party nights and to say that the almost graduates were well spent by graduation day was no exaggeration. Nevertheless, they did show up in caps and gowns for the big day! It was fun filled, but things would never be the same. There was a war going on and many of them would be off to fight, some never to come home again. The goodbyes on this final day at the University of Florida were extremely difficult. The young men, who had given a solid handshake, now hugged. There were few dry eyes. The next stage of their young lives had begun, but not as they had expected four years earlier when they first arrived at the Gainesville campus. It would now become a time when changes occurred almost on a daily basis.

Both Steve's and his father's pickup trucks were needed to haul his belongings back to the Stardust Ranch. Ray Carmichael could not believe the things that Steve had accumulated during the past four years at the university.

"Let's just drive straight to the dump!" kidded his father.

"There's good stuff here, Dad."

"Well, I guess it's okay to sort through it first, then to the dump," returned Ray, with a wide grin on his face.

Steve was the first in his family to graduate from high school, let alone college. He had been one of the most successful athletes from the area and the folks of Kissimmee had followed his sports career through both high school and college.

Ray Carmichael was very proud of his son. Ray was a man of pioneer stock. His own father had come to Central Florida in 1869 as a 19-year-old, looking for his fortune. He found enough work to enable him to purchase some good government land and start a small cattle ranch. The first customer for beef on the hoof was the U.S. Army. He did well enough to buy more land and expand the ranch.

Ray was born on the ranch in 1878. He grew up in the rugged life of a Florida cowboy and learned cattle ranching inside out.

Ray was just past 40 years old when he married a beautiful showgirl who had come to town as a cast member in a play. Life on a ranch was really too much for her. In 1921, a year after Steve was born, she left her family to continue a life in show business. She wrote for a while, telling of the wonderful places she had been and then the letters came less and less often and finally stopped. Ray obtained a divorce. He had heard that she had married again, but by now he just did not care; he had Steve. The closeness was more than a father–son relationship. They were also best friends.

Ray had planned a huge party at the ranch with what seemed to be half of Kissimmee in attendance to celebrate Steve's graduation. The party not only came off well, but with everyone enjoying themselves so much, it lasted well into the night. The warm hospitality Ray always offered to visitors showed on this important night. It would also be the last party for some time because many were off to war.

As the last of the guests left, Steve came over to his dad with a cold beer. The long-neck bottle was still dripping from the ice-filled tub. Steve wiped his wet hands on his pants.

"Let's take the Stinson up for a flight tomorrow," said Steve as he handed the bottle of beer to his dad.

"Early," came the reply. "About eight," continued Ray as he lifted the bottle in salute to Steve.

"I'll be ready," answered Steve.

The Stinson referred to the old bi-wing mail plane that Ray had purchased at a government auction years before. It was a veteran of the old mail routes throughout the South and was in terrible disrepair when Ray bought it for less than a hundred dollars.

"What the hell do you want with an airplane?" someone had asked him.

"I don't know. Maybe I'll fix it up and get someone to teach Stevie and me to fly the damned thing," had been his reply.

Steve had been just 12 years old when he first soloed. Flying was a wonderful part of his life and he had become quite a skilled pilot.

It was after breakfast, the needed chores completed, when the sound of an airplane engine coming to life broke the silence of an otherwise quiet beginning of a beautiful day. Steve was at the controls and his dad sat relaxed, "playing passenger," as he liked to say. They taxied to the end of the makeshift runway and lifted off into the bright Florida sky.

They first flew northeast over the city of Orlando, then took a southwest heading toward Lakeland, Plant City, and Tampa, before landing in St. Petersburg to gas up and return to the ranch. Neither Steve nor his dad said anything during the flight. The noise of the loud engine along with the plane's open cockpit kept them from talking. They would each point out a part of the landscape or a building as they flew over it. The simple enjoyment of each other's company seemed to be enough.

After they landed and taxied to the tie-down area, Steve opened the conversation.

"Dad, we need to talk about what's going on with the war."

"What branch of the service do you plan to join? The Air Corps?"

Steve looked at his dad with amazement. They climbed down from the plane, tied it down and walked over to the nearby equipment chest. Ray sat on the chest while Steve picked up some weeds, tossed them into the air, as if checking the wind direction. He looked back at his father.

"You knew that I planned to join?" he questioned.

"I know you," answered Ray as he got off the chest and gave his son a hug.

"I was thinking of the Army Air Corps," started Steve, pausing for a moment. "You know that at six foot one and 185 pounds, I'm probably too big for the pursuit planes, so I figured bombers, hopefully the B-17. She's the queen of the fleet."

"Well," Ray began, taking a long time before he continued, "I don't like the idea of you going off to war, but I do understand." As they walked back toward the ranch house, he asked, "What about Elly?"

"She has another year at the university," answered Steve as he held the screen door for his dad. "She was my girl in high school and college. It's not the same as it was. I caught her out with some guy from the football team. I just can't go off thinking she'd be there for me, because she won't and I believe that to be a fact, Dad."

"I'm sorry, son. I thought you and she would be . . . "

"I thought so too," interrupted Steve, who thought for a moment, then continued, "I just don't think that I could trust her and if I was overseas, well, I don't need that kind of worry on my mind."

"I'm going to brew a pot of coffee . . . want some?" asked Ray as he put his hand on Steve's shoulder.

Ray did not say any more about Elly; he understood completely.

"I'll get the cream. I'm hungry too. Looks like Lillian baked us a coffee cake. She must have known," said Steve as he placed the cream pitcher on the table and pinched off a piece of the coffee cake.

"Use a dish," scolded Lillian as she came into the kitchen. "Both of you sit down, I'll serve you. You'll just get crumbs all over my kitchen," she continued, half mumbling to herself.

Ray and Steve sat down at the kitchen table. They were handed cups and saucers as well as napkins. Lillian cut man-sized slices of coffee cake, placed them on dishes and gave the piece with the chunk out of it to Steve.

"You about to retire, Lillian? Go off and live the rest of your life having fun in the sun and give us some peace and quiet?" kidded Ray with a wide smile. He took a sip of coffee and a bite of cake.

"I'm only 77 years old and I'll live long enough to bury you, old man," was Lillian's reply. "My retirement is right here on this excuse for a ranch and besides, I helped raise that boy. Not to mention you'd consider other people's cooking as poison after all the meals I've given you over the years. Now, if you figure I've got a pension coming to me after 21 years, then put it into my paycheck and I'll thank you for it!"

"Like I've always said, Lillian, we love you, darlin'. You stay here as long as you want," answered Ray to his longtime housekeeper.

"I've got things to do. You put the dishes in the sink when you're through and, by the way, when my time does come, plant me under a good shady tree," stated Lillian as she left the kitchen.

Steve took his last bite of cake and thought of getting another piece but saw that Lillian had put it away, so he just poured a refill of coffee for Ray and himself.

"I was thinking about the 15th of June, over in Orlando . . . like to come along?"

"That's only 10 days away, but yes, I'll drive there with you. Do you leave the same day?" questioned Ray.

"No, from what the guys told me, I'll have another 10 days or so to clear away things before I leave for basic training."

"For sure you'll fly. Hell you've been doing it since you were twelve, even younger," said Ray who took another sip of coffee, thought for a moment and continued, "I sure don't like this war stuff. Big planes like the B-17 make big targets."

"It's not time to worry yet, Dad. It will take close to a year before they would send me overseas and I might not go to Europe at all. I could wind up in a B-24 with longer range than a 17 and be sent to the Pacific," answered Steve.

"I'd prefer you stay at home." After a short pause and sigh, Ray said, "But I know what you've got to do and I respect it. We can talk when we know more."

Steve nodded, patted his dad on the shoulder as they got up from the table and left the kitchen. Ray had some things to do around the ranch and Steve had to finish unloading the pickup trucks.

The next 10 days were spent, for the most part, working on the ranch. Steve also caught up with friends from his high school days as well as area friends from college. Like Steve, many were about to enlist in the service or were waiting for the draft call. Some had already left to serve their country. One boy from the area who was a couple of grades ahead of Steve in high school had been killed during the attack on Pearl Harbor. It had brought the war right to the doorstep of the little cattle town of Kissimmee. The military burial at the cemetery after they brought the body home showed the locals just how far the war had reached.

On a quick trip to Orlando, a few days before he was to enlist, Steve ran into Elly at the post office. It was the first time they had seen each other in more than a month. The chance meeting was a bit awkward.

"I had heard that you were going to enlist," started Elly, attempting to break the ice.

"In a couple of days. The Air Corps," Steve replied.

"Were you going to call me?" questioned Elly with a half-smile.

"As a matter of fact, no, I wasn't."

"We've been together a long time. I had hoped that we'd have the summer to patch things up."

"No, I don't think so . . . the summer with me, and then back to college in the fall with your new friend, anyway, I'll be in the service."

"You are . . . angry with me," said Elly, who then took a deep breath.

"Angry, no, mostly hurt. We were together for a long time and I just thought that we meant more to each other than you running off with someone else. Maybe we were together too much, too long," explained Steve.

"It was only a couple of dates. I was attracted to him and he asked me out." She continued after a short pause, "I want to be with you for the long term, like we had planned."

Steve didn't say anything for what seemed to be longer than it actually was, then he half stated, half asked, "Did you and he—"

"Make love? I won't lie . . . yes, but just once. I wasn't a virgin. You made sure of that years ago . . . with my help, of course," answered Elly. "Look, let's get together for old time's sake."

"Look, Elly, you've changed the way I feel about you, think about you. Sorry to say, but things can't be the same with us. I guess that I'm a bit old fashioned, but after I found out I was crushed. I knew from the guys what was going on and that you'd been with someone else. Your new boyfriend brags."

"This sounds so final, Steve. How about if I just write to you . . . letters from home, so to speak?"

"I'm starting a new part of my life. I don't think that letters from you would do anything for me, except make me wonder about . . . " and he let it drift. Steve thought for a moment and continued, "I mean, let's just let it all go and just remember the good times we had together. I'm glad we met today. It sort of clears the air, lets us be free of the situation."

"Well, I really didn't want to be free, but I've got no choice," answered Elly.

"You did have a choice, Elly, and you made it," replied Steve, as he left the post office where he and Elly had spent the last few minutes talking. He walked to his truck, opened the door, slammed it in anger and stared through the windshield for a few minutes before driving back to the ranch.

During the drive, Steve could not help but reminisce. The miles back to the ranch gave him thinking time. He forced himself to remember all of the good times: the dates, dances, football, baseball, and basketball games he had played in during high school, with Elly being one of the cheerleaders. Steve remembered how proud he was when she joined him at the University of Florida. But then how dreams and plans could be crushed in such a short period! Steve just shook his head. *Things will be better.* He would certainly have to concentrate if he wanted to become an Air Corps pilot. It was the best thing for now.

Just as he was pulling into the ranch yard, Ray came out of the house to greet him, "How'd you make out?" Looking at Steve, he continued, "Son, you have a problem, I can see it in your eyes. You've shed a tear."

Steve half-smiled as they walked up onto the porch and into the house, with Ray holding the screen door for his troubled son.

"I met up with Elly," said Steve and he proceeded to tell his dad about the conversation and the results, asking if he had done the right thing.

"For now you have," said Ray, who paused for a minute. "Time has a way of healing, forgiving. It's best to let it rest for a while. You never know how things will turn out."

Steve did not answer, there was nothing more to say. In his mind, at this point, he had closed the door on Elly. It hurt, well, it just plain hurt.

During the next two days, Steve said goodbyes to friends who lived on outlying ranches by way of flying the Stinson. He would drop in, as he had done so many times before, with a low slow flight over the ranch house, then landing in a field, or sometimes, landing on the lane that leads to the house from the highway. This was a bit trickier, but it always brought great satisfaction to Steve to kid about driving up to the house "in his airplane."

Finally, the big day arrived. Steve and his dad drove into Orlando, parking across the street from the post office. Enlistment posters caught their eye as they crossed the street and walked into the post office. The most vocal, through its printed message stated "I Want You!" with a picture of Uncle Sam pointing directly at you. Ray walked over to greet the postmaster while Steve climbed the stairs to the second floor where the enlistment offices were located. After a brief hello, Ray joined Steve.

"The Air Corps office is over here," stated Steve, as he pointed to an office that had a sign over the office reading *U.S. Army.*

"That's for the Army," said Ray, as he looked down the hallway for another sign that might read *Air Corps.*

"The Air Corps is the Army Air Corps, Dad. It's a branch of the Army," returned Steve. "I'm a bit nervous about this."

"Me too," replied Ray. "Me too!"

Inside the office, a man in an Army uniform got up from his desk and came around to greet Steve and his dad. "I'm Staff Sergeant McConnell. Which one of you gentlemen is interested in enlisting?" he said as he shook hands, first with Ray, then Steve.

"He is," both Steve and Ray said almost simultaneously.

They had a good laugh. "I hope things are not so bad that they need a 64-year-old man flying those machines!" joked Ray.

Steve presented his diploma from the University of Florida and spoke about his flying background and his desire to fly the B-17 bomber as a pilot.

Sergeant McConnell was quite familiar with Steve through his sports activity, even before Steve had phoned to make an appointment for his Air Corps enlistment. They went through all of the formalities. Steve had a copy of the most recent physical that Dr. Hughes had given him. Dr. Hughes liked to say to Steve since he delivered Steve he was the first to smack him on the behind! Steve wanted the physical to make certain there would be nothing that would keep him from flying in the Air Corps.

Steve then completed all of the forms that Sergeant McConnell placed before him in order to become part of Uncle Sam's forces. Steve was told to report in nine days for induction. He would undergo eight weeks of basic training, then after a short leave, he would be off to flight school. If all worked out and he did not wash out of pilot training, Steve would then have the opportunity to go on to multi-engine planes and finally to four-engine school where he would fly either the B-17 or B-24 bomber. He would also become an officer with the rank of second lieutenant, having earned his pilot's wings.

Nine days can go rapidly when that is all you have. They also go slowly when you want them to go fast. For Ray, the days seemed to almost flash by, but to Steve, the nine days passed at a snail's pace. Steve, of course, was anxious to get going, but helping his dad was also important. It was a case of duty verses duty—the ranch versus the military.

Fort Dix, in Wrightstown, New Jersey, was where the basic training would take place. It was the major army training facility in the eastern part of the country and became a topic of conversation with Ray and Steve.

"I am not very happy that they would be sending a Florida boy all the way to the New York City area," stated Ray.

"The Army will have first call and if I did get some kind of a pass, New York City also has Yankee Stadium and major league baseball."

"Well, all right, just stay away from that Times Square area," stated Ray.

"Look, Dad," kidded Steve. "Now that you've pointed it out, I'll just have to see Times Square! Hell, I can take care of myself. I'm 22 and besides, I'll have other soldiers with me."

That stopped Ray cold. He looked at Steve and said, "You're right, I sometimes forget that you're full grown."

Steve had also informed the Detroit Tigers of his plans and hoped they would still be interested in him when he returned home from the service. He received a telephone call from Mr. Briggs himself, owner of the Tigers, wishing him the best and telling him that the Tigers would keep in touch with his dad. They had every desire for Steve to become a Tiger.

Ray carried the small suitcase down the stairs to the front door for Steve. Outside waiting for Steve were the seven ranch employees, including Lillian, who had prepared a bag of food that looked more like a bag of groceries for his long trip. Steve shook hands with each, but when it became Lillian's turn, a hug, kiss and tears from both marked their goodbye.

Ray drove Steve to the designated meeting point, the Orlando train station. As they arrived and parked the pickup truck, they could see that more than 20 other young men were already there. Steve knew a few, just a few. Staff Sergeant McConnell was there with an envelope of papers for each individual. Another sergeant would make the trip north with them. Steve's group of recruits was assigned to rail-car coach number 1043. The train would make stops in Jacksonville, Savannah, Raleigh, Richmond, Washington, D.C., and Baltimore before the final destination of Philadelphia, 30th Street Station. It would be from there that a bus would transport the newly sworn-in soldiers to Fort Dix.

Ray shook hands with his son but also wiped away a tear as Steve boarded the train. The train inched its way out of the Orlando station, bound for cities along the route, picking up more young soldiers and likewise sailors who would leave the train in Baltimore for the Bainbridge Naval Base.

With the stops in route, it took almost two days for the trip. A highlight for Steve was when the train passed through Washington. He could not only see the important government buildings, but also Griffith Stadium, home of the Washington Senators baseball team. Steve and his dad had come to Washington for a baseball tournament in which the University of Florida had participated. It took place in Griffith Stadium with the highlight for Steve being a high long fly ball that carried into the grandstands for a home run. It was quite a thrill, one to be remembered, to get a home run in a major league ballpark. He and his dad had stayed over for a couple of extra days at the Mayflower Hotel to enjoy the nation's capital. But that was last year——the summer of 1941. Things had changed quite a bit since that fun-filled time.

Steve had fallen asleep; however, he was awakened by the slowing of the train as it made its way through the train yards and approached Philadelphia's 30th Street Station. He had great views of the Schuylkill River, the boathouses and a large museum that sat atop a hill. Someone pointed out to him that the large building was the Philadelphia Art Museum. The skyline of Philadelphia was visible for just a short time before the train entered the station.

The recruits walked through the main part of the 30th Street Station, noting that with its high ceilings and décor it was everything a train station should be. It even smelled like a train station. Outside they boarded buses. Steve's was a dark royal blue with gold lettering that read Wood Bus Lines. In small print, it showed the city of ownership to be Woodbury, New Jersey. Other buses had the name of Public Service printed on the side. Steve sunk into a comfortable seat for the journey to Fort Dix, about 70 miles away. They passed through Philadelphia and crossed into

New Jersey on the Delaware River Bridge, stopping only for a pause at the tollbooth on the Camden side of the Delaware River. The journey finally came to rest at the main gate of Fort Dix in Wrightstown.

Basic training had begun! The issuing of uniforms made it official. Things were a bit confusing for the first few days, but then they settled into the training routine. This becoming a soldier was hard work. Lucky for Steve, he was in much better shape than most of the men. The physical part was somewhat fun for him, although he dare not say that. Playing baseball at the university and working on the ranch had kept him in excellent physical condition.

Steve wrote to his dad, telling him of the trip north and of the past grueling weeks of basic training. He told him that they woke up very early and he was counting the days until he could catch up on some sleep at home. He did not think that there would be time for him to take a trip to New York City. As soon as he got leave from basic, he was heading home!

Steve spent some of his free time over at the Fort Dix companion military establishment, the Army Air Base. He was able to talk airplanes with the ground crews and the men who flew the planes. This would work out well for Steve because when basic training ended, he was offered a flight down to MacDill Air Base in Tampa, Florida. They had training missions going there and he was just another piece of cargo.

Steve met his dad at the main gate at MacDill. They did not stop to shake hands. A big bear hug was in order.

"Let me look at you," said Ray. After a long look at his son he continued, "You look simply great in that uniform. Have they made you a general yet?"

"Not quite," answered Steve, a big smile spread across his face. "In fact, I pretty much have to salute everyone now. Even the sheriff and the postman for all I know."

Ray motioned he would carry Steve's bag, but Steve said no and carried it to the pickup truck. It was more than an hour back to Kissimmee and the ranch, but it seemed like a short trip with their nonstop conversation. Ray asked about the training and Steve gave a blow-by-blow description of the different things that happened, some quite funny and some not so humorous. He was glad that basic was behind him. He had a ten day leave after which he was to report to Maxwell Field in Alabama for preflight. He was full of excitement, but now there were ten days to relax and to sleep in a real bed.

Lillian, of course, had prepared a wonderful homecoming dinner and Steve's favorite dessert of hot apple pie with loads of vanilla ice cream melting on top. There was constant talking up to around nine o'clock, when Steve stated that he had hit the wall and needed to get some sleep. As Steve was about to drop into the bed, he remembered that his dad had mentioned something about taking the plane up; something about gassing the old girl up and doing some flying, maybe tomorrow afternoon!

Steve came downstairs for breakfast dressed in his old comfortable civilian clothes. Lillian had prepared a huge breakfast of eggs, over easy, country ham with red-eye gravy, grits and fresh biscuits, plus a homemade coffee cake that both he and Ray enjoyed so much. Lillian did warn Ray not to expect the same service after

Steve went back into the service, but she was just kidding. She hummed a tune while cleaning the pots. Lillian was happy that Steve was back, if only for a short while.

Ray mentioned to Steve that he did an overhaul on the Stinson's engine and she was running just like new. Taking the plane up for a flight over the familiar country-side was something Steve had thought about the entire time he was going through basic training. The old bi-wing plane roared to life with the sound of a solid engine. She never sounded so good, or was it that he was so anxious to fly that he thought the plane sounded better than ever? No matter, it was probably a combination of both.

Steve taxied to the end of their makeshift runway and turned the plane into the wind, pushed the throttle in, and off they started, lifting into the midday sky. It was a warm summer day and being off the ground felt good. The cooler air and the slip-stream even at the slow speed of the old Stinson made Ray and Steve feel almost as if they should have brought jackets. Steve headed due west. He wanted to stay clear of the Drew Field restricted area, a training base in Tampa.

Florida had several military pilot training fields so both he and Ray kept a good lookout for traffic in the air. The coast of the Gulf of Mexico came into sight as they approached Tarpon Springs, the sponge capital and fishing community. Steve flew just over the coast and started south. He continued along the Gulf Coast past Clearwater and the barrier islands. It was a beautiful ride, with the plane's solid but loud engine running smoothly. It was not a very fast ride because the old girl stayed below 100 miles per hour, but it was good for sightseeing. With the Pink Palace, the Don CeSar Hotel, coming into sight in Pass-A-Grille, it would soon be time to turn to the east. The area around old Fort De Soto and Egmont Key was being used for bombing practice. It was not the place to be.

Flying back to the Kissimmee area and the ranch was just as enjoyable. After getting the plane settled in one of the barns turned hangar, it was time to relax with a cool beer before Lillian called them for supper.

The next few days, which seemed all too short, were spent helping around the ranch and visiting with friends. Steve also managed to fly some each day, even if it was just for an hour. There was a short list of friends to visit because many of them were also in various branches of the service and scattered all over the country, receiving their own training.

"It's hard to realize, Dad, that not all of my friends will make it back here to raise their own kids," said Steve, as they sat at the kitchen table having breakfast. "I'm not concerned about myself . . . I think I'll make a pretty good pilot, but enough of that stuff. I think I'll drive into Orlando and see Sergeant McConnell and let him know in a few months he'll have to salute me."

Steve took his pickup and headed down the lane and onto the road to Orlando. He had a good meeting with Sergeant McConnell at the recruiting office. As Steve was leaving the post office, he turned as he heard "Hi, soldier," and spotted Elly. As he walked over to greet her, she continued, "You look great in that uniform. It fits you to a T."

Steve had to smile to himself, thinking that this was not a chance meeting. "It's not exactly tailor-made, but when I make second lieutenant, it will be a good fit."

He gave Elly a hug and light kiss on her forehead. He was glad to see her, despite the recent past.

"Got time to buy a girl a cup of coffee?" questioned Elly. "Sure." They walked across the street to the drugstore and took a booth in the back.

"This wasn't a chance meeting, you know. It was an ambush," started Elly, who paused for a moment as the waitress brought two cups of coffee. She continued after the waitress left, "I'm on my way back to college. I leave for Gainesville in a few days and heard that you were home on furlough and just had to see you. I am so sorry that I hurt you. Maybe things won't be the same, but please don't shut me completely out. At least, can we still be friends?"

"Well, I don't see why not," answered Steve as he sipped his coffee. Then he continued before Elly could say anything, "If you write, don't give me any detailed descriptions of things going on in your life. I'll have enough to think about learning to fly the Air Corps way. You understand what I mean?"

"Agreed," stated Elly with a wide smile. Their eyes met.

"I'm going up for an hour or so this afternoon, want to fly with me?" asked Steve as he picked up the check, left a tip for the waitress and stood up to leave.

"I'd love to." Elly grabbed Steve's hand. "No charge for you, son, and good luck in the service," came the reply when Steve started to pay the bill. After they left the drugstore Steve said, "We can drop your folks' car at your house, then take my truck. I'll bring you home after we buzz a few ranches."

Elly nodded her head, then walked to her parents' 1941 Ford and drove over to her house just a few blocks away. Elly's family operated the hardware store in Orlando and they lived in town. After parking the car in the driveway, Elly ran in the house to drop off the keys and to pick up a warm jacket for the flight. She also took a little time to freshen up and to put some perfume on, not too much, but enough to catch Steve's attention. She also left a note letting her folks know where she was. After just a few minutes, Elly bounced out of the house and into Steve's pickup truck, curling her feet up on the seat as she moved to the familiar spot she had occupied so many times before.

They talked for most of the ride out to the Stardust Ranch. It was nothing special, they just talked. Elly did ask a lot about Steve's basic training. "What do you think it would be like flying in the military? How dangerous will it be?"

"I really don't want to get into that right now. Combat flying is just that, flying in a combat situation. If the war wasn't going on, I'd be busting my butt trying to make the Detroit Tigers baseball team as their next catcher," answered Steve and he squeezed Elly's hand as if to say, "I'm sorry for the little speech."

Steve checked with his dad to see if he was needed for anything. Ray's answer was to simply have a good time and that he would place a phone call to Elly's parents telling them that she was staying for dinner. You could tell that Ray was glad that Steve and Elly had settled some things. It had been a somewhat abrupt ending to their relationship and clearing the air, so to speak, would take a load off Steve's mind. He would have enough to think and worry about in the coming months as he learned to fly Uncle Sam's way and to get his hands on a B-17.

Steve and Elly climbed up into the plane and were off touring the countryside from 1,000 feet above the plain. It was a beautiful afternoon for a flight. Nothing was said because it is hard to be heard over the roar of the engine in the old open cockpit biplane.

After they landed, Steve taxied to the tie-down area just to the left of the little hangar. He climbed down from the plane and helped Elly plant her feet on solid ground. She helped him tie the plane down for the night.

"Thanks for the flight, the afternoon and thanks for—" started Elly, but Steve cut her off with a quick kiss.

"Come on, let's head for the house. There are a couple of cold beers in the fridge and dinner shouldn't be too far away," Steve said as he took Elly's hand and they walked toward the ranch house.

Lillian had set the table with the "good" dishes, the guest china place settings. She liked Elly. Lillian had even baked a special fresh apple pie for dessert. Ray handed Steve a letter, which had arrived earlier in the day. It was from the Detroit Tigers Baseball Club, Briggs Stadium, Michigan and Trumbell Avenues, Detroit, Michigan. The letter stated that they would like to send a scout to meet with him but knew he was busy with the military at the moment. It further stated that enclosed was a contract in order to have him signed as a Tiger when his military service was complete. Upon signing the contract, he would be sent a bonus check for $5,000 as good faith from the Tigers. It was not the $40,000 bonus the Tigers gave to Dick Wakefield a couple of years earlier, but it was a fair sum of money and certainly the main topic of conversation during dinner.

"Well, after the war, you can play baseball during the summer and be a rancher the rest of the year," commented Ray.

"I just hope the war doesn't last too long," answered Steve, who thought for a minute and then continued, "a ballplayer's career is only so long and I'm already 22."

"Wow, that old," joined in Elly, who chuckled. In a more serious tone she said, "Baseball players make pretty good money, so even a few years is like a small gold mine. If the Tigers want to give you a signing bonus, they must figure you're in their future plans. They don't want other teams looking at you."

"She's right, you know," Ray agreed. "The Tigers have been scouting you since high school."

"Well, some can play into their mid-30s, but catcher is a tough position and . . . hell, I haven't even seen a day in the minor leagues yet. But if they believe in me this much, I'd be a fool not to sign the contract," stated Steve.

Lillian interrupted, "Do you want dessert or not?" They answered a unanimous yes, followed by Ray's comment, "And decent-sized slices too!"

The comment was not unnoticed by Lillian who brought the entire pie into the dining room and ordered Ray to cut it. Actually she said, "Okay, old man, you cut the pie and place the ice cream on the slices. I'd better give you soup bowls, so you don't make too much of a mess!" Elly moved to get up and help clear the dinner dishes, but Lillian shook her head. She would take care of that. Ray complied and cut a good-sized portion for Lillian and looked up to notice that she approved.

After dinner, Steve helped his dad complete the chores. Elly, as she had done many times before, tagged along.

It was not too long before Steve and Elly headed the pickup truck down the lane towards Orlando. They seemed to take the long route home. It was more than three hours before Steve drove back up the lane to the ranch.

The visit home had been wonderful. It was all too short, but Steve got to see some of his buddies, spend time on the ranch with his dad, flew every day, and well, he and Elly patched up things a good bit and at the very least would remain friends.

It was now time to head to Montgomery, Alabama, and Maxwell Field for the next important step in his flying career—the road to becoming an Army Air Corps pilot. He felt quite confident that he would make a very good pilot. There was the Air Corps way of doing things and he knew he had to go along and try not to show off the fact that he had been flying for over ten years.

At Maxwell Field, in the air cadet quarters, there were four men to a room. Steve became friends with one cadet in particular. His name was Howard Barclay Van Dyke III and he was a recent Yale graduate. Steve simply dubbed him Howie, which was just fine for the young man from Glen Cove, Long Island, which was just outside of New York City. Howie was from a wealthy, prominent family and appreciated the friendship, especially since with his name everyone else seemed to keep their distance from him. Howie had played on the Yale baseball team as an outfielder, although most of the time he was not in the starting outfield. Even as a backup, he received his athletic letter. Howie almost apologized for not being a starter, but Steve reminded him that a college team carried only so many players and he was good enough to make the varsity team at a highly respected baseball program. Some recruits tried to put Howie down because of his family's money. Steve simply considered them on the same level and enjoyed his friendship.

At dinner, in the mess hall one evening after they had been at Maxwell Field for a little more than a month, Howie opened the conversation with, "Man, I just made a passing grade on the written test and you skimmed right through it! I do appreciate the help you've given me."

"No problem, Howie. Remember I've been flying since I was about 11 years old," Steve said. "My dad and I had a good instructor and I've had a license for several years. I just need to learn everything the Air Corps way and any help I can give you . . . consider it done. We'll both get through this just fine!"

Steve soloed in just five hours and went on to fly the Stearman PT-17, the primary trainer. The Stearman was so much fun that Steve never wanted to land. She was also much faster than the old Stinson. The instructor explained to Steve that the Stearman had been designed to duplicate the much bigger and faster Air Corps planes. It was one great trainer. Steve did find, however, that it was a bit tricky to fly and you always needed to pay attention. He and Howie talked every night about the day's activity. Howie had to work so very hard just to keep up.

"I hope I don't wash out. My family is counting on me being a pilot," stated Howie. "Glen Cove and the country club might not be the same if I wash out."

"Stick with me, kid. We'll both get through this. I'll help you any way I can, you know that."

"I know and it is appreciated," said Howie as lights-out was called in the barracks. While resting in bed he continued, "This flying, then more ground school, then the hour or so of physical training is really making me tired, you know?"

Steve did not answer. There was just the sound of someone who had already fallen into a deep sleep.

Howie soloed in a little over 10 hours, which was close to average. To solo was a great confidence builder. It was also most important in terms of not having been placed on a list of hopeful pilots who would wash out of training. Howie was on his way!

An important part of the advanced ground school training took place in the Link Trainer. This is a stationary, on-the-ground instrument flying trainer in which the instructor closes the hood after the student pilot enters. The lesson acted out an actual flight, as if the pilot was flying at night or in cloudy, bad weather, and made him rely solely on his instruments without outside references. When weather conditions called for instruments, the skill of flying with them made the difference—period! Both Steve and Howie did very well with the Link Trainer.

The fun of flying was really beginning in earnest, especially with the solo cross-country flights. Steve had flights of 164 miles, all the way across Georgia and back to Maxwell Field. He enjoyed these much more than the 106-mile flights that were conducted while flying on instruments under a hood with an instructor. Steve, like all instrument students, wore a hood which let him see the instruments but nothing outside of the cockpit. The instructor kept an eye out for disorientation, obstructions, and other planes in the area, or looking out for traffic, as they say. Becoming an expert at instrument flying would certainly pay off when flying over the often-cloudy skies of England and Europe.

Steve caught up with Howie at mess, having supper. They sat next to another flying cadet by the name of Wright Gerke. Wright was from Camden, New Jersey, and just across the Delaware River from Philadelphia. Wright had been around airplanes since he was a kid and would work for free plane rides at Camden's Central Airport, just beside the Airport Circle. Often, a pilot would let him have the stick and control the plane for a few minutes each flight. He, like Steve and Howie, was working his butt off to become an Air Corps pilot. Wright also wanted to go to Four-Engine School and fly B-17 bombers.

"Are you having as much fun as we are?" Steve asked Wright, as Howie rolled his eyes.

"I really am," Wright replied. "It's work, really hard work, but the cross-country flights make it fun. I do sweat while under the hood on the instrument flights, but—" and before he could say more, he was interrupted.

"We all sweat the instrument flights," said Steve, with a nod from Howie.

The flying part of the training was on an everyday basis. Seven days a week they were up flying local or cross-country and doing instrument training. They spoke about the fact that they were now getting to the point where serious flying would be done.

Steve wrote to his dad as often as he could. In a letter he recently posted, he told of rolling the plane, peeling off and flying just as you see in the movies! Steve also received many letters from his dad, Lillian, old family friends, and several from Elly. Steve asked his dad to share his letters with the others, saying, "Frankly, Dad, I'm entirely too busy flying and studying to write much." Steve did answer Elly's letters. He likewise told her how busy he was and not to take it personally if he did not write very often.

Steve now had more than 30 hours in the Stearman PT-17. This meant that he would now incorporate another important phase of his flight training, night flying. The night flights entailed flying cross-country over a total distance of 180 miles, usually lasting at least two hours.

Finally, Steve and his two friends were ready to move on, not really too far, just over to Valdosta, Georgia, as they went to Advanced Two Engine School. Steve, Howie, and Wright spent a lot of what spare time they had together. With the move to Valdosta, they managed to be billeted in the same barracks. While each worked and flew independently, it was nice to get together for some relaxation and to bolster each other. Actually, Advanced Two Engine School went well for all three men. Howie was not quite the pilot that Steve or even Wright was. Still Howie worked just as hard and kept up. Steve enjoyed flying the twin-engine plane and looked forward to his goal of flying the four-engine B-17. He felt at home flying. The hard part was working and getting used to all of the handles, dials, and whatnot. The important thing to remember was that it did get easier each day.

At last came the big day, graduating to Advanced Four Engine School. It had taken months of very hard work, concentration and learning the skill of flying the Army Air Corps way. Some classmates who did not make it out of primary flight training went on to navigator school or to bombardier training. There were also cadet pilots who were better suited to fly pursuit planes—fighters, such as the P-40, P-47 or even the twin-engine P-38s. Some cadet pilots would continue in twin-engine bombers, such as the B-25 Mitchell or B-26. Still others would go on to fly transport planes such as the C-46 or C-47. While all of those jobs were important, Steve, Howie, and Wright were just where they wanted to be: Hendrick's Field in Sebring, Florida, in Advanced Four Engine School with the B-17.

They managed again to bunk in the same barracks. Things, as expected, were getting tougher. They flew every day, with some flights lasting up to six hours. Ground School was also advanced. The subject line-up included navigation, radio, meteorology, and engineering, what the B-17 is all about, plus aircraft and naval identification and a "ton of other stuff," as the saying goes.

Steve wrote to his dad, telling him that the B-17 was a dream to fly. He went on to say that the hardest part was getting used to all of the instruments in the cockpit, especially now with four engines to control. The fun, though, began once the big bomber was off of the ground and flying.

Cross-country flying was becoming most enjoyable. Steve was now at a point in his flying that the B-17 felt like a comfortable pair of shoes. It just felt and fit so well. He was completely at home in the left-hand pilot's seat. The four Wright Cyclone engines had a distinct sound of their own and Steve was tuned in to just how they were supposed to sound and feel, not unlike an automobile mechanic knowing exactly how a car engine should sound.

Howie joined Steve's crew as a copilot on several of the cross-country flights, which was fine with him. Howie had said that Steve is one hell of a pilot and that he felt quite comfortable flying the right seat. During the flights they would take turns flying the plane. Howie quietly told Steve that, at this point, he would rather fly in Steve's crew than have his own plane. While he felt confident in his flying, he would rather not be an aircraft commander, or A/C, right now.

Steve, of course, told Howie that he would be welcome in the right seat, but that he felt that Howie would make a fine A/C. Wright, in the meantime, was also flying the cross-country flights.

On a beautiful Florida morning, they and several other B-17s took off from Sebring and flew up to Columbia, South Carolina, and back. Steve flew an E model. They had some old C, B, E and a couple of the newer F models. The F model B-17 was the one currently flying combat missions overseas. It had a greater bomb capacity and armament. The most enjoyable part of the flight was when Steve flew north from Sebring and right over the ranch in Kissimmee. Steve was quite certain that Ray saw the B-17s pass over and would figure that Steve was one of the pilots. Ray called them a flock. Steve would later try to correct his dad that he would prefer that they be known as a flight or formation.

Finally, they received some time off, a three-day pass. It was not difficult to determine how the short time would be spent. Steve had invited both Howie and Wright to the Stardust Ranch. Ray would meet them at the Hendricks Field main gate with a car. Ray, like Steve and so many other cattle ranchers, did not own a car. They just had pickup trucks. Therefore, needing a car for this adventure, Ray borrowed one for the occasion. With the three cadets waiting at the main gate, Ray pulled up in a four-door 1941 Buick Roadmaster.

Steve walked over to greet his dad and to give him a big hug, "Hey, Dad, I didn't know that you knew anyone with a Buick; I'm impressed!" Steve then pulled back a little and motioned for his buddies to come over. "Dad, I'd like you to shake hands with Howie Van Dyke and Wright Gerke."

"Hello, Mr. Carmichael," said both Wright and Howie, as if on cue.

"I'm Ray. Nice to meet you boys. Let's head for the ranch." He helped load the gear into the Buick's trunk. There was a lot of conversation while driving to the ranch. Ray certainly enjoyed having the boys talk of flying, which somehow now included flying over the ranch whenever they could. Mostly Ray enjoyed hearing Steve's voice again. Letters were fine and welcomed, but having him home, even for a short stay, was very meaningful.

Lillian was on the porch as the Buick drove into the ranch yard.

After giving her a big hug, Steve introduced Wright and Howie to Lillian.

"I hope you boys like steak and cake," said Lillian, knowing that they would certainly enjoy a meal on the ranch.

Steve took his friends up to the guest room. It was quite roomy, had two single beds and its own private bathroom. Steve also brought out a mixture of his and Ray's ranch clothes to wear while on the ranch, figuring that it would make them much more comfortable during their stay, rather than wearing their uniforms.

Lillian called Steve to the kitchen. She had a fresh baked cake and just brewed coffee, something to hold them until dinner. Ray joined them at the kitchen table and had a piece of cake with his coffee. The young pilots consumed the rest of the cake.

Steve showed Howie and Wright around the ranch using his pickup truck. He said that they could see other parts of the ranch by horseback tomorrow if they liked. It would be just a short ride, though, because he did not want them to go back to the Air Corps with saddle sores. They all had a good laugh. Wright said he was okay with riding, because his Aunt Martha and Uncle Emery owned a 450 acre ranch farm in New Jersey known as Sleeter's Ranch, where he had ridden many times. However, Howie said he would follow on foot or in the pickup truck. He was not getting on a horse to ride. In fact, the only horses he was familiar with were those that pulled carriages through Central Park in New York City.

Lillian, of course, set out the good china for dinner. She had prepared a huge dinner for this special occasion.

The three-day pass was a wonderful stay at the ranch, even though it was certainly not very much time. Ray took the boys, fine young men, back to Hendricks Field. The stay at Hendricks would not to be very long. It was here that they would receive the gold bars of a second lieutenant and their wings as an advanced four-engine B-17 pilot. Then they would move on to Boise, Idaho, and Gowen Field to pick up what would become their crew. The B-17 bomber operates with a ten-man crew. While Steve was learning the skill of flying the B-17 and the job of aircraft commander, which entailed being not only the first pilot, but in addition, the commander of the crew both in the air and on the ground, his future crew members were also learning their skills.

The crew of a B-17 bomber included the pilot, copilot, navigator, and bombardier, all officers were in the front of the plane. The pilot and copilot were located in the cockpit or flight deck. The navigator and bombardier were located below the flight deck in the nose of the plane. This was their office, so to speak. The pilot and copilot were joined on the flight deck by the engineer, usually a staff sergeant, who helped the pilots and was also the top turret gunner. Behind the flight deck in a B-17 was the bomb bay, where the bombs were loaded. Then behind that compartment were the radioman, the ball turret gunner, two waist gunners, and a tail gunner. They all carried the rank of sergeant. The B-17 was a most formidable piece of equipment, which was one of the reasons why she was called the Flying Fortress.

Once he arrived at Gowen Field, Steve was also told, as if he didn't already know, that not only was he in charge of a flight crew, but that he was being placed in charge of a piece of military equipment valued at $300,000.

Howie and Steve were together in Boise; however, Wright was sent to Blythe, California, to pick up his crew. They would try to stay in touch through Steve's dad at the ranch. Things were moving rather fast now and they would all be on the move.

Steve received his crew and held his first meeting with them. "I'm Lieutenant Steve Carmichael," he began. "They haven't assigned a copilot to my crew yet, but we'll get started by way of introductions. Some of you men already know each other, which, of course, is good news to me because if there is one thing that we all need to do in a 17, it's to be a well-oiled machine, a solid team. I played some college baseball, so I know all about teamwork and how once a team gels, there is no stopping it. This is how we will operate. Some of us are officers and on the ground, normal military protocol will prevail, but in the air, each of us has a job and I expect that job to be done in an expert way, with respect and help to others, if needed. As the A/C, I am responsible for each of you on the ground, as well as in the air. If there is one thing that I can do it is fly the B-17, so all of you can count on me as your first pilot. We have a tough road ahead as we prepare to fly combat and I expect nothing less than your very best. Any questions?"

However, before the first hand could go up, in walked Howie Van Dyke. "Sorry I'm a bit late, but, well, I'm your copilot, Steve. I had to complete some paperwork." Howie had a wide grin on his face.

"You okay with that, Howie?" asked Steve, knowing full well that Howie should have a crew of his own. He motioned for Howie to follow him to another part of the Ward Room. "Excuse us for a moment, gentlemen."

"Look, they told me that they didn't think that I was quite ready to assume the role of A/C and, that while I was fine as a pilot, they thought I'd be better off starting as a copilot," explained Howie. "So given that, I asked if they could place me in the Carmichael Crew . . . a little paperwork and here I am."

They walked back to where the other men were sitting. "Well, it seems as if we, especially me, have had a huge stroke of good luck. Howie Van Dyke, who was an outstanding classmate of mine, has been assigned to our crew. He will be our copilot. The crew is now complete. I'll give you my speech later, Howie," said Steve, with a wink to Howie. Then Steve continued, "Okay, time to introduce everyone. I'll start and what I want from each of you is your name, your position in the plane, where you are from, what you did before the service and anything else you'd like to say. As I've said, my name is Steve Carmichael, I'm 23 years old and from Kissimmee, Florida, where my dad and I have a cattle ranch. I have been flying since I was about 11 years old. I graduated last May from the University of Florida, where I also played some baseball as a catcher. I enlisted with one goal and that was to fly the B-17. Howie?"

"I'm Howard Barclay Van Dyke III. Howie, if you don't mind. I'm from Glen Cove, Long Island, outside of New York City. I graduated from Yale University and had begun law school when the war broke out. I enlisted, went on to pilot training and will be your copilot. Oh, and Lieutenant Carmichael is a bit modest about his baseball ability. He will become a Detroit Tiger at some point. While we're giving ages, I'll be 24 in 10 days."

"I'll go next," said a red-haired second lieutenant. "I'm Bob Courtney from Bangor, Maine. I graduated from the University of Maine a couple of years ago. I'm 26 and was working in Portland for an engineering company. I tried for pilot training, but couldn't quite make it, so went on to Navigation School."

"I'm Russ Parker," said the fourth officer in the crew. "I'm from San Francisco, graduated from Stanford University, and like Bob, started flight training, but I washed out and went to Bombardier School. I'm 23 years old."

"Okay," said Steve, "Jim, it's your turn."

"I'm Staff Sergeant James McFarland from Buffalo, New York. Old Man in the crew, I guess. I'm 28 years old and joined the Army out of high school. I was an Army aircraft mechanic but wanted to fly. I'm the flight engineer and top turret gunner."

"I'll go next. I'm Eddie Anderson from Tioga, Texas. My family has a ranch outside of Tioga where our best-known citizen is Gene Autry. Well at least the ole singing cowboy was born there. I was also a ham radio operator, so guess who your radio operator is. By the way, Jim, I am a year older than you are. They wanted me to teach radio and I did for a while, but really wanted to get into a flight crew, so here I am."

Looking around as to who was to go next, Jack Kowalski saw Steve nod toward him. "I'm John . . . Jack Kowalski, a plumber from Chicago, the family business. I'm 21 and fresh out of gunnery school, so I am listed as a waist gunner."

"My name is Joe DeMatteo, from Philadelphia, South Philly, as we call it. I worked as a mechanic for the PTC—Philadelphia Transit. I'm 19 and a waist gunner."

"You can see by my size that I'm the ball turret gunner. My name is Willie Burnett from Seymour, Indiana. I'm 22 and worked in the warehouse for a food chain called John C. Grub Company."

"Looks like I'm last," said a small but rugged-looking man. "My name is Roger Earp from Phoenix, Arizona, and yes, I'm related. Wyatt was my great uncle. I knew him but not very well. I was minding my own business riding bulls, calf roping, doing the rodeo circuit when Uncle Sam said he wanted me, so here I am, a tail gunner in a B-17. My age is 23, but I know, you all think of me as looking like a teenager!" he joked.

Roger had made them all laugh and Steve was quite satisfied that he had the crew he wanted. He was especially pleased that he had a solid backup in Howie.

"Okay, thanks, men," started Steve, as he looked at his crew with a smile, "I'm really pleased that we are all together as a crew. I believe that I could not have done better if I had hand-picked each of you. Tomorrow, we will go up as a crew and will concentrate on high altitude flying . . . up to 35,000 feet, that is, if they give us a bird that will get that high. We also will be doing cross-country flights of more than 1,000 miles. We will not be here very long either, because they tell me that we will be assigned a new B-17 F model and fly to Tampa, Florida, at MacDill for overseas training. Of course, what I've just told you about near future plans is to be kept within the crew. That is all for now, gentlemen."

The crew split up after the meeting. The non-commissioned men gathered in a group as they made their way to the evening mess for dinner. Steve and Howie were huddled for what seemed like a long time, but it was just a few minutes. Lieutenants Bob Courtney and Russ Parker stood to the side, not certain if they should go on to the officer's evening mess or to wait for Steve and Howie. While Steve and Howie were talking, Steve became aware of the awkward situation and said, "Russ, Bob, please wait for us, this will only take another minute."

With the mini-meeting over, Steve and Howie walked over to the waiting men.

"Sorry, fellows," started Steve, who paused for a moment and then continued, "As I had told all of the crew, Howie is an outstanding pilot and to me should have his own crew. He just would rather not have that responsibility right now and I'm damned pleased to have him as my copilot. Howie and I agreed that when he feels the time is right, he puts in for his own crew. That is what we discussed. I have no secrets from you. I just wanted to clear the air with Howie."

Bob and Russ understood. "Quite frankly, having two pilots like you gives a certain comfort," stated Bob Courtney. Russ nodded in agreement as Bob continued, "Being an engineer, I'm all for improving the odds."

It was a short walk to the officer's mess and after settling down at a table, in addition to the dinner, the conversation was light and pleasant, non-military. They spoke just about home, jobs and life before there was a war to contend with that placed their individual plans on hold.

Friday, March 19, 1943, was cold and windy but clear, high sky in Boise, Idaho. The complete crew was assembled inside a well-worn B-17 E model number 41-26322 for the first of high-altitude flights. This would enable Steve to be certain that each of the airmen could handle the altitude as well as start the work of making them bond as a solid crew.

Steve gave a little talk while they were still on the ground waiting to board the aircraft. This would be something that Steve continued to do each time they were to fly. He wanted his crew to be as comfortable as possible, under the circumstances, and to ready them for the task at hand. The talk was a bit reminiscent of his days as co-captain of the University of Florida baseball team and here on the hardstand by the plane, he wanted his men to know and have confidence in the officer in charge.

The fact was that Steve and Howie had been at the hardstand where the plane was parked for some time. They had completed a walk around check of the ship with the ground crew chief, who had also warmed up the engines.

The men climbed aboard the B-17. The officers entered through the nose hatch up front and were joined by Staff Sergeant Jim McFarland, the engineer and top turret gunner. It would not be long before he was simply called "Mac!" The other men came aboard through the door in the rear of the plane. Steve and Howie went through the long checklist. Steve finally gave the familiar "clear" signal out of the pilot's left side window while Howie did the same from the right copilot's sliding window. They then started the outer port side engine, number one. The engine coughed a little, tried to start, smoke exhaust came pouring out and then the 1,200 horsepower Wright Cyclone caught and roared to life. It was much the same for the other three engines. Soon, the engines had that solid sound of a B-17 bomber. That sound is like none other! At the flare signal from the control tower, their flight of eleven B-17s lined up and began taxiing to the active runway for takeoff. When it was their turn, they started rolling down the runway. Jim, as the engineer, called out the speed from the air speed indicator and when it reached 110 miles per hour, Steve called out "rotate," eased the yoke back and the big plane went flying. They gained altitude and joined the formation that was headed on a northwest course toward Washington state.

Four hours later, the big bird settled back to earth at Gowen Field in Boise, where they taxied to the hardstand, turned the plane around and brought it to rest, engines now silent. Steve and Howie went through a quick checklist and soon the crew was outside of the plane awaiting the ride back to the operations hut. Steve spent some time with the crew chief and then spoke with his crew, thanking them as a group and telling them that dinner was on him and Howie at the Texas Steak House, even though this was Idaho!

The routine was pretty much the same for the next couple of weeks, except for the morning that Steve was called to operations and placed in command of a new B-17 F model. He would fly this plane to Tampa, Florida, and MacDill Air Base for overseas training. It was getting that much closer, this flying into war.

Flying the plane to Tampa was a dream come true for Steve. He had phoned his dad to tell him he was on the way and had received permission to deviate slightly from the flight plan and do a fly-over the Stardust Ranch in Kissimmee, before flying onto Tampa and landing at MacDill.

It seemed as if all of Kissimmee was on hand as the big B-17 flew low over the town and ranch. The word had spread around town that Steve would do the fly-over and many sets of eyes looked skyward as the plane roared overhead.

Ray and the ranch hands were glued to watching the plane, plus a photographer from the Orlando newspaper took photos of the plane and the ground scene—a local boy was now a B-17 pilot!

Finally, the crew reached and landed at MacDill and taxied to the appointed hardstand. With gear and duffle bags in hand, they were driven in a truck to the operations office for further instructions and assigned quarters. As the officers settled in their assigned quarters, a voice was heard at the door.

"About time you showed up," called Lieutenant Wright Gerke as he walked over to shake hands with Steve and Howie.

"Ike," said Steve and Howie at almost the same time. The name Wright had been changed to the boyhood nickname name he carried, Ike.

"How long have you been here?" asked Steve.

"One entire day," came the answer and, with a grin, Wright continued, "flew in yesterday. I've got a great crew. Really good bunch of guys."

"Have you seen your wife?" asked Howie.

"Not recently, but I'll see her before going overseas, we write most every day. By the way, we're going to have a baby."

"Wow, congratulations! That's terrific," said the two friends. Steve asked, "When do you expect the baby?"

"I believe early August," replied Wright. With a sad tone in his voice, he said, "We'll be overseas by then."

"Well, hopefully we can get this thing over quickly and you'll be back home before you know it," said Steve, understanding Wright's frustration.

"It's chow time, anyone ready for some supper? I know I'm hungry," Howie said as he pointed toward the officer's mess hall.

"I'll be along in a minute . . . waiting for my guys to show up," answered Wright. "How'd you guys do with a crew?"

"I lucked out," answered Steve, nodding toward Howie. "Got Howie as my copilot!"

"It's the way I wanted it, at least for now. Who knows, once we're overseas I might want my own crew," added Howie.

"You did luck out," said Wright. "I did too. My copilot is Tommy Read from Pottsville, Pennsylvania. My navigator, Joe Costa, is from New York City and Jack Little is our bombardier. Jack is from Butler, Pennsylvania. They are a great group of guys."

"We'll see you inside," said Steve, as he and Howie spotted Bob Courtney and Russ Parker waiting in the mess hall.

In the meantime, on the other side of the large mess hall were the enlisted men. Steve was pleased to see that the rest of his crew had all gathered at one table. It was a good sign. Through the light chatter within the plane and through the intercom system while on the flight from Boise to Tampa, he had a good feeling that the crew would gel nicely.

After going through the officer's chow line, Steve and his officers were motioned by Wright to join him and his officers. When everyone was settled at the table, Wright introduced his copilot, navigator, and bombardier and Steve did likewise. It turned out that Russ and Jack had been in the same bombardier class. The same was true with Joe Costa and Bob Courtney with Navigation School. Conversation was lively throughout supper and likewise as they all enjoyed a couple of beers later in the base Officer's Club.

Intense flying, bombing practice, and classroom instruction was the structure for the next couple of weeks with the B-17 bombers. There were cross-country flights, many of which were more than 1,000 miles, plus the constant aerial gunnery and bombing practice as they prepared for duty overseas.

Steve worked his crew very hard as he pressed for perfection—the only acceptable way of doing things—as he prepared them to fly in harm's way over the enemy sky of occupied Europe. As their instructors had driven home, those veterans of the early raids over occupied Europe had proved teamwork and perfection gave them a much better chance of staying alive, a cold hard fact in war.

"Howie, have you noticed the different smell of this plane from the old Es we trained in?" asked Steve as they shut things down after a long day's flight.

"Of course," was Howie's answer and after a short pause, he continued, "This ship smells like a new car. No one has really sweated up the place and the odor of hydraulic fluid hasn't set in yet. Just wait until we get overseas. From what they're telling us . . . " His voiced drifted off as though he didn't really want to finish the sentence.

Steve understood, especially the last part of what Howie said, but he smiled as they left their seats and started to exit the plane. He said, "I wish we could keep this ship, she has such a nice balance, so easy to trim, but, I hear that after we arrive over there, they'll take her as a replacement and assign us to a bomb group where we'll fly whatever they have."

As the training neared an end, they would receive a ten day pass and when they returned, their training would be completed. Then, it would be off to the overseas flight and the war. They knew they were going to England to the area known as East Anglia, northeast of London. This was where all of the American bomber groups were based.

Howie would head to Long Island to be with his family. The rest of the Carmichael Crew also disbanded, heading for family visits before going overseas. Wright Gerke and his navigator, Joe Costa, were bound for the Camden, New Jersey——Philadelphia, Pennsylvania area. They would meet up with their wives and families. The wives were sharing an apartment together near Park Avenue in the little town of Merchantville. Park Avenue was not quite the same as the one in New York City, but it's a fine family-oriented street, as was the town, located six miles from Camden. Wright had graduated from Merchantville High School, before going on to Drexel Institute in Philadelphia, an outstanding engineering university.

Steve's dad, Ray, drove from the ranch to pick up his son. There would be no big ole Buick ride this time, just the pickup truck.

"You look very professional all decked out in that officer's uniform," said Ray as he and Steve shook hands, then hugged.

"They tell me that I'm a gentleman as well as an officer." He and his dad had a good laugh as Steve turned around to show off his uniform.

Steve placed his officer's bag into the back of the pickup's bed, which Ray assured him was perfectly clean and he also noted that Steve now carried a fancy officer's suitcase, rather than just a duffel bag. Most of the conversation on their way to the ranch focused on what it was like flying a B-17.

"I tell you, Dad, the plane is a dream to fly and with those four engines you have 4,800 horsepower!" said Steve.

"Maybe, but remember that our old biplane will get you to where you want to go on a lot less fuel, but I sure would like to fly one of those big birds myself," kidded Ray.

With several of Steve's flights having passed over the ranch, Ray had a bird's-eye view, well, from the ground, but he did have a pair of powerful binoculars.

Once at the ranch, all of the ranch hands as well as Lillian were there to greet Steve. There was also one other person. Elly had come home from the University of Florida to spend time with Steve. She was standing next to Lillian on the porch.

"My, my," said Lillian to Elly as Steve climbed out of the pickup truck, "Doesn't my boy look handsome in that officer's uniform? Just look at him!"

Elly did not answer, but quickly moved off the porch to plant a kiss on Steve to go with a hug. "It's so good to see you," said an excited Elly.

"That was a nice hello. I'm surprised to see you. I thought you were up at school. I'm glad you're here," answered Steve.

"Well, I took some time off of school to be here. There's nothing important going on up there, nothing," answered Elly.

Steve did not bother to answer the last part of what Elly said, but simply answered with, "Let me get out of this uniform and into some ranch clothes."

"No way," stated Elly, who with camera in hand continued, "First we take some photos of you with those gold lieutenant bars on your shoulders and the pilot wings on your chest. You look so handsome."

"Good idea," reasoned Ray, "Elly, your idea and camera, so you go first. You two get together . . . good," and Ray snapped the first of several pictures of Steve and Elly.

It was not long before everyone had a picture taken with Steve and perhaps the most meaningful were the ones taken with Ray. Although the photo with Steve's arm around Lillian brought tears to her eyes. She had been both a mother and grand-mother to him since he was a baby.

Afterwards, Steve bounced upstairs to unpack. He was also quite happy to be back in ranch clothes.

Dinner was a lively, noisy, happy event. Lillian had cooked a special meal, used the good dishes and Elly had stayed to join them.

The ranch seemed to come alive with Steve's ten day furlough.

He figured to be flying out of England on bombing missions for six months or even more. These ten days were golden!

Elly had her mother drive her out to the ranch, of course, so Steve would drive her back home later that night. It was a beautiful, clear but moon-less night and the stars seemed to touch the earth on the horizon. Steve would take the long way home with Elly.

On Steve's sixth day home, he, Ray, and Elly took a drive over to Lakeland and Henderson Field, the spring training home of the Detroit Tigers. Ray had borrowed the Buick for the occasion. Steve had his summer khaki uniform on, wanting to show the Tigers management that he had made second lieutenant and had received his pilot's wings. They had a good meeting. Later, Steve put on a Tigers uniform, number 26, and they had him take some batting practice. As a catcher, Steve threw right handed, but batted from the left side. This was one of the things that the Detroit Tigers initially liked about Steve. With the "short porch," as they called the right field fence and second deck overhang in Briggs Stadium, Steve's power to right field meant that a lot of long high fly balls hit that way would drop into the upper deck seats for a home run, rather than into the outfielder's glove below.

Steve did not disappoint during his time in batting practice. Some of his down-time from flying was spent playing baseball at the airfields. He actually hit four balls that cleared the right field fence in Lakeland, while several bounced off the wall. He had a nice level swing that the coaches like to see, a line drive type of swing, with just a bit of lift.

It had been a great day. Elly, camera in hand, had taken a full roll of film. The Tigers players, coaches and management could not have been nicer. Mr. Briggs seemed very pleased that he had signed Steve before he went to the open market.

There were just three days left, then two, and finally the day came when Steve was to return to the MacDill Air Base in Tampa. Ray had once again exchanged his pickup truck for the borrowed Buick. Elly would drive with them and keep Ray company for the long drive home. The goodbye at MacDill was a sad scene. Ray, Elly, and even Steve had tears in their eyes. Steve would call home from Tampa and Bangor, Maine. Then it would be letters from England. Once his crew was assem-bled, it would be just days before they were on their way overseas.

Howie was the first to meet up with Steve. They had a long conversation about the time spent at home. Howie was telling Steve that he had impressed the Glen Cove crowd at the country club. Even his old girlfriend showed up, but Howie said she was even too country club for him. "She told me that the past year in the service had made me almost cavalier, and she did not care for it! Hell, she wanted to get engaged before I left for flight training." Howie went on to say how lucky he was to have put off that engagement. "You know, I sat at the country club bar, Scotch in hand, watching her dance with some 4-F and wishing they'd fall in love!" Steve laughed.

Howie continued, "Come on, let's go to the O-Club. Bob and Russ are already there." Steve and Howie met with them and they all relaxed over a drink before calling it a night.

During the next few days, they completed the overseas training program. It was then time to get ready for the long journey. Some of the men completed their wills in case they didn't come back, which made the dangers of war all that much more real.

Steve made a phone call to his dad, telling him that he was off to Bangor, Maine, for the first leg of the flight. The small formation would fly directly over the ranch. "Don't ask how it was arranged. I'll flap my wings." That way Ray would be able to see which plane was Steve's.

As the planes flew overhead, Ray, binoculars in hand, stared at the formation, and then one of the B-17s rocked his wings. Ray was proud but also sad. In addition to the boy killed at Pearl Harbor, four Marines had come home to be buried from the Pacific, two airmen from the sky above Europe, and two more were listed as Missing in Action. The war was at their front door in Kissimmee and nearby Orlando. Ray would worry until his boy was back home to stay.

At 8,000 feet, the formation flew on, heading north. It was while they were over Pennsylvania, near Allentown, according to the map, that second lieutenant Wright Gerke put in a call to the leader and said he was having trouble with one engine. He would feather it and land at Allentown, check out the trouble and be back on his way. He would see them in Bangor.

Steve looked over at Howie, who had a giant grin on his face. With Ike, as they now called him, from Camden, and Tommy Read, copilot from nearby Pottsville, well, of course they did not foul that engine on purpose! Later, Steve and Howie talking quietly to Wright found out that two carloads of family had driven to Allentown and Tommy had a family visit, as did Joe Costa. Wright proudly showed the B-17 to the family. His nephew and godson, Wayne, even sat in his pilot's seat!

Once in Bangor, Maine, it would be a few days before the overseas flight began. With Bangor being home for Steve's navigator, Bob Courtney, Bob arranged for a special lobster dinner for both the Carmichael and Gerke Crews. It was a feast. They also received permission to go to the town of Old Orchard Beach, just south of Portland on the Atlantic coast. The early days of May were warm enough to be on the beach, but the ocean water was too cold for most of the men, Steve included.

CHAPTER TWO

Engines roared to life and the planes left the United States soil for the last time. At the current rate of plane losses to date, these beautiful B-17s would soon either be shot from the sky or be so heavily damaged as to end up in the boneyard, giving pieces of themselves so that other less-damaged planes could continue the bombing missions over occupied Europe. The aviators flying in these Flying Fortresses were off to war and war is a very deadly business.

The first stop was at Gander, Newfoundland. At this point in the trip, frankly, Steve and his crew were really excited. They were going to places they had never dreamed of being. For Steve, flying a new B-17 F model these great distances was a dream come true.

Howie, a man of the world, had traveled to and from England before, out of New York on both of the Cunard liners Queen Elizabeth and Queen Mary with his family. He promised to show them around London. It was his kind of town.

The balance of the flight, with a stop in Iceland, brought them finally to Prestwick, Scotland. The flight went flawlessly. As the plane crossed over the North Atlantic, the crew pointed out small icebergs floating in the icy waters below. They arrived in Prestwick on Monday, May 17, 1943.

Steve was thrilled to fly into Scotland. He was of Scottish origin. His ancestors came from Oban, Scotland, on the west coast. Ray Carmichael would tell young Stevie stories about the family history, about their tartan, and that Stevie even had Viking blood in him.

He would tell Steve about the castle that his ancestors' clan owned. Dunollie Castle was in ruins, however, it was a castle where battles had been fought. It is north of Oban's center and they were members of the Scottish Clan MacDougall. Steve took a slight deviation from the flight plan as he passed over Oban and spotted the castle ruins, which as his dad said, were just north of the town center. He then set the plane down in Prestwick. "Just some slight complications in coming on down the coast, but we corrected them and here we are," explained Steve to a somewhat upset major after they reported to operations.

After landing in Prestwick, Steve was told that he and his crew would be moving down to Bovingdon, northwest of London, for a couple of weeks or so at "finishing school." Here they would learn the British way of flight control. There was a single system in order to maintain organization in the sky and they needed to learn it quickly.

After two weeks of practice and learning the proper way to do things in the sky over wartime Great Britain, Steve learned that he and his crew had been committed to the 305th Bombardment Group and their 366th Squadron. The 305th was stationed in Chelveston, England, in the area known as East Anglia. Steve was to learn that the 305th Group consisted of four squadrons: 364th, 365th, 366th and 422nd. The Carmichael Crew was replacing a crew that had been shot down. Things were becoming very real, so to speak—quite serious.

Steve was pleased to learn that the Gerke Crew had been assigned not only the 305th Group, but also the 366th Squadron. The 305th Group had the motto "Can Do."

The 305th already had a proud history. The first commander was Colonel Curtis LeMay, who was now in command of the 102nd Provisional Combat Wing. He turned the 305th over to Lieutenant Colonel Donald K. Fargo.

Steve and his crew officially became part of the 305th on Friday, June 11th. They settled in with the new surroundings and seemed to be comfortable with the routine. They were to fly a few practice missions before being committed to an actual bombing mission.

The practice missions would also let them become familiar with the farmland turned air base and exactly where Chelveston, their base, was among all of the Eighth Air Force bases in East Anglia.

Within this area, there were bases for fighter planes: P-38s and P-47s, plus B-17 and B-24 (H) heavy bombers and B-25 and B-26 (M) medium bombers. In addition, there were bases for the C-46 and C-47 cargo planes. With so many American air bases in East Anglia, the sky could become quite crowded in the summer of 1943.

Finding your way home in a crippled aircraft was most important, especially if you had wounded aboard. The flight pattern for each base had been established, both outbound and inbound in order to avoid midair collisions. The practice flights took place while those committed to the mission of the day were away fighting their way to the target, as well as the running air battles that often took place as they worked to make it home.

Steve and his crew would watch the B-17s leave for the mission and likewise would be near the control tower as they counted the returning ships. A flare fired from a plane as it worked its way into the landing pattern meant that there was wounded aboard. Those planes had priority and would land first with the ambulance following on the ground to where they could extract the wounded and rush them to the base hospital.

Some of the returning planes struggled to remain in the air, often with one or two of the engines feathered and the others coughing, trying to keep running. Still others simply landed as if it were a routine flight. It was the luck of the draw, no hits by flak and no fighter attack on that particular aircraft, at least on this day, Sunday, June 13th. The mission for the day was Bremen, Germany. One plane was missing in action, B-17 serial number 42-5125, the Higgs Crew. Their crew was the 30th lost by the 305th to date.

To be sure, being here at Chelveston was a wake-up call. Steve's letters home talked about the flight over the ocean, the Dunollie Castle in Oban and adapting to the British flying patterns. Steve did not write about the serious part of the war. He had not actually started his missions, yet he saw firsthand the results of a mission when the plane and crew did not come back. Steve knew that as aircraft commander of his ship and crew, he would have to put up a convincing front in order to have them be confident that all would be well in the air.

His squadron commander told Steve that he might fly the first couple of missions as a copilot in order to become familiar with the battle scene in the air. Afterward, he would have his full crew back together. There was also the rumor that the quota for flying missions for each crew member would increase from 25 to 30 missions before being rotated home because the air crew's loss was high and replacement crews were slow in coming. The rumor referred to those crews that arrived May 1st and later. "Just ducky" was the general comment. Some of the veteran crews, the ones with as many as 10 missions behind them, did some figuring and found that the life expectancy of a crew was between 8 and 10 missions, a sobering thought. They all spoke of the luck that the B-17 *Memphis Belle* had. They were the first intact crew to complete the required 25 missions. They would soon fly back to the States.

"Mail call!" The mail had finally caught up with the Carmichael Crew. Steve had quite a few letters to read and answer. He sent one answer to each person using V-Mail. V-Mail, short for Victory Mail, was a microfilmed three-by-three-inch letter. Steve sent two to his dad, and asked how the Tigers were doing this season.

Three of the Carmichael Crew had already flown bombing missions. Eddie Anderson, the Texan and radio operator, flew with the 305th July 4th mission to Nantes, France, and on the July 14th mission to Caen, France. A crew was short a radioman. The plane sustained damage on the Caen mission from a fighter attack and the right waist gunner was killed. Eddie told Steve, "I thought I was pretty tough, but when they are shooting right at you, it's all you can do not to pee in your pants."

In addition, on the same two missions, Jack Kowalski, the plumber from Chicago, and Joe DeMatteo, the kid from South Philly, were pressed into action as waist gunners on two different crews. Joe described one incident where he had a German ME-109 fighter bearing in on him: "I opened fire right away to let him know I'm alert and he holds off until about 300 yards away. Man, he opens up firing away, then flips over on his wing and breaks off at maybe 200 yards, maybe less. I could see the bright yellow engine cowling and I could almost make out his face. It all happened so fast . . . not at all like I thought it would be."

Jack sat quietly as Joe gave the blow-by-blow description of the battle in the sky. Joe seemed excited about the action. Jack, however, was not sure that this action was the place to be. The copilot in his plane on the Caen raid was killed by machine gun fire. The ME109s, also with yellow cowling paint, formed a finger-five formation and flew directly at the front of the plane, firing away with 37-millimeter cannons that fired through the propeller hub. The pilot did all he could just to bring the crippled bomber back to Chelveston.

The weather kept the planes grounded for a few days. On Tuesday, July 27th, Steve was called into operations and told that he would not fly as a copilot on any missions, but would fly as aircraft commander, with his full crew. He would be alerted for tomorrow's mission. While Steve was pleased to have his own ship, he also understood that they were short of pilots because of recent losses.

Steve and Howie were at the Officer's Club when Bob and Russ joined them for a beer. "Tomorrow's the day. I'd like to know where, but we'll all know soon enough," said Steve, as the other officers settled in.

"Are they letting us use one of those new planes?" asked Howie.

"No, she's a war-weary bird, number 42-29555 . . . already has 22 missions on her," answered Steve. He took a sip of beer and continued, "Our crew chief is Master Sergeant Walter O. Creamer, career Army Air Corps and one tough old bird himself. He is in his mid- 40s, I guess, and explained to me today that the plane is his and I just fly it! We had a meeting of the minds, finally, and agreed it was our plane and we'd do our best to protect her and bring her home. Oh, and we can call him Pappy!"

"Is he going to be trouble?" asked Howie.

"No, quite frankly I like his attitude. He'll prepare the ship well for the mission . . . tune the engines, warm them up for us, check out the pressures and temperatures and have her already to go," answered Steve. "He also told me he'd dress her wounds and keep her flying. He's like a mother hen to *Image of War.*"

"That's her name, *Image of War?*" asked Bob Courtney.

"He named her . . . sounds like a plane with a bad attitude. I like it," added Steve, who finished his beer. "Let's get some sleep, tomorrow will come early."

As Steve, Howie, Bob, and Russ walked back to their Quonset hut they met up with Wright Gerke and Joe Costa. "Are you alerted for tomorrow, Ike?" asked Steve.

"Yes, like you this will be number one and to be honest, I'm kind of glad to get started," answered Wright. "We've been doing a lot of practice flights while waiting for this one to come." He thought for a second, and then continued, "What plane are you flying?"

"Number 29555, *Image of War.* She's already had 22 missions. What about you?"

"We also have a 1942 plane, number 42-29553, ARKY. She likewise has been to battle with 23 missions and has that smell, if you know what I mean," answered Wright.

Steve simply shook his head. The difference between the old B-17 E model and the newer F model he had flown across the Atlantic Ocean was quite evident. He imagined that the main difference between the *Image of War,* an F model and the older ships he had flown in the states was that the sweat in this plane was from real battles and not from new pilots getting practice. They all said their good nights, and then headed off for what they hoped would be a good, well, decent night's sleep.

It was just before dawn that the orderly entered the quarters. "Okay, gentlemen, everyone up, you men are alerted for today's mission."

After shaving very closely so that the oxygen mask would fit snugly, it was off to the morning mess and, tray in hand, have some breakfast. This was a time when some could eat, while others simply could not. Those who could, for the most part, would eat in silence, each with his own thoughts before a mission. Butterflies were in everyone's stomach; the first mission, the 10th mission and so on, it did not matter.

After breakfast, it was off to the briefing hut for the mission. They entered the hut and took a seat. Pilots, copilots, navigators and bombardiers attended the briefing, usually sitting up front, with the rest of the crew also in attendance. In addition, pilots, navigators and radiomen attended their special meetings for updated information and radio codes. Then additional gear was picked up for the ride out to the flight line. Here, equipment was checked and guns rechecked, as they tried to keep nerves in balance. The crew chief worked with them, helping to prepare for the coming mission. He had already been at the hardstand for some time, going through the checklist and warming up the engines. Pappy also understood the feelings of the young men about to fly to war. He had sent many a crewman off in the *Image of War;* some came home wounded but others were not quite so lucky.

When they were at the briefing hut, the men stood at attention as 305th Group Commander Lieutenant Colonel Donald Fargo entered the room. He stepped up onto the small stage. Behind him was a large map covered by a blanket. He told the men at ease, and they all sat down. Beneath the blanket was the course for today's mission on Wednesday, July 28, 1943. An aide took the blanket away and the map revealed that the mission, charted to the target in red yarn, would be to the German city of Kassel. There were some quiet wisecracks and groans by some, but there was simply silence by most, including Steve. *Hell, this is for real,* he thought.

"Settle down," were the words spoken as the bomb group's intelligence officer took over the briefing. He explained where to expect the worst concentration of flak and enemy fighter planes.

They would have a P-47 fighter escort. However, with the limited range of the fighters, they could only be escorted to just across the English Channel and inside the Dutch coast. The formation would be on their own to the target and back to the coast, where they would be picked up once again by an escort of British Spitfires. They had to maintain and fly the protective box formation in order to give each ship maximum protection from their combined firepower.

At the additional briefing, pilots were given assembly points for the flight formation after takeoff, with the navigators and radiomen attending their own briefing. While the men were trying to digest everything they had just heard, the trucks brought them out to the hardstand to join the rest of the crew, where their ship awaited them.

Steve felt a bit overwhelmed, but dared not show it. *I'll be glad when this day is over and mission number one is in the book,* he thought to himself.

While the men were getting ready to board the plane, Crew Chief Creamer took Steve to the side. "I've seen you fly. They tell me you're one of the best and I believe it. Try to relax and fly the tightest formation you can muster. It will give you and my old girl here the best protection. You'll do just fine. I'll see you this afternoon."

"Thanks, Pappy. I'll bring her home to you," answered Steve and he patted Pappy on the shoulder.

Steve called his crew together and said, "Howie and I are going to board and do our checklist to make certain that all is well. Then, we will come back out and do the ground inspection with Pappy. We will all board when we see the flare from the tower for start time. If you want to board and check out your responsibility again, well, do whatever makes you feel comfortable. I know that some of you are a bit unsettled about this first mission as a complete crew, but we'll do just fine. Relax and remember the training you've had. It will see you through. I, for one, am glad to be on our way . . . any questions?"

"It's tough just sitting here waiting," stated ball turret gunner Willie Burnett.

"I agree," answered Steve. Then nodding his head toward Eddie Anderson, radioman, and Jack Kowalski and Joe DeMatteo, the waist gunners, he continued, "We have three experienced combat men in our crew. They'll take care of us."

"Don't look at me," exclaimed Jack, "I'd rather fix a toilet full of shit!"

Everyone had a good laugh, which seemed to cut the tension.

Steve and Howie walked over to the open nose hatch, threw their gear up into the plane and swung themselves inside. They made their way up to the flight deck and went to work.

A few minutes later, they came back down through the nose hatch. The ship's flight engineer, Jim McFarland, and Pappy joined them as they gave the plane the ground inspection. The inspection was really almost unnecessary because Pappy had been with the plane for quite some time before the crew arrived and had completed a full inspection, including a warm up of the four engines. However, for Steve, as the aircraft commander, along with his copilot, this was an important part of the preflight procedure. Howie, for good measure, also kicked one of the main tires, which brought a smile to everyone.

It was not long before a brilliant green flare from the control tower signaled it was time to board the plane and start engines. The officers, Steve, Howie, bombardier Russ Parker, and navigator Bob Courtney, along with top turret gunner–flight engineer Staff Sergeant Jim McFarland, all entered through the nose hatch. The rest of the crew, radio operator Eddie Anderson, waist gunners Jack Kowalski and Joe DeMatteo, along with ball turret gunner Willie Burnett and tail gunner Roger Earp, boarded through the rear door of the plane.

Those up front settled in. Bob was at his navigator's desk and Russ, who as bombardier, wouldn't have too much to do until they were well on the way to the target, when he'd arm the bombs and check out his other duty, which was to work the twin .50 caliber machine guns that stick through the nose's Plexiglas.

This particular aircraft has been fitted with the twin 50s because the nose in a B-17 was the only unprotected area of firepower, having just the cheek gun. German fighters quickly exploited this with frontal attacks, especially coming in with a figure-five formation in order to take out the pilots and kill everyone else up front. This war is becoming serious business!

Steve and Howie, along with Jim McFarland set up for the start of the engines.

"Clear!" came the call out of the windows in the cockpit by both Steve and Howie, as the ground crew stood by with fire extinguishers ready if needed.

Steve called out to Howie, "Mesh one, Start one!"

Howie, from his copilot's seat, labored with the primer pump for each one of the four engines as they coughed, spit out smoke, and finally roared to life. With the engines running smoothly and warmed up at 1,000 RPMs, they checked the prop feathering, and then ran each engine up to maximum in order to test the magnetos and turbochargers.

In the meantime, after a final check of their guns, the four rear gunners gathered in the radio room with Eddie Anderson for taxi and takeoff. This was done for two reasons: one, it was the safest place in the plane should there be a crash during takeoff, and two, it brought their collective weight more to the center of the plane, which made it easier for the pilot to control the ship during the takeoff and climb out to altitude.

In the cockpit, Steve and Howie watched as other B-17s moved past their dispersal site. Finally, they spotted the tail number of the plane they were to follow. Howie released the parking brake and the *Image of War* left her hardstand once more. This time with a new crew she rolled onto the taxiway, lumbering along to take her turn for takeoff. During taxi, the two inboard engines were set to idle at around 800 RPMs and the two outer engines were used for maneuvering. The sound of squealing brakes could be heard as the big bombers waddled their way to the takeoff point of the runway.

Finally, it came time for Steve to maneuver onto the runway. He lined the ship up for the takeoff. Howie, as copilot, locked the tail wheel. Then he kept his eyes on the instruments as Steve advanced the throttles to maximum power, pulling 2,500 RPMs per engine. Brakes were released and with the nose pointed straight down the runway the big bomber started to roll, laboring with a full bomb load aboard.

As flight engineer, Jim McFarland, who stood just behind and between the pilot and copilot seats during the start and run-up of the engines, now called out the airspeed readings so that Steve could concentrate on keeping the plane headed straight down the runway.

Steve, who had already pushed the yoke forward in order to lift the tail wheel off the ground, called out, "We'll hold her on the ground until 115 miles per hour."

Howie and Jim heard him, but did not respond. Steve's concentration, especially for this new experience of flying off to the first mission, was too important for additional chatter.

At 115 miles per hour, Steve pulled the big plane off the runway. "Gear up," called Steve. The *Image of War* was flying once more.

Howie brought the wheels up and while doing this, he touched lightly on the brake pedals to stop the wheel spinning. Steve glanced over to Howie for just a second and each smiled as the plane continued the climb out at 140 miles per hour. In the meantime, Bob and Russ, who had left the nose area in order to take up their brace position behind the pilot and copilot during takeoff, now squeezed back into the nose of the aircraft to assume their normal positions as navigator and bombardier nose gunner.

After heading straight out for a minute, Steve started a climbing left turn and flew the course to the assembly point where the 305th Group formed over East Anglia. They were at this time just below the altitude where oxygen would be required. This entire endeavor had been quite tricky, especially for a pilot on his first combat mission, and both Steve and Howie gave a sigh of relief as they eased into their position within the formation. Almost an hour had passed during this period, but now being in position only meant that they had to be continually on alert until they once again settled back on English soil.

Everyone was now at his assigned position. Steve told the crew to go onto oxygen as they passed 12,000 feet on the way to 20,000. Howie had the men check in to be certain that everyone was on oxygen and okay. The plane shuddered as guns were tested. The Continent was now in sight and the formation climbed up to 25,000 feet. The escort fighter planes, P-47s for this element, were still with the formation but would have to turn back after being just inside of enemy territory. They did not have enough fuel to go deeper and the formation would be on their own to and from the target. British Spitfires would pick them up as they exited the Continent and flew back to their home base at Chelveston.

So far, so good; no enemy planes had appeared. Light antiaircraft fire appeared as black puffs in the sky as they passed over the coast, but it was not accurate. Luck was still with them. Howie motioned to Steve that their fighter escort was turning back toward England. Steve acknowledged and spoke on the intercom, "Our fighter escort is leaving us so let's be on the alert. Give us exact locations of enemy aircraft. Remember your training and we'll all do just fine." Then Steve continued, "Wyatt, Are you okay back there?" as he spoke to the tail gunner.

"A bit lonely, Skipper, but I'm sure awake," was the response. Although his real name was Roger Earp and Wyatt Earp, the famous lawman from the old West was his great uncle, the crew dubbed Roger "Wyatt" because "roger" was part of the vocabulary spoken aboard the plane. "Quite a view, Skipper, you should see it sometime," added Wyatt.

Steve laughed to himself and saw the smile on Howie's face. "I'm a little busy right now, but maybe sometime we'll trade places and exchange views."

"For sure not right now, Sir, I've spotted six, no, make that eight or so ME-109s," came the excited voice of the tail gunner. "They're just sitting out there; haven't made up their mind which plane to jump."

"I see them . . . looks like they're spreading out. Willie, get ready if they turn over and dive down past you," called Jim McFarland from his top turret position to the ball turret gunner.

Steve did not say anything as he worked to fly as tight a formation as he could in order to maintain protection from the other planes' guns. He was pleased that the crew was alert and working as a team. At the same time, he was concerned for their safety, especially with this being the first time under enemy fire for most of them.

"They're coming in," yelled Joe DeMatteo from his right waist position.

The ME-109s, with the 37-millimeter cannon, which fired through the prop hub, started their run at the B-17s. The leader did not fire until he was less than 300 yards away. The ME-109s, with their bright yellow engine cowlings, dove through the formation. It was frightening to see the tracer bullets headed your way.

Guns from both their ship and others answered the fire. The leader flipped over on his wing and broke off the attack as he dived under the plane. Wyatt, Joe and Willie all fired their guns, but were not certain if they got in any hits; everything happened so fast.

"Let's keep alert," called Howie's voice over the intercom. "They're also setting up for a frontal attack . . . everyone okay?"

Each position checked in, everyone was all right, although there had been the sound of a loud thud. The ship had been hit, somewhere!

ME-109s bored in, this time with a figure-five formation, cannons firing as they raced through the formation. Guns from the nose, top turret, and ball turret blazed away from the *Image of War* as she defended herself. Steve and Howie looked on in horror as a plane on their right went down in flames, out of control, and only two parachutes were seen deployed. Just ahead on their right, another B-17 exploded in a huge yellow and orange fireball, no parachutes. Then the fighters were gone; they were getting close to the initial point, or IP, for the bomb run on Kassel. The B-17s were greeted by the ugly black puffs of smoke from the exploding anti-aircraft flak shells.

Steve placed the plane on autopilot and told Russ, as bombardier, that the plane was his. Along with the other planes, they made the bomb run. "Bombs away," called Russ. *Image of War* lurched upward as the weight of the bombs were released and the bomb bay doors were quickly closed. "Let's get the hell out of here!" he yelled.

Steve, now back in control of the ship, turned away from the target for the long trip home. The flak was still heavy and fairly accurate. The German fighters were nowhere to be seen, at least for now. They knew not to fly into their own flak field. The *Image of War* bounced as a flak shell exploded just below them and to the left. Pieces of the exploding shell—shrapnel—banged against the fuselage of the big ship, tearing small holes in the skin. Lucky this time, a direct hit would have brought them down.

The flak subsided, but off in the distance specks could be seen that, as they moved closer, became German planes. They were ME109s and FW-190s. Unlike the 109s, the FW-190s had their cannons mounted in the wings. Both were deadly fighter planes with outstanding pilots.

There was a running battle as the planes of the 305th fought their way across Germany and Holland, trying to get back home to English soil and their base at Chelveston. Finally, over Rotterdam a gaggle of British Spitfires rushed to the rescue and the German fighters decided it was better to break off and fight another day.

Steve and his crew were quite exhausted. They had been to battle and now, with the sky empty except for the B-17s and their "little friends," the Spits, they could relax a bit. Steve motioned to Howie to take over the controls. Howie had flown the plane during some of the early part of the flight, with Steve flying the ship while they were over enemy territory. They formed a good team of pilot and copilot.

As they let down through 10,000 feet, Steve, who now acted the role of copilot, announced that they could come off oxygen. Off came the oxygen masks and they wiped the sweat from their face. It had been tense.

"The fuel looks a bit touchy," stated Jim McFarland, who had come down from his top turret position and once again was behind Steve and Howie, as the flight engineer.

"She wouldn't dare quit on us," answered Steve, as he took over the controls once again in order to line up for the landing in Chelveston. He went on to say, "We'd all have to explain to Pappy. We'll be on the ground in less than 15 minutes. The others with wounded aboard will land first."

"Well, I'm not one to worry either, Stevie ole boy, but that damn fuel warning light just came on," quietly stated Howie.

"You guys, hell, you want fuel to taxi as well as land," answered Steve, who at this time was flying the downwind leg of the flight pattern, then turned onto base and with Howie working the flaps and lowering the landing gear, brought the ship onto the final approach. Steve made a picture-perfect three-point landing, four engines still running.

Steve taxied the plane to their hardstand where Pappy was waiting. Steve and Howie went through the shutdown procedures and turned the big ship over to Pappy and his ground crew.

After the crew had exited the plane, they all did a walk around and spotted several shrapnel holes as well as two cannon shell holes in the vertical stabilizer.

"How was it?" questioned Pappy to Steve as he took him aside.

"Well, I didn't see as much as the other fellows. Keeping in tight formation is tough, but with the ME-109s and FW-190s trying to knock you out of the sky and the flak being shot up at you, things are more than a bit scary," answered Steve.

"You brought her home with no wounded aboard . . . must be some good flying," said Pappy as he patted Steve on the shoulder.

"We saw two planes go down. I think luck plays a big part. Some flak was just a few hundred feet from our ship, really just seconds of flight time. We get hit or we don't. We have 29 more trips before we go home. Well, one down anyway," Steve replied.

A grounds crewman walked over to Pappy and reported that in checking the fuel tanks, the plane had less than 10 minutes of flying time left. Pappy looked over to Steve, who just smiled. It had been a close call.

The rest of the crew had jumped aboard the waiting Jeep, but before getting in the right passenger's seat, Steve gave the plane a pat, "Thanks for bringing us home, ole girl," he spoke quietly, almost to himself.

It was a quiet ride back to operations. The 305th's intelligence officer interrogated the crew. They were questioned about the details of the mission. Some things they were asked to comment on included the level of anti-aircraft fire, flak, plus when and how many enemy aircraft had attacked them on the way to the target and on the way home. Did they see the other planes get hit? How many parachutes were deployed, if any?

A double shot of whiskey was served to everyone who wanted it. Everyone in the Carmichael Crew, even 19-year-old Joe DeMatteo, took the shots of whiskey. They had all been through a lot on this day . . . some of the crew were still rattled as they tried to settle down from the mission.

Steve, Howie, Bob, and Russ were completely exhausted as they stumbled from the debriefing hut. They went directly to their barracks, as did the enlisted men of the crew.

For some, a flop onto the bed with a few winks of sleep would serve as an additional cure to keep the nerves in check. Still others would place pen to paper and write a letter home.

Steve wrote a letter to his dad. He spoke of finally getting into battle and that his crew had acted under fire just as he hoped they would. There were not too many details in the letter to avoid worrying his dad. Steve censored his mail, and as aircraft commander, it was his duty to spot read all of the mail sent by his crew. Vital information was not supposed to be put into a letter, in case it could fall into the hands of enemy spies.

After Steve and his officers went for the evening meal at the officer's mess, they then met up with the Gerke Crew at the base Officer's Club. The eight officers gathered at a table near the unlit fireplace. The O-Club was always well stocked with gin, rum, and good Scotch whisky, but on this night, beer was what they all drank. Each, with a mug in hand, talked about the mission to Kassel. It was so important to have that first mission behind them, the hell of baptismal fire.

"Just 29 more to go," said Steve to the group, as he raised his mug and took a sip of beer and set the mug on the table.

"I just hope the results are the same, that we can all sit here and have more beers together. Today was no picnic," said Tommy Read, Wright Gerke's copilot.

"I was too busy keeping a tight formation to really get a good look at what was happening," said Wright.

"Know what you mean, Ike. I was doing the same," stated Steve, who thought for a minute and continued, "I was so pleased that the crew stood up under real battle conditions. They acted and reacted just as they've been trained to do. I think we'll be all right."

"Flying the tight formation helps keep the bandits at bay, but that damn flak! It seems that they've picked you out of the pile to shoot at," added Howie.

"I agree with you," said Russ Parker, who paused for a moment to take another taste of his beer. "From the nose, I could see some of those shells coming up from the ground and even saw one zoom by on its way up to the high squadron."

"We lost one ship from the 364th. The old-timer crews told me that we may last about eight missions. I don't know if they told me that to scare me or not, but they did," said Bob Courtney, who emptied his mug and then looked around at the others to see if they also wanted a refill.

"Here, I'll help you," said Joe Costa, navigator on the Gerke Crew, as he reached for some empty mugs to refill.

Just then, an announcement was made that the bar would close at eight o'clock because there was a mission on for tomorrow! The line for last call was four deep.

Most of the crew members went to bed early. They didn't know which crews would be scheduled for tomorrow's mission. In addition, they were just plain tired.

Very early the next morning, well before daylight, the crews who would fly the mission of the day were awakened. The Carmichael Crew and Gerke Crew were among those to fly. Briefing would be in one hour.

Steve bounced out of bed, as did the others. Well, some didn't exactly bounce out of bed, they sort of sleepwalked through the motions. It was first to the latrine, then a quick shower and close shave so that the oxygen mask would fit tight to the face and not cause chafing. Then, it was off to breakfast at the officer's mess before heading to the briefing hut.

They were somewhat used to the routine. After all, they were here yesterday. When the blanket was pulled away from the map during briefing, it showed the target to be Kiel, Germany. Kiel was located in the most northern part of Germany, not too far from Denmark. There were U-boat submarine pens in Kiel, as well as other ports. The mission flight plan would be a long trek over the North Sea. The date was Thursday, July 29, 1943. It looked to be a long day.

Steve, at the advice of a veteran pilot with 11 combat missions completed, was told to always study the flak map. It gave, for the most part, flak locations. This was an important piece of information for B-17 pilots because it showed whether to continue flying straight before turning away from the target or if it was best to turn right away, depending on the location of the flak batteries within the range. He was told that he would be in a flak field for long enough so why give the enemy additional shots at you? It certainly made sense to Steve, who decided to make this a habit before each mission.

Pappy was waiting for the crew. He briefed Steve on the plane. She was armed, warmed up, and ready to go. The scene was familiar as they went through the walk-around, waited for the first flare for start-up and the second flare to start taxiing out of the hardstand for their proper slot for takeoff and assembly in the formation. Then it was out over the North Sea and toward Kiel.

There was a layer of stratus clouds at 12,000 feet for more than 100 miles out into the North Sea. Finally, the clouds started breaking up and the formation climbed to the bombing altitude of 25,000 feet. The German coast was in sight, but they kept their distance from it, continuing to fly over the sea. The intended course also kept the formation just west of the Frisian Islands where flak batteries were located.

"I like this course," said Howie to Steve, as he acknowledged Steve's motion for his copilot to take over the controls for a while.

"Me too," said Steve as he stretched, then settled in to relax a bit before retaking the controls of the plane. "Let's keep alert for bandits," Steve told the rest of the crew over the plane's intercom.

Steve no sooner said those words than Joe DeMatteo from his right waist gunner's position and Jim McFarland from the top turret called out, "Bandits at three o'clock!"

It looked as though the six ME-109s were almost flying along with the formation. However, they were scanning the B-17 formation over to figure out a weak spot to attack. The ME-109s made a wide turn well out in front of the formation of B-17s and prepared for the familiar frontal attack: six enemy fighters wing to wing.

"Heads up, here they come," called Steve, as he took control of the plane in order to set up for the bomb run at Kiel.

The twin 50s through the Plexiglas nose, along with the top turret and ball turret guns, were ready and started barking fire as the ME-109s made their move. They made just one pass and kept on going, looking for another formation to attack. The reason for one pass was quite evident as the flak batteries opened up. Black puffs of smoke were now all around as the anti-aircraft shells exploded, sending deadly fireball chunks of shrapnel showering the planes. A direct hit could bring a B-17 down.

"They've got us zeroed in, Skipper . . . want to kick her around a bit?" called tail gunner Roger "Wyatt" Earp.

"Just a bit," answered Steve, as he took some evasive action to move the ship around so that the flak gunners on the ground would have a more difficult time trying to shoot them down. Steve knew that they were well past the IP and going onto the bomb run, so he had to keep the plane on course.

The plane was turned over to the bombardier from the pilot as he prepared to drop the bomb load. The clouds at their level were scattered, but the main target, a torpedo factory, was in plain view. Smoke screens that had been set were blown away by the surface winds. "Bombs away," called Russ over the intercom.

"Four flak shells just exploded, not 150 yards behind us, Skipper, at our altitude," called the excited tail gunner.

Steve took some immediate, severe evasive action just after leaving the target area in order to escape the flak being shot up at them.

As they pulled away from the target area in Kiel, the flak was shifted to another Group whose bomb run included the submarine pens.

It wasn't too long before they once again encountered German fighters. A group of ME-110s approached the formation, just out of the range of the B-17s' gunners. They seemed to just sit out there and then launched rockets toward the B-17s. Luckily, there were no hits and with no more enemy planes in sight, the formation made its way back toward English soil.

The long, over-water flight home to Chelveston was uneventful. Steve handed the controls over to Howie, who would fly the plane back home, with Steve taking them back to land. They had completed mission number two; just 28 more to go. That number seemed so far away. The Carmichael Crew had been lucky. No one injured! The long mission had taken seven and a half hours to fly. Steve took over the controls, flew downwind and finally set the *Image of War* once more onto British soil. After bringing the plane to a halt on their hardstand, doing the final checks and turning the ship over to Pappy, it was off to debriefing for the exhausted crew.

After resting up some and going to evening mess, Steve, Howie, Russ, and Bob walked over to the Officer's Club to join the Gerke Crew, who had already settled in. The 305th Group had lost no planes this day. Wright Gerke's tail gunner, Eddie Keesling, had claimed an ME-109. "I tell you, he keeps up our spirits," stated Ike, who took a sip of his beer. "He calls out the action as if we were at a prize fight."

The gang stayed at the O-Club until around nine o'clock. They were all simply tired and the bunk, such as it was, looked inviting. Needed rest was now the order of the evening.

There was no mission scheduled for the next day. The English weather had brought the bombing missions to a halt.

Steve, like most others, took the off day to not only rest and catch up with his nerves, but also to reread the letters from home and answer them. Steve wrote to his dad, telling him that two missions were now behind them and that he could not be more proud of his crew. He also asked his dad to drop a line to Mr. Briggs, owner of the Detroit Tigers, and let him know that his future catcher was doing well. Steve also wrote to Lillian and Elly. He had received four letters from Elly. He wanted to let her know that he could not answer one for one, but he would do his best, as time permitted. Steve also kept the letters to Elly light, so to speak, not wanting to scare her about combat flying. She had also kept them in a lighter manner, as Steve had requested. He did not want to know about her dating, or especially about the fellow he heard she was dating. It would be perhaps a long time before he saw her again and, well, there was a war on.

The weather continued to be on the foul side with no missions scheduled again for Saturday, July 31st. That night, there was a dance on the base, with a live band. It was a good time to relax and enjoy the hospitality of the attractive British women who came by train from London to Chelveston to attend the evening's event.

All of the men had a good time. Steve met a young beauty, three years younger than he was. Her name was Margaret Steele. She was from Sandown, Isle of Wight, an island town just off the coast of Portsmouth, England, in the English Channel. The Isle of Wight was quite a historic place and one of beauty. It had a little bit of all of England on one 60-mile-around island as she explained. Margaret, or "Maggie" by evening's end, was a nurse, currently serving at St. Thomas' Hospital in London. They had an enjoyable evening together and while the girls were supposed to dance with several of the young airmen, somehow, Steve and Maggie spent the whole night together. Steve and Maggie decided to keep in close touch and she would make some time for him, should he come to London.

During the first week in August, the weather still did not favor flying. It also seemed that flying conditions would not improve for at least a week. Steve, his crew, the Gerke Crew and some other crews received permission to go to London. It was a stroke of luck! While preparing to leave, Steve held a meeting with his crew. He wanted them to enjoy themselves, but there was a limit and he wanted them to be in good shape for when they did fly again, and to be careful of the ladies around Piccadilly Circus.

Steve and his officers made their way to the Stafford Hotel on St. James Place in London. It was where most of the 305th officers stayed on trips to the city. They found an American-type bar at the hotel, a home away from home. The Gerke Crew caught up with them at the hotel.

Howie took everyone on a tour of London. As he had said so many times, it was a favorite city of his and his parents. They took in the Tower of London, the Tower Bridge, and visited a couple of pubs for refreshment, before going on to Westminster

Abbey and Buckingham Palace. They also walked the London Bridge before stopping again for some refreshment at a pub.

When the gang returned to the Stafford Hotel, there was a note from Maggie. She would be happy to see Steve and join him for dinner.

Steve showered, shaved, and looked just like the officer and gentleman they place on recruitment posters. His silver pilot's wings and second lieutenant bars were shining as though there was an inspection.

As he came down in the lift and into the lobby, whistles greeted Steve from both his crew's officers and those of the Gerke Crew. Steve took it all good naturedly and simply spread his arms and did a slight bow.

"Where are you heading?" kidded Wright Gerke. "Ah, I know, dinner with General Eisenhower."

"Well, if he does show up, I'll at least offer to buy him a drink. But, he can't stay for dinner. I want to get to know Maggie a little better," answered Steve.

"Seems like you made an impression on each other," stated Howie.

"I know, we'll see," was Steve's reply to his copilot.

"Where are you going for dinner?" asked Russ Parker.

"I really don't know. We're meeting at the Victoria Train Station. Maggie has a place in mind." Steve walked toward the door. "Maybe I'll catch you later at the Simpson Club on Piccadilly Road."

"Well, we'll wind up there or here at the Stafford Bar," said Russ as he waved to Steve.

Steve, knowing that it would be difficult hailing a taxi, left on the early side in order to give himself plenty of time to walk to Victoria Station. He could have taken the London Underground from the Green Park Station, but it was just as easy to walk.

With umbrella in hand on a misty afternoon in London, Steve cut through Cleveland Street and part of Green Park, went down the Mall, past Buckingham Palace, continuing down Buckingham Palace Road, stopping briefly to peek at the exercising horses at the Royal Mews and on toward Victoria Station. Just a couple of blocks to go, then Victoria Train Station came into sight.

Steve entered the huge train station, taking in this beautiful historic old place, along with the smell of a train station. To those who love trains, it was a wonderful, hard-to-describe aroma, coupled with the thought of distant places where trains travel. He was all eyes, looking at everything at once.

Maggie, who also wanted to be there on the early side, spotted Steve and ran over to him.

"My you look quite handsome in that uniform. How about a date, soldier?" whispered Maggie as she gave Steve a big hug, backed off a second to look at him and then they kissed.

"It's great to see you again, very sharp," said Steve as he looked at the beautiful girl he was holding and they kissed again. It was a scene that did not look out of place in Victoria, but a quite familiar one as couples said hello and goodbye.

"I didn't realize until now how much I missed you," said Maggie, as she squeezed his hand and motioned for them to leave the train station. They walked arm-in-arm through the light rain under Steve's large umbrella. Tucked under the umbrella one could see that, as their eyes met, there was more than a casual relationship brewing. She continued, "I've got to be careful, this thing, whatever it is, could get out of hand with you."

Steve smiled, thought for a moment and answered, "I know, maybe it's the war, maybe not, but I'm willing to find out."

It wasn't too long before they were standing in front of the Ebury Wine Bar and Restaurant.

"My parents always came here when they would take the train up to London from Portsmouth Harbor. After riding the ferry, of course, from Ryde Pier on the Isle of Wight. It's a very friendly restaurant," explained Maggie.

They walked in and were greeted by an older lady who smiled and said, "Why hello, Margaret, and I see you've brought a guest."

"Yes. May I present Lieutenant Steven Carmichael, a pilot in the American Army Air Corps. We met at a dance in his air station a couple of weeks ago. Steve, say hello to Mrs. Cox."

"Nice to meet you, Lieutenant," said Mrs. Cox as they shook hands. "Welcome to the Ebury. Is this your first time in London?"

"Yes and I hope the first of many."

"How are your parents, Margaret?" asked Mrs. Cox, as she motioned for them to follow her to a table. "We don't get to see them as often these days."

"You know how it is with the war and restrictions leaving the Isle of Wight for the mainland," answered a proper Margaret. Mrs. Cox did not know that Steve nicknamed her Maggie.

"This table in the back corner is probably more comfortable for you young folks," said Mrs. Cox as she handed them menus.

"Thank you, Mrs. Cox," said Steve and Maggie at the same time and they had to smile at each other.

It was not long before a waiter came over. "Hello, can I bring you anything to drink or some starters?" he asked.

"Let's figure out what we'd like for dinner, then I'd like to see the wine list," was Steve's reply.

"I'll give you a few minutes," stated the waiter as he opened the wine list book and handed it to Steve. "Here is our wine list. It is not what it was before the war, but there are still some good wines in our cellar."

"The specialty of the house is roast beef with Yorkshire pudding," said Maggie. Then thinking for a moment and she added, "The beef is from Scotland."

"Sounds good to me," answered Steve. He looked over the wine list and selected a bottle of Claret. It is an enjoyable dry wine with a deep-garnet color and smooth tannins, as stated in the wine list. "In the States, Claret is Cabernet Sauvignon. It comes from California, just north of San Francisco. Wine Country is what they call it."

Steve and Maggie ordered the specialty of the house, accompanied with peas and potatoes. The dinner, wine, and steady flow of conversation made the evening not only a pleasant affair, but one could easily tell, especially when their eyes met, that much more than a social encounter was taking place. They lingered for quite some time after supper, engaging in small talk, just to spend a moment more enjoying each other's company.

Mrs. Cox rang up a taxi for them at a little past nine o'clock. Maggie had an early shift at St. Thomas' Hospital. The taxi took them past Parliament and Big Ben, then just over the River Thames by way of the Westminster Bridge. Steve asked the taxi driver to wait for him. He said a long goodbye to Maggie. She would be off duty around tea time and they agreed to meet at Harrods department store, in London's Knightsbridge area, at the Georgian Room Restaurant on the fourth floor at 3:30 p.m. the next afternoon.

Steve took the taxi back to the Stafford Hotel and walked into the cocktail bar to see if his or the Gerke Crew were about. They must still be out on the town, he thought to himself and settled at a small table in the corner. He ordered a pint of English Bitter.

The barman brought the freshly pumped beer and a bowl of peanuts.

"I know you Yanks like to munch on something with your beer," said the barmen, as he placed the pint and bowl of peanuts on the table.

"Thank you," was Steve's reply, as he handed the barman money. Steve added, "And please, one for yourself." He had learned that this was a proper way of giving the barman a tip.

"Thank you, sir," answered the barman, who smiled and walked back to his position behind the bar to wait on an officer who had just arrived.

The officer, also a second lieutenant, had a pint in his hand and looked around the room for a place to sit. Steve motioned for the officer to join him.

"I'm Steve Carmichael, 305th Bomb Group, and by way of your chest, I see that you're a navigator from the . . . " said Steve, as the lieutenant sat down and shook hands with Steve.

"Don Perry, 306th, just down the road a bit from you," stated the tall, reddish-haired navigator.

"Have you been over here for a while?" asked Steve.

"It's hard to say, Steve. How long is a while?" said Don, who took a sip of his beer. "Came over the end of March and have 11 missions behind me, but I've come to the point where I don't look forward much. We're losing too many crews. I guess I'm not supposed to talk like that."

"I understand," answered Steve. "I have just two behind me and 28 more to go before I'm finished with this tour, that is, if you can call it a tour. Neither Kassel or Kiel was a picnic."

"I was on Kiel and Kassel a month ago and to me they all are rough," said Don, who had a faraway look on his face. "I'm now with my third crew. But, what can I say?"

"Where are you from?" asked Steve, wanting to change the subject.

"Atlantic City, New Jersey . . . my parents have a grocery store on Connecticut Avenue, just off of Pacific Avenue. I grew up on the beach. In New Jersey, we call it the Shore," replied Don, now with a smile on his face. "How about you?"

"Central Florida, town called Kissimmee in Florida's cattle country where my dad and I have a cattle ranch just out of town. We have to go many miles to get to a beach. The Atlantic Ocean and the Gulf of Mexico are a few hours away."

Just then Howie, Bob, and Russ came into the bar. Howie and Bob walked over to the table while Russ gestured that he was going to order a few pints. Steve held up two fingers and Russ gave a high sign, also ordering for Steve and Don. The barman told Russ that he would deliver the beer to the table, so he could go and join his mates.

Steve did the introductions. Bob Courtney and Don Perry had met at Navigation School. Don was a class ahead of Bob and they knew each other in passing.

"Where's that Gerke Crew?" asked Steve.

"Still at the Simpson Club," answered Russ.

Howie and Don talked about Atlantic City. Howie's family had vacationed there a few times. Howie described that they had stayed at the Claridge Hotel and about the times he enjoyed on both the Steel Pier and the Million Dollar Pier and that his folks would go to the Garden Pier to hear a concert. Don told Howie that he had worked summers at the Garden Pier.

Finally, as the conversation settled down, Howie turned to Steve and said, "Well, I haven't fallen in love yet, how about you?"

Steve smiled at his copilot, then saw that Russ and Bob were also interested in his answer. "Close, I say, but this thing we're all caught up in has a way to go and hell, she's from the Isle of Wight and I'm from Florida. But, to her credit, she does know about baseball," he replied. "Her dad played tournament cricket. In 1939, when her father was in New York on business, he went to Yankee Stadium to see Ted Williams and the Boston Red Sox play a baseball game against Joe DiMaggio and the New York Yankees, so that does count for her!"

Everyone had a laugh and Howie said, "Well, it's hard to make plans now. You have time, Stevie my boy."

It was about then that they all decided to head upstairs and get some shut-eye. Before walking to the lift, Howie asked if anyone had plans for tomorrow. Steve stated that he was due for tea at 3:30, but was free up until then. Don was invited to join the group but needed to decline since he had to get back to his squadron. Howie told them that he would show them Speakers' Corner, where a speech for the day centered on "Sack the lot of them!" He would also take them to Trafalgar Square, and yes, there would be pub time. The next time they were in London, Howie said that he would take them to places of refinement. They needed some culture!

Steve and Howie shared a room at the Stafford, as did Russ and Bob. They all met for a late breakfast and joining them were Wright Gerke and his officers. After breakfast, Howie played tour guide. The weather gave them a break and even the sun popped out occasionally. Other crews told them that the weather was still not clear enough over the Continent to fly bombing missions. Good weather, bad weather, they would have to leave London for their base at Chelveston the following morning.

Steve left everyone just after lunch, took the Underground train and worked his way back to the Stafford Hotel to clean up once again, before going over to Harrods to meet Maggie. He walked from the Stafford back to the Green Park Underground Station, checked the map on the wall and counted how many stops there would be before he "minded the gap" as he alighted from the carriage. After leaving the carriage car, Steve walked for a while, climbed some stairs, rode an escalator and climbed some more stairs to the street level. A short walk on Brompton Road and Steve was standing in front of the world-famous Harrods. Since he was a little early, Steve decided to stroll through the ground floor and found himself amazed as he gazed around the food halls. It was fascinating and he could only imagine how it might look if there were no war on, no ration coupons in order to purchase things. He remembered his dad telling him that ration stamps were now the order of the day in the United States. Steve priced a fresh peach. The cost of just one was three shillings and three pence, about 65 cents U.S., for one peach! A British pound note was almost equal to four American dollars.

Steve checked his watch, walked over to a lift and told the operator that he would like the fourth floor, where the Georgian Restaurant was located. The lift operator smiled, figuring that this was his first time in Harrods.

Maggie had been waiting and walked over to greet Steve. They embraced, kissed and hand in hand they were off to see the maitre d'. He greeted them and took them to a table on the right side of the room, so they could look out onto the terrace and be just far enough from the older gentleman playing the piano to hear each other talk. A waitress came over to them and Maggie told her that they would like a "Cream Tea" accompanied by a pot of Darjeeling. "It is very pleasant afternoon tea," replied the waitress.

Maggie then turned her attention directly to Steve. "I hope you don't mind me taking charge," she said. Steve simply reached over, took her hand and smiled.

"I'm taking mental notes, so that the next time I'll know what to ask for," was Steve's reply.

"When is the next time?"

"Well, they usually give you a pass after 10 missions. I pretty much know that for certain. Depending on the weather and with some flying luck, I hope it will be soon."

"It's nearly impossible to reach either one of us by telephone. I will write and perhaps, if I am able to get some time off, I could travel up there, for a dance or something," and Maggie's voice trailed off as her eyes started to tear.

"We will work something out. Don't concern yourself."

The waitress returned to the table with the pot of Darjeeling tea. "We'll let it steep a little more before pouring," she said, then left for just a moment, returning with the several-plated tower containing mini-sandwiches, scones with a small dish of strawberry jam, a dish of clotted cream and a plate that held an assortment of mini-desserts. While Steve and Maggie looked over the decorative food, the waitress poured the tea.

"Wow, this Cream tea is something . . . can't wait to describe this to Lillian," said Steve as he reached for one of the tiny sandwiches.

"Now this is the time for you to be a gentleman," said Maggie softly. "There are two of everything. If you eat both of the salmon, I'll break your arm!"

"No worries, my dear, if you're still hungry, we'll order another tray!"

Steve and Maggie worked to keep the conversation on the lighter side. It was a hard thing to do for young people who seemed to be falling in love yet had no certain future. Steve asked about the Isle of Wight, her parents and her childhood. He told her all about Florida, the ranch and how much he loved flying. It was a pleasant late afternoon spent in Harrods. When they left, a Harrods doorman helped them into a taxi.

"Please take us to the Mall entrance of St. James Park," Maggie told the driver. Then she turned to Steve as the taxi pulled away from the curb saying, "This is my most favorite park. Ever since I was a little girl, my parents would bring me here when we were in London. Now, I'll share it with you and make a memory."

Steve paid the taxi fare, then with hands intertwined he and Maggie strolled down the path to the park lake. Maggie walked over to a vendor and purchased some cracked corn and a very large muffin.

"Still hungry?" kidded Steve.

"The cracked corn is for the ducks and the muffin will be shared by the squirrels and wild birds," replied Maggie, as they settled in on a park bench overlooking the water.

Steve could see the joy Maggie took in feeding their new friends. She had a wide smile as the ducks ate the cracked corn from her hand.

Even from a distance, it was easy to see that they were happy in each other's presence. Neither Steve nor Maggie wished to rush things, even though it seemed like the thing to do during war.

They talked, laughed and held one another, but all too soon, it was time to leave the park.

In leaving St. James Park, they strolled along Bird Cage Walk toward Big Ben and the Westminster Bridge. At about the midway point of the bridge over the River Thames, Steve stopped and handed Maggie an American quarter and also held one in his hand. Then, at the signal from Steve, they threw the coins into the rushing tidewaters of the Thames. "Now, we'll both have to come back to this spot," said Steve.

"Some old American folklore custom?" questioned Maggie.

"No, not really, I just made it up. It sounds good, though, don't you agree?"

Maggie gave Steve a light punch on the arm, as they continued arm-in-arm across the bridge to St. Thomas' Hospital. Just across the street was London's County Hall. Once at the hospital, now that it was supper time, Maggie suggested that they have a light dinner in St. Thomas' dining hall. Steve agreed that he was still full from the late afternoon tea and that perhaps some soup and bread and butter would be just right.

While they were dining, two of Margaret's nurse friends stopped by their table and were introduced to Steve. To say the least, the girls were curious to know who this man was who appeared to be dating Margaret. One of the nurses, as Maggie explained to Steve, was a friend who also came from the Isle of Wight. She lived in the next town to Sandown, Shanklin.

"I'm not going to invite you to join us. Maybe the next time the lieutenant comes to London he'll bring a friend for each of you," stated Maggie. Her message brought about an exit of the nurses with a "nice to have met you" and they found another table.

"Did I sound rude?" asked Maggie.

"No . . . but what could be called direct," answered Steve.

"Well, we don't have much time and I want you all to myself."

Afterward Steve and Maggie walked outside toward the river, then holding hands walked a few yards out onto the Westminster Bridge. They did not say anything; nothing needed to be said as they kissed and held each other. It was getting late and Maggie was once again on early call at the hospital. Steve also needed to get to the hotel and be ready for the early trip back to Chelveston. They spoke quietly as they walked back to the hospital. Maggie lingered a few minutes to watch Steve's taxi as it drove out of sight, across the Westminster Bridge on the way to the Stafford Hotel.

Howie called to Steve to join Russ, Bob, and himself in the Stafford's bar. As Steve sat down, Russ placed a pint in front of him. Steve raised his glass in salute to his friends and enjoyed a long sip of British Bitter. They talked for a while, had one more round of pints and after leaving a wake-up call at the front desk, hit the hay. The fun trip to London was over. Now it would be back to the business of war.

CHAPTER THREE

Even though they were now back at the Chelveston base, the weather for flying combat missions over the skies of the European continent was cloud covered and too dense for meaningful bombing raids. The local weather in the East Anglia area of England, however, permitted some practice missions. With the complete crew back together once again, Steve welcomed the opportunity to fly a practice mission in order to keep everyone sharp. He wanted to have his crew focused on the job at hand and like it or not, it was back to war.

Excitement broke their lull when Lieutenant Wright Gerke returned to the barracks with the wonderful news that he was a father. "It's a baby girl!" he said. Wright passed out cigars all around and took some good-natured razzing, however, as he stated, having a boy would not have made him any happier. He was such a proud papa. Wright told everyone that he was dreaming of the things he now had to come home to. He was waiting to see pictures of his newborn daughter.

Steve made time to catch up on his letter writing. The first, of course, was to his dad. He told his dad that he had met a nurse named Maggie at a base dance and that he spent time with her while in London. He added that she was from the Isle of Wight: "Check it out on a map, Dad. From London, look south, down toward Portsmouth and the Isle of Wight is just off the coast, about six miles into the English Channel." From reading the letter, Ray would certainly know that the young lady had caught his son's eye.

In addition, Steve wrote that a friend from the University of Florida had sent a letter telling him that he had enlisted in the Navy, would be commissioned an ensign and had passed tests permitting him to go into the PT Boat Program at Melville, Rhode Island. Also knowing that Steve was part of, well sort of part of, the Detroit

Tigers organization, his friend brought Steve up to date on the Tigers' 1943 season. He also told Steve that he had been on a date at the movies and ran into Elly, who was with a guy he knew from the football team. He went on to say that while he knew Steve and Elly were close at one time and had some problems, he did not want Steve to feel guilty if he met someone overseas. Steve told his dad that it was ironic the letter should arrive just as he actually had met someone whom he was beginning to care about. Steve further wrote that the bad weather had been a blessing because after the recent missions; the crew was a bit on the jumpy side. The trip to London had been a little reward. "You wouldn't believe it, Dad," he wrote, "but after just two missions, I almost consider myself a veteran. Knowing what to expect in combat takes away the wondering. Now we know what's happening!"

Steve also wrote V-Mail letters to friends who were kind enough to write. Mail from home was so important. One of the V-Mails, kept on the light side, was to Elly.

Word came as both the Carmichael and Gerke Crews sat at their favorite table by the fireplace in the Officer's Club that a mission was on for tomorrow. The O-Club would close early. They were all sure to fly.

The crews were awakened early the next morning with the usual schedule. After breakfast, it was off to the briefing hut to learn about the mission for Thursday, August 12, 1943.

There were sounds of gasping and moaning as the blanket was pulled away from target map. It would be one of the toughest missions to date: Gelsenkirchen, Germany, located well near the center of the heavily armed Ruhr Valley. The flight plan would carry them over the North Sea, across part of Belgium, where they would continue to have fighter escort, P-47s. The escort, however, would need to turn back at this point because the fighters' range did not permit further penetration into enemy territory. The B-17s would be on their own as they continued across the Netherlands and into Germany. The bombing altitude would be from 31,000 feet for the high squadron. With so many flak batteries in the Ruhr Valley, at least this would make it a bit tougher for the anti-aircraft gunners to lock their sights in on them. It certainly seemed that on this mission the B-17 crews would have to fight their way in and out of the target area.

As the crews left the briefing hut for the ride to their planes, Steve walked over to Wright Gerke to congratulate him on making first lieutenant. They had quite a long conversation together, shook hands, and said they would meet up at the Officer's Club later. Hopefully the baby pictures would arrive today.

Then Steve joined his crew, who were waiting at the Jeep that would take them to the hardstand to get ready for the mission at hand. Pappy was completing his preflight duties as the crew arrived. He went over to Steve and brought him up to speed on the plane's preparation. The old girl had been warmed up and was ready to go. They completed the preflight and at the signal from the control tower, the crew boarded the *Image of War*.

Just before Steve swung up into the forward hatch to enter the plane, Pappy said, "I hear that you've got a rough one today."

"From what I've observed and heard, they're all rough. Just some are tougher than others," answered Steve as he patted his ground crew chief on the shoulder and boarded the B-17.

Howie was already in the copilot's seat going over the checklist as Steve settled into the left-hand pilot's seat. They completed the preflight checklist. In just a few minutes, with engines roaring, they taxied in line to the end of the runway. The takeoff and climb to join up with the formation was normal. The weather had cooperated to this point and allowed a more relaxed routine rendezvous with the group, before heading out to sea and toward the Continent.

The P-47s were right on time. For now, the formation of B-17s was under the protection of their little friends. The P-47s would also pick them up on the way home. It was the time between, when the escort had to leave and before meeting them again on the way out of the Continent, which was of greatest concern. They could expect German fighters to try to work them over during that period. In addition, they had to contend with the flak.

Steve flew a tight formation, keeping his ship in its designated slot to afford the best protection by the group's firepower. He did not have much time to look around. Puffs of exploding flak started to appear as they crossed the coast and ventured into the Continent. So far, the flak was not very accurate. The Luftwaffe had not sent up any fighters to intercept the bomber stream; however, they would arrive when the escort P-47s had to turn for home.

"Little friends are heading back to England," said Howie.

"Let's be sharp. We're on our own now," reminded Steve to his crew over the plane's intercom.

Steve had no sooner spoken when his top turret gunner, Jim McFarland reported "Some specks out there at 11 o'clock, looks like they're headed our way." Jim swung his twin 50s around to greet them if they came in for a pass.

As the objects grew larger, it was clear that there were more than 30 ME-109s. They made a pass at the low squadron, made up from a composite of two other groups.

"One B-17 on fire, out of formation. Oh Christ, he exploded!" exclaimed the ball turret gunner, Willie Burnett.

"Okay, let's continue to be alert. We've got a long way to go," said Steve, not wanting his crew's minds to wander, but to keep vigilant about the danger unfolding before them.

"Bandits at 12 o'clock, looks like a dozen or so are making a frontal attack," said Howie in as calm a voice as he could muster with all that was going on.

It looked as though the ME-109s were breaking into three groups of five fighters for the frontal attack, which was planned for killing everyone up in the front of the B-17 bomber, or more specifically, the pilot and copilot.

Russ Parker was at the twin 50s in the nose. The top turret and ball turret guns swung around into position to ward off the frontal attack. Guns from the *Image of War* started firing even before the ME109s were in range to let the enemy fighter pilots know that they were alert and ready for action. The ME-109s bored in, firing at the formation in the frontal attack. Killing those at the controls would certainly disable the Flying Fortress. Just before flying through the formation, the ME-109s turned over and dove below the B-17s. The waist gunners as well as both the tail and ball turret gunners continued to fire at the diving enemy fighters.

"One's smoking!" yelled Willie.

"Everyone okay?" Steve's voice came over the plane's intercom. "Check in."

All of the crew checked in; everyone was all right. Just as Bob completed each position's response, the German fighters turned away from the formation.

The bomber stream was about to enter the heavily fortified flak area of the Ruhr Valley, the heart of German industry. At their altitude, the B-17s hot engine exhaust was leaving a long, white trail of condensation, a vapor trail seen and easily tracked from the ground. It was not long before all hell broke loose. A steady barrage of 105-millimeter shells, along with 88s, exploded in clusters all around them. The German defensive anti-aircraft artillery was uncomfortably effective even at their altitude.

Steve heard his crew's calls to "shake the plane around" a little to ward off the trackers. The exploding shells were very close and showered the *Image of War* with dirty black fragments of flak. Steve did his best to do exactly that: shake the plane around. He would drop 100 feet, climb 100 feet and move the plane side to side to keep the ground battery gun crews guessing, however, he also had to keep his slot within the formation. This was no easy task. Steve also wondered if it did any real good. The flak batteries were not shooting directly at their plane, but putting up the barrages in hopes that a B-17 would fly into one of the exploding shells. If the crew felt a little better with him shaking her around, fine!

"Skipper," called radio operator Eddie Anderson. "The primary target is clouded over and they also have smoke screens there. We're to follow them to the secondary."

Steve looked over at Howie, who had an exasperated look on his face. "Okay, Eddie," was Steve's reply.

"I don't think we should be taking a tour of the Ruhr Valley," said Howie to Steve.

"Maybe we'll have better luck in Cologne . . . Köln, they call it," was Steve's reply as the formation made its way south.

They continued to fly with flak shells exploding around them. The plane, even with all of its weight, bounced from the concussion of the explosions. Suddenly a shell burst several yards in front of their plane. A piece of flak, about the size of a prune, came crashing through the Plexiglas nose and glanced off the right shoulder of Russ Parker, slitting his "Mae West" life preserver. From there, it ricocheted up and into the pilot's cockpit with its direction shattering a flight instrument directly in front of Steve. Both he and Howie jumped a foot!

"You okay?" asked Howie.

"I'm all right," answered Steve as he looked at the instrument that was no more, and then he continued, "Russ, Bob, okay or what?"

"A bit of what, but we're all right," answered Bob. He paused, then continued over the intercom, "Piece of shrapnel hit Russ in the shoulder, did no damage to him, but ripped a hole in his Mae West. It's also a little drafty with all the holes in the Plexiglas. Got something we can shove in the holes, Skipper?"

Steve looked over at Howie and both of them understood that this had been a close call. The formation was lining up in the new IP and preparing to bomb an airfield just east of Cologne. The heavy flak continued. There was not a thing they could do about it. Steve had handed the plane over to Russ for the bomb run. While the target was somewhat clouded over, there was enough of a break in the clouds to drop the bomb load.

"Bombs away, bomb bay doors coming up, let's get the hell out of here and go home," called Russ as Steve once again took control of the B-17.

Just off the target, there was a huge flash to the left of Steve's pilot seat.

"Ike's been hit! It looks like a direct hit in the right wing. Hit the gas tank!" exclaimed Steve.

Howie, looking over to the left from his copilot's seat said, "Goddamn, get out of there, guys! Oh shit . . . goddamn son of a bitch!"

"B-17 knocked out of formation, fire in the right wing is swelling badly," reported Willie Burnett, who turned his ball turret downward to try and fend off the six ME-109s that had pounced on the crippled ship.

It was no use. The half-dozen ME-109s were shooting the hell out of the B-17. Their attack was to the front, back and sides of the doomed bomber. Soon there was no return fire from the B-17 named *ARKY.* Finally, after maintaining control for a few minutes, the big ship went into a spin and exploded.

"Anyone see parachutes?" asked Steve as he tried to gain control over his emotions.

"Just two that I saw, Skipper," answered a stunned tail gunner, likewise trying to regain his composure. They knew that it was the Gerke Crew going down. "Both from the bomb bay, just before she exploded. I saw only two," repeated Wyatt.

"Me too. That's all I saw, Skipper," said Willie.

The German fighters that had finished off the Gerke Crew and sent their plane plummeting from the sky continued to harass the B-17s in the lower squadron, rather than climb back to their altitude that was now 31,200 feet.

The formation continued back toward England. They skirted Rotterdam in order to avoid their flak guns. The P-47 fighters picked them up just off the Dutch coast and escorted the bombers back across the North Sea. Their little friends flew with them until the battle-weary

B-17s peeled off to land at their home base.

A stunned, silent Carmichael Crew withdrew into their own thoughts at the loss of a crew who, dating back to initial training, had become close friends. Steve motioned for Howie to take over the controls as they let down past 12,000 feet and went off oxygen.

Steve took off his oxygen mask, wiped tears from his eyes and slowly shook his head in disbelief. "My god, Howie," he said, "Ike just became a daddy."

Howie nodded his head slowly as he flew the B-17 toward their home base at Chelveston. Finally he said to Steve, "We've been lucky so far . . . Russ and Bob and that damned flak."

Steve looked over at Howie, understanding what he meant. He took over the controls before starting the downwind leg and brought his crew home for the third time.

The mission had taken almost eight hours to complete. Fatigue clearly showed as they left the debriefing. Steve did not go directly to his barracks, but over to the one that had been occupied by First Lieutenant Wright Gerke. Howie went along with Steve and made the motion to Bob and Russ that they would meet up with them later.

As the two entered the barracks, a sergeant and a corporal were placing Wright's personal things into his trunk.

"You move fast. Wait a minute," said Steve to the sergeant.

"But, sir, we have our orders," was the response.

Howie, seeing that Steve was in no mood to discuss anything, said to the men, "Go outside and take a smoke break. You can come back in a little while," and he escorted the two men to the door.

The sergeant, now understanding the situation, said, "Please take your time, I'm sorry."

Steve sat on Wright's bed. He did not know what to do other than to sit in silence. He looked around the room, up toward the ceiling, but he was not really staring at anything. His thoughts were, *Only two parachutes and not likely one that belonged to Ike. He would have been the last to leave the crippled ship.*

After about 15 minutes, Steve stood up, patted Howie on the shoulder and said, "Thanks for coming over here with me. I just cannot believe it, Howie. Last night we were all together. Wright was just talking about his newborn daughter. Damn!"

Howie did not answer. What was there to say?

After evening mess, Steve, Howie, Russ, and Bob made their way to the Officer's Club. They gathered at their favorite table, less four chairs this night. No one spoke. Russ helped Bob bring four pints of beer to the table.

Before they had taken a sip of their pints, Howie, holding a small piece of paper in his hand said, "I've brought this little list with me and I'd like us to raise our glasses to the Gerke Crew: pilot Wright Gerke, copilot Tommy Read, navigator Joe Costa, bombardier Jack Little, engineer Harry Fullerton, radio operator Jim Chalker, ball turret gunner Joe Hall, waist gunners Herb Kalwa and Joe Rowlinson, and tail gunner Eddie Kiesling, that wonderful clown, who shot down that ME-109. To that wonderful group of guys that we'll miss and who we'll think about for the rest of our lives . . . to them."

They raised their glasses and there was not a dry eye.

There was not a mission scheduled for the next day. The local weather and that over the Continent was poor again. Steve, for one, was glad. It would give him and his crew a day or so to rest and catch up with their feelings.

Steve wrote just one letter. It was to his dad. "Dear Dad, I've got some mighty bad news to tell you. Wright Gerke and his crew are missing in action. We saw his plane get hit and frankly, I don't think he made it. At least Ike knew he was a daddy and did that ever make him happy. Dad, I'm so sad." Steve also said that he would write again in a day or so, when his thoughts were clearer, but for now, he had to pull himself together for the sake of his crew.

Steve was also able to reach Maggie. He had telephoned St. Thomas' Hospital several times before finally speaking with her. He told her about the loss of their close friends, the Gerke Crew. Even though the phone call with Maggie was fairly short, it did give Steve a chance to talk. It was a comfort to hear her voice.

There was a mission scheduled for August 15th. It was to the Flushing area in Belgium, bombing an enemy airfield. The mission would be of just the length where they would have a P-47 fighter escort all the way to and from the target. Sunday or not, a war was on and the mission would take place.

Everything on this day went off without a hitch. They returned to Chelveston with all four engines running smoothly. Mission number four was in the books. It was a good day for the 305th Bomb Group. All of the planes dispatched for the mission returned safely to base.

There was, however, not much time to reflect on the mission because while the Carmichael Crew officers were at the O-Club that evening, word came that a mission was on for the morning. The club would once again close early.

At briefing, very early the following morning, they were told that the target would be to bomb an airfield at Le Bourget, France. The flight would take them to the outskirts of Paris. This airfield had become famous in 1927 when Charles Lindbergh landed here after his historic solo flight across the Atlantic Ocean from Long Island, New York. Now German fighters flew from the airdrome.

When the crew arrived at the hardstand, Pappy rushed over to Steve. He spoke quickly, "We can't get the number three engine to turn over. As you can see, the cowling is still off and I'm trying to figure out what's wrong. We're working on her, Lieutenant, but damn, she just won't kick in."

It would not be their day to fly. The spare B-17 was in the J hangar, also being repaired. They would just have to sit this one out. It was a great disappointment to the crew because this mission, like the one yesterday, would be of the length in which they would have escort fighters to and from the target. It would not be considered a milk run, but it was a good one to put in the books as one more combat mission behind them. The 305th Group left for France as the Carmichael Crew watched from their plane's hardstand.

The mission to Le Bourget went as planned. Bombing the target was right on. It was, in fact, some of the best bombing to date. In addition, all of the group's B-17s returned home safely once again. Steve and the crew gathered by the control tower as one by one the 305th planes landed.

The Carmichael Crew was posted to fly the following day, August 17th. The target was the long-expected visit to Schweinfurt. The 305th Bomb Group had been scheduled to bomb this target twice before, but each time the weather forced them to scrub the mission.

There was a heavy fog on the field at Chelveston as dawn was breaking and the crews filled the briefing hut. The mission on this Tuesday morning would be a maximum effort. The 305th would use 100 percent of the available planes. Most missions called for 75 percent of the planes with one squadron standing down for a day of rest, but not today! All squadrons would fly this mission. The 305th Bomb Group Squadrons, 364th, 365th and 366th would fly as the 305th Group, while the 422nd would join a composite group made up from planes of both the 305th and 306th Groups.

Colonel Fargo did not have very much more to add after the blanket was taken from the mission map and the yarn stretched all the way to Schweinfurt, Germany. The intelligence officer had made things quite clear in his mission briefing. The solemn look on the crew member's faces let Colonel Fargo know that they understood what the mission meant. They also understood one particular fact: that this would be an extremely rough one.

The mission called for a dual effort as well. A double strike would have the Fourth Bomb Wing under the command of Colonel Curtis Le May hit Regensburg and the ME-109 factory, while at the same time the 101st Bomb Wing, formally the First, under the command of Brigadier General Robert Williams, would be bombing Schweinfurt where 50 percent of the ball bearings Germany needed were manufactured.

The flight to the target would fly the 305th over Belgium, just a small portion of Holland, near Maastricht and a little south of Aachen, where they would enter German skies as they flew on toward their target. Success of the mission would largely be due to the strike forces as they coordinated bombing both Schweinfurt and Regensburg. Both targets were to be bombed simultaneously. By coordinating the mission in this way, the B-17s would benefit because the German fighters would have to deal with attacking two formations of bombers rather than one. While this was not exactly a bonus from the viewpoint of the bomber crews, at least they would only have to fight off half the number of enemy fighters they would have otherwise encountered.

Regensburg would be attacked by between 145 and 150 bombers, made up of B-17s and B-24s. The strike at Schweinfurt would be made by 230 to 235 bombers. The number of planes flying the mission was to be determined by how many aborted due to mechanical problems that forced them to return to their base. The fighter escort for the dual mission was to consist of American P-38s and P-47s, plus the outstanding British RAF fighter, the Spitfire. The Allied fighter force would number over 250. The escort would use their maximum range to protect the bombers as best they could. The bombers, however, would be on their own for a good part of the long, tedious mission. The time over enemy territory was estimated to be over four hours.

When the Carmichael Crew arrived at the plane's hardstand, as usual, they found the maintenance crew making the final checks on their B-17. She was repaired and ready to go. With the impending flight due to be a long one over enemy territory, the armorers had quipped each gun station with extra boxes of .50 caliber ammunition. The bomb bay was loaded with special British firebombs, rather than the usual 500 pound bombs.

Fog continued to hang over the field at Chelveston. The delay from the original takeoff time made several crew members nervous. They wanted to get on the way and place one more combat mission behind them. Steve, seeing this, decided to keep the crew loose and busy playing catch with the baseballs, gloves and bats he kept in the maintenance tent near the plane. They mainly played catch because hit balls would disappear in the fog, although a couple of the fellows did bunt the ball back to their crewmates.

Finally, after a delay of more than two hours, the fog started to lift and at the signal from the control tower, the Carmichael Crew climbed aboard the *Image of War* and went to their respective stations for one final check before assuming their takeoff position.

With the aircraft forward hatch and rear door now closed, the wait was not long before the flare to start engines was seen from the control tower. Another flare and the planes started the taxi toward the takeoff position at the end of the runway. The control tower fired the flare to take off and one by one, the big, heavily loaded bombers labored down the runway. They lifted off into a sky now filled with broken clouds and formed up for the raid to Schweinfurt, Germany.

Steve continued to have the bomber climb, as Howie, from his copilot's seat kept an eagle eye out for other planes that might stray into their air space due to the poor visibility. The 305th Group passed over the Splasher Seven beacon on the coast of England. The 366th Squadron would fly as the low squadron of the group this day. Steve leveled the B-17 off at 24,250 feet. Howie motioned to Steve that the P-47s were right on time, even with the delay. The little friends would work to escort and protect the bomber wing as much as they could. Some of the fighters moved in close to the bombers, while others fanned out and took up positions on each flank. The bombers in the higher squadrons were likewise protected by the British Spits, as well as American twin-engine P-38s and P-47s. From the flight deck, Steve and Howie exchanged silent greetings with the escort fighters as they maintained radio silence. The English coastline slipped slowly behind them as they traveled further out over the Channel toward the Belgian coast.

"Pilot to crew, you can test your guns. But, don't shoot down any of our escorts," called Steve over the plane's intercom.

Howie broke into a wide grin as he looked over to Steve and said, "Good thinking. They don't get credit for a kill if it's one of ours."

The chatter and vibration of guns test firing a short burst brought about the serious nature of what was about to happen. Each crew member checked in and everything was in working order. The bomber stream was now halfway across the channel. The P-47s slid in and out of the formation, dipping their wings so that the B-17 gunners would recognize them as friendly rather than enemy fighters.

Black puffs of anti-aircraft cannon fire alerted everyone that they had entered enemy territory. So far, the flak batteries had not honed in on the bomber stream and their fire hadn't been very accurate.

"Okay, let's keep on our toes," Steve said to his crew.

He no sooner completed his statement when over the intercom from the tail gunner's position, came an excited call, "Enemy fighters coming in from the rear."

The German ME-109s roared in, ignoring the P-47s, but holding off firing their 37-millimeter cannons until they were less than 300 yards away. The Carmichael Crew returned fire as the enemy fighters flipped over on their wings and broke off the attack at less than 150 yards. Cannon shells ripped into the *Image of War*, scoring hits on the vertical stabilizer and just behind the radio room. Eddie Anderson checked in that he was all right; however, there were pretty big holes where the shells came in and then out the other side of the plane without exploding. Wyatt was also okay, but something had sure as hell hit the plane above him.

The bright yellow ring on the ME-109s' cowling and spinner hub on the engine let everyone know that the boys from Abbeville were here today! The P-47s, also caught by surprise, drove off the enemy fighters. The friendly fighters were now reaching the limit of their range. Soon the B-17s would be on their own. It would be more than two hours before they see their little friends again.

Flak exploded once again throughout the formation as they passed near Antwerp. It continued as the flak batteries on the ground tracked the flight of B-17s. So far, Steve and his crew had been fortunate. The plane was flying fine, engines running smoothly and what damage that did occur to the vertical stabilizer was not affecting them. To the right, left, and in front of them, B-17s were falling from the sky as deadly anti-aircraft fire found their targets. This, coupled with the intense fighter attacks, was taking a terrible toll on the bombers. Parachutes filled the air as crews tried to escape from their burning B-17s.

The B-17 at their level and a little to the right exploded into a bright-orange fireball. Six crew members made it out, just six. What of the other four crew members? Six parachutes opened, but one was on fire and collapsed. What a terrible death. The other five were lucky, but they would be in German hands tonight.

In the meantime, Steve had to concentrate on keeping in close formation to best protect his ship.

They passed Maastricht, Holland, and entered German skies just south of Aachen. A squadron of German ME-210s now joined the battle. They stayed just out of range with twin-engine ME-110s leading them.

"The son of a bitches are firing rockets at us!" said Howie in an excited voice.

Steve took a quick peek, however, he was too busy keeping the big plane tucked in. He really had no time to take a long look around at this chaotic scene.

"What's it look like, Howie? Should we kick her around a bit?" questioned Steve.

"I don't think so, they haven't picked us out of the pack, at least not yet," came Howie's reply. He kept an intense eye on the rocket-bearing enemy planes, then added, "No sense drawing attention to us."

Directly ahead of them, perhaps a half mile in front, another B-17 was hit by flak in the left wing, which became engulfed in flames, knocking it out of the formation. It was immediately attacked by six FW-190s who chased it, firing away as the B-17 spun out of control on the way down. No parachutes were seen.

As they flew on toward the target, further ahead still more B-17s were seen to fall from the sky. The deadly accurate flak was taking a terrible toll and the fighter attacks continued as they pressed to shoot down the bombers before their bomb loads could be released on German targets. It seemed as though the Luftwaffe was throwing every available type of plane at them on this day. The two targets were vital to the Allies, but they were just as important to the Germans.

There were certainly more fighters than had been predicted at the briefing. Perhaps the delay in leaving due to local fog had let the Regensburg portion of the mission take off on time, thus permitting the Luftwaffe fighters to land, refuel, pick up more ammo and come back to fight this formation headed for Schweinfurt. At least this was the thought of the Carmichael Crew as they watched the largest group of German fighters they had ever seen. The delay was proving costly.

Finally there was a slight breather from the fighters, who had now gathered nearer to the target area in an attempt to shoot down the invading B-17s before they could drop their bombs on the ball-bearing factory at Schweinfurt. The heavy flak continued to explode all around them.

The Luftwaffe fighters were so intent on stopping the bombing that they even flew through their own flak in order to press the attack on the bomber formations.

The *Image of War* shook and bounced as the exploding flak shells spewed chunks of hot shrapnel into the thin skin of its aluminum fuselage, tearing numerous small holes in the side and belly of the plane. So far, no direct hits. There was little that Steve could do. It seemed as though luck was either with you or not. There was no divine guidance that said this ship will be shot down and that one will not be shot down, at least on this day. All of these planes carried good, solid, young men, who by other means would be back home on the farm, working their job or perhaps attending college. Nevertheless, they were all here, fighting for their very lives.

Another B-17 dropped out of formation with two engines on fire. Get out of there! was the thought of all who could see the big bomber flailing out of control, falling toward the earth. Seven escaped from the crippled plane; three did not.

Finally, the target came into sight and Russ Parker said, "Bombs away, bomb bay doors coming up. Skipper, your airplane . . . get us the hell out of here!"

"Okay, Russ, I've got her. Let's go home," came Steve's reply as he once again took control of the plane from his bombardier.

The heavy flak continued, with shells exploding at their altitude. Shrapnel pounded and showered the plane. More holes in the skin. So far, the plane had still not sustained a direct hit and no one had been injured, although a small piece of flak hit the jacket of Jack Kowalski, spinning him around.

"Are you okay?" yelled Joe DeMatteo as he quickly moved over to check on his fellow waist gunner.

"I think so," came Jack's reply. "But look at my flak jacket." One glance at Jack and his flak jacket showed that he came close to not being okay.

"Check in. Is everyone all right?" called Howie over the intercom. Everyone was all right, some shaken a little, but otherwise alive and still intact.

The flight back to Chelveston would be a long one. It was still 475 miles back to the base. At cruising speed, a B-17 flew at 2.5 miles per minute. There were a lot of minutes in 475 miles.

The B-17 formation, or what was left of it, had not counted the number of planes lost in this battle. That would come later at the debriefing. The tally of those planes that did not return to English soil would increase. Planes were still being blown from the sky by both direct flak hits and enemy fighter planes. The German fighters were pressing attacks from the frontal finger-four, or even six, formation trying to kill those up front who fly the plane, or from behind to take out the tail gunner and then the wing struts and engines. The German fighter pilots were extremely aggressive on this day.

Suddenly Bob Courtney shouted over the intercom, "Oh, geez, Doug Mutschler's plane has been hit. Bill Bagwell is their navigator."

"Count the chutes," called Howie into the intercom.

"I see three, no, four," stated Willie Burnett from his ball turret position. Then he corrected himself, "I now count seven, that's it, seven!"

"That ship is from the 365th," said Bob.

"Okay, let's keep a sharp eye and do our jobs," came the word from Steve and he tried, in as calm a voice as he could muster, to have his crew refocus on the task at hand.

No sooner had everyone settled down, than a huge explosion jolted the plane. The flak hit just behind them and showered the tail gun position.

"What the hell was that?" called Eddie Anderson from the radio room.

"Shell exploded just where we had been," stated Jim McFarland from his top turret position, where he had a good view of everything, except below the ship.

"Wyatt, are you all right?" called Steve over the intercom.

"Okay back here, Skipper," answered an obviously shaken tail gunner. "But there is a big hole just above my head. I must have ducked when the flak exploded. The flash blinded me for a minute. I'm all right."

"She's still flying . . . no cables destroyed," stated Steve to Howie, referring to the hits in the tail section. Howie, with a worried look on his face, half-smiled and said, "I thought with a hit like that, we would have lost some cables."

"Howie, take her for a while," said Steve.

Howie took over the controls and continued to fly in close formation, keeping her tucked in, so to speak. It gave Steve a breather and he figured Howie needed some relief from being the official worrier. He now had flying the plane to concentrate on.

"A 366th ship is in trouble, two engines not functioning. I don't know what happened to him," said Jim McFarland.

"It's Roth McKeegan's plane," said Steve.

"Looks like we're slowing down a little so that he can try to keep up with us," said Howie to Steve.

Once again, ME-110s were leading the rocket-firing ME-210s into position. The rockets were being fired just out of gun range. The B-17s could do nothing but hope they missed. A blast went off near their ship, but no damage occurred. The ME-210 fired another rocket toward the formation, this time from behind the B-17s.

"Tail gunner to pilot. Pull up . . . pull up . . . quick!" yelled Roger "Wyatt" Earp.

Howie didn't wait for an explanation, he simply pulled hard back on the yoke and the big plane, now much lighter without a bomb load and half of the gasoline used up, climbed upward at a rapid pace.

Two rockets whizzed underneath and darted out in front of the plane. Howie, Steve, Bob, Russ and Jim saw them as they flew on out of sight.

"Nice going, Wyatt," said Steve, who thought for a moment, but did not say anything more. He just looked over to Howie, flying the plane from the copilot's seat and shook his head in relief. "Damned good flying, kiddo," said Steve to Howie.

Howie, who had leveled off by now, turned to Steve and said, "I'm sweating and baby its cold outside!"

"Good flying up there, Skipper, you saved our ass," exclaimed Willie Burnett from his ball turret position. The rockets had passed just below him. "Think I did something in my pants when I saw those rockets. Someone want to help me change?"

"It was Howie," said Steve, amused by Willie's comments, before he continued, "but let's keep focused. We're not out of the woods yet."

Just then, they saw Lieutenant McKeegan's plane head toward the earth, out of control. It looked like two crew members did not make it out of the ship. Eight parachutes were seen.

"Fighters," but before Jack Kowalski could say more from his left waist gunner's position, Jim McFarland interrupted him from the top turret and shouted, "P-47s!"

The little friends were a welcome sight. They were at the very limit of their range. The American fighter planes went after the German fighters at a torrid pace. While the P-47s shot down several enemy fighters from the sky and forced the Germans to call it a day, the enemy had done quite a job mauling the B-17s during the long air battle to and from the targets in and around the city of Schweinfurt, Germany.

Flak from the Belgium coastal city of Oostende was once again not very heavy or accurate, perhaps on purpose. The formation, now made up of many stragglers from different groups, had formed because their own had been dismantled by flak and fighters. They saw a beautiful sight in front of them: England. Once over the English coast, they broke away in several directions as they each headed for their home base.

With Steve once again at the controls, he and Howie noticed that the number three engine was overheating. "Feather it!" called Steve to Howie.

Steve brought a battered *Image of War* back to English soil at Chelveston.

As they went through the shut-down procedures, Steve, Howie, and Jim were drained of all energy. The crew had spent four hours and 33 minutes over enemy territory and it was evident as each staggered out of the plane.

The men gathered to survey the battle damage. Besides the large hole behind the plane's radio room, a portion of the tail rudder was missing, there was a good-sized hole just above the tail gunner's position, and there were well over 100 holes throughout the fuselage from flak and fighters. The maintenance crew had a job ahead of them.

Pappy's comment was, "Well, Lieutenant, at least you brought her home to me."

"Pappy, this was as rough as I'd like to see," answered Steve. "We were damned lucky to come home in one piece this time. There were a couple of very close calls up there. We must have seen 18, maybe more, planes go down. I don't know what the final count will be, but it will be high." Steve then headed for the truck that was waiting to take the crew to the debriefing hut.

Debriefing took longer than usual because of the questions concerning the downed B-17s. A great many of the questions centered on the loss of the 305th's two aircraft. With the loss of the Mutschler Crew and the McKeegan Crew, the 305th now had 40 crews missing in action. Lieutenant Rothery McKeegan had also been the operations officer. In that position, he could pick his own missions to fly. He certainly chose a tough one in Schweinfurt.

Strike photos showed that the bombing had been very good. They would, however, based on what the photos also showed, have to visit Schweinfurt once again.

For most of the Carmichael Crew, this was their fifth completed mission and they were awarded the Air Medal. That was fine, however, 25 missions still lay ahead. Having completed their seventh mission, Eddie Anderson, Joey DeMatteo, and Jack Kowalski told the rest of the Carmichael Crew that they did not consider their crewmates "rookies" anymore. There was some good-natured kidding all around, which was fine with Steve.

Reports that came in the following morning told a meaningful story. Losses at the Regensburg portion of the dual mission showed that 36 bombers were lost, and at Schweinfurt the enemy had destroyed 24. In total, the Eighth Air Force had lost 60 bombers and 600 crew members in one day! Almost 20 percent of the striking force was lost on the dual mission of Tuesday, August 17th. It had been a savage air battle. Mission planners now questioned whether losses would have been less had there not been a weather delay. The time difference in flights arriving over Regensburg and Schweinfurt, which was to be coordinated, allowed the Luftwaffe to fight at one target, land, refuel, rearm, then set out to defend the other target.

There was no mission scheduled for Wednesday, August 18th. It gave the crews time to write letters home, play a little baseball and generally relax before the next call came.

The officers of the Carmichael Crew, Steve, Howie, Bob, and Russ, received permission to leave the base for a few hours. They hired a taxi to take them to the town of Rushden, a short distance away. The men took a walk in the downtown area, small as it was, but it gave them at least a little freedom. They stopped to speak with some of the local folks. It was time to restock one's thoughts and feelings. Now, with it being lunchtime, they sought out an inviting pub.

"Gentlemen, welcome to the Four Lions," said the proprietor.

"This is very nice," said Howie as the men gathered at a table in the corner by the side window. "A table with a view," said Howie as they all sat down.

Steve walked over to the bar and ordered four pints of Bitter. "Do you have a menu that we can look over for some lunch?" he inquired.

"Well, son, I've got some very good fish and chips, a ploughman's lunch, some pies and see up there on the board," said the proprietor, now turned barman, as he pumped the four pints of English Bitter.

"Do you want to take a look at the board?" said Steve to the men.

"Fish and chips sound good to me," said Russ Parker.

The others agreed and Steve walked over to the barman and said, "This will be easy. Four orders of fish and chips."

Bob Courtney got up from his chair and helped Steve deliver the pints of beer to the others. Each pint had a "proper fill" and they carried them very carefully so as not to spill.

"This seems so peaceful," said Russ, who after a slight pause in which he gazed around the cozy pub, continued, "I'm glad you thought of coming over to Rushden, Skipper."

"It's not far, but far enough to kind of catch up with ourselves," answered Steve as he took a long sip of his beer. "It takes a little getting used to, but I like this English Bitter."

"I'm still a fan of good ole American beer. Some of this stuff tastes to me like it has pond life floating in it! I'm even more a fan of a good dry martini in a New York establishment like the Stork Club," kidded Howie.

"Well, when this war is finally over, the drinks are on you at the Stork Club in New York City," said Russ.

"It's a deal and I'll even introduce you to some very rich women!" answered Howie.

"I couldn't afford your lady friends from the country club! Just bring some good-looking gals," stated Bob, as he took a sip from his pint.

The conversation ended for a while as the barman brought out the plates of fish and chips, mushy peas and bread.

Howie made a face at the peas.

"Now, Howard, eat your peas, they're good for you," teased Steve.

The conversation for the balance of the time in the pub was kept on the light side. The men had, as Steve hoped, become almost as close as brothers.

Later that evening, when Howie and Steve were alone, Howie asked if he thought that Ike and his crew could have made it back today, if they had been able to make it through to the Schweinfurt mission. Steve's reply was that he didn't know. Fate takes over on whether you survive or not. He had come to think that pure luck and nothing else figured in the equation: right place at the right time or wrong place at the wrong time, no religious thing involved. But to others who felt differently, it was okay with him.

The following day, August 19th, would be another day spent on a mission. Steve thought that they would have the day off since their plane was not ready to fly yet. He was informed that his plane was still in the hangar being repaired. He would, however, fly the mission in number 42-29556. This B-17 was a base unit ship that was just transferred to the 305th and assigned to the 366th Squadron. The plane had not been named, and they could name the ship if they desired. Those remarks brought Steve to the realization that he would not be flying number 42-29555 anymore. That plane was not damaged enough to become a "hangar queen" and he wondered aloud about her fate. He had come to trust that plane, especially since they had been through quite a lot together in just five missions. Steve was told that the *Image of War* would be transferred to the 422nd Squadron when she was completely repaired. He and Pappy would have number 556 to worry about for flying any future missions.

The mission of the day for Thursday, August 19th, was a trip back to the Flushing area. They would have fighter escort cover the entire mission. It was a comfort to know that the little friends would work to keep the Luftwaffe at bay instead of having to fight their way to and from the target as they had done just a few days earlier.

Steve had his crew out to the hardstand earlier than usual. Pappy greeted them and assured Steve that this was a good ship. She had been well maintained. This would be the plane's first combat mission. Both Steve and Pappy were also pleased that twin .50 caliber machine guns had been installed in the nose of the B-17. They would at least afford a little more protection from those deadly frontal attacks.

"She has no name. Have you thought of one, Lieutenant?" questioned Pappy.

"Yes, I have," said Steve. He put his hand on his crew chief's shoulder and declared, "Paint *Pappy's Pack* on her after we get back this afternoon!"

The crew quickly entered the ship. The initial ground checklist had been completed. In the cockpit, Howie, while going through the final checklist and also looking out of his copilot's window, noted to Steve, as he climbed into his pilot's seat, the smile on Pappy's face when he was told the name of the ship.

This mission could not be called a milk run. There were German fighters and the anti-aircraft flak to worry them. The P-47s kept most of the ME-109s away from the bombers, but one plane was lost to a direct flak hit. The B-17, number 42-29807, was from the 364th Squadron. Lieutenant Ralph Miller piloted the ship. Only two parachutes were seen from the burning plane as it tumbled out of control. Eight of the crew did not get out of the plane.

The Carmichael Crew landed their new ship back at the base in Chelveston, four engines running. Mission number six was now in the books.

The 305th mission, scheduled for Friday, August 20th, was canceled due to weather. The same was true for the next few days. Even though it was wet and miserable, the lull in flying missions was welcomed by the combat crews. As usual, it was letter-writing time. Steve wrote several, using V-Mail for most except his dad. That letter, in which he wrote of receiving a newer plane, some battle descriptions and praise for his crew, was written on normal stationery.

Steve also managed to get through to Maggie on a phone call to St. Thomas' Hospital in London. They had exchanged short letters, well, Steve's were short and Maggie's were quite a lot longer. She told Steve on the telephone not to worry about writing anything other than that he was safe. They would certainly meet in London on his next leave. She also hoped that Steve would have a leave around the time of her 20th birthday on September 28th. It would be nice for him to help her celebrate.

On Tuesday, August 24th, the mission called for a bombing run on the airfield at Villacoubley, France. It would not be a deep penetration and the 305th would have P-47 air cover throughout the mission. All planes returned. The Carmichael Crew was relieved to be on a mission like this. Number seven was now behind them, but there were 23 more to go before heading stateside! The interesting thing was that with just seven missions flown, the Carmichael Crew was now considered one of the veteran crews; a sobering fact.

The newness of being over here in England was now gone. The Carmichael Crew, for one, had settled in and while not as comfortable as they would have liked things to be if back home, they simply made the best of it. The British people had made them feel welcome and often invited the young aviators into their homes for a home-cooked meal. The folks in the Chelveston area had adopted the 305th. The young airmen, it seemed, were now a little older as well, not in years, of course, but flying combat missions had made them more mature. Fighting for your life at 25,000 feet will do that.

It was a pleasant evening at the Officer's Club. The mission had gone well. The new plane, *Pappy's Pack*, was performing just as they hoped it would. It was a nicely balanced, easy-to-trim ship. Both Steve and Howie were pleased with how she flew. The strike photos of the target showed that the bombing accuracy had been good. The rain was coming down hard again and the word was that there would be no mission scheduled for tomorrow. They could relax tonight at the O-Club.

Steve, Howie, Russ, and Bob sat at their familiar table near the fireplace. Russ and Bob did the honors and brought the pints of beer to the table. Steve produced a brown bag with more than three pounds of roasted peanuts in it.

"They're lightly salted. I have another bag here for the shells," said Steve as he placed the full bag on the table and pulled over another chair, placing the empty shell bag on it.

"How did you come by these?" questioned Howie as he took a handful.

"Package from my dad, but the cake Lillian baked didn't fare too well. It had the look of blue cheese. I carefully dropped the cake over the fence near those hay stacks and the birds loved it."

"How is your dad doing?" asked Howie.

"Well, he's okay," Steve replied. "The ranch is a lot to handle, but he's got good people who have worked there with him for years, so he's getting along. He said that beef prices are running quite high. Beef is rationed for everyone and the government is purchasing a great deal of it. He is running more cattle than ever before. He says that the ranch is making money, so coming from my dad, we must really be raking it in! I had written to him about Ike. He was upset, even though he only knew Wright for a short while. I guess he looks at Ike's going MIA and thinks that it could also be me. I imagine it's hard on him, wondering if I'm all right. He reads the papers about what's going on over here."

Russ and Bob didn't have anything to add to the conversation, so they sat, listened and happily munched on the peanuts and enjoyed their pints.

Finally, as the evening was drawing to a close, Bob Courtney became serious and said, "You know, it's hard to get close to the new replacement crews that are being assigned to us. I talk to them, especially the new navigators, to kind of help them over the rough spots, but well, I just don't want to make friends and then lose them like we did the Gerke Crew."

"I know what you mean," stated Russ, as he pushed back in his chair and slowly nodded his head as he stood up. "But the Gerke Crew was special. We knew those guys since training days."

Steve spoke as he also stood up from the table, "While it is hard and you really don't care to make solid friendships, we do need to help the new crews as best we can. Remember, it wasn't that long ago that we were one of the replacement crews."

Steve then picked up the still half-full bag of peanuts and pushed his chair in toward the table. Howie took the other bag with the shells and placed the extra chair they had used back where it belonged.

The last call came for the O-Club, but the Carmichael Crew officers did not get in line. They were tired and headed for a good night's sleep, one in which there would be no early wake-up call for a mission.

The next mission was on for Friday, August 27th. At briefing, the target was described as a "special mission" on a specific installation.

There would be no secondary target. This installation was the only one to be bombed. Bombing would be at lower altitudes with different groups bombing from 16,000 feet to 25,000 feet. The target was to be an aero works at Watten, France. The bomb load seemed to point to something made from reinforced concrete. It was a comfort to know that on this shallow intrusion into France, their fighter escort would consist of RAF Spitfires, plus P-47s, who would be with them the entire time that they were over enemy territory. The groans at briefing came as the altitudes were announced. German 88s were quite accurate at the lower altitudes. Watten was not too far from Calais. It was also close to the town of St. Omer, where flak batteries protected the area from intruders in the sky. This would not be an easy mission, even though the planners considered it a shallow penetration.

The 305th Group took off, formed up and headed for France. The sky was somewhat hazy and there were scattered clouds as they approached the French coast. Even with the fighter escort, 18 ME-109s and a dozen FW-190s slipped in from the cloud cover to make a tail-end run at the formation of B-17s.

"Watch out . . . bandits are making a run at our tail," yelled Jim McFarland from his top turret position. He swung his twin 50s around to meet the attack.

"I see them," called Roger Earp and the tail gunner started to fire just before they came into range. The tracer bullets were letting the enemy fighters know that he was right on them.

Cannon fire from the enemy fighters ripped into the right wing and tail section of *Pappy's Pack*. Guns from the top turret, bottom turret and tail gunner returned fire at a feverish pace.

"We got one," called Jim. "Look at him smoke!"

"I'm hit . . . damn it, I'm hit. Oh shit!" screamed Roger Earp into the intercom from the tail section, but he continued to fire his twin 50s at the approaching ME-109, which turned over and dove well below their formation.

"Jack," started Steve, but he was interrupted by Howie.

"I'll handle it," said Howie over the intercom to Steve and the crew. He then continued after a slight pause, knowing that Steve was busy enough trying to fly in close formation as a burst of flak exploded near the ship. "Jack, check out Wyatt. Eddie, take over the left waist for a minute."

"It's okay here, Eddie, stay put for now. I can handle things here," called the right waist gunner, Joe DeMatteo.

The enemy fighters broke off the attack as the flak became more intense. They would be waiting on the other side of the target to continue the battle.

The Spitfires and P-47s had been kept quite busy all during this time as evidenced by several falling ME-109s and FW-190s. Two P-47s and one Spitfire were also shot down as they fought the Luftwaffe in trying to protect the bombers.

Jack Kowalski worked his way around the tail wheel well and into the tail gunner's position. He carried one of the portable oxygen containers with him.

"Hey, Jack, nice to see you," said Roger. He was bleeding from his left arm and shoulder. In addition, his face had been hit by shattered fragments of the shell and ship metal. "If this was the O.K. Corral, I'd be in serious trouble," he continued.

"If you had been at the O.K. Corral with your great uncle and with that pair of twin 50s, the Clantons would have shit their pants and run like hell the other way," answered Jack as he tried to keep Roger's spirits up. "Let's get you out of here." It looked bad, but he really could not tell.

In the meantime, the group had reached the IP and the bomb run began. It was a long straight run with nowhere to hide from the flak batteries of nearby St. Omer. Flak continued to explode around them.

Steve turned the plane over to Russ for the run on the target. It seemed like a long time to the pilot as he impatiently waited for the bomb load to be released so that he could once again be in control of the plane.

"I'm bringing Wyatt up. Joey, I'll need your help," stated Jack over the intercom as he started to drag him out of the tail gunner's position.

Without saying anything, Eddie Anderson left his desk in the radio room and motioned to Joe that he would help Jack. He placed the first aid bag just outside of his compartment and helped bring Wyatt to the area behind the radio compartment's open door.

"Bombs away, Skipper," came the signal over the intercom from Russ. At that, Steve took over the controls once more.

The formation made a turn away from the flak batteries of St. Omer and started the trip home. Enemy fighters started to swarm in for an attack, but the Allied fighter escort planes drove them off. A battle ensued, but it was among the fighter planes. The escorts did a most effective job!

Eddie checked Roger "Wyatt" Earp's arm and shoulder, gave him a shot to hold off the pain and did what he could to dress the wounds. Eddie then started to clean Roger's face, but saw that fragments had penetrated the skin, so just gently wiped some of the blood away and made him as comfortable as possible.

Joey crawled back around the tail wheel well and took over the tail gunner's position for the trip home. By the radio room, both Eddie and Jack continued to talk to Wyatt so that he would not pass out. It seemed as though he was going into shock.

Eddie motioned to Jack that he had to get back to the radio. Jack nodded that he understood and would stay with Wyatt. He also walked back and forth, checking on his waist gunner's position and then back to Wyatt.

In the meantime, as they closed in on the British coastline above the English Channel, Jim McFarland left his top turret gunner's position and came through the bomb bay and radio compartment to check on Wyatt.

"How you doing there, pal?" remarked Jim as he knelt down beside Wyatt.

"This is the lousy shits! I'm busted up enough to miss out being with you guys. I think this damn arm is busted too. It doesn't hurt right now, but I can't move the damn thing," answered Wyatt as he teared up a bit.

"We're almost home," was Jim's reply. "Don't worry about it right now. Let's get you fixed up and take it from there. At least those shells were not dead center, if you know what I mean. I've got to get back up front. See you in a little while."

Jim reported to Steve and Howie, told what he saw and took his position as they set up for the landing, firing a flare to alert those on the ground that they had wounded aboard.

As they came to a stop just off the runway, an ambulance met them. Wyatt was carried from the plane and into the waiting ambulance.

"His name is Roger Earp, but we call him Wyatt. His great uncle was the real Wyatt Earp. Take good care of him . . . there's a big tip in it for you," said Howie to the medics with a wink to Wyatt. "We'll see you later," he said to Wyatt as the medics closed the ambulance doors and pulled away toward the base hospital.

During the debriefing everyone complained about bombing at low altitude, especially one in which the flak gunners could be terribly accurate. They also learned that one B-17 from the 305th did not return. Lieutenant Don Moore's plane from the 365th Squadron was shot down with seven parachutes seen . . . just seven.

Mission number eight was now in the books, but with the loss of their tail gunner. Steve was particularly upset. It was his crew and this was a loss of one of the family. "It could have been worse," Howie told him. "He has some pretty bad wounds with a broken arm and shattered shoulder, plus the facial wounds, but he is alive!"

The crew went over to the base hospital to see Wyatt. They were told by one of the nurses that he had just come out of surgery, was in recovery and to check back tomorrow. It seemed as though Staff Sergeant Roger Earp would be headed back to the United States.

There was no mission scheduled for the 28th. At different times Joey, Jim, Eddie, Willie and Jack visited with Wyatt. Likewise, Bob and Russ visited. Steve and Howie went together. There was a steady stream of crew members; however, only so many were permitted to visit at one time and nine at once was too many.

"How are things? Are you at least comfortable?" asked Steve when he and Howie had their turn, gathering one on each side of Wyatt's bed.

"I'm all right, sore, but really okay," came the reply from Wyatt as he tried to be strong.

"Well, from what I understand, you have some personal appearances to make after you heal up," stated Steve.

"That's the way it looks. I'd rather stay here and get back in the crew," answered Wyatt.

"Look, you did your job as well as anyone," said Steve as he gently patted his tail gunner. "You protected our behind very nicely. I'm just glad that you can go home. You know what is going on over here and that people do get hurt. You . . . you did not get killed. Your next job is to visit our love ones and let them know that we're doing our best and that we will see them soon. If you're still taking orders from your old Skipper, then that's an order."

"From you it's not an order, sir, it's done," answered Wyatt.

"What a welcome you'll receive from the crowd at Glen Cove and then there's the ranch in Florida. Come to think of it, you will feel at home on the ranch," stated Howie.

"Do you think that they'll send me back here after I mend?" questioned Wyatt.

"It could happen, but you've got an immediate job of getting yourself back together," answered Steve. "You will probably take several months to heal completely. Quite frankly, you'd be of more value to the service as an instructor. There are enough guys coming out of training to man the guns in these bombers."

"Do you have a replacement yet?" asked Wyatt.

"The replacement will be at right waist gunner. Joey went back to the tail after they got you out of there and liked the view. He asked if he could take over until you got back. So Joey is now officially our tail gunner," replied Steve.

"That kid is a fighting fool. He'll do well for you," said Wyatt.

Just then, a nurse came in and said, "Enough gentlemen, Sergeant Earp needs his rest."

"We'll catch up with you before they ship you back to the States," stated Howie as he and Steve gave a wave and left the hospital ward.

"He's headed home, but that arm and shoulder, they're busted up pretty badly," said Howie as he and Steve left the base hospital.

"They'll take good care of him," said Steve. "It will be several months though before he's ready for his next assignment. I just hope to hell that they do make him an instructor; Wyatt would make a good one, especially with his combat experience. I think that coming back into a combat situation as a replacement would be tough on him."

"When do we get the replacement for our ship?" questioned Howie. Steve flagged down a Jeep for a ride back to the 366th Squadron area.

"I guess we'll know about the replacement just before our next mission," said Steve and he shrugged his shoulders.

"Are you headed for the motor pool?" called Steve to the driver of a Jeep.

"Yes, sir," came the reply. "This one may or may not make it in for repairs. We may have to walk part of the way."

"Well, we're headed for the 366th," said Steve.

"Hop aboard, sirs," was the answer.

That evening at the O-Club much of the conversation centered on Wyatt and his narrow escape. They also spoke about the replacement. Everyone was quite comfortable with Joey taking over as tail gunner. Other things discussed while they relaxed, at least for the moment, were the weather and when would it permit them to get on with completing the required 30 missions, plus the fact that even short missions were becoming extremely dangerous. They never thought in years past that they would be spending the summer of 1943 fighting for their lives and the freedom of others.

The following morning, even though the weather still did not let them fly, Steve was called into operations. He was introduced to an 18-year-old youngster named Ronald Lattamus, who would be joining his crew as a gunner.

Steve told Ronald to grab his gear and he would take the young replacement over to the enlisted men's hut and introduce him to the crew.

As they were being driven over to the 366th area, Steve thought to himself, *This is just a kid, must be fresh out of high school.* Steve looked over to Ronald, smiled and asked, "When did you join the Air Corps? We'll also shorten your name to Ron."

"Day I graduated high school, sir. June 1st. I was the best in my gunnery class and put in for immediate overseas duty and here I am," stated Ron. "With being top in my class, I was made a private first class right out of gunnery school and now, since I've been assigned to a combat crew, I've been promoted to sergeant. Wow, isn't that something!"

Steve did not tell Ron that in a combat crew all of the enlisted men were sergeants. It seemed that if a plane was shot down and the crew became prisoners of war, the Germans treated those of that rank much better than a lower one.

Steve caught up with his enlisted crew members just before they left the barracks for the mess hall to have lunch. He also sent word for Russ, Bob and Howie to meet the new replacement. They all met in the day room where Steve introduced Ronald Lattamus to his crewmates.

"Gentlemen, shake hands with Sergeant Ronald Lattamus," began Steve. "He tells me that friends simply call him Ron. He is now officially the youngest member of our crew, having graduated from high school in Sterling, Illinois, this June. Sterling is west of Chicago. He was first in his class in gunnery school and has been a National Guard soldier during his last two years in high school. With Joey moving back to the tail, Ron will be the right waist gunner. By the way, Ron, left waist gunner Jack Kowalski is from Chicago. Okay, men, help him get settled and take Ron under your wing. He's now part of our crew."

Ron started to salute the officers, but Howie told him that they only did that when formalities called for it. "We are a crew, a team, and Lieutenant Carmichael is our Skipper."

Steve, Howie, Bob, and Russ left the day room and walked over to the officer's mess to have lunch. Steve told them the record stated that Ron was a pretty good gunner and should work out just fine and that he liked the setup with Joey asking to make the move to tail gunner. Steve said that he would have placed Joey there anyway.

In the meantime, back at the day room, the enlisted crew members took Ron over to the hut before they also went to the mess hall for lunch. Jim McFarland, as the engineer, had taken the lead and reintroduced Ron to Joey, Eddie, Jack, and Willie. He also explained their individual positions in the plane.

Ron, of course, had 100 questions to ask. "What is combat like? Is it exciting?" He wanted to hear the war stories!

Jack was the first to stick a pin in young Ronald's balloon. "Ron, let me explain a couple of things to you. Most of the crew has completed eight missions and have 22 to go before they get to go home. Joey, Eddie and I had to fly two earlier missions before rejoining our crew because of losses. We just lost our tail gunner who is headed back to the States, busted up and lucky to be alive. This is no picnic. It's not like target practice back home. They shoot back at you over here and then there is the flak, exploding shells that can rip a plane apart. I don't mean to scare you, but this is serious business, as you will come to know. We'll take care of you, as we do for each other."

Ron was a little more subdued as they ate lunch. The crew tried to make him feel at home by asking about his life before the Air Corps. Ron told them that his family owned a restaurant in Sterling. He had worked there since he was a little kid and was a pretty good cook. They all kidded him: "A cook, of course, you're now a waist gunner. That makes perfect sense!"

There would be one more day of rest because of the weather. Actually, it was not a total day of rest because there would be routine duties to perform as well as lectures on security and aircraft recognition. Steve made certain that his crew attended the lectures. They were, of course, most important to the newest member of the crew, however, Steve felt that part of air discipline included keeping sharp on every detail.

The weather started to break and a mission would be scheduled for Tuesday, August 31st. At their briefing, the crew found out that the mission was to attack an airfield and depot located east of Paris, France. The target lay at Romilly-sur-Seine and it was to be an afternoon strike.

Pappy had everything in order as usual. He was introduced by Steve to Ron Lattamus. Steve also made extra time to show Ron the ship during the walk-around that he and Howie normally did, accompanied by Pappy. As part of the crew now, Steve wanted to instill a feeling of pride not only in his crewmates, but also with the B-17 that Ron would be flying in and fighting to protect. Ron was also told by Pappy that the ship, *Pappy's Pack,* was also Pappy's pride and he expected everyone to do their job to bring his plane back to him. Steve had let it go. His duty, as far as he was concerned, was to bring his crew back home.

Flares were fired, engines started, and the heavily laden bomber joined the taxi and takeoff. Everything was normal so far. The climb to formation was completed through broken clouds. As the flight of B-17s joined up with other formations of the wing, clouds gathered and Steve noted to Howie that they might be recalled due to the weather closing in on them.

Eddie Anderson, from the radio compartment, informed Steve and Bob that he had received detailed instructions on a change in the target, in code, of course. The original target, Romilly-sur-Seine, was completely engulfed in clouds. They were to make a turn to the north and the new target was an airfield at Amiens, France. Bob plotted the course as the 305th Group made the turn and headed for the new target. It seemed as though things were mighty confusing because some of the bombers simply turned toward England and home. The 305th made a good bomb run. This mission also must have confused the Luftwaffe, because today, they were not seen. Flak over the target was considered moderate and no planes from the 305th sustained any meaningful damage. Ron Lattamus did though show some real panic on his face as the exploding anti-aircraft flak shells went off between *Pappy's Pack* and the ship to the right. He had the look that everyone has when they actually see one of the 88-millimeter shells explode nearby. Jack simply gave him a high sign to calm Ron. They weren't hit by the shell burst. Luck was with them this time.

Steve had Howie fly the ship back home with four engines running. Just before going into the landing pattern, Howie motioned for Steve to take the controls once again, but Steve shook his head no and had Howie bring the B-17 in for the landing, taxi and to a halt at their hardstand. Steve took over the duties of copilot. For Steve, Howie, Russ, Bob, Jim, and Willie, mission number nine was completed and in the books. For Eddie, Jack and Joey, number eleven. Ron was all smiles as he came out of the rear door of the B-17. He had a combat mission in the books! It seemed that he would have to buy a round of drinks that evening at the Enlisted Men's Club.

Some of the conversation after debriefing centered on the fact that movie star Captain Clark Gable was stationed at a nearby base. He had flown combat missions. In addition, he was making a military film about aerial gunnery. It was quite an inspiration knowing that he was on missions, taking his chances like everyone else in a combat crew.

Later that night it was learned that a B-17 from the 422nd, 42-5376, Eager Eagle, Truesdell Crew, had collided with a British Beaufighter while still flying over England. Somehow, the two waist gunners and a British observer who was aboard the B-17 managed to escape. Lieutenant Floyd Truesdell, the pilot, plus seven crew members were killed in the collision.

August was gone. Now it was September of 1943. May 17th was the date when the Carmichael Crew first landed a B-17 on British soil in Prestwick, Scotland. It was less than four months ago, but it seemed like forever as Steve reflected on how so much could have taken place in such a short time. In his letters to his dad, Steve thought carefully before placing pen to paper. Steve knew from his father's letters that Steve's safety was of utmost concern. Though he never expounded on it, his dad certainly knew of the danger his son was in.

Steve wrote about the normal things that took place. He told how he managed to get a team together for a softball game. His team, of course, won the game. The score was 23 to 2. "I hit three home runs and two doubles, so you can write to Mr. Briggs that I am keeping in baseball shape. However you do not have to tell him that it was softball and that we played only one game. Just let him know that I will be ready to play for the Tigers when I get home."

Steve also wrote that he had not heard from Elly lately and surmised that she was becoming more involved than she let on. He told his dad in the letter that he had not mentioned to Elly about meeting someone. It was not important to say anything at this point because things would simply take a natural course. Steve mentioned that guys were receiving "Dear John" letters all the time and he was glad that he and Elly had agreed just to be friends for now. "It makes life easier for both of us, Dad, plus quite frankly I've grown up a little these past few months and I'm not interested in a juvenile relationship anymore, if you know what I mean."

There was no mission scheduled for September 1st. The weather also canceled the mission on the 2nd. The crews were up early though on the 3rd for what they learned at briefing was another try at Romilly-sur-Seine.

The path of the strike force carried the formation past Paris. The target, as before, was a Luftwaffe airfield. The fighter escort of P-47s was with them almost to Paris, before they had reached the limit of their operation and had to turn back. The flak encountered was moderate to, at times, heavy and fairly accurate. *Pappy's Pack* had luck with them once again. Some exploding shells were close and there was damage from flak, but the ship came through just fine. No one was injured. For some reason, the Luftwaffe was not up in force on this day. The 305th came home with all of the planes dispatched. Steve later wrote in his diary that mission number 10 was now behind him with still 20 left to fly.

The following morning Steve was called into operations. He was told that normally he would be entitled to a pass to London after completing ten missions, however (and Steve waited for the "however"), losses had been higher than expected and a mission calling for maximum effort would be required. That was it: keep flying!

At afternoon mess, Steve caught up with his crew. He first broke the news to the enlisted men, catching up with them just before they had entered the hall. Then Steve went through the luncheon line and spotted his officers waving from the table where they were seated.

"Gentlemen, I wish that I could somehow explain about our now in the future leave for London. It will not be for a while," stated Steve as he started eating his lunch.

"Future leave as in not now after 10 missions?" questioned Howie.

"Are we allowed to go on strike?" asked Bob Courtney.

"I don't think so, something about simply shooting you . . . something like that," said Russ Parker.

"Well, let's see, what could I say that sounds like the aircraft commander is in charge of the situation," mused Steve. "Gentlemen, at the O-Club this evening, I'm buying!"

A mission was scheduled for Saturday, September 4th. However, in the early morning hours it was scrubbed due to weather conditions over the target area. It would be a day of rest, letter writing and generally catching up with one's self. Combat and flying into harm's way to a target would have to wait.

Sunday, the 5th, was no better. It rained all day long. Steve, his officers and most of the crew attended services at St. John the Baptist Church, just off the base at Chelveston. Others caught a truck ride over to Rushden for services at St. Peter's Catholic Church.

After lunch, the order of the day was to attend lectures on security, aircraft identification, plus some other general subjects. One of the gunners did point out that if he identified a plane shooting at him, he would most likely return fire! Everyone had a good laugh, except the instructor.

The O-Club closed early as word came that a mission would be scheduled for tomorrow. "Pinetree" was ordering what it called a deep penetration into enemy territory. As the officers finished their beer, having responded to "it's time, gentlemen," they understood why the leave for London had to be canceled. Tomorrow would not be a fun day.

The morning came very early for the Carmichael Crew. They were pulled from under warm covers at three o'clock. Breakfast would be served at four, with the briefing at five. Back home, these were milkman hours!

Once in the briefing hut, when the new, fancy curtain started to be lifted, a complete hush came over the crews as they saw the yarn extend further and further.

With the curtain now completely back, the map of England and Europe showed that this mission would be the deepest penetration into enemy territory since the August 17th raid to Schweinfurt. The target was Strasbourg, France, which was located quite near the German border and the city of Stuttgart, Germany. After crossing the Channel, the flight path of the bombers would take them all the way across France. In addition to being right at the German border, Switzerland was less than 200 flying miles to the south.

Word had gotten back that planes on previous missions that had been badly shot up or were low on fuel and could not make it back to English soil had pointed their planes for the safety of Switzerland, a neutral country. International law dictated that the aircrews were to be interned for the duration of the war. It was also found out that the aviators were not placed in a prison, but were free to do as they desired, so long as they did not leave Switzerland. Those particular men had spending money, sent by our government, plus they had good quarters to live in and plenty of good food. It was like being on holiday in Switzerland! Some of the interned airmen even went to Swiss ski resorts. While it is true that many crews had to make for Switzerland or perish, others did fly to Switzerland to escape the war. Interestingly, the B-17s or B-24s, if capable of flying, were being returned to the Allies to fight another day.

Reports were that General Hap Arnold was in England for a look-see on daylight bombing and that this deep penetration mission was to show that they had recovered sufficiently enough from the August 17th Schweinfurt raid losses and could undertake such a mission as was on for Monday, September 6th. The canceled London trip was all General Arnold's fault!

Takeoff was scheduled for 6:06 a.m. The crew of *Pappy's Pack* would be part of the maximum effort that would include more than 450 (H), heavy bombers, B-17s and B-24s. The 305th Bomb Group would make their bomb run on targets in Strasbourg, while other groups would venture into Germany and target Stuttgart. In addition, diversionary strikes near these targets hopefully would break up the concentration of fighter planes from the Luftwaffe and spread them out.

Flares were fired from the control tower. Engines were started and it was off to war once again for Steve's 11th mission. It certainly seemed like this would be a rough one with no sugar coating. Fighter support would only be with them for less than a third of the mission. The bombers would then have to fight their way to and from their respective targets, until once again they would welcome the little friends supporting the withdrawal from enemy territory.

Pappy had made sure that they had a full load of fuel. The gunners also made certain that extra ammunition was on the plane. For weight and balance purposes, the extra ammo was stored in the radio compartment. Pappy alerted Steve about the extra weight and that, coupled with a full bomb load, made for a very heavy plane. The old girl would surely be waddling down the runway trying to lift off the ground.

Steve noted to Howie as they started the engines and ran through the final checks that they were certainly heavy on this day. "Pappy said we're really loaded down, so let's hold the brakes and build as much energy as we can. We'll need to get some speed quickly so that we don't run out of runway, if you know what I mean."

Howie understood and just nodded his head rather than answer over the roar of the engines. It's a mission where dismissing the weight and balance check was in order.

Jim McFarland, who had just come down from checking out his top turret gunner's station now took up his other job of engineer. Knowing that Steve liked to takeoff at 115 miles per hour rather than 110, he said to his pilot, "115, Skipper?"

"Maybe a little more; it depends on where we are on the runway," came Steve's reply.

Howie motioned to Steve that it was time for *Pappy's Pack* to leave the hardstand and join the long line of B-17s as they waddled noisily toward the end of the runway. Engines roared, brakes were released and the shuddering bomber started her trip. Jim called out the numbers on the air speed indicator as *Pappy's Pack* headed straight down the runway, gaining speed very rapidly now. Steve pulled back on the yoke and they went flying, wheels up very quickly. Even with all of the extra weight on board, the plane performed perfectly. What a beautiful ship. The pilot, knowing his airplane, made the takeoff look routine.

It took a while for the climb and to join the formation. Once together, the 305th now joined other groups, including their neighbors, the 306th, and the First Bomber Wing headed out over the Channel. The escort met them right on schedule and joined the bomber stream. Some of the escort fighters flew with them while others flew out in front, above and below the B-17s. More than 150 P-47s would work to protect the bombers as best as they could for as long as possible before having to turn back to England due to their maximum range.

On this day, the sky was filled with Allied aircraft. There would be a show of strength. In addition to the heavy bombers (H), groups of medium bombers (M), B-25 and B-26 twin-engine planes would be part of the overall diversion. They would bomb enemy airfields in Holland and France with the hope that they could destroy the Luftwaffe fighters on the ground before they had a chance to get airborne.

So far, as the formations started across France, the little friends had been able to keep the enemy fighters away from the bombers. At this point the diversionary mission of the medium bombers was working rather well since few of the Luftwaffe was present, at least for now.

With the bomber stream now more than halfway across France, Steve took a break, turning the plane over for Howie to fly. The bombers continued to fly in close formation. The weather, however, was starting to become a factor. The formation climbed to get above the clouds that had closed in at the previous altitude. *Pappy's Pack* was now at 25,000 feet.

Flak was now becoming a problem. The anti-aircraft shells fired at the formation were exploding at their level. The crew was asking those in the cockpit to shake the plane around a bit. Steve, at this time, took over the controls once again and did take some evasive action, as did other nearby B-17s. With trying to keep a tight formation for the best protection, kicking the plane around too much was hard on the wingman on either side who was also trying to keep his ship from receiving a direct flak hit.

Finally, the formation was nearing the IP of the bomb run. Steve turned the plane over to his bombardier, Russ Parker, for the bomb run itself.

"The clouds are covering up the goddamn target, Skipper, but if I see any kind of break, I'm dropping the load," stated Russ in a disgusted voice.

"Do your best. We've got a long trip home and I don't want to run out of fuel over the English Channel," answered Steve, as he impatiently waited to get the plane back.

Howie looked over at Steve from his copilot's seat, nodding in agreement with him that this was not the time to take a tour of the French–German border.

Just then, a huge flash and explosion of an 88-millimeter shell burst just to the right of the plane, showering it with dirty, black shell fragments that put several small holes in the ship's skin as the plane bounced from the concussion.

"Geez, that was close," said Steve to Howie.

"We just lost a wing tip, Stevie ole boy," said an excited Howie as he glanced out of his side window and looked at the damaged wing.

"Damned good thing it wasn't more inboard," stated Steve.

"Bombs away, Skipper. Let's go home. Damned shell was close . . . almost makes you shit your pants. I'm buying tonight if you get us out of here," called Russ over the intercom.

The plane lifted quickly with a surge upward as the weight from the bomb load was now on its way down from 25,000 feet.

Steve took control of the ship once again from his bombardier as the flak continued to explode at their altitude. Just as they pulled away from the target, a B-17 off to the right took a direct hit, knocking it out of the formation.

"It's *Rigor Mortis* . . . Ray Holliday," exclaimed Howie.

"Here come the ME-109s trying to finish him off," called Joey from his tail gunner position. He fired a few rounds from his twin 50s toward the attacking fighters, but they were just out of his range. Joey continued, "Flak knocked him out of formation, Skipper, left wing on fire, two engines out . . . oh damn!"

"Okay, calm down, count the chutes," stated Steve in business-like voice.

"I see four, no, six," said Ron Lattamus from his right waist gunner's position.

"I count nine all together, Skipper," stated Willie Burnett from the ball turret position. Then after a long pause, he continued, "I think one of those flak shells took out the ball turret."

"Okay, Willie, now everyone be alert for fighters in case they come back to our altitude and try to work us over," said Steve over the plane's intercom.

"Looks like we're losing a couple of ships from our squadron. They're headed for someplace other than England. *Madame Butterfly*, MacSpadden, and *So What*, the Glaiser Crew . . . I guess for Switzerland," stated Howie.

"Skipper, those two planes reported that they were running low on fuel and couldn't make it back to England," called radioman Eddie Anderson.

Bob Courtney was taking all of this information down, as part of the duties of the navigator.

"Good thing that Pappy made sure we were topped off," said Steve with a look to Howie.

"I don't know, I hear those that can make it to Switzerland have a pretty good deal," answered Howie.

Steve was about to continue the conversation with Howie, but over the intercom, as the crew of *Pappy's Pack* continued the trek back across France hoping to see their escort, came Mac's voice from his top turret, "Looks like a line of ME-109s at 11 o'clock. Head-on attack coming!" called Mac.

"Okay, let's be ready for them," stated Steve, who also quickly looked to his left to see if his wingman had seen what was coming. He could see that both the top turret and ball turret had rotated their guns in order to face the enemy fighters and the intended attack.

Howie, from his copilot's seat, in the meantime, looked to his right and likewise saw that the B-17 was also prepared. Before Howie could tell Steve that everyone was on to the ME-109s, Russ broke in on the intercom.

"Here they come," called Russ, as he prepared to fire the twin 50s mounted in the nose.

At just about the same time, Mac in the top turret and Willie in the ball, opened up firing a few rounds with the tracers flying out, even though the ME-109s were still just out of range. Russ also let go with a burst of fire from the nose-mounted twin 50s as the finger-four frontal attack bore in on them.

"Be alert as they pass," called Jack Kowalski from his left waist position to young Ron Lattamus at his right waist position.

Everything was happening so fast it was almost a blur. The ME109s closing in on the formation of B-17s took just seconds. To the crew of *Pappy's Pack*, the aerial battle seemed to last an eternity, although perhaps in real time less than a minute had passed. The B-17 shuddered from the recoil of her guns. The noise, especially in the cockpit, was deafening. The two gun positions, top turret and twin 50s in the nose, were incredibly loud.

Just as the 109s flashed by the side of the B-17 and then did a half roll under *Pappy's Pack*, Ron put a burst of fire into the enemy fighter he had picked out of the flight of ME-109s. The enemy fighter started to smoke from the engine compartment. Bits and pieces of the ME-109 were being ripped away as Ron's bullets found their mark. The plane flew on for just seconds, then seemed to almost stop, shudder a bit, before becoming engulfed in a huge orange ball.

Willie was also firing away at one of the 109s that was diving, placing a burst toward the canopy. It continued to dive, but now trailed smoke. No parachute was seen. The plane went straight into the ground, exploding as it hit the earth.

"I got one!" shouted Ron.

"Me too," stated Willie in a more calm voice.

"Nice going, guys. Check in . . . everyone all right?" called Howie.

From each position, the crew responded. Everyone was still in one piece.

"Skipper, looks like one of the ships over on the right took some hits in the number one. It's smoking a bit and they've feathered the engine," stated Mac.

"Right, Mac, we'll slow down a little to stay with him. Everyone, keep a sharp eye. We've still got a way to go," stated Steve, as he motioned for Howie to take over the controls for a while.

"I can see the English coast and those beautiful white cliffs. Here comes a flight of Spitfires to ferry us across the Channel," stated Howie as he took over flying the big bird home to station number 105—Chelveston.

Steve took over the controls once more as he set up in the pattern to land *Pappy's Pack*, four engines still running smoothly.

Mac, now down from the top turret and at his other job as engineer, said, "Skipper, we're coming in on a tea cup of fuel."

"If one of the engines starts to cough, feather it," said Steve to Howie.

"What if they all fail, Stevie?" kidded Howie to break a little of the tension as they were now on final approach.

"Then we've got one big, expensive glider," answered Steve as the plane crossed over the threshold and settled onto the runway.

As they left the runway and worked their way toward the plane's hardstand, the two inboard engines were shut down, as was procedure.

Pappy, of course, was on hand to welcome them back home. He would work through the night to get the old girl ready for the next mission.

The flying part of the mission was completed. Now, it was to the debriefing and interrogation hut where details of the mission plus information on those who did not make it back would be given and assessed. It was also the time for both Ron and Willie to get credit for each downing an ME-109.

The crew, to say the least, was exhausted. Perhaps a little sack time before evening mess was needed. They were, however, also elated that their ship had two enemy kills to brag about and paint on the ship.

That evening while the officers gathered at what had now become their table in the O-Club, not that some superstition was somewhat involved, which may well be true, they toasted that mission number 11 was now in the books. Russ, true to his word while they were flying over Strasbourg, France, bought the drinks! They were also informed that the club would close early as a mission was on for tomorrow.

It was a clear, cool September 7th as the crew of *Pappy's Pack* boarded the heavily laden B-17 for another trip across the English Channel. On this Tuesday, the target was Brussels. They would be bombing an airfield suspected to be loaded with Luftwaffe aircraft, hoping to catch them still on the ground. The good news about this mission was that they would have fighter escort for the entire time. Steve was looking forward to putting number 12 behind him.

With clear weather, the takeoff, form-up, and formation flying was routine, even though most often routine was not quite the word explaining how, somehow, things really did work out. There were no mishaps on this day and the escort of P-47s and the twin-engine P-38 fighters was right on schedule. The group entered the European continent just north of Oostende, Belgium, a coastal city that had been heavily bombed at the very outset of World War II, during the period of May through June of 1940 by the British.

Flak started to appear as they crossed into the airspace of the enemy. The flak shell bursts were considered both light and inaccurate. The flight path of the B-17s took them over the city of Ghent as they worked their way toward Brussels. So far, so good: no Luftwaffe in sight. So far, that is!

Howie pointed out to Steve that next to Paris, Ghent, or "Gent" to the Belgium people, was the most important city in Medieval Europe. In the 13th century, it had a population of over 60,000 and was the mill city that manufactured the famous Flemish cloth that the aristocrats wore. "You see, I did pay attention during European history classes in school," Howie said.

The approach to the IP, plus the bombing, was going much easier than anticipated. It was almost like waiting for the other shoe to drop as *Pappy's Pack* pulled off the target. Many individual fires could be seen and were reported by Joey from this tail gunner's position. "Looks like we hit a fuel depot . . . burning like hell down there," called Joey as he continually scanned the sky for specks that could turn out to be enemy aircraft.

"Looks like Goering's flyboys decided that we had too much of an escort to tangle with us today," remarked Howie.

"Fine with me. Take over for a while," answered Steve.

Howie, now flying the plane from his copilot's seat, pointed out that the English coast was coming up. It had been a good mission. *Pappy's Pack* had not fired their guns. They landed back at Chelveston, Howie at the controls, four engines running.

After leaving the debriefing hut, Steve told the crew that he would catch up with them a little later; he was told to report to headquarters. Steve advised the crew to stay loose because he might have to meet with them after the headquarters visit with Colonel Wilson.

CHAPTER FOUR

When Steve left headquarters, he sent word that the crew was to meet with him in the day room. His meeting had taken more than an hour and now it was just before everyone went to the evening mess. The men arrived a little before Steve. As he entered the room, he held up his right hand, which was holding passes that would let the crew go down to London. Steve was also sporting the bright, shiny, silver bars of a first lieutenant.

"I'll be damned, they finally found out that you can lead men into combat!" stated Howie, pointing to Steve's first lieutenant bars. "Congratulations, Stevie old boy . . . this is terrific," continued Howie.

Russ and Bob also came right over to shake hands and congratulate their pilot on his promotion.

"Congratulations, Skipper," was the voice from the rest of the crew members. For them, it was somewhat neat to have a first lieutenant as their pilot.

"Well, first, thank you . . . thank you for being the crew members that you've become," Steve responded. "With the promotion that I've received because of our overall performance, I was told that we would be one of the lead crews on future missions. It is, of course, more responsibility, but I know that we are up to the challenge. In the meantime, the passes are set to start tomorrow morning, the eighth, and we are due back here for evening mess on Sunday, the 12th. Now, for those going to London . . . you know the drill, be careful, be smart, and be back here on time."

For the officers of *Pappy's Pack* it was an early night at the O-Club. They left the Club and went back to their quarters to pack for the trip to London. Oh, that wonderful pass!

Some, including Steve, also made time to write letters to the folks back home. The letter to his dad included the big news that he was now a first lieutenant and that he was traveling back to London for a few days.

It took three telephone attempts for Steve to reach Maggie. He was coming to London! Maggie said that she would see to it that they had plenty of time together. Her friends would change shifts and even work her shift in order to give them more time with each other. The numerous letters and infrequent telephone calls simply did not make up for time together, even if only for a short visit.

Steve had arranged for a taxi to take the officers over to the Wellingborough Railway Station for the train trip to London. He and Howie also split the cost of a taxi for the other crew members. It was much faster than the bus. It's better to be at the train station early and wait for the train, rather than count on a bus getting you to the train on time.

The trip to London was completed in comfort. The English first-class train car compartment was spacious, comfortable, and private. Russ asked if anyone else wanted a cup of tea and a scone as he stood up and opened the compartment door to the aisle. That sounded like a good idea to everyone. Bob went with Russ to the snack car to bring them back to the compartment.

Finally, the train slowed to a crawl as it approached and entered King's Cross Train Station. The crew gathered on the platform for a couple of minutes. Steve simply told them to have a good time and to take care of Ron Lattamus. It was the kid's first time in London! In a flash, they were off, wide-eyed Ron looking all around as he trailed the bunch headed for the Underground tube station.

Howie, in the meantime, had left the train platform saying that he would meet them in the main part of the terminal. As Russ, Bob, and Steve left the platform and entered the main part of King's Cross Train Station, Howie motioned for them to follow him toward a side door of the station and not to follow the crowd to the taxi stand. They left through the side door and a uniformed chauffeur driver from a local livery company met them and offered to carry their officer's suitcases. They declined, saying that it was okay and that they would carry their own bags to the waiting late-1930s Rolls Royce limousine. The driver opened the "boot" and placed the bags inside what the Americans knew as the trunk.

"I thought this would be easier for us," said Howie in a matter-of-fact tone. Then to the chauffeur he said, "You know the way to the Stafford Hotel . . . St. James Place?"

The driver acknowledged and they were off through the streets of London toward the Stafford Hotel.

Howie told the others that this little arrangement was his gift and that the hire was on call during all of their time in London. They were not to ask if they could chip in for the cost of the limousine or the extra petrol he and the driver had to secure. They were better off not knowing! Steve did state that if Howie and the driver wound up in jail, he would at least bail out his copilot. Howie explained that the livery company was the same one his father had used on business trips to London and all would be okay.

Once settled in the Stafford, Steve and Howie sharing one room with Russ and Bob in another room, they all went downstairs to the hotel bar for a drink and some lunch.

Maggie had left a note with the desk clerk, ringing up to say that she would meet Steve at Victoria Train Station at six o'clock as before, with dinner reservations at the Ebury Wine Bar and Restaurant. The note, which Steve brought into the Stafford's bar, also mentioned that on Friday night, the 10th, she had lined up three other nurses and had made reservations for dinner and dancing at the Savoy! She further suggested that they not spend all of their leave money because they would need it for Friday night.

"This is one sharp lady . . . can't wait to meet her," said Howie, who paused for a moment then continued, "you've kept her away from us long enough."

"I tell you, between the letters, phone calls when we can get through, and our time together, this thing is getting more serious than I thought," stated Steve, who munched on some peanuts while waiting for his ploughman's lunch.

"For now, you go with the flow. It sounds to me that what you two have might be more than just the war," answered Howie as he made room on the small table for the luncheon plates.

Neither Bob nor Russ offered any thoughts on the matter. Howie and Steve had become more like brothers and could talk about things that were of a personal nature.

"Well, it's amazing how one's life can change in such a short time," stated Steve as he began eating his lunch. "I find out that the girl I thought I would spend my life with is off with someone else. Instead of playing major league baseball, I am in England, flying a bomber, and fighting for my life. Then I meet a nurse who knocks my socks off . . . crazy!"

"I'd call a lot of what you said 'lucky,'" stated Howie, who paused for a moment, then continued after munching on his lunch. "Hell, you found out about the girl back home before you got a Dear John, and you're fortunate enough to meet some-one who seems to care a lot for you. You're one lucky guy!"

"I'd say that I agree with Howie," joined in Bob.

"Received my Dear John letter just as I started schooling as a bombardier and we were engaged. A 4-F is what she ran off with. I hope the bastard gets drafted," shared Russ, who paused for a moment, slowly shook his head and took a drink of his beer.

When they finished with lunch, Howie took Russ and Bob to see some of the sights in London that they hadn't visited on their last trip which, of course, included a couple of stops along the way for what they called refreshment: pub time!

Steve said, quite frankly, that he had hit the wall. He was extremely tired and would stay behind, take a nap and then shower for his date with Maggie. It was better to do this than fall asleep in his soup!

Howie, Russ, and Bob started for the hotel door and their waiting driver. Steve walked to the lift. They had agreed to meet later that night in the hotel bar for a nightcap.

Steve took the lift up to the third floor. As he entered the room he shared with Howie, Steve felt like just falling onto his bed; however, before lying down, he set the alarm clock for four o'clock. In almost no time, Steve was in a deep sleep.

Even though it had been three hours since Steve laid down for his nap, the ringing of the alarm clock startled him awake. It seemed as though he had just placed his head on the pillow. He was glad that he had set the alarm.

When Steve left the Stafford Hotel, he walked the now-familiar trek. He went down Cleveland Street, walking through part of Green Park, down the Mall, stopping for a moment to take in the view of Buckingham Palace before continuing down Buckingham Palace Road. Steve then walked past the Royal Mews where he was going to stop to see the horses, but noticed that the large gate was closed, so he continued walking on to Victoria Train Station. Steve checked his watch and saw that he was close to 10 minutes ahead of the time for meeting with Maggie.

Just as he took up a position to wait at the meeting spot in Victoria, he felt arms from behind encircle his waist with a tight hug.

"Hello, soldier," said Maggie as she came around and held Steve before they kissed.

Steve took a moment, as they separated, to take a special look at the girl who was becoming such an important part of his life. Her shoulder-length, dark-brown hair had a natural shine to it. Maggie's eyes, a beautiful blue that could light up a room, and her complexion suggested that generations ago a Roman influence was part of her ancestry. She was indeed a beautiful young woman and Steve was taking in the total picture standing before him.

They embraced again and as they stood back taking in each other, Maggie suddenly noticed the silver bar on his uniform shoulder. "You've been promoted!" she said in an excited voice.

"Yes, from second lieutenant to first lieutenant . . . next step up will be two silver bars joined together and the rank of captain, but that will take a bit longer. Then, hopefully the rank of civilian after this damn war is over and getting on with a real life," said Steve.

"Could I be a part of that real life?" asked Maggie as she looked into Steve's eyes.

"I'd certainly like it to be that way," answered Steve as he squeezed Maggie's hand and they left Victoria Station, walking toward the Ebury Wine Bar and Restaurant. It was, as Steve remembered, a fairly short walk on Ebury Street and then there it was, number 139.

Just as they reached the Ebury, Steve told Maggie to stand in front of the restaurant so that he could take a photo of her. He meant to take one back at Victoria, but in the excitement of being with her again he forgot to take the picture. Maggie, in turn, wanted one of Steve, especially with his new first lieutenant bars. When this was finished, Steve stopped an older gentleman who was walking a large, brown, tail-wagging dog and asked if he would take a photo of the two of them. He said he would be delighted and took two photos. The extra one for good measure in case one did not turn out well. The dog, wanting to be petted by his new friends, somehow wound up in the picture, sitting nicely in a very proper manner.

Once again, as they entered the Ebury, Mrs. Cox greeted them. "It's so nice to see you two again," she said as she showed Steve and Margaret to their special table in the back corner. After they were seated across from each other at the small table, Mrs. Cox handed them the menus and then asked, "Have you seen your parents lately, Margaret?"

"Yes, I was able to spend a couple of days at home in Sandown last week," answered Margaret. "There are, as you know, restrictions for visiting the Isle of Wight, but as a resident, I was able to receive special permission for the visit."

"Oh, I'm so glad . . . it's hard to travel around these days," said Mrs. Cox.

"I told my parents that Steve and I had dinner here at the Ebury. They said to give you their very best," said Margaret. "Did you notice that Steve has been promoted from second to first lieutenant? I'm so proud of him!"

"Why that is wonderful, congratulations," stated Mrs. Cox, who really knew nothing about British military ranks, let alone what American ranks represented. She did know that from Steve's uniform that he was an officer.

Soon, the older gentleman who had waited on them the last time came over to the table with two wine glasses and a bottle of British Claret. "This is what you young folks had before," he said. "Would you care for the same wine?"

"Thank you for remembering," answered Steve. After a pause while the bottle of wine was being opened and poured, he continued, "The roast beef with Yorkshire pudding is what we'd like for dinner, and whatever you're serving with it." Steve knew that the accompaniment would include potatoes and for certain peas, with mushy or not mushy being the surprise.

The conversation between Margaret, now quietly Maggie so as not to raise the eyebrows of Mrs. Cox, was very relaxed. They were just two young people who were falling in love, even though circumstances were almost unrealistic as the dangers of war haunted their future together. They did talk about a future. They hoped for a future together.

Steve and Maggie lingered for a while after enjoying a dessert of sherry trifle and just the simple company of the other and held hands across the table.

Mrs. Cox arranged for a taxi that would take them to Maggie's quarters at St. Thomas' Hospital. The streets of London were dark, of course, by wartime restrictions. The taxi driver, like all of the London taxi drivers, knew every street in the city and it was not difficult for them to manage driving through the darkened streets. The taxi drove past the Parliament buildings and Big Ben before crossing the River Thames on the Westminster Bridge. They slowed to almost a halt just over the Westminster Bridge and then drove onto the war-damaged hospital grounds.

Steve paid the taxi driver and was about to ask him to stay for a little while when the chauffeur Howie had hired for their stay in London approached him.

"Good evening, Lieutenant," he said. "I was sent by Lieutenant Van Dyke to fetch you back to the Stafford Hotel when you, as he stated, were completely ready. There is no hurry, sir. I have a good book that I'm reading," and he motioned for the taxi driver to drive on. The chauffeur then walked back to the Rolls.

It was now past 10 o'clock as Steve and Maggie walked into St. Thomas' Hospital lobby. She knew where an empty admissions conference room was and the two spent a little more than three quarters of an hour there. After Maggie walked Steve to the hospital door, he took the waiting limousine back to the Stafford.

The drive back to the hotel took several minutes. Even though it was a short drive, it was important to take the safest route in returning to the Stafford, especially at night. Steve thanked the driver, who said that it was his pleasure. Lieutenant Van Dyke had paid him very generously for the entire officers' stay, and he was on call!

Steve entered the hotel lobby and then ventured into the bar where, upon his arrival at the table occupied by Howie, Russ, and Bob, the barman set a pint of freshly pumped bitter on the table in front of the lone empty chair. Steve sat down, picked up the pint, saluted his mates, and took a long, refreshing sip of the popular English brew.

"Thanks for the ride," said Steve to Howie.

"My pleasure," answered Howie, who paused for a moment to take a taste of his own pint and to pick up a handful of shelled peanuts. "Are we all still on for Friday night or did you screw it up?"

Russ and Bob had a wide grin on their faces as they enjoyed the banter between Howie and Steve.

"Bob and Russ have the good-looking nurses . . . yours, well . . . let's just leave it at she is a very nice lady," kidded Steve as he reached for some peanuts.

Howie had a good laugh. "Story of my life . . . things still okay with you and Maggie?" he asked.

"Well, it's decided that we'd kind of like to be a part of each other's future, if there is one," answered Steve in a sober voice.

"It's tough, but nothing to worry over. Things will work out for you two, I'll take bets on it," stated Howie, knowing what Steve meant. It was a dangerous war with many more missions yet to fly before solid plans could be made. They both knew of the big family plans that their friend Wright Gerke had before he was shot down on August 12th.

Bob and Russ wondered to themselves in private moments if the new 30-mission requirement could be completed when losses were running so damned high.

Finally, Steve said, "I think that we're all tired; let's figure out what's on for tomorrow and then get some sack time."

"We've taken in a lot of the sights of London, so let me see, how about a little high culture, say the British Museum," answered Howie.

"What time do you meet Maggie?" asked Bob.

"Not until six o'clock. She's on duty at the hospital until five," was Steve's reply, as he pushed his chair back and stood up.

They left the bar and just before they reached the lift, Steve said, "Oh, the reason why Maggie set up the dates for Friday night is because she figured that if you hit it off well with the lady she chose for you, perhaps you might also want to see her on Saturday too, rather than have to wait for the next leave."

The men entered the lift, went to their rooms and retired for the night. A leave to London could tire one out. Trying to do so much in so little time did that, plus with so much adrenaline being used during the flying missions, the coming down, so to speak, could also make one feel equally drained. A good night's sleep would work wonders.

After a "full English breakfast," the chauffeur picked up the vagabonds and they were off to the British Museum where they spent a little more than three hours. It was, of course, not enough time to see everything, but as Russ pointed out, culture must be taken in small doses, so as not to warp the brain. Besides, it was getting toward lunchtime.

Howie told their chauffeur, now "Michael" to everyone, to take them over to Covent Garden. Michael said that he had a favorite pub that the men might enjoy. They let him choose the spot and, of course, he would join them for lunch.

"Ah, there are a fair amount of good drinking pubs here in London, but, for a good meal, gentlemen, we need one that also serves delicious food," stated Michael as he parked the car.

"Okay, Michael," remarked Howie, as they all walked toward a corner with three pubs in view. "Which one has good ale and food?"

"Gentlemen, may I introduce you to the Drunken Dirty Duck Pub," answered Michael as he held the door for the aviators.

As they entered the pub, which was filled with both British and American servicemen, plus the businessmen and locals, it certainly looked to be a very popular public house.

Steve and Howie started to look for an empty table in this very crowded establishment, as did Russ and Bob who had gone to another part of the pub.

The search ended as Michael motioned for the men to follow him. The owner of the Drunken Dirty Duck came over to speak with Michael, who introduced him to his wards; however, with the noise level of the pub no one really caught his name.

They all went behind a large, burgundy-colored curtain and up a staircase to a large dining room on the second floor. This dining area seemed much more formal than downstairs, although in looking at the tables and chairs, they had the rustic well-worn appearance of solid wood furniture that had been in service for many years. There were a few other people dining up here, but it was easy to see that they were businessmen. The owner went back downstairs to tend to his thriving business.

"Nice and quiet up here," stated Michael, who thought for a moment, then added, "Much more civilized than downstairs."

"This is nice . . . a rugged man's pub . . . and probably with a lot of history," stated Bob.

"This is one of the independent pubs, not owned by a brewery, so they have several, ales, lager, and bitter to choose from," stated Michael. "There has been a public house on this particular corner since 1789."

"What do you suggest?" asked Steve.

"Good question," started Michael. He thought for a moment and then continued, "Here on the next table, hand me the menu card . . . it shows what they serve."

"They have Tetley, that's a good bitter," said Bob, as he handed the card to Michael, now satisfied that he knew what he would order. Bob also went over to another table and picked up a food menu to bring back for everyone to look at.

"Yes, Tetley is good and they also have Gale's Best Bitter, Gale HSB, Bombardier Premium, Wadworth 6X, Toby and Worthington plus if you like a nice light ale, Tennents is good," stated Michael as he went down the list. "They also have Scrumpy

Jack Cider, but it is very strong and most Americans need to acquire a taste for it."

"I've had Worthington Best Bitter before. A pint of that would taste good," said Steve as the waiter approached and started to write down the order for pints and food.

In a few minutes, everyone was raising their pints and soon after, lunch was delivered to the table. Russ, who had ordered Bombardier Premium, joined with Bob in ordering the steak and kidney pie and chips. Howie and Steve went with the fish and chips. Michael chose bangers and chips. Somehow, mushy peas were served with everyone's lunch.

Conversation at lunch was light and lively. Michael pointed out that if the young airmen should find themselves with a powerful hangover from the drink, well, a dear friend of his named Graham, from up in Birmingham, stated that the solution was to have an order of extremely greasy fish and chips. "No matter what the hour is, it will cure the hangover, enough at least to function."

After a most enjoyable lunch, the group spent some time walking all around Covent Garden. They checked out what was for sale in the different stalls and, before heading back to the Stafford, stopped at the Jack the Ripper Pub for some refreshment.

While at Jack the Ripper's, Michael told them about spending time in Wales before the war. His family would go on holiday to the seaside town of Llandudno. While there, they would also spend time up in the Snowdona Forest. He remembered his father taking him to see the castles of Caernarfon and Conwy. Later, as an adult, business brought him to southern Wales and the city of Cardiff.

"They also brew good traditional bitter in Wales," continued Michael, smiling as he recalled days gone by. "A standout good one is called Allbright. Another, Hancock's HB, is produced at the old Crawshay Street Brewery in Cardiff. William Hancock brewed a mighty bitter . . . the 'sign of hospitality' stated the pub emblem."

"Did you ever go on holiday to the Isle of Wight?" questioned Steve.

"Ah, yes, they have a good sandy beach at Sandown," answered Michael. "The beach is in Sandown Bay and runs down through the town of Shanklin. We also used to go to Ventnor. There was a really good restaurant that overlooked the sea. Some bombing took place over on the Isle, so I don't know what has happened. Wartime rules will not let you travel there. They have a pier at Sandown, which I understand they rather cut the middle out of so that in the event the Germans tried to sneak onto the island by quietly landing at the end of the pier, they would be in for a surprise when they got halfway toward land. That is quite clever! I think that the entire pier is closed now even to the public. Unfortunately, anyone looking to go back to the Isle of Wight will have to wait."

"Steve is dating a nurse who is working at St. Thomas' Hospital. She is from the Isle of Wight," joined in Howie.

"Of course, your young lady, Maggie, you call her. What town is she from?" asked Michael.

"Sandown," was Steve's answer.

"It's a spectacular place, Lieutenant. One fine day you must have a visit," said Michael, who had put down his pint and used both voice and hands to describe a place that he was both familiar with and fond of. "You can get lost in the beauty of the place. I call the Isle of Wight a little of all of England, on one island. It is larger than most folks think. I believe it is about 60 miles around . . . a good stretch of the legs if you are walking! From the rugged Needles Rocks, the chalk cliffs near Sandown, old Carisbrooke Castle, St. Catherine's Lighthouse, Queen Victoria's Osborne House, the yachting town of Cowes and over in what is called West Wight, Yarmouth and Freshwater. Then inland, a beauty of a town with the name of Godshill, with those lovely thatched roof houses. The capital is Newport . . . I could go on and on. At one time, I owned a company that used to take people on holiday tours there and when this damned war is over, I hope to retire and spend out my days on the Isle of Wight."

Just as they were leaving the Covent Garden area, Michael stopped for a moment at a tobacco store to purchase two "Hamlet Special" large Panatelas cigars, telling Howie that from what he was paying for his services, he could afford two—just two!

Later, after everyone was settled back at the Stafford, plans were made for the evening. Steve, of course, was spending the evening with Maggie. Russ, Bob, and Howie had a reservation at one of London's finer restaurants. Howie had been there with his parents and told Russ and Bob to save their money because dinner at Rules on Maiden Lane was on him. Howie explained to his mates that Rules was a fine, old Edwardian restaurant that featured the very best of British cuisine.

In the meantime, Steve and Maggie were also going to enjoy dinner at a very special place. The long evening would start with dinner at the Connaught in Mayfair. The Connaught is, simply put, one of London's timeless classics.

It was quite late when the evening finished, even though Maggie had an early call for her shift at St. Thomas' Hospital. She said that sleep could be made up after Steve had gone back to Chelveston.

Finally, it was Friday, September 10th. Date night would be tonight. Maggie had her three friends adjust their hospital schedules so that they would have Friday evening and all day Saturday, plus Saturday evening, off duty. She felt that Friday would be just a teaser and from what Steve had told her about each of his comrades, they would hit it off with her friends and therefore want to extend the time to include all of Saturday.

During Friday, the men visited Madame Tussauds Wax Museum on Marylebone Road. It was a favorite destination for all the American military visiting London.

Michael, who had become a friend in addition to his job as their chauffeur, decided that for lunchtime they needed to visit a special pub he knew. On the way to the pub, he described its history: "The place I'm taking you to was erected in the 1850s right on the site that was once the old Fleet Prison. I will have the owner, a mate of mine, show you the dungeons deep down in the cellar. They are a bit creepy, but I believe you will find it interesting to see where men were tortured and murdered. It is a real place that Madame Tussaud speaks of in the wax museum. They do have an excellent luncheon buffet and serve a good bitter. Ah, look, they have laid out the parking space for me. It pays to ring ahead. Gentlemen, here we are at the fine, old Victorian pub . . . Old King Lud! I know it's been a bit of a drive across London to arrive here, but believe me, it is worth it."

Michael was quite correct. The men enjoyed the buffet, bitter, and even the trip down into the cellar to see where the prison and dungeon had been. The owner kidded that they had just stopped the torture down there last week! From the looks of the dungeon, it was just as well now that the place was simply a fine pub.

Michael drove them back to the Stafford. He would meet them once again at six. As instructed, for this evening, he would also have a second chauffeur-driven limousine. Eight people certainly would not fit comfortably in one car, large as it was. Steve quietly informed Howie that the second limousine was on him.

Returning to the Stafford at three gave the men time to shower, shave, and have their uniforms pressed. They all wanted to look their best for this evening.

Michael was right on time, as usual. With him and driving the second car was a chauffeur named Clarence. Steve and Howie would drive with Michael while Clarence would drive Bob and Russ. Soon they were off, negotiating the streets of London. Right before the drive, the men questioned Steve about the girls they would be dating. He stated that all he really knew was that they were nurses. Steve did say that he might have briefly met two of them while he and Maggie had a light dinner in the St. Thomas' Hospital dining hall. Both of them seemed to be quite attractive and he surmised that they would be for Russ and Bob. The other one, well, would be very nice and Howie surely would have a pleasant evening!

The limousines passed over the Westminster Bridge and drove into the entrance of St. Thomas' Hospital. Steve could see that Maggie was already in the lobby. The American aviators looked sharp as they left the cars and smartly walked the short distance to the hospital lobby.

Steve started the introductions, "Gentlemen, say hello to Margaret Steele, the lady I lovingly call Maggie, and ladies, may I present Lieutenants Howard Van Dyke, Robert Courtney and Russell Parker. They are officers, gentlemen, and almost housebroken."

Maggie gave Steve a light punch on the arm and then started her introductions. "I think that we are all going to have a wonderful evening, we've certainly been looking forward to it. Lieutenant Courtney, your date for this evening is Catherine Wilkes. She, like me, is from the Isle of Wight. Lieutenant Parker, your date is Emily Graham. Emily is a country girl from Kent, not too far from Leeds Castle, and Lieutenant Van Dyke, your date is Elizabeth Anderson. Elizabeth is from York. Her father was a professor at Trinity College in Oxford. I believe you are a Yale man! Elizabeth's father is now in the business world. Me, I've got a cowboy and flier from Florida!"

The remark by Maggie brought about a wide grin on the faces of Steve's officers. They understood almost immediately why Steve fell for Maggie. They really belonged together and it showed as they looked at each other.

It seemed as though everyone was satisfied with Maggie's pairing of couples.

Steve then suggested that they go to the waiting cars and proceed to the Savoy Hotel on the Strand, where there was a reservation at the Savoy River Restaurant. While they were driving over to the Strand, Howie inquired if the reservation was for the Savoy Grill. Steve said that no, the Grill, with its wood-paneling, had more of a men's club type atmosphere. The River Restaurant was more formal and had a dance floor. There would be dancing at the Savoy!

It was not a long ride to the Savoy. In no time, the limousines were turning off the Strand and into the covered entrance area. Even with the war on and a darkened London, the Savoy had done a remarkable job of keeping up their tradition of excellence, one that began when the Savoy Hotel first opened in 1889.

A somewhat elderly uniformed gentleman opened the limousine doors and helped the ladies as they exited the cars. Steve figured that before there was a war to be considered, the age of the men performing these particular duties would have been a tad younger. However, they were very efficient and quite cheerful. The doorman made them feel right at home as he gave directions to the River Restaurant.

The maitre d' greeted the party as they entered the elegant River Restaurant. Supper at the Savoy had been legendary over the years. It was one of those things that would be thought about as memories were recounted. Everyone was wide eyed as they took in the scene, noting that the dining tables surrounded the dance floor. The maitre d' escorted them to a very large table in the corner. There were more intimate tables located by the dance floor, but none that would seat eight people. The table was set beautifully with three place settings on each side and one on each end. Steve and Howie took the end seats with Maggie at Steve's left and Elizabeth at Howie's left. Russ sat in the middle, to Maggie's left, with Emily sitting next to Russ. On the other side of the table, Bob sat to the left of Elizabeth and Catherine sat next to Bob. Howie did the directing of seating assignments and kind of shook his head, now satisfied that everyone was where they belonged. Steve asked if they all should take a moment to remember where they were supposed to be seated when they returned from the dance floor, but Howie said no problem, he would remember in case anyone got lost!

"Okay, boy, girl, boy, girl. Yes, Steve, everything is all right," stated Howie.

"We know that Maggie, I mean Margaret," started Bob, who was not quite certain what she should be called in front of her British friends, which brought about a laugh from the girls. He continued, "Anyway, are you ladies nurses as well?"

"That we are," answered Elizabeth before Emily, who had taken a sip of the bottled spring water that had been poured by a waiter, could answer. Catherine sat silent as Elizabeth took the lead. "My friends simply call me Beth. Catherine is Cathy and we all call Emily . . . Emily," continued Beth.

The table captain came over, greeted everyone, thanked the American fliers for taking some of the pressure off the British fliers and told them how welcome they were at the Savoy River Restaurant. The Americans appreciated the comments.

Howie asked that champagne be brought to the table. He noted that just a piano was being played as background music and asked what time the band started for dancing. He was informed that a four-piece band would also be playing during dinner; however, music for dancing would not begin until nine o'clock. It was now just past seven, so they could have a relaxing meal before trying out the dance floor.

Conversation during starters or appetizers, as the Americans called it, was kept light and lively as everyone, except Steve and Maggie became acquainted. It certainly seemed that they were all having a wonderful time. At least for this night, the war was being placed on hold.

Not often was there the opportunity to have beef, in this case delicious Scottish beef. To the civilians, rations of nearly everything needed special stamps in order to purchase food and merchandise. This was true in the United Kingdom and now true in the United States. With grilled Scottish Chateaubriand on the menu, Steve made the suggestion and everyone agreed that it would make a wonderful dinner choice. The maitre d' asked if everything was all right. He pointed out that the Savoy received special Scottish beef from contracted suppliers in Scotland. During the main course, they enjoyed a 1937 vintage Bordeaux. Howie especially noted how good the wine was. When it came time to think about dessert, the party was divided. Four elected to have the lavish Crêpes Suzette, while the other four ordered the famous Savoy Peach Melba. Steve said that back home they would not believe what they were having! There would be sharing of the dessert, with exclamations of "Let me have a taste of that!"

The long, relaxing dinner was ending. It was now time to join other couples who had moved onto the dance floor. Hand in hand, it was a natural move for Steve and Maggie to lead the party as they danced at the Savoy.

Howie and Beth were getting along just fine. They genuinely seemed to enjoy each other's company and were still chatting as they began to dance. Russ and Emily were somewhat more subdued, but one could see that there was a connection between them, especially on the dance floor. Russ told Emily about growing up in the San Francisco area and Emily spoke of a wonderful youth spent on the Isle of Wight. They laughed when they realized that as kids they had been separated by about 6,500 miles, but here they were dancing together in London. Bob and Cathy talked nonstop. She had family who lived in the state of Maine, just south of Portland in the community of Scarborough. Bob would look them up when he went home. Cathy said that she would like to visit Maine when the war concluded and people could once again travel.

Maggie was very pleased that through Steve's descriptions of the men she was able to choose the dates so well. Everything just flowed in such a natural way.

It was quite late when the evening was over and no one wanted it to end. With Maggie, Cathy, Emily, and Beth all having Saturday off duty, a reasonable time was arranged for everyone to meet at the Victoria Train Station for a day's outing to Brighton, the famous seacoast resort.

There was a pleasant 50-mile train trip through the English countryside from Victoria to Brighton. When the train arrived at the Brighton Railway Station, the men started to look for a taxi to take them to the seafront, but the girls said that they would prefer a more leisurely pace walking down Queens Road. In about 15 minutes, the fun-loving group arrived at the promenade and the beach area. At the beach, which was made up of mostly stones and not sand, Steve paused to watch a young boy who was standing by the water's edge throwing stones into the English Channel.

"If I had a camera with me, I'd call the photo 'Boy Throwing Beach'!" said Steve.

Everyone continued to walk on the promenade toward the Palace Pier. The pier, which was built around 1900, was a popular amusement destination. Only about one-half of the pier was open. The section further out to sea was removed from the main section for security wartime purposes. The idea was to keep the enemy from trying to use the pier to off-load saboteurs into Brighton.

They spent an enjoyable time on the pier playing some of the games. Soon it was getting close to lunchtime. They all decided to have a simple lunch of fish and chips. A small local family-type restaurant just off the promenade seemed perfect. It was not a place with white tablecloths where one would have a special sit-down dinner of Dover sole, but it had a view of the Channel and was perfect for their lunch.

After a most enjoyable lunch, they wandered over to the Royal Pavilion at Castle Square. Here they took in the extravagant building and a little later the art gallery. The gallery contained only about half of the paintings they normally would display. Because of the war, only the paintings they could quickly remove to safety in the event of an air raid were on exhibit.

At tea time, there was one place the girls wanted to go and the men simply went along. They would enjoy a cream tea at the Grand Hotel.

The Grand Hotel in Brighton was just that: grand! It opened at Brighton's seaside in the year 1864. In addition to the grandeur of the hotel, which looked more like a palace, the afternoon tea was legendary.

The hotel also bragged that it swifted guests by way of five elevators, or lifts, as the airmen were now calling them, having become used to some of the British terms.

The party of eight settled near the windows in order to enjoy the seaside view as they had their cream tea. They opted for the Darjeeling tea as the focal point. The Darjeeling, as pointed out by Maggie, was the champagne of teas. Her grandfather was a tea buyer and taster who had worked in Ceylon and England during his business career. He eventually brought the entire family to the Isle of Wight when he retired from the business world.

The tea, much like that at Harrods' Georgian Room, consisted of several food towers, enough to accommodate eight wide-eyed customers. There was, of course, the assortment of mini-sandwiches: cucumber, egg and watercress, potted meat, tomato and elegant, little smoked salmon pinwheels. The tower had scones with both strawberry jam and the famous Devin clotted cream as accompaniments. Also, a section of the tower had an assortment of miniature cakes and tarts.

After enjoying their time at the Grand Hotel, they took a taxi back to the Brighton Railway Station for the train trip back to London's Victoria Station. The ride, with everyone crowded into a single compartment of the train coach, was a cheerful, noisy event. Everyone had become, at the very least, friends. They talked, joked, and laughed for most of the trip. It was, for now, a diversion from the war that the men fought over enemy skies, and the war that was so devastatingly brought to London, where the nurses worked and lived.

At Victoria Station they all parted company for a while. Maggie, Beth, Emily, and Cathy said that they did not need an escort back to St. Thomas' Hospital. They wanted to freshen up before going out for dinner. Maggie also told Steve that the girls would meet them at the appointed restaurant. It was just as easy for them to take a taxi.

Steve, Howie, Bob, and Russ decided to walk back to the Stafford. It would be a good stretch of the legs. They, like the girls, wanted to freshen up before going out for the evening. They also wanted to be clean shaven.

Michael and Clarence brought their limousines to the Stafford, fully expecting to pick up the airmen and then go on to St. Thomas' Hospital for the nurses. Howie told the chauffeurs about the change in plans, so with Steve and Howie in one car and Bob and Russ in the other, they drove directly back to the Strand and just down the road from the Savoy to the Victorian institution called Simpson's-in-the-Strand.

As with most first-timers, walking into Simpson's and seeing the high ceilings, rich paneling and the magnificence of the crystal stopped them cold. It was a restaurant where most certainly, a memory was about to be made.

The maitre d' greeted them and showed the gentlemen to a table on the left side and near the back, which was already set for eight people. Much like the Savoy River Restaurant, the place settings were arranged with three on either side and one at each end. Howie joked that they were to have the same seating arrangement, but could they remember how it was or did he have to take command once again? They remembered, or at least said that to Howie, figuring that everything would work out!

Steve told Howie, Russ, and Bob to "hold down the fort." He would go outside and meet the ladies' taxi.

It was not long, just a few minutes, though to Steve watching taxis come and go, it seemed longer. Finally, the black cab carrying the girls arrived in front of Simpson's. Steve walked over to open the taxi door but a quite formally dressed doorman motioned to him that he would do the honors, so Steve went to the open taxi window and paid the driver.

Steve then ushered the girls into Simpson's to the table where the men were waiting. As the "hello agains" were exchanged, the girls easily moved to their seats without being prompted. The arrangement of the seating was the same as at the Savoy and at the Grand Hotel.

Howie ordered champagne as a starter. This was an expensive leave, one that both Howie and Steve could afford because they had means beyond their military pay. This simple fact had been discussed with Russ and Bob. When a tab was picked up by either Howie or Steve, they, in a matter-of-fact way, stated to the other men that they would settle it later, so as not to embarrass Russ or Bob in front of the girls.

The cuisine at Simpson's, as well as the motif, suggested it was somewhat of a male bastion. The waiters, formal as they were, went out of their way to make the ladies feel important and comfortable.

For dinner, the meat was carved from trolleys carrying huge roasts. Everyone except Cathy and Emily elected to have large portions of roast beef served with the traditional Yorkshire Pudding. Emily and Cathy ordered Simpson's famous roast saddle of mutton topped with red currant jelly. It was a fine meal, enjoyed by everyone.

Howie once again did the ordering of wine and settled on British vintage Claret. The dessert was long and relaxing. No one was in a hurry to leave and the staff at Simpson's was quite accommodating. The ladies elected to have treacle roll with custard while the men ordered two trays of cheeses from Great Britain, mostly fine cheddar and the famous Stilton. They shared, tasted each of the desserts and enjoyed a fine vintage port.

All too soon, the evening was at an end. It was quite late and with everyone having such a good time, they did not want to leave! Michael and Clarence drove everyone to St. Thomas' Hospital. Once there, the couples split up with each going in somewhat of a different direction so that some private time could be spent. Clarence said his goodbye to everyone, especially the officers. He wished them well. Michael would wait and drive the men back to the Stafford Hotel.

More than half an hour passed before the group once again gathered to say goodnight. Steve and Maggie had the hardest time leaving each other. It was not too difficult to see that Maggie's eyes were wet from tears as she and Steve were the last to say their farewell. She cried harder as the limousine pulled away from St. Thomas' and made its way across the Westminster Bridge. Emily, Beth, and Cathy did their best to help comfort Maggie.

Once at the Stafford, the men said goodnight and thanked Michael. He would see them in the morning for the ride to King's Cross Train Station for the trip back to Chelveston and the war. In the hotel, the men gathered in Steve and Howie's room for a nightcap. Steve placed four glasses on the small table. Howie, already with the bottle in hand, poured a dram of special Oban Single Malt Scotch Whisky in each glass.

"Well, I don't know how to thank you, Steve," started Howie, as he, Russ, and Bob raised their glasses.

"We concur," agreed Russ and Bob almost in chorus.

"You and Maggie certainly did a great job of matching us up with the right ladies. I don't remember when I've had a better time," continued Howie.

"The really great thing is that we'll stay in touch and, hopefully like you, have something special to come back to London for," stated Bob as he stood up from his chair, took a sip of his Scotch and stretched his shoulders.

"You're welcome, I'm glad things worked out for everyone," Steve said.

It was not long before Russ and Bob made their way to the room they shared. Everyone was exhausted and the morning trip back to base would come soon enough.

Just as the men were finishing an early breakfast at the Stafford, Michael drove up to the hotel with a passenger. Steve didn't know it, but Maggie had quietly spoken to Michael last night about picking her up so that she could spend just a little more time with Steve. Michael would bring Maggie back to St. Thomas' Hospital after the trip to King's Cross Train Station. While Emily, Cathy, and Beth would be on duty this morning, Maggie had set her schedule so that she had an afternoon shift at the hospital.

With officer's bags in hand, the men exited the Stafford once again. The hotel had become a home away from home. The staff of the hotel made everyone feel special and this was important for those who had just a few days away from the dangerous war they were fighting.

As the men walked to the limousine, a smiling Maggie left Michael's side and as Steve put his bag down, she reached up and placed her arms around his neck. They embraced and kissed.

"Needed to see you again before you left town, soldier," said Maggie as she gave a slight wave to Howie, Bob, and Russ.

The men and Maggie climbed into the limousine while Michael placed the officer's bags into the boot, which was not as large as most American car trunks. With a tug here and a push there, Michael managed to close the boot's lid.

Russ and Bob sat in the jump seats while Steve and Howie sat on the large back seat. Maggie also sat on the back seat, but so close to Steve that Howie had a lot of room.

On the drive to King's Cross Train Station, Russ, Howie, and Bob spoke about the time they had spent with the nurses and thanked Maggie for making the London stay so memorable. Maggie told them that Emily, Beth, and Cathy also had a wonderful time and looked forward to the next time they could be together.

Maggie went on to say, "I don't want your egos to climb too high, but the girls had a fabulous time and they were all properly impressed with each of you. They would like to keep up a correspondence until your next leave, if that is okay with you."

"Agreed!" was the answer.

At King's Cross they did not have long to wait for the train back to Wellingborough. Steve and Maggie stayed on the platform for as long as possible. Howie handed Steve's bag up to Russ as he and Bob claimed a compartment in one of the great old trains where the compartment doors open directly onto the platform. Howie climbed into the compartment and placed his bag above the seats in the luggage rack, moving Steve's slightly to the left so that his bag would also fit in the rack. The carriage compartment door was kept open for Steve. There was one last kiss and hug. The train then slowly made its way out of King's Cross Station. Maggie, stayed on the platform watching the train disappear from view.

Maggie then left King's Cross and walked to Michael's waiting car. He gave Maggie a fatherly hug and told her that she and the lieutenant were very fortunate to have found each other. For most of the trip back to St. Thomas', Maggie was quiet with her own thoughts.

Maggie was thankful for her afternoon shift. She needed the time to unwind before her nursing duties.

In the meantime, Steve, Howie, Bob, and Russ had settled into the compartment. They ordered tea and a sandwich from the elderly woman who pushed the trolley up the aisle outside of the compartment.

A taxi was waiting, as had been arranged, for the trip back to the 305th base at Chelveston from the Wellingborough Train Station.

After unpacking, Steve, Howie, Bob, and Russ made their way to the officer's mess for the evening meal. Conversation during dinner centered on the enjoyable trip to London. That particular subject of conversation continued later, as they gathered at their favorite table in the Officer's Club.

Weather for a mission on Monday, September 13th, did not look good. It was windy and a continuous rain started just past midnight. The Carmichael Crew would not have been scheduled anyway. They would, however, be expected to fly a practice mission, weather permitting. As it turned out, on the 13th classes were held in the morning and attended by the full crew. Steve also met with his crew. The enlisted men had a wonderful time in London. Some needed to catch up on lost sleep or just get over a plain old hangover.

Steve wrote some letters to answer the mail he picked up upon his return to the base. There were, of course, letters from his dad and Lillian as well as a few friends from the Kissimmee area. There was no letter from Elly, which was just as well. Steve knew that she was otherwise involved and he was not sure how he would answer a letter from her anyway. Things had certainly changed since he last saw Elly, and to him, what he had now felt much better. When Maggie asked if there was someone back home, he replied that there might have been, but that circumstances had ended the meaningful part of the long-term relationship. Perhaps they'd just be friends, but nothing more than that. Maggie told Steve that there had been just the usual school crushes, but no one like him had ever come into her life.

The following day, another letter from Steve's dad arrived. In this letter, his dad described the usual things that were going on around the ranch. He mentioned that Lillian had come down with a very bad cold and that she had to stay in bed with a high fever. Ray went on to say that Lillian was fine now, but milked her illness for all of its worth. He reckoned that he would deduct sick money from her pay and when she told him that she didn't care, he knew that she was really sick, so he just shut up and got her some more tea and toast.

In one paragraph Ray told Steve that he had been in Orlando and needed some things from the hardware store, so he stopped at the store owned by Elly's father. Both of Elly's parents were in the store at the time and had asked how Steve was doing. Ray said that he gave the usual response of "fine," adding that Steve was flying dangerous missions over the skies of Europe. He told them that Steve was doing well enough as far as the Air Corps was concerned and he had been promoted to first lieutenant, which impressed them. Ray had not seen Elly, but her mother said that she was now going steady with a nice, young man at the university. Ray also wrote that while in Orlando for some shopping, Lillian bumped into Elly and her young man. Lillian was introduced to him, but Elly was clearly embarrassed. In Lillian's words, it seemed to her that "Elly wanted her cake and Stevie too." Ray said in the letter that the reason he wrote this was that he did not want Steve to have any feelings of guilt about meeting someone in England for whom he cared.

In a return letter, Steve wrote of being so proud of his entire crew. He told of how close Howie, Russ, and Bob had become to him and that Howie was actually more like a brother. On the subject of Elly, Steve said that whatever Elly did was all right with him. They both had simply moved on. Steve wrote that he observed the somber effects of the war in the past few months, both to those in combat and to civilians who lived in harm's way, like the fine folks of London and other English cities. The same, he guessed, was probably true with those living on the other side of the English Channel. Steve said that he felt for the people of Holland, Belgium, France, and even the people he was bombing in Germany, but that they had a job to do to bring this war to a close as soon as possible. But now he was getting a bit philosophical. Steve asked his dad to post the letter so that everyone on the ranch could read it because he appreciated everyone's letters from home.

The bad weather continued throughout the next couple of days. A mission was on for the 15th to Romilly-sur-Seine; however, the crew of *Pappy's Pack* would fly only a scheduled practice mission. This gave the Carmichael Crew time to get back into the combat mode, so to speak. They would be back at war soon enough.

Soon enough came the next day. They were alerted for the mission of September 16th. At the briefing, the mission for the day would be the German submarine U-boat pens at the slightly inland port of Nantes, France. There would be P-47 escort fighter cover for most of the mission. The worry was, as always, for the rest of the mission when the only fighters in the sky would be wearing enemy insignias on their wings. Flak batteries would also be active from the time they flew over the enemy coast until the group was flying safely back over the English Channel. Weather was reported to be excellent for the duration of the mission on this fall day. The 305th would take off beginning at 11:44 a.m.

All went according to plan and *Pappy's Pack* joined a good assembly in the clear sky. The flight plan would route the 305th just east of the English coastal city of Portsmouth.

From Howie's copilot seat, he pointed out the Isle of Wight to Steve, who dipped his wing a little so that he could also view Sandown Bay.

The P-47s kept the FW-190s away from the group's B-17s and shot down one of the four that tried to break through the fighter cover. Several additional dogfights ensued, however, Steve and Howie were too busy flying their plane and keeping in the tight formation to follow the action that was going on around them. So far, as they crossed the shoreline and entered enemy territory; the flak was somewhat light and not very accurate.

"Let's keep our eyes peeled. Our escort is heading home," warned Howie over the intercom to the crew.

Steve looked over in approval as Howie spoke up before he made the statement over the intercom. The two worked as well as a pilot and copilot could. Steve was grateful to have a partner on the flight deck of Howie's caliber. Steve knew that Howie was certainly capable of having his own crew, but he would not push it. Howie would let Steve know when he felt he was ready.

"Skipper, I've got two FW-190s trying to sneak up on our tail," called Joey DeMatteo from his tail gunner position. "Willie, keep alert in case they pass under us," he stated to the ball turret gunner.

"If the bastards get close enough, knock them off," came Steve's reply.

All of the crew was alert. The tension could be felt as each crew member dealt with his own feelings and thoughts while the enemy fighters tried to pick the right time for an attack on the B-17. The gunners were at the ready and trigger fingers poised for the action that was about to unfold.

"They're coming in!" called Joey.

"Show them you're on the ball, Joey," advised Jim from his top turret position.

Joey, who usually fired a burst to let the enemy fighters know that he was alert, held back, letting the two FW-190s come in a little closer. *Just a little more . . . a little more,* he said to himself. Then with the cross-hairs on the FW-190 on the left, Joey let go with a long burst of his twin 50s aimed directly at the red-painted engine cowling. Joey hit his mark. The engine immediately began to smoke and flames started licking out from under the engine hood. The plane then broke down and to the right, rolling over with the FW-190 now becoming engulfed in flames. With the FW-190 upside down, the pilot's canopy opened and the pilot dropped out of the burning plane. His parachute opened a short time later, but the FW-190 continued its spiral toward the earth. It hit the ground with a small explosion.

Joey started to swing his twin 50s just after he saw flame coming from the engine of his kill, but the other FW-190 darted away down and to his left, trying to escape. He drew fire from both Willie in the ball turret and Jack from his left waist gunner's position. Both were certain that they had done some battle damage, especially when they saw parts of the plane flying off into the air. The enemy fighter did, however, manage to fly out of range to fight another day.

"Everyone . . . chalk up a kill for Joey," called Willie over the intercom.

"Good going, Joey. Now we've both got a kill," shouted Ron from the right waist.

"Okay, let's settle down and cut the chatter and get back to business. We've still got a long way to go," stated Steve in a calm, steady voice.

The formation was closing in on the IP. The enemy fighters disappeared, but only because of the flak that was coming up to meet the bombers. Shells were exploding around the ships as the group flew nearer to the target.

"Your plane, Russ," called Steve to his bombardier as he handed over the B-17 for the bomb run.

There were just a few clouds over Nantes. The smoke screen, which had been put up over the city, was not very effective on this day. In addition, flak was unusually light and, for the most part, inaccurate.

Nantes was a difficult target to bomb. The River Loire and shipping harbor, including the U-boat pens, were located somewhat near the center of the city. Both sides of the river and port were occupied by industry, plus civilian homes. Poor bombing could make civilian casualties run high.

Russ was right on the target though. "Bombs away, Skipper," called Russ in a business-like manner.

With the bomb bay doors closing, Steve once again took control of the B-17. The plane easily made a climbing right-hand turn away from the target area now that it was without the weight of the bomb load. The 305th formation tightened up once more and made straight for the coast, leaving the Continent as they flew over the Bay of Biscay. The formation of B-17s flew well out to sea now and away from the French coast. It would take a little longer to fly home to England, but it was much safer to stay at least 50 miles clear of the coastal area and the flak batteries.

ME-109s and 110s were spotted going after another group, but luckily, none came after the 305th formation. This route, all the way back to England, was to be over open water. The flight plan home called for them to go completely around the Brest Peninsula before making for England. More than 450 miles lay between them and the 305th base at Chelveston. Not only was it a long trip home, but cloud cover with a low ceiling had forced them to fly most of the way at less than 1,200 feet. While no enemy planes harassed the formation as they withdrew and crossed the open water, they were still glad to see an escort of British Spitfires meet them a hundred miles from the English coast.

Finally, the formation crossed the English coast at Plymouth, flew over Weston, just east of Cardiff, Wales, and then made straight northeast for Chelveston and home. The fuel tanks were all reading close to empty as they flew over the threshold. All 305th planes landed safely with weary crews.

At evening mess and later at the Officer's Club, Russ, Bob, Howie, and Steve were a little on the subdued side. It had been a long day and as Steve liked to say, "I'm not really tired, just a bit overextended."

Some referred to the just completed mission as having flown number 12-A. Others simply said that they had 13 missions behind them. To the officers of *Pappy's Pack*, they just knew that there were 17 more missions to complete before they could go stateside!

They all decided to hit the sack early, but not before hearing the sound of B-17 engines during taxi and the solid sound of Wright Cyclones during takeoff. A mission also was taking place that evening. It was the fourth bombing mission for the 305th that was a night operation. The target area was Modane, halfway across France.

Weather the next morning brought operations to a halt for that day and several days to come. Missions scheduled for September 17, 18, 20 and 21 were all canceled.

The lull in operations gave Steve some time to answer all of those who sent mail. In a letter to his dad, Steve asked how Rudy York was doing. Rudy was an American Indian who played first base for the Detroit Tigers. He was particularly kind to Steve when he visited the Tigers' spring training camp in Lakeland. Rudy had come up to the major leagues as a catcher, the same position as Steve. The last that Steve had heard, Rudy was leading the American League's 1943 season in both home runs and runs batted in. He also wrote to Maggie, answering four letters with one. Steve also reached her by telephone. They were not able to talk for very long, but any time they had was meaningful.

The usual classes were also being held during the bad-weather break in the action. Aircraft identification, especially for those with a trigger finger ready to fire at enemy fighters, was an important class.

One would not want to shoot up a friendly P-47, Spitfire, Hurricane, or the twin-engine P-38 thinking it was an enemy aircraft. The P-38 was distinct in itself, but a gunner could mistake the others for a ME109 or an FW-190, especially in the excitement of battle or with a green gunner flying in his first combat mission. Things happened so quickly; there was not much time to determine friend or foe. Instructors reminded the crews of the grim reality that in combat, about 15 percent of the casualties were from friendly fire. This was especially true in aerial combat where instant life-or-death decisions were made based on identification of head-on silhouettes of aircraft, which with minor modifications could represent half a dozen types, both friend and foe.

In addition, because of the weather conditions, gunners had to check and inspect their weapons frequently. The weather often played havoc with the metal and moving parts, rusting them almost overnight. Cleaning and oiling them kept the guns in combat condition.

Steve also took the time, as the aircraft commander, to hold a crew meeting. It involved going over such subjects as: the dos and don'ts in the use of oxygen; care of the electrically heated suits; shoes and gloves; the bail-out procedure; proper use and care of the parachutes; ditching over water procedure; a drill on proper release; and use of the dinghies and first-aid treatment of wounds for bleeding, fractures, shock, anoxia, frostbite, and burns. In addition, Steve had Bob Courtney, as navigator, review proper intelligence reporting. Howie also assisted, speaking about evading capture in the event they were shot down. He spoke and reviewed the equipment the crew was issued: the aid box, which contained many useful items, like the purse with foreign money, maps and compass and the photos that each crew member had taken in the photo lab wearing civilian clothes. Steve then picked up where Howie left off and concluded the meeting with how, if possible, to evade the enemy soldiers and work their way to neutral Spain, where they could expect a return to England in due time.

While much of the meeting would seem redundant, especially for a trained combat crew whose next mission was number 14 over enemy territory, Steve, a taskmaster on details, felt it extremely important for the safety of his crew to keep these things fresh in their memory. If a crisis did occur, they would do the necessary tasks automatically. They would be prepared. In a combat crew, everyone depends on everyone else; simple as that!

There was a night operation on the 22nd. The target was Hanover, Germany. While Steve and his crew did not fly that mission, they were alerted for a mission the next morning, Thursday, September 23rd. It turned out that the bombing operation to Nantes did not get the job done. They would once again be on a long flight to complete the task.

Everything went according to plan. The assembly was completed on schedule and off went the formation to finish the job. British Spitfires stayed with them as long as possible until their fuel gauge demanded that they must return to the base. The mission itself fared little better than the one a week ago. This time the smoke screen worked. The actual target at the port, aside from the sub pens, was a German supply ship that had escaped serious damage. This time the ship could be seen burning, even through the haze.

About a dozen ME-109s followed the Group as they came off the target. They made only a couple of passes and damaged one plane, a 366th Squadron ship flown by Lieutenant Norman Drouin. The plane, 42-30647, *Polly Ann,* crashed on landing at Chelveston, killing the entire crew. It was a tragic end for the mission to Nantes, France.

To the crew of *Pappy's Pack*, they now had 14 in the books and 16 to go! They wondered after the tragic loss of the Drouin Crew if they could make it. They just never knew when they left for a mission if they would be coming back. You were attacked, or some other plane had that misfortune. It was up to the German fighter pilots which plane they picked out of the sky, or which plane passing through a flak barrage got shot up at 25,000 feet from a gun battery on the ground.

Steve once again had to convince his crew that all would be okay. Pappy wouldn't permit the Germans to destroy the old girl that he nursed back to health and sent off to fight for another day. As much as the plane was their baby, Pappy looked after her like an old mother hen. "Don't tell him what I said about the old mother hen part!" Steve warned his crew.

Missions scheduled for September 24, 25 and the 26th were canceled due to the weather. Mother Nature was having her way, grounding all air operations.

Two missions were on for the 27th. The Carmichael Crew was alerted for the daylight operation to Emden, Germany, a port city. It was an historic mission in that it was the first operation to use the Pathfinder radar-trained bombardier in which all planes would release their bomb load on the lead ship's signal.

The mission went off as planned. The flight path of the formation carried the 305th out over the North Sea, staying away from the coast and outer islands until they reached the IP and started the bombing run. It was almost complete cloud cover. The Pathfinder-led ship, however, could peer through the clouds and on the flare released by the lead plane, away went the bomb load, dropping onto the dock area and port of Emden. The cloud cover kept the enemy fighters grounded. While flak was put up, it was not at the formation's altitude and, for once, it was harmless. The trip back to Chelveston was the kind they wished they all could be: uneventful. *Pappy's Pack* landed, four engines running. Mission number 15 was now behind them. They had reached the halfway mark.

The Carmichael Crew learned the next morning at the officer's mess that an old friend had been lost on the night mission to Hanover.

"Steve, have you heard, a crew was lost last night on the mission to Hanover. Our old ship, the *Image of War* was shot down," said Howie as he set his tray on the table and sat down.

"No, I hadn't heard," answered Steve, who took a sip of his coffee. "Remember that they transferred her to the 422nd? I wonder if Pappy knows. She was his baby. She must have had at least 40 missions. What crew was it?"

"I don't know, but someone told me that they changed her name . . . I'll find out," stated Howie as he started in on his breakfast.

Russ and Bob joined them for breakfast and received the news about the *Image of War*. It was like the loss of an old pal. That plane had seen them all through the early days of their combat as they learned about flying in a shooting war.

No mission was scheduled for today, September 28th. It was Maggie's 20th birthday, so Steve tried to place a phone call to her at St. Thomas' Hospital in London. After several attempts, he finally reached Maggie at the nurse's station where she was on duty.

"Hello, Nurse Steele here," spoke Maggie's voice. "Happy birthday to you, happy birthday to you . . . " sang Steve in his best voice.

"Thank you . . . wish you were here!" replied Maggie.

"Me too, will you have a chance to celebrate?" asked Steve.

"Cathy, Emily, Beth, and I are going over to the Ebury Wine Bar this evening. Want to join us?" answered Maggie. After a slight pause, she continued, "Are you okay?"

"I'm fine, the crew is fine as well. We are halfway through the missions now," stated Steve.

"I've got to go now, but think you might be interested to know that I've fallen completely in love with you," said Maggie.

"Me too . . . I'm in love with you, Maggie. I can't wait for my next leave," answered Steve.

"Okay, I'll be right there," Maggie was heard saying to someone in the hospital. Then she said to Steve, "Please take care of yourself. I love you."

"I will . . . love you and happy birthday. Bye for now," answered Steve as he hung up the telephone.

The weather once again closed in and the mission scheduled for the 29th was canceled. There was no mission slated for September 30th. One more month had passed. A night mission set for the first day of October was also scrubbed. The ever-changing British weather was keeping the B-17s grounded. One could say that boredom would set in as mission after mission was canceled due to the weather; however, it was also a fact that if a mission was postponed for that particular day, it would still be flown on another.

The Carmichael Crew was alerted for the mission of October 2nd. It turned out that they would be making another very long trip, back to Emden, Germany. Once again, it would be a bombing mission using the Pathfinder-trained bombardier. There would be some comfort, because they were told that P-47s with long-range drop fuel tanks would accompany them on the long journey. For the P-47 pilots, cramped in their cockpits, it would be a long journey. The 305th formed up with other groups and headed once again out over the North Sea. The target, as before, was completely cloud covered. Bombing took place again on the lead Pathfinder ship.

"I'm not a happy camper just being a toggler," stated Russ as he threw the switch and dropped the bombs on the Pathfinder B-17's signal.

"Well, if it weren't for the Pathfinder, we'd have to fly someplace else and find a target that we could bomb," answered Steve as he took the ship back from his bombardier after the bomb run.

Just as before, it was a long flight home, but all planes of the 305th landed safely. *Pappy's Pack* was once more landing on British soil with all four engines running. Number 16 was now in the books for Steve, Howie, Russ and Bob.

The 422nd Squadron flew a night mission. It was a Saturday night bombing raid to Munich, Germany. All of their planes returned safely back to Chelveston.

The mission set for October 3rd was scrubbed. It was just as well, for the crews were very tired from the long flight to and from Emden. There would be, though, a bombing mission scheduled for Monday, October 4th.

October 4th dawned bright and clear. It was also quite cool. Leaving the warmth of the blankets for Steve, as well as others, was always difficult, especially on cold mornings. After shaving and dressing for the mission, it was off to the mess hall for breakfast. For Steve, as a crew member who was flying a mission on this day, fresh eggs and bacon were served. Conversation at the breakfast table was always the question of where the bombers would be off to today. The speculation was somewhere deep into Germany, but they would find out soon enough at briefing.

At the briefing hut just before the curtain was pulled away from the mission map and the route to today's target was unveiled, crew members sat, anxiety showing in their faces while knots welled up in their stomachs. Would the mission today be easy or one in which the bombers would have to fight their way to and from the target? How long would they have to fly beyond the protection of the escort fighters? Soon those questions were answered. The red yarn reached across the channel, past Brussels, Belgium, Maastricht, Holland, entering Germany just south of Aachen and south of Bonn to the target area of Wiesbaden and Frankfurt.

This would be the 79th trip into enemy territory for the 305th Bomb Group. It would be a difficult mission. The sky would be filled with B-17s and B-24s from other groups as several targets in the Frankfurt area would be attacked at the same time. With more than 200 American bombers to shoot at, from both the ground flak batteries and the ever-present German fighters, the crew of *Pappy's Pack* hoped that their ship was not one of those picked out of the crowd. Then, that was also the feeling of every bomber crew!

Pappy was waiting at the ship as the truck dropped off the crew. Steve walked over to Pappy to discuss the readiness of the plane. The flak holes had been patched, engines warmed up, fuel had been topped off and the ole girl was ready to take on the mission at hand.

With everyone aboard and flares fired from the control tower, Pappy gave Steve the all clear and, one by one, the engines roared to life. The brakes were released and *Pappy's Pack* left the hardstand to join the taxi for takeoff. Finally, it was their turn and the loaded B-17 started down the runway once again. The lift off, just before they were out of runway, went smoothly as the plane with four engines straining, carried them up toward the formation that will head out across the English Channel. The escort of P-47s met them right on schedule. It is a comfort to have them fly cover, at least to Brussels. This was where they would once again have the protection of their little friends for the flight back to England.

The formation entered the Continent just south of Oostende, Belgium. The flak was, so far, light and not very accurate. In fact, it was not even close to the altitude they were flying. The Luftwaffe had not shown up yet. Perhaps they were simply waiting until the escort was forced to leave the bomber stream because of having just enough fuel to fly back to England. The formation continued past Brussels, flying south of the city between Brussels and Charleroi, trying to avoid flak as much as possible. It was here that the escort of P-47s dipped their wings and started for home. Still, there were no enemy fighters. Perhaps they were attacking other groups as they flew toward their assigned targets or maybe, with more than 200 American bombers in the air, they could not find this formation.

When the IP was reached, the bombing run on the airfield at Wiesbaden began. Steve handed the plane over to Russ. Bomb bay doors were opened and the B-17 surged upward a bit as the weight of the bomb load was released on the target 21,500 feet below them.

With the bomb bay doors coming up and closing, a sharp, climbing left-hand turn was started as Steve once again took over control of the plane. He tried to avoid the flak that was bursting around the ship. A shower of dirty, black flak fragments hit the plane as a shell burst went off about 20 yards from *Pappy's Pack*. The big plane bounced from the concussion of the blast.

"Check in . . . is everyone okay?" called Steve over the intercom.

Everyone checked in. No one was hit by the flak. They were lucky once again. In the meantime, Bob was plotting the course back to England. It would take them north of Luxembourg and south of Aachen and Liege as the formation worked to stay away from the industrial areas, which would hold the greatest concentration of antiaircraft fire.

Just before the formation reached the Brussels area, a barrage of deadly flak hit a plane from the 305th.

"Number 741 just took a flak hit," called Ron over the intercom from his position as right waist gunner.

"That's Bailey . . . a 366th ship," said Steve.

"She's knocked out of formation and, oh hell, here come the 109s," stated Howie as he looked over his right shoulder. "Bastards are shooting the shit out of her."

"B-17 going down," called Joey from the tail.

"Count the chutes!" called Howie.

"Some from up front and some from the back. I count four, no five . . . wait a minute, seven. I count seven that got out," stated Willie from the ball turret.

"I'll confirm that, seven parachutes," said Joey.

"That makes three that did not get out of the ship," said Howie quietly to Steve. Steve acknowledged Howie with a nod of the head as he continued to fly as tight a formation as he could.

Bob noted in the logbook that a 366th ship, 42-37741, the Bailey Crew, was shot down near Brussels by flak and fighters and that seven parachutes were seen escaping the doomed bomber. He would report this at the debriefing.

The enemy fighters did not return to fight the formation, but broke away. They might have needed to refuel themselves or possibly, like the crew of *Pappy's Pack*, they saw that the escort that would ferry them home, the P-47s, were joining up with the group.

In reaching the coast, the flak was light and inaccurate. Steve turned the plane over to Howie for the rest of the flight home. They could place mission number 17 into the books as being completed.

A tired group of officers gathered that evening at the O-Club. They had thought of going over to a pub in Rushden, but Russ, Bob, Howie, and Steve decided that they would do that another time. For now, the Officer's Club was fine.

"The weather is closing in; I think we'll have tomorrow off," said Bob as he and Russ each brought two pints over to their favorite table.

Howie placed a large bag of unshelled peanuts on the table. "They just arrived . . . told my folks to send them . . . didn't want us to run out," he said.

"Very good, Howard my boy," said Steve as he reached in the bag for a handful.

"I'd better get that trash can over there," said Russ and he walked over to the bar and took one of the two trash cans back to their table.

There was happy munching going on and Steve, along with Howie, delivered the next round of beer to the table. They stayed until the club closed.

During the night, it became known that a 422nd Squadron plane was lost over Frankfurt. The Seay Crew, 42-3091, did not make it back.

The weather again played a part during the next few days as the 305th stayed on the ground. Night missions scheduled for the October 5th and 6th were canceled, as was the daylight mission of the 7th. The 422nd, however, flew a leaflet mission to Paris on that night.

The Carmichael Crew was alerted for Friday, October 8th. The weather had cleared and they would fly.

At briefing, they learned that the mission would be to Bremen, and it was the first trip that the Carmichael Crew would make to this German port city. From the groans and the looks on the faces of the crews who had already been to Bremen, this certainly had the sound of a difficult mission. Other groups would form up to become a wing and make the long trip. In all, the men were informed, more than 300 B-17s would bomb the specified targets. In addition, there would be a diversionary force of 100 B-24s bombing other targets in the Baltic region.

"What the hell is a diversionary target?" whispered Howie to Steve.

"All I know is that they shoot at you no matter what," answered Steve in a very quiet voice.

"I don't want to be shot down as a diversion. What would the folks at the country club say?" whispered Howie back to Steve.

That brought a wide grin on Steve's face, but he didn't answer Howie for fear he would break out laughing; bad time to laugh!

Pappy, as always, had the plane ready for the trip across the North Sea. He informed Steve that additional ammunition was aboard, stored as usual in the radio compartment.

"They've got several hundred fighters stationed around the area you're going today," stated Pappy to Steve as they completed the walk-around procedure. "I figure that your gunners will be quite active."

"Thanks, Pappy," replied Steve as he prepared to climb aboard the B-17 through the nose hatch. "A few hundred flak batteries are also in the Bremen area, so I'm told, but don't worry, we'll bring the ole girl home, and as always, we know that she'll carry us home."

Howie, in the meantime, was in the cockpit doing some of the preflight checklist and was waiting for Steve to climb into the left pilot's seat to complete the list.

It was not too long before the flares were fired, engines started, taxi and takeoff completed, and the Group was forming up and joining the wing for the Bremen mission.

The First Wing climbed to 25,000 feet as they crossed the North Sea. They would climb to 27,000 feet for the bomb run, hoping that it would take the flak batteries on the ground a little time to figure out that the formation was 2,000 feet higher than originally estimated. Perhaps the altitude change would save a ship or so from receiving a direct hit by the exploding 88-millimeter flak shells sent up from the gunners on the ground.

The P-47 fighter escort, which had met them right on schedule, now had to turn back just inside the Continent as the wing approached Leeuwarden. So far, the flak was light and inaccurate. As the First Bombardment Wing flew on, individual pilots now moved their B-17s a little closer to each other, seeking the protection of the tighter formation as the little friends turned toward home. Now over Groningen, the crew spotted what looked like tiny specks on the horizon. Those specs grew larger; enemy FW-190s were bearing in on them.

"Bandits at one o'clock, FW-190s," called Jim over the intercom from his top turret position. Jim then swung his twin 50s to the spot where the 190s were coming from, ready to open fire as soon as they were in range.

"Heads up, everyone!" alerted Howie.

Steve automatically moved the heavily loaded *Pappy's Pack* a little closer to his wingman, flying as close a formation as he could for the protection of the ole girl.

Flak shells were now exploding around them as they continued to fly over the German landscape. They were now close to the IP and the bomb run on their Bremen target, a submarine construction and repair yard.

The FW-190s had decided to attack a formation flying below them and off to the right. Sometimes, when the formation was really tight, the German fighter pilots would seek out B-17s that were spread out a little more.

So far, the flak gunners on the ground had not found the correct altitude; luck was still with them.

Russ had taken over the plane and the bombardier dropped the load through scattered clouds. There was also a haze over the target, a munitions factory, which Russ thought was either smoke pots to form a smoke screen or the smoke from factory chimneys.

Just off of the target, as Steve was making a climbing, left-hand turn away from the target area, they spotted a 305th plane that took a flak hit in the right wing. It must have hit a gas tank because both the number three and four engines were on fire. The wing was starting to swell, with fire coming out of both engines on the right side of the plane. It was clear that the crew would have to leave the ship before it exploded.

"I think that's the Emmert Crew from the 365th," said Howie, who looked for a moment and then stated through the plane's intercom, "Count the chutes!"

From the ball turret, Willie stated, "They're coming out from everywhere. I count 10 chutes. They all made it out."

It was a relief that ten parachutes were seen and that the crew had safely evacuated the burning plane, but it was also a fact that soon they would be in German hands instead of flying home to Chelveston.

Not long after leaving the target area, the formation was jumped by what appeared to be 40 or 50 enemy fighters. The FW-190s were joined by ME-109s, ME-210s and even some JU-88s that tried to stay just out of the B-17s gunners' range and fire rockets toward the formation.

The fighters made several passes, firing away at the formation, with the B-17s returning the fire. Two FW-190s flew right into a stream of fire as they tried to make a snap roll and dive under the B-17s. Both were hit, one losing a good part of his left wing as it continued to spin down toward the ground. The FW-190 exploded on impact. The pilot did not get out. The other plane continued to dive out of range and was last seen leaving the area of combat, the pilot trying to make it back to his base in the damaged plane.

Then the German fighters all disappeared. They broke off the fight and headed to see what damage they could do to another formation of B-17s, which was flying below and off to the right.

A huge explosion shook *Pappy's Pack* just when Bob started to give his navigation position of Assen as they prepared to exit the European continent and start the over-the-water trip back to England. The flak shell, which hit near the number three engine, knocked it out of commission and started a fire. In the cockpit, Steve and Howie reacted automatically. Fire extinguishers put out the blazing engine, which was also feathered. Steve also increased the RPMs on the other three engines and tried to work his way back into the formation. The explosion had bounced them out of the position they had occupied.

Shrapnel also ripped into the side of the plane, puncturing the skin just in front of the radio room, as well as shattering some of the ball turret Plexiglas.

"Check in . . . everyone okay?" called Howie.

"I think we're all okay. We are pulling Willie out of the ball. It was shattered a bit and he's bleeding," answered Ron Lattamus from his right waist position.

Steve started to call for Jim McFarland to leave the top turret, go back and see what was going on, but Russ, who said he could leave the nose and take care of things, interrupted him.

Russ came out of the nose and went along the catwalk in the bomb bay. He noticed a gaping hole in the right side of the plane and was glad that the bomb load had been released before they took the hit. Russ went through the open door into the radio room and saw that Eddie Anderson was already cleaning Willie's face where some Plexiglas had hit him in the forehead. Jack Kowalski was also kneeling down as he administered first aid to Willie.

"I'm okay, Lieutenant . . . just might have trouble parting my hair for a few days," said Willie as he forced a smile, knowing that it could have been much worse.

Eddie nodded, and told Russ that there were no other injuries. They all wondered if everyone was all right up front. That was a close one.

"We're fine, just lost the number three engine, but the ship is okay," stated Russ coolly. In moments of stress, everyone observed a calm, business-like manner and looked out for each other.

Russ came back through the bomb bay and into the cockpit. He reported everything he had seen to Steve. As he was talking to Steve and Howie, the P-47s arrived to escort them home.

Aside from losing an engine, the plane was flying well. There was no real damage that might affect the way the plane behaved. The formation had slowed down a little in order to let Steve keep up with the others. He was even able to let up a bit on the power of the three good engines.

Pappy observed the flare from *Pappy's Pack* warning that wounded were aboard. He also saw that the ship was coming in on just three engines. With the priority of landing first, the ambulance and Pappy met the plane. Willie was helped into the ambulance and driven to the base hospital. Once there, he would be examined thoroughly and his wounds treated by a doctor.

Willie would be the second crew member to receive a Purple Heart for being wounded in action. The other was their former tail gunner, Roger "Wyatt" Earp, who was now stateside and recuperating in a military hospital near Philadelphia, in Valley Forge, Pennsylvania.

Instead of having Steve taxi the plane to the hardstand, Pappy said that he should shut everything down; it would be towed. There was no sense taking a chance on a potential fuel leak that could set the entire plane on fire.

Pappy and the crew looked the damaged plane over while they waited for the tow.

"We were lucky once again. She is one sweet airplane . . . knows when to duck. And she brought us home," said Steve to Pappy as they surveyed the holes in the side, the shattered ball turret and the ruined number three engine.

"Well, looks like I'll be up late tonight, but we'll get her patched up," said Pappy as he patted Steve on the shoulder. "I already have an engine hidden away that no one knows about."

A truck arrived to take the crew to the debriefing interrogation. On the way they discussed the close call and wondered if Willie would be able to continue with his missions or if he'd have to sit out a few.

Pappy, in the meantime, supervised the B-17 as it was towed back to its hardstand. He walked behind the plane as it was being towed to look for the telltale drops of fuel on the concrete. Surveying the damage, he really did not think the job could be completed overnight. He might need two days to get her back into combat flying condition.

After interrogation, the crew left the hut and went back to their quarters to clean up before mess.

Three other 305th ships had wounded aboard and the medical team had plenty of work to do. However, late in the afternoon, there was a visit by a concerned crew to see how Willie was getting along. They managed to all file in to see him, but it was not long before a nurse showed up and broke up the crowd. She would let two at a time spend five minutes with her patient. Willie would be all right, but with the deep lacerations, especially on his forehead from the shattered Plexiglas, he would be laid up for at least a week, maybe two.

"I'm going to be way behind in my missions. Maybe I'll even have to fly with another crew," stated an anxious Willie Burnett to Steve, as he and Howie stood on each side of his hospital bed.

"We'll need a replacement, but you are an important part of my crew, Willie, and when you're ready, the job is waiting," Steve told him as he and Howie left to let others come back to visit.

Howie and Steve waited for Russ and Bob, and the four men made their way over to the O-Club for a drink and some relaxation. Nevertheless, as usual, conversation included the mission and how, once again, lady luck was with them. None of the 422nd Squadron flying officers were at the club. They were flying a night leaflet mission to Rennes, France.

A mission was scheduled for the following day, October 9th. It would be a long trek over the North Sea to the port city of Gdynia in Poland. The flight plan would take them north of Kiel in order to avoid as much of the flak area as possible. Several other targets would be bombed at the same time by other formations.

The Carmichael Crew was to stand down for the mission to Gdynia. As far as Steve was concerned, it was just as well. *Pappy's Pack* was not quite ready to fly, despite the fact that the holes had been patched, a new engine hung in the number three position and the ball turret had been repaired. The ground crew was still working on her, putting in the remaining touches to make her airworthy and ready for combat. The flak explosion had also caused some damage to control cables and the wing flaps.

Steve was glad that they were not ordered to fly a replacement aircraft like they had with his first plane, *Image of War*. *Pappy's Pack* was now their aircraft and she had been a lucky plane to fly into combat. Superstitions arise when a crew changes planes. Now they were all used to their ship! The crew did not want another change.

All of the 305th planes returned from bombing the Port of Gdynia. It was always a good day when all the Group's B-17s returned home safely. Other Groups bombing targets in Prussia and in other parts of Poland were not so fortunate. Losses ran higher than expected. More than 50 B-17s had been lost during the past two days and 500 men were missing in action.

Sunday, October 10th, would see some crew members attend church services before a scheduled briefing for the bombing mission that would take place. The target, Enschede, Holland, was east of Amsterdam. The Carmichael Crew would lead the low element. They preferred the high spot, but a crew takes what is assigned to them. Other groups would be bombing targets further east in the area of Munster, Germany. For them, it would be an even longer trip over enemy territory.

Steve, Howie and Bob studied the flak map. The flight course would have them enter the Continent on the Dutch coast south of Amsterdam and just north of Scheveningen. Bob would keep them on a flight path that would avoid as much anti-aircraft flak batteries as possible. A P-47 escort, with the greater range drop fuel tanks, was going to take them almost to the target. They could keep the Luftwaffe fighters at bay, but would have to drop the extra fuel tanks if they engaged the enemy.

Steve also met replacement ball turret gunner, Vincent Campalone. At the hardstand, Vincent told the crew that he came from Blackwood, New Jersey, and had been a baker at an Italian bakery known as Mighty Bread in Camden. He had not been assigned to a regular crew yet, but had flown four missions. This mission, his fifth, would earn him an Air Medal. Vincent was 18 years old. He had quit school when he was 16 and was drafted into the service.

"It seems right," stated Howie, who thought for a second. "We have a cook as a waist gunner and now a baker as our ball gunner. I wonder what the actual Army cooks and bakers were doing before the war."

Steve explained to Vincent that he would, at this time, be on temporary duty with the Carmichael Crew, and that when Willie was healed, he'd most likely return to combat duty back at his old position. Vincent understood the situation. He had been a fill-in on all of his previous missions.

Eddie Anderson, the old man of the crew (after all, he was 29), put his hand on Vincent's shoulder and told the little guy that they'd all take good care of him and that after the plane took off and formed up, they'd tuck him neatly in the ball turret. Jack told Vincent that he was lucky to be flying with the best crew in the 305th, with the best pilot in the Air Corps. Then, of course, each crew felt the same about their crew and pilot.

Flares were fired from the control tower and it was off to war once again. This time, the Carmichael Crew had more responsibility as a lead crew. They would be much busier than usual on a normal mission, but to say the least, the crew was up to the challenge. The assembly was completed and the wing headed out over the North Sea toward the Netherlands. Escort P-47s darted above, below and around the bomber stream as they sought to protect their big friends from the Luftwaffe. The German fighters were seen, but they were after another formation of B-17s well off to the right and above them. They could be the group headed to raid the Munster area.

Seeing enemy fighters will automatically motivate a pilot to move his ship in just a little tighter for the greater protection the formation's guns afford. The flak, so far, had been light. Bob was doing a good job of following the flight plan that would, they hoped, keep flak at a minimum for at least part of the mission.

The IP was reached at Haaksbergen, with bombardier Russ Parker taking over the ship for the bomb run. As they lined up for the target the flak became more intense. The bomb load was released on the enemy airdrome 21,000 feet below them, the bomb bay doors came up and Steve once again took control of *Pappy's Pack* by banking the plane hard to the left as they flew away from the reported flak batteries, which were just beyond the target area.

"Let's head for home," called Steve in the intercom after bringing the big plane level once again. "Keep a sharp eye. Jerry's out there waiting to shoot down our cute little ass."

"I've got our ass covered, Skipper," called Joey from the tail gunner's position.

"Ronnie and I have the waist covered," chimed in Jack Kowalski.

"Old Buffalo Jim has the top covered," called Jim McFarland in a jovial voice.

"I've got the nose covered . . . twin 50s at the ready," yelled Russ from his other duty of nose gunner.

"What about you, Vincent?" asked Eddie Anderson from the radio compartment.

"Gentlemen, I am ready," returned Vincent in a firm voice.

"If any Jerry fighter pilots are listening . . . you've been forewarned. I pity you bastards if you tangle with us," taunted Howie. "Hey, we didn't hear from Robert. Mr. Courtney, are you with us?"

"Oh, I'm just up here looking out the window and searching the horizon for England, you know, playing navigator," answered Bob.

So far, the Luftwaffe had not shown up, although there were some specks far out on the left of the formation. Flak continued to be light and sporadic. The route in and out of this target was working, at least up to this point.

"We've got company," called Russ.

"They're friendlies . . . P-47s that have come to ferry us home . . . a helping hand," called Jim.

The flight back over the North Sea was routine, engines running smoothly and with Howie at the controls, the plane headed for Chelveston and home. Steve took over as they set up for the landing. Mission number 19 was completed for much of the crew. Eddie Anderson, Jack Kowalski, and Joey DeMatteo, who had been called upon to fly as replacements before the assembled crew flew together, had two additional missions to their credit. Ronnie was catching up and was now considered by the crew as a veteran. Vincent had completed number five and would receive his Air Medal.

The weather became a factor once again, this time both in England, where there was a dense fog, and in Europe, where a steady rain covered the target areas. The missions scheduled for October 11th and 12th were canceled.

A mission was on for the 13th, but the 366th Squadron was to stand down. It turned out that the mission was recalled due to weather conditions over the target area.

Just as before, the lull in the action gave the bomber crew's time to, as they say, catch up with themselves. For some, extra sleep was in order, while others caught up on letter writing or just relaxed from the pressure and anxiety of combat.

Steve wrote several letters. The most important and longest was to his dad. He told of having 19 missions in the book and with just 11 more to go. Steve wrote, "No matter how hot Central Florida got in the summertime, I will never again complain. The dampness and cold in this part of England goes right through a poor ole Southern Boy!" Steve spoke of Maggie as well, but asked his dad not to broadcast anything about their relationship. It was not time yet to do that. Steve also wrote to several friends, plus Lillian, but used V-Mail for those letters. He answered Maggie's four letters that she had written. She understood that Steve could not answer each one. Her main concern was simply knowing that Steve was all right.

Steve tried and finally was able to get a telephone call through to Maggie at St. Thomas' Hospital, and caught up with her at the nurse's station. He told her that perhaps after the next couple of missions he was hoping to wrangle a pass to London. Maggie questioned the new word entered into the English language, "wrangle." She sometimes kidded Steve that he spoke American and not English!

The Officer's Club closed early on the 13th. The weather was clearing and word was that a deep-penetration bombing mission was on for the 14th. In addition, word was passed around the club that the former 305th Commanding Officer Curtis LeMay had received his first star. He now held the rank of brigadier general and was commander of the Third Bombardment Division.

On the morning of Thursday, October 14th, the crews at Chelveston were awakened at five and breakfast was served at the mess hall at six o'clock. The sound of feet shuffling through the chow line, along with the banging of metal trays as the airmen set them on the table to try to eat were, for the most part, the only sounds heard among more than 180 men. They had heard that the mission for this day called for "maximum effort." This meant a long and dangerous bombing raid would be taking place. The short lull in the action had ended. Most of the men ate quietly. Briefing for the mission would be just about an hour away at 7:30. As before each mission, eating breakfast was a meal that left stomachs churning as nerves had the men dwelling on what lay before them.

Steve, Howie, Bob and Russ ate their breakfast mostly in silence, but there was some conversation between them. It never got any easier, but this was mission number 20 for them and they had been through enough together so that they were not as nervous as the newer crews. Therefore, it was not really for concern of the mission that they ate quietly, but more for the morning hour. Howie always kidded that their crew was not made up of morning people.

"We've got fog and a steady drizzle, we're not going any place today," said Russ as he placed his coffee mug back onto the table after taking a sip of the morning brew. "They should have let us sleep. Where did they get the idea that the weather is clearing?"

"Well, maybe it's clear over the target area, wherever that might be," answered Steve.

"If we have to lift off in this stuff, it certainly will be an adventure until we get above the weather," chimed in Howie.

"Are you kidding?" started Bob, who paused a moment as he took a drink from his coffee mug. "Hell, this is the kind of weather us navigators dream of!"

They all started to laugh at Bob's remark, which broke the silence of the tables around them.

"Come on, let's get to the briefing, after all, we want to get a good seat," said Steve as the officers of *Pappy's Pack* started to leave the mess hall for the briefing hut.

At the briefing, Lieutenant Colonel McGehee gave the opening remarks, but they were short. Everyone would soon find out what he knew about the mission. Then, the operations officer pulled the drawstring to reveal the map showing the path of the mission. The red yarn line extended from England, across Belgium, part of Holland and well into Germany. Oh my . . . it was back to Schweinfurt!

The officer, standing on the small stage, then announced, "The target for today is Schweinfurt!"

There were some groans, as there were for every mission, but mostly there was a stunned silence at this gathering of the 305th aircrews as they listened to the details of the mission. They were right at breakfast. This would be a long and dangerous mission. There was fright in many eyes as the thought of perhaps not coming back from this one set in.

The intelligence officer told them that the August 17th raid on the ball-bearing factory at Schweinfurt had been only partially successful. The plant was back to operating at almost 70 percent of capacity and they were going back to put them out of business. The war, they were told, would be shortened by six months because of this mission.

Howie whispered to Steve, "I didn't realize they already had a timetable. Maybe the intelligence officer should go along on the mission in order to get a firsthand look at the target."

As the briefing continued, the intelligence officer spoke of what they could expect along the route to and from the target area. It did not sound comforting. Beside the expected flak batteries firing at them from the ground, there would be more than 1,000 enemy fighters to contend with along the route to the target and back. Help would come from an escort of P-47s that were fitted with extra external fuel drop tanks. The drop tanks would give welcomed extra range for the American fighters and permit them to extend to a few miles into Germany. They would be able to escort to just north of the border city of Aachen. Then, of course, the little friends would have to turn back toward England. The Flying Fortress B-17s of the 305th would be on their own until they once again reached the Dutch–German border where both P-47s and British Spitfires would cover the withdrawal, helping them to reach the Channel and English soil.

Major Charles Normand, the commanding officer of the 365th Squadron, would be leading this important mission. The 366th would fly as the high squadron and the 364th would fill the low position. The 305th Bomb Group would send 18 planes on this mission.

Just before leaving the briefing room, Steve, Howie, and Bob checked the map showing the expected flak along the planned route. It showed that they would see light to moderate anti-aircraft fire until they flew over and entered the Ruhr Valley. Some crews referred to the Ruhr as Flak Valley. It was here, on the August 12th mission to Gelsenkirchen that their close friend, First Lieutenant Wright Gerke, and his crew were hit by the flak that knocked them out of formation, only to be finished off by attacking ME-109s. It now seemed so long ago, but it was just two months.

After the briefing had concluded, many of the airmen gathered with their chaplains. Then it was time to pile into the waiting truck that would take them to the hardstand and the airplane that would once again fly them into the war.

Once at the hardstand, the crew went about the particular things each man does to put the finishing touches to prepare the plane and its guns for the mission. Pappy had made certain that the fuel tanks were topped off, knowing that on a long mission, each gallon was important. He also loaded in extra ammunition, because the crew would spend far too much time over enemy territory. The extra ammunition would not be a luxury, but for all practical purposes very necessary. On this mission, *Pappy's Pack* was loaded with six 1,000-pound bombs. With the extra weight, they would be using a lot of runway before lifting off and getting airborne.

The light rain now became much harder and the heavy fog persisted. The Carmichael Crew had been waiting for more than an hour for the order to start engines. Most of the crew was convinced that the mission would simply be scrubbed. Schweinfurt would have to wait at least another day for their visit.

At 1000 hours, or 10:00 a.m., the order was given to start engines. It was hard to believe. The roar of B-17 engines coming to life filled the air and planes began to taxi. This was one of the missions in which the tail gunner in each B-17 had to use the Aldis blinking light that flashed from the tail section so that the pilot and copilot in the plane behind, inching its way along the taxiway, could see the plane in front of him. Several such missions flown from England when fog was a factor required use of the Aldis lamp.

Steve and Howie were having trouble getting the number three engine to start. Pappy did have all four running smoothly before, so perhaps it was the weather playing hell with the old number three position.

No more planes taxied past their hardstand and Steve was now concerned that they would have to abort the mission. Finally, after a tremendous amount of smoke and coughing, the number three kicked in and soon had smoothed out. Number four easily came to life and Steve started to inch his way out of the hardstand. However, after just a few feet he stopped the plane, slid open the window on his left and shouted to Pappy, "I can't see a damned thing. I don't want to run off the taxiway and put this ship into the mud!"

Pappy acknowledged Steve and told one of his ground crew to get the spare Aldis lamp from the service tent. Pappy usually had a spare everything.

Soon the spare lamp was retrieved. Pappy told the corporal to drop the canvas roof on the Jeep and climb into the back seat with the lamp. It would be a very wet trip to the end of the runway for the two of them as the rain drenched the men in the now open Jeep. They would guide the B-17 with the blinking Aldis lamp to the takeoff point.

As Steve brought the plane onto the end of the runway, it dawned on him and Howie that they were the last ship to leave for the battle. "This is a hell of a way to have to play catch up," noted Jim McFarland from his engineer's position, as the three of them peered into the fog in front of the plane.

The B-17s brakes were held. The big bomber shook from the vibration as the engines were run up. The tail wheel locked, brakes released and *Pappy's Pack* started to lumber her way straight down the runway, lifting off into fog and very low clouds.

Howie was looking for other aircraft that might drift into their air space during the climb. He pointed out, "It's thick as soup out there. If we do see a B-17, it will be too late to do anything!" This was not very comforting.

Finally, after the climb-out that took a little over 25 nerve-racking minutes, in which you depend on the instruments because outside is just a whiteout, they popped out of the clouds.

There were no other aircraft in sight. With their ship being so late, the other planes had formed up and were on the way to Germany. *Pappy's Pack* leveled off at 12,000 feet and applied additional power in order to try to play catch up with the specks they saw off in the distance. Steve, Howie, Russ and Bob hoped that the specks were the 305th planes, but with radio silence enforced, Bob just set the course that would let them intercept the bomber stream closest to them. They would need the protection of other B-17s as they entered enemy territory.

"It's going to take a while to catch up," stated Howie to Steve. "We're all alone out here."

"I know, but I don't want to abort if we can help it," answered Steve. He also was worried if they could indeed reach whatever formation was out in front of them. In addition, he was concerned about the extra fuel they were consuming.

Steve called to his navigator over the plane's intercom, "Bob, when do you figure we can meet up with the formation?"

"Just after we cross the Belgium border," replied Bob.

"We've got company," called an excited Joey from his tail gunner's position. Then after just a few seconds he continued, "Friendly . . . they're Spitfires!"

Two British Spitfires cautiously moved in position off the left side of *Pappy's Pack*. They dipped their wings in salute. Steve gave a wave and thumbs up signal back at the Spitfires. They were certainly a welcome sight.

Apparently, the British Spitfires had been on the lookout for any bombers that might have been forced to turn back and abort the mission. They would escort them safely back to England. However, in this case, the job would be of a different nature as they escorted the lone B-17 that was trying to catch up with a formation and go into battle.

Radio silence was maintained and the Spitfires continued to fly with *Pappy's Pack*. So far, so good; there were no encounters with enemy aircraft. Puffs of dark black flak explosions, which were directed toward the bomber stream they were trying to catch, appeared in front and throughout the formation. It seemed to be light and so far inaccurate.

Pappy's Pack entered the Continent just south of Oostende, Belgium. Finally, they had caught the bombers in front of them. It was not the 305th Group, but at least they had some protection and would fly as part of this formation.

"We're going to be in a lousy position, Stevie ole boy," stated Howie, as *Pappy's Pack* prepared to join up with the formation of B-17s and fill a vacant slot. The bomber stream was at 23,000 feet and climbing to what Steve figured would be 25,000 feet.

"At least we're no longer alone," answered Steve as he slid in behind and to the right of the bomber nearest to them, tucking *Pappy's Pack* neatly into the formation as they made their way across Belgium.

"We've hooked up with the 384th Bomb Group; look at the triangle P on the tail," called Bob over the intercom.

As Steve maneuvered the ship within the group, he dipped the big bomber's wings slightly and waved to the Spitfire pilots "thank you." They also dipped their wings and headed back toward the sea and a return to the original assignment they were scheduled to fly.

"I count just 13 ships with a P . . . must have had some aborts," said Howie.

"Well, they've got 14 now. A triangle G has come to save the day," kidded Steve. He referred to the big painted triangle with a G in it on the large vertical stabilizer, or tail as some people simply call it that signifies the Group to which the plane belongs. As the formation reached 25,000 feet, the flak became more intense. The bomber stream was now just north of Brussels. So far, though, the flak was not accurate. They knew this would change as they crossed into Germany.

The P-47 escort, along with a flight of twin-engine, twin-tailed P-38s, was doing battle with the yellow nose painted FW-190s. Usually the German fighters would wait until the American or British escort fighters had to turn for home as they neared the limit of their range, but on this day, waves of enemy fighters swarmed in after the P-47s and P-38s as they tried to break up the escort and expose the bombers.

"Keep on the ready. They're plenty aggressive today. Make your ammo count. I think we're in for a long battle," called Howie over the intercom.

Steve eased his plane a little closer to his neighbor. It seemed as though all of the other B-17 pilots had the same idea. They closed up their battle-tested combat box formation which afforded the best protection for their planes against attacking fighters. German fighter pilots loved to see a strung-out formation. It enabled them to isolate individual targets and destroy the bombers, which had much more vulnerability sitting out there alone.

Just after the formation flew north of Maastricht, Holland, and entered Germany at Aachen, the escort of P-47s and P-38s had to turn for home, leaving the B-17s to fend for themselves until withdrawal, when hopefully they would see the little friends once more.

German fighters continued to harass the American escort fighters as they started to make their way back across Holland and head for England. Perhaps they were hoping to make the Americans use up precious fuel and not make it across the English Channel.

German flak gunners kept up a steady stream of anti-aircraft fire from ground positions. It was becoming more intense as the bomber stream worked their way toward Schweinfurt to unload their deadly cargo on the ball-bearing factories 25,000 feet below.

Steve took what evasive action he could from the bursting flak explosions that seemed to surround the plane. It was as though the enemy had picked *Pappy's Pack* out of the formation. It was difficult because he and the other planes were tucked in as close as they dared without colliding. Steve and Howie now worked as a team with Howie easing the B-17 back toward the left if they got too close to the plane on the right and Steve doing the same if they got to close to the plane on the left.

Many of the pilots, Steve included, wondered if the evasive action made that much of a difference when it came to flak being shot up at them. Were they maneuvering the plane out of the path of the shell being sent up at them or were they placing the ship in the path of the next exploding 88-millimeter or 102-millimeter cannon shell? The crew liked the idea of "shaking the plane around a little," so Steve thought that if it made them feel better, well, then no harm done.

The men up front in *Pappy's Pack*—Steve and Howie on the flight deck, Jim at his top turret gunner's position plus Russ and Bob in the nose—watched in horror as hundreds of German fighter planes of all types were decimating the formations in front of them. They could be easily seen in the now perfectly clear sky. German fighters were attacking four, five and even six planes abreast. They were coming in on the bomber stream from all angles. German planes could be seen sitting just out of B-17 machine gun range, firing deadly rockets into the formation.

There were exploding B-17s and still others on fire dropping out of formation, headed earthward. In addition, there were many still under German fighter attack, engines smoking as they reached the IP at Wurtzburg, just southeast of Schweinfurt. Parachutes were filling the sky as the American aviators tried to escape from their falling B-17s.

"This sure as hell doesn't look good," stated Howie.

"Keep a sharp eye, they're sure after us today . . . in a big way," Steve warned into the intercom as the loaded heavy bomber bounced and shook from a near-miss flak explosion.

Shell fragments from the flak showered *Pappy's Pack*, sounding like rain on a tin roof. Another shell made the ship bounce upward as it exploded a little below the left front side of the plane. It tore a lemon-sized hole by the pilot's seat with some of the tiny fragments hitting Steve in the left leg. His flying suit ripped and blood seeped into his pants.

"Part of that damned flak shell hit me; take over for a minute while I see what's going on here," called Steve to Howie as he looked down at his leg.

"Want me to have Eddie come up here with the first-aid kit?" questioned Howie.

"No, it's not too bad. I'll be OK . . . close though, if you know what I mean," answered Steve as he settled back into the seat once more.

"Your plane, Russ," called Howie as the plane passed over the IP at Wurzburg.

Russ set up for the bomb run, taking the plane from Howie, who was piloting the ship.

"We've been pretty lucky so far, the fighters have been concentrating on the other formations . . . not to mention the flak, of course," stated Howie to Steve as they prepared to take the plane back after the bomb drop.

With the weather so clear, it was not difficult to pick out the ball-bearing factory targets in Schweinfurt. Heavy smoke and burning fires showed exactly where previous formations had placed their bomb loads.

Flak was now becoming even more intense as *Pappy's Pack* came off the bomb run. They had made an individual attack on the ball-bearing factory, since they were not flying with their normal 305th Bombardment Group.

Enemy fighters, for the most part, had stayed outside the range of their own flak batteries. They were waiting for the B-17s as they exited the target area. A few of the fighters ignored the flak and attacked the B-17s as they made their bomb run.

"Bombs away, Skipper, bomb bay doors coming up . . . let's head for home," called Russ as he handed the much lighter bomber back to Steve.

Steve did not mention to anyone else in the crew that he been hit by some shell fragments. He did not want to worry anyone. They had a long way to go in bringing the ship back to English soil and they needed to concentrate on their own jobs.

Steve took evasive action as he pulled a sharp, climbing right-hand turn away from the burning target below. He climbed 500 feet during the turn to try to avoid the rockets being fired at the formation by the enemy planes sitting outside of the B-17 machine gun range.

Just to the left of *Pappy's Pack*, a B-17 exploded from a direct rocket hit. It was in the position vacated by *Pappy's Pack*. No parachutes were seen as the big bomber broke apart and dropped toward the ground.

Steve stayed with the 384th Bomb Group for protection. The overall flight plan called for an exit route, which would take them south to Heilbroun, across the southern tip of Luxembourg, north of Paris and withdrawing from the Continent a little north of Dieppe. They would cross the English Channel and enter England at Beachy Head, near Eastbourne, then home to Chelveston. The trick, it seemed, was to complete this mission in one piece.

"There are 109s coming up at us," reported Joey DeMatteo from the tail.

"Four abreast, coming for a frontal at 12 o'clock," called Jim as he swung the top turret around to meet the frontal attack.

"Swinging in at three o'clock . . . here they come," called an excited Ronnie from the right waist gunner's position.

Steve and Howie looked at each other. All hell was breaking loose, but they had an airplane to fly.

"Pick out a target, seems like there are plenty to choose. Don't waste ammo, we have a long way to go. Make them pay for attacking us," ordered Steve in the calmest voice he could muster under the circumstances.

Pappy's Pack now shook from the recoil of the plane's .50 caliber machine guns as they fired at the approaching enemy fighters. The noise in the cockpit was deafening from the top turret twin 50s overhead and the twin 50s mounted through the nose that Russ, as the bombardier, was handling.

Steve dropped the nose of the plane as the ME-109s made their four-plane-abreast frontal attack, aiming to kill the pilot, copilot, navigator, bombardier and top turret gunner. While dropping the nose slightly made their gun platform a bit unstable, Steve's maneuver forced the enemy fire go above the B-17, while still letting the bombardier operate the nose-mounted twin 50s and the top turret guns struck the fast-approaching enemy aircraft.

Smoke streamed from the engine compartment of an attacking ME-109 as the firepower from *Pappy's Pack* hit the mark. The continuing machine gun fire from the B-17 brought the frontal attack to a halt. The ME-109s broke off the battle and headed toward another B-17. Everyone was too busy to see what happened to the disabled 109.

Joey let loose with a hail of .50 caliber fire at the ME-109s that were closing in on the tail section. In addition, Vincent had swung the ball turret guns around and was firing at the approaching enemy fighters. They also broke off to try to find another prey.

Suddenly, *Pappy's Pack* shook as cannon shells from an attacking FW-190 ripped into the right side of the B-17 at the right waist gunner's position.

"Ah . . . I'm hit . . . oh damn!" cried Ron Lattamus. He was hit again, spun around and thrown down onto the pile of expended .50 caliber shell casings on the floor of the plane.

"Eddie, get back here now," called Jack Kowalski from his left waist gunner's position as he continued to pour firepower at the attacking FW-190s, which were now attacking from both sides.

The attack was sudden, brutal and then gone. The 190s continued their attack, but on another B-17.

Eddie came out from his radio compartment, first-aid kit in hand. There was not a thing he could do. The young man from Sterling, Illinois, was dead. The hail of bullets from the FW-190 had killed the young aviator.

Meanwhile up on the flight deck, hearing what had been said over the intercom, Howie asked Steve, "Do you want me to check out things back there?"

"No, I need you up here," was Steve's reply to his copilot.

"Skipper, Ronnie's been killed. We've moved him by the radio room," stated Eddie over the intercom to Steve.

"Everyone else okay, Eddie?" Steve asked to his radioman as things quieted down for the moment.

"Yes, Skipper," was the reply from the distraught radioman.

Steve looked over to Howie in disbelief. Howie just shook his head. Roger "Wyatt" Earp and Willie Burnett had been wounded, but now a crew member killed. Any further thoughts had to be placed on hold as another attack was coming from the rear of the plane, as well as a frontal attack.

Machine guns blazed away once more as *Pappy's Pack* was forced to defend herself again. Cannon shells from an attacking ME-109 ripped into the number four engine. It started to smoke as oil gushed out of the crippled engine.

"Hit the fire extinguisher and feather it," called Steve to Howie. He acted quickly to prevent an engine fire. This was no time for an engine fire to engulf the wing and force the crew to leave the plane, especially over enemy territory.

Steve applied more power to the three remaining engines in order to keep up with the other B-17s as they fought their way back across the Continent. A straggler would surely not make it back to England.

The running battle cost the formation two additional B-17 bombers. Seven parachutes were seen from one ship and eight from the other. They would be in German hands by nightfall and a POW camp for the duration of the war. One wounded B-17 had turned south, trying to make it to the safety of Switzerland, but being a wounded straggler made it an easy target for the Luftwaffe pilots. The B-17 did not make it and was shot down.

Even with just three good engines running, it was not very difficult to keep up with the withdrawing B-17s. Several others were operating with just three fans turning. Those with four engines running slowed just enough to maintain a practical working formation for the safety of all planes.

"Thunderbolts coming into view," called Jim from the top turret, as the P-47 fighters arrived to escort the formation home.

"The 56th Fighter Group has come to carry us home," stated Howie over the intercom.

"Let's keep on the alert. We still have a little way to go before we get to the Channel," stated Steve as he also welcomed the sight of the escort fighters.

It was time to breathe again, knowing that they would make it home once again. It was also a time of sorrow with the loss of a valued crewmate and friend. Ronnie would be missed. Steve knew he had a letter to write, but how could he express his thoughts to the mother and father who would never see their son again?

The P-47s of the 56th Fighter Group fanned out and some flew deeper into enemy territory, expecting more B-17s than they saw. The mission to bomb the ball-bearing plants at Schweinfurt had taken a terrible toll as the P-47 pilots could easily see . . . and what of the missing planes? Had that many been lost?

"Well there is Beachy Head and way over to the left, the Isle of Wight. Let's go home," said Steve.

"How's the leg?" questioned Howie to Steve.

"Sore and now that I've got time to think again . . . a bit stiff," answered Steve. "You want to take over?"

The formation was now over English soil and Howie made straight for Chelveston. Fuel was now a concern and this was no time to run out.

As *Pappy's Pack* started to make the approach, Steve noted to Howie that most of the 305th Group planes must have still been out on the mission because just a few planes were visible on the ground. A flare was fired signaling that wounded were aboard. Steve did not want the attention, but Howie insisted.

Howie brought the plane in and taxied to their hardstand. Pappy and the ground crew were waiting. An ambulance was also on hand.

As Steve and Howie slid out of the plane's nose, Pappy came over to greet them. One look at the plane told the story that it had been a rough mission.

"Who's hurt?" asked Pappy.

"I caught some shrapnel in the leg, but it'll be all right. We lost Ronnie to machine gun fire," Steve told a stunned Pappy.

"Where is the rest of the group?" asked Howie.

"Gone . . . of the 18 who got off on time three aborted and 15 flew the mission," answered Pappy. "Only two of the aircraft made it back, 13 planes were lost."

"What do you mean *gone?*" asked a non-believing Steve.

"Seven ships from the 364th: Kenyon, Holt, McDarby, Dienhart, Eakle, Murdock and Kincaid Crews," replied Pappy. "The 365th lost two crews: Bullock and Maxwell. And from the 366th, you lost four crews: Lang, Fisher, Willis and Skerry. The Kane Crew of the 365th with Major Normand leading and the Fred Farrell Crew of the 366th were the only ones to come back. Your plane was not counted since you took off late. How in the hell did you survive? We gave up on you until we heard engines."

"We caught up and flew with the 384th," answered Steve. "We all took a pretty good beating. Luck was with most of us, but not Ronnie. It's such a shame . . . so young."

"Go with them over to the hospital," said Howie to Steve as he pointed him to the waiting ambulance and motioned for them to take charge of Steve. "I'll handle things here and take care of Ronnie."

Steve stepped into the back of the ambulance and it was off to the base hospital. Three small fragments of flak were still in his left leg and he said he wanted to keep them as a souvenir. He also received a tetanus shot, which was not pleasant. Steve told them that he had one before, but gave in when the nurse insisted. They would also keep him overnight just to be certain that there was no infection. Steve said that he would rather go to the O-Club, have a beer and check back with them tomorrow. He lost the argument.

It was around seven o'clock when Howie, Russ, and Bob came into the base hospital ward to visit Steve.

"Are you okay?" asked Howie as he picked up the chart at the end of Steve's bed and pretended to know what he was reading.

"I'm out of here tomorrow . . . need a pair of pants," answered Steve.

"There is no mission on for tomorrow or for that matter, at least a few days," stated Howie. "Hell, we have no airplanes or crews to fly them. The toll was pretty bad. From what I've heard, we are lucky to have made it back. Word is that about 60 crews were lost today. That's 600 empty beds and so many parachutes that the Germans must have had a hard time rounding up all of the guys. It's a real mess; hope it was worth it to the brass."

Steve took in everything that Howie had said, then handed him a piece of paper on which Steve had written a letter to Ronnie's parents. "Read this and tell me what you think."

Howie read the letter, handed it to Russ and Bob for them to see what Steve had written. "Excellent letter, Stevie. His folks will appreciate what you've said," stated Howie. Bob and Russ agreed.

Steve would wait a few days before mailing the letter to Ron Lattamus' parents. The War Department would be the first to contact them with the awful news by way of the dreaded telegram: "We regret to inform you . . . " it began.

Howie and Steve talked about the fact that Ronnie was just 18 years old. While many other young men had also lost their lives, Ronnie's loss hit close to home. He was a crew member and a lively, enjoyable friend. Just as with the Gerke Crew, the hurt was deep for *Pappy's Pack*. Those young men would never know the joy of a fulfilling life. Such is the horror of war.

CHAPTER FIVE

Steve spent two days in the base hospital recovering from his wounded leg. He took the opportunity, not that he had a choice, to catch up on mail. He read the several letters that had arrived and answered them. Steve wrote a little about the mission to Schweinfurt to his dad. He gave no real details, but said that it had been a rough, deep-penetration mission and that Ronnie had lost his life. He noted that mission number 20 was now completed. There were just 10 to go before being eligible for a stateside journey. Steve did not mention that mathematically most of the crews would never make 25 completed missions, let alone the now 30 in effect. He did write one line about some flak ripping the pants of his flight suit and that a couple of pieces of flak had penetrated the skin. "It was nothing serious," he wrote, "and a cheap way to receive a Purple Heart!"

Being confined to the hospital gave Steve the time to write a long letter to Maggie. He mentioned several of the subjects included in the letter to his dad, but also wrote about personal things that were just between them. Steve attempted several times, but was unsuccessful in reaching Maggie by telephone. He would keep trying.

Steve also wrote to Lillian, several friends and Elly. The letter to Elly was in answer to a short one from her. It was clear, by Elly's carefully worded letter, that she was more involved with someone else than she let on. This was fine with Steve, as he had stated in a previous letter.

On Sunday, October 17th, Steve was released from the hospital. He had just finished breakfast when the doctor told him that all was okay, but that he wanted to see him in five days. Steve was informed that he would not be on flying status until the doctor saw him.

Steve hitched a ride back to the 366th Squadron. He caught up with Howie, Russ and Bob as they were returning from breakfast.

"Still a little stiff I see," said Howie as he stuck out his hand, rather than a salute.

"They asked me if I wanted a cane," answered Steve as he shook Howie's hand.

"Let's stop at the orderly room for a minute and I'll bring you up to date," suggested Howie.

The four officers entered and sat down; Russ and Bob on a sofa with Howie and Steve settling into individual armchairs.

"Willie is back with the crew," stated Howie. "He is a little leery of climbing back into the ball turret, so he'll take over at right waist and I've had Vincent permanently assigned to our crew. He will continue to fly in the ball."

"Good going . . . sounds fine," answered Steve. He appreciated the way that Howie had handled things.

"Oh," started Howie, who paused for a moment figuring out how to put the following, "I knew you were having trouble reaching Maggie, so I made the call as a Colonel Somebody . . . doctor's medical emergency and had her tracked down. She is aware of your medical status and happy that it is not serious. I told Maggie that you had tried to reach her and that you wrote her a letter of explanation. With the call being of a medical nature, I also spoke with Elizabeth, who can't wait for me to come back to London!"

"Thanks . . . Colonel Who!" kidded Steve.

"To touch on a serious subject, do you want to talk about the arrangements for Ronnie now or later?" asked Bob.

"Now is fine," answered Steve, who paused for a moment, then continued, "they are going to bury Ron at the new American Cemetery in Cambridge on Tuesday the 19th. I have arranged for a couple of Jeeps so that we can drive over."

"Good . . . just fine," was Howie's comment. Bob and Russ agreed.

"I will let the rest of the crew know the arrangements," stated Bob.

"Steve, after you're settled, we can hitch a ride out to the hardstand," Howie said. "Pappy has been hard at work patching up the old girl. I think the new engine will be installed later today or tomorrow. The number three also needed some extra maintenance. If the weather doesn't cooperate, he will move the ship into the J hangar."

"They've got some coffee over there, let me get a cup and then we can go see Pappy," said Steve as he started to get up from his chair.

"Stay put, I'll get it . . . anyone else?" asked Russ.

"Coffee sounds good, I'll help you. Howie, do you want some too?" asked Bob.

"Only if you also bring some donuts," responded Howie.

Coffee and donuts were brought to their little corner and after a couple of sips of coffee and a bite of a donut, Steve said, "I still can't believe that we lost 13 planes on the Schweinfurt raid," and he slowly shook his head.

"Three aborted with just two of the 15 that flew across the Channel managing to come home. It's being looked into," answered Howie. "It seems as though some of the upper brass have questions. Something was surely wrong to have lost 13 of 15. They don't count us because we got off so late and wound up with another Group."

"They're starting to fly in replacement aircraft tomorrow," said Russ. "It might be a couple of additional days before we are back to full strength. With the new replacement crews, I think that there will be some practice missions flown to get them oriented. You know, we're surely getting to be a senior crew around here."

"Well, if nothing much is going on for us, maybe I'll push for a few days in London. I think we've earned a little break," said Steve.

The four commandeered a Jeep and drove out to the hardstand. They were greeted by Pappy, who took them on a tour of the ship, pointing out the new patch-work. Some of it actually covered old patches on the plane's fuselage. Most of the bullet and flak holes were repaired, however, the ground crew was still covering some.

"There were more than a 100 new holes in the old girl," stated Pappy as he proudly looked over *Pappy's Pack*.

"We had to fight like hell to get her home," answered Steve as he surveyed the battle damage. "Too damn many didn't make it."

"I'm so sorry about Ron Lattamus . . . fine, young man," said Pappy as he looked down at the ground, then lifting his head, wiped a tear from his eyes. "He enjoyed talking about the family restaurant and some of the crazy customers they had. Ron was always so upbeat. He was just a kid." The plane was Pappy's charge to keep flying, but the tough old top sergeant had also adopted its crew as his own.

Steve patted Pappy on the shoulder. He knew that while Pappy put on the tough act, he did truly care about the young men flying the B-17 into battle.

Replacement B-17s were landing on the morning of the 19th as the crew of *Pappy's Pack* left for the trip to Cambridge and the American Cemetery to say fare-well to Ron Lattamus. The day was clear; no rain to contend with. The military ceremony was impressive and Steve would include this in the revised letter to Ron's parents. Still, it was difficult to write. He hoped that during the next ten missions there would be no more such letters.

A daylight bombing raid was scheduled for the 20th, but it was abandoned. The night leaflet mission that the 422nd Squadron would fly to Paris, Caen, and Rouen was completed, with all planes returning safely to Chelveston. There were no missions scheduled for the 21st and the night mission to be flown by the 422nd on Friday, the 22nd of October, was canceled due to weather. In addition, bad weather conditions kept missions from being flown on the 23rd.

Despite the weather, replacement B-17s were being ferried to the 305th Bomb Group. Also arriving in Chelveston were the new replacement crews that would fly the aircraft. On days that minimum weather conditions permitted, practice missions were being flown in order to familiarize the new 305th Group members with their surroundings, which included instructions pertaining to the flying patterns of the area. With the 306th Bomb Group just down the road, so to speak, the air space patterns and their closeness to other groups leaving and returning made the integrity of every flight pattern a must to be maintained. The greatest importance was in keeping order in the sky to avoid in-flight collisions from occurring.

While still at breakfast on Sunday morning, the 24th, Steve sent word to the enlisted men of his crew to meet him in the orderly room at 7:00 a.m. With only a night leaflet mission on the schedule board, the 366th Squadron would once again stand down. Actually, the 364th, 365th, and 366th Squadrons were still being brought up to strength because of the losses on the second Schweinfurt mission.

"I've got some passes," stated Steve as the men gathered around him.

"Well, Skipper, we all know what to do with them. London, here we come! We also know the drill to be careful, be smart, and be back here on time," said the smiling Jim McFarland, Steve's engineer and top turret gunner.

"They're well deserved, we've been through a lot these last few missions, so enjoy your time away from the war," said Steve as he handed out the passes to his crew.

Just after Steve had secured the passes, he telephoned Maggie at St. Thomas' Hospital in London. It being a Sunday morning, she was much easier to reach than on a normal hospital day. Both Steve and Maggie were obviously looking forward to even the short time that they would have together. Steve also mentioned that Howie, Russ, and Bob would be in London and looked forward to meeting up with Elizabeth, Emily, and Catherine if it was possible, schedules permitting.

Howie had taken it upon himself to arrange for a taxi for the ride over to the Wellingbourgh Railway Station. Steve, Russ, Bob, and Howie relaxed in a first-class train carriage car. The train was otherwise fairly crowded because the Sunday schedule meant fewer trains traveling the rails.

Like before, during the trip to London's King's Cross Train Station, the four officers decided they would like a snack with a cup of tea. A good hearty cup of Twinings English Breakfast Tea and a scone with strawberry jam hit the spot. "Enjoying a cup of tea," Howie pointed out, "is a very civilized tradition the British have, especially when one considers the violent world that surrounds them on an almost-daily basis."

Steve gathered the enlisted crew together on the platform just outside of the entrance of the main terminal at King's Cross. This time, instead of looking after young Ron Lattamus on his first trip to London, Vincent would be their charge. Since the passes had been secured rather quickly, Steve was concerned that not all of the men might have spare cash with them. Steve took Jim McFarland aside. As the top turret gunner–flight engineer, he was the senior enlisted man in the crew. Steve handed Jim several British pounds saying, "Just in case it's needed . . . otherwise, have a dinner on me!"

Russ, Bob, and Howie had left the scene and headed on into the King's Cross main terminal. If any of the crew was a little short of cash, it would be a little embarrassing to the individual if the officers were standing around. The skipper alone took care of his crew. Steve also made it known where he and the other officers were staying in London, in the event they were needed in an emergency or to bail them out of jail.

After the enlisted men left the platform and headed out of the train station, Steve made his way to the familiar side door where Bob, Howie, and Russ were waiting by the old Rolls Royce limousine.

"Hello, Lieutenant, welcome back to London," greeted a smiling Michael as he reached for Steve's officer's bag and placed it in the limousine's boot.

"Hello, Michael, hope all goes well with you," answered Steve as he waited for the boot lid to close, and then shook hands with their chauffeur.

It felt good to be back in London and the men took in the sights as Michael drove them over to the Stafford Hotel on St. James Place.

After they signed in at the hotel's front desk, the desk clerk handed an envelope to Lieutenant Carmichael. It was from Margaret Steele. Instead of immediately going up to their rooms, the men went into the hotel bar where they ordered a light lunch and had the barman pump them a fresh pint of British Bitter. Steve pulled the envelope out of his inside coat pocket, opened and read the note to himself. Russ, Bob and Howie waited for Steve to finish before questioning what the plans were with the girls.

"Well, from Maggie's note, for some unexplained reason, Elizabeth indeed wants to put up with Howie while we are all in London. Catherine is looking forward to spending time with Russ, and Emily can't wait to see Bob again . . . some impression you gentlemen have made," grinned Steve as he placed the note back into his pocket.

Just then, the barman delivered the pints of English beer. "Gentlemen, to your health," he stated and went back toward the kitchen to get the luncheon platters.

"Do the girls have a tight schedule or can we spend some meaningful time with them?" asked Howie.

"We'll have to make the time meaningful. Tonight we'll all have dinner together, then because of the short notice, we'll have to catch them on their off-duty time," answered Steve. "It won't be so bad because we'll all have them on a one-on-one basis, which for Maggie and me is just fine, if you know what I mean."

The men liked the idea of spending some quality time alone with the girls. Russ, Bob, and Howie had been corresponding with the nurses since they met them on their last leave in London.

"Dinner tonight will be at a restaurant where Maggie took me on our first date," announced Steve. "It's a lovely little place called the Ebury Wine Bar and Restaurant. You will enjoy it. Maggie has made reservations for six o'clock. That will give us a chance to settle in and wash up."

Howie telephoned Michael and told him of the plans. Michael had anticipated the use of two autos, so he had Clarence keep the evening open. They would be at the Stafford by five, which would give them time to pick the ladies up at St. Thomas' Hospital and drive on to the Ebury.

Steve and Howie once again shared a room as did Bob and Russ. They just had enough time to shower, shave, and dress because of the hour. Five o'clock comes quickly to those who linger over lunch with a couple of pints. However, it was also time spent relaxing in a dangerous war-torn world where not much relaxing was permitted. Those everyday dangers were also true for the citizens of London who had endured bombings and now had to contend with the horror of the dreaded German buzz bombs.

Michael was, as usual, right on time. Clarence shook hands with the men and seemed genuinely glad to see them again. In times like these with so many young men being lost in action, Clarence was glad to see that they had survived, which was not easy in itself. He, like Michael, was a veteran of the First World War and both had lost many friends in combat.

As the two limos pulled up to St. Thomas', the nurses, dressed quite elegantly, at least they thought so because they were not in uniform, came out of the hospital's dorm and walked to meet the cars. Howie and Steve did not wait for Michael to come around and open the limousine door, nor did Bob and Russ wait for Clarence. They opened the doors and greeted the girls!

While Howie, Bob, and Russ gave a light kiss to their respective dates, Maggie flew into Steve's arms. It was quite clear to see that they were a couple. While the letters and infrequent phone calls kept them in touch with each other, when their eyes met it told volumes of what was becoming a love affair . . . perhaps for life.

After all of the greetings were exchanged, with Maggie tightly holding onto Steve, they were off to the Ebury Wine Bar and Restaurant for their six o'clock reservation. Mrs. Cox, though, did not hold them to an exact time.

The limousines drove across the Westminster Bridge, past Big Ben, the Parliament buildings and on toward Victoria Train Station. They drove past Victoria and, within a short distance from the train station, they were at the Ebury.

Maggie and Steve led the way up the short flight of stairs to the restaurant. Mrs. Cox greeted the group, especially Margaret and her lieutenant. She then took them toward the back of the restaurant where tables were placed together for the eight people.

Everyone settled in with Steve and Howie taking each end of the tables. With everyone comfortable, Steve ordered two bottles of champagne to start. They could order some "pickers" to go with the champagne and determine what they would like for dinner in a little while. Maggie suggested a specialty of the house which was their roast beef with Yorkshire Pudding. It seemed that Maggie's choice would be fine with the group.

Steve ordered the special Claret wine to go with the meal. Everyone was relaxed and comfortable. Lively conversations filled the air with much laughter as the group thoroughly enjoyed the evening. The war would have to be placed on hold once again. This was an evening of celebration in which the young people enjoyed being alive.

Finally, at close to 11 o'clock, Michael and Clarence drove the party people back to the dormitory at St. Thomas' Hospital. Clarence said good night to everyone and drove away in his limousine. Michael would stay and see to it that the aviators were safely returned to the Stafford.

Each couple went in a different direction to say good night. They agreed to be back at Michael's limousine in 20 minutes, well, surely in 30 minutes!

While Catherine and Russ, Emily and Bob, and Elizabeth and Howie did not go very far, Maggie led Steve to a bench along their walk near the River Thames, where they could spend some time alone.

With the cool night air, Maggie cuddled close to Steve. He placed his officer's coat around her. It was hard to fall in love, really in love, because of the war with its uncertainty. The cultural differences between a Florida rancher with that of a girl raised on England's Isle of Wight made for a strange couple; however, they were indeed in love. If the war permitted, Steve and Maggie would work it out, somehow.

Even though Steve was 23 and Maggie had just turned 20, the war itself has forced them to mature well past their years. In fact, the war made all young people grow up sooner than expected. It was like bolting from winter into summer without any springtime.

After a final good night and with each couple making their own plans, Michael drove the men back to the Stafford Hotel. Before going up to their rooms, they stopped in the bar for a nightcap.

The barman was about to pump an ale for them, but Steve stopped him, saying that he would like a brandy. It sounded good to the others, so brandy was poured for everyone.

"Another wonderful evening set up by your lady," said Howie to Steve as the four settled by a table not too far from the bar.

"I second that for sure," said Russ.

Bob did not say anything, but one could easily see that he concurred. He and Emily had made plans for tomorrow, as did Russ and Catherine. Howie and Elizabeth had not hit it off like Steve and Maggie, but things were progressing toward a more than casual situation. They also would be spending as much time as they could together while he was on this short leave from flying missions.

After a second brandy, the men stood up from the table as the barman announced, "Last call, gentlemen." They were a tired group and instead of answering last call, they made their way to the lift, which would carry them up to the rooms. It was time for a good night's rest.

Maggie had quickly rearranged her schedule so that she and Steve could spend an entire day and night together. The others had also made plans. Bob and Emily's date would have to be a daytime one. The same was true for Russ and Catherine, as both nurses were on duty during the night shift. The four of them had made plans to spend the day together. Howie and Elizabeth would have the evening for a dinner date, as she was working the day shift and had the night off.

Steve quietly told Howie that he would have their room at the Stafford to himself. Plans with Maggie called for them to be together. He would be back at the Stafford by 10 o'clock the following morning for the trip back to Chelveston.

Steve packed his officer's bag and left the Stafford at 11 o'clock. Michael drove him over to the dormitory area at St. Thomas' Hospital. Maggie, who had completed early morning rounds, was waiting in the nurses' lobby with her overnight bag in hand. She spotted Michael's limousine, left the building and walked to the car. Steve and Michael greeted Maggie, with Michael taking the overnight bag and placing it into the boot next to Steve's officer's bag. Steve helped Maggie as they settled in the back seat. Then, it was off to the Connaught Hotel on Carlos Place in London's fashionable Mayfair section. The Connaught, built in 1897, was a 92-room luxury hotel.

Michael pulled up to the Connaught's beautiful entrance. The elegant lobby was buzzing with activity. It was now just past noon and several people were seen walking toward the Drawing Room for lunch. Check-in time at the Connaught was listed as 1400 hours; however, this rule was waved for the lieutenant and his lady. Steve had reserved one of the five junior suites for their overnight stay. After they checked in, the bellman took hold of the trolley with their luggage and directed

Steve and Maggie toward one of the hotel's lifts.

Their suite was on the fifth floor of the six-story hotel. Simply said, it was everything a suite should be; luxury at hand!

Neither Steve nor Maggie was hungry enough to eat lunch. Steve said that he would order room service, but Maggie declined. They would go down to the Red Room for afternoon tea. This, for Steve and Maggie, would be the time both dreamed of, their time together. It was a time when they could feel the love they had for each other.

It was just past 3:30 in the afternoon when the young couple emerged from their suite. They took the lift down for afternoon tea in the Connaught's Red Room. Before going in for tea, Steve stopped by the Concierge's desk to make an eight o'clock reservation for dinner in The Grill Room that is noted for their famous French cuisine.

Even with a war raging, the tradition of British afternoon tea was a step above elegance at Connaught's Red Room. First, Steve and Maggie had a champagne toast followed by a large pot of Darjeeling tea, delicious mini-sandwiches, scones accompanied by clotted cream and strawberry jam, plus, of course, the delicate little pastries.

Later, around seven o'clock in the evening, Maggie and Steve came down once again from their suite to have a cocktail before going into The Grill for the evening meal. As the dinner progressed, Steve remarked, "This dinner is more like a banquet!"

They spent the rest of the night as a couple much in love, ignoring the fact that the war would once again separate them.

Steve ordered breakfast to be served in the suite. It would give them some additional precious time alone and together.

At nine o'clock, Michael arrived to take them first to St. Thomas' where Steve and Maggie would say farewell until his next leave. They held each other for quite a while, not saying anything. Finally, Steve had to leave. As Michael drove the limousine onto the road and across the Westminster Bridge toward the Stafford, Steve, sitting in the back seat, looked out at the River Thames, but really not looking at anything in particular. He was deep in his own thoughts. The war made things so difficult, however, he would not have met Maggie if not for the war, and Maggie was becoming everything to him.

Howie, Russ, and Bob had already checked out of the Stafford. They were waiting in the lobby as Michael and Steve drove into the hotel's driveway. Michael loaded the additional suitcases into the boot and they were off, driving toward King's Cross Train Station. Not much conversation took place during the ride. The flyboys were simply tired.

At King's Cross, they said goodbye to Michael, who once again wished them well. He knew the dangers of war and could only imagine the horror of being shot at from 25,000 feet below or being attacked by enemy aircraft as they fought their way to and from their targets.

The train trip back to the Wellingbourgh Railway Station was quite uneventful. Steve had packed up most of the pastries from breakfast and along with some sandwiches and tea from the trolley that passed through the train, they all had a decent lunch. At the Wellingbourgh Station, the taxi, which had been previously arranged for, took the men back to Chelveston and the 305th Bomb Group.

The following morning was socked in by a dense fog, coupled with a steady drizzle. The light rain soaked everything. There was no mission scheduled.

After breakfast in the mess halls, Steve had his crew assemble in the day room for a meeting. He wanted to be certain that everyone was still in one piece after the leave. In addition, it was a time for the crew to relax and talk about their adventures in London and enjoy the moment. The crew would be back at the business of war soon enough.

When he left the meeting, Steve paid a visit to the base hospital in order to have a final check-up on his leg so that he could resume flying status. Later, after lunch, he caught up with some mail and a package from his dad. It seemed to Steve as though his dad wrote a letter every day, but in reality there were only three or four letters a week with the return name of Ray Carmichael.

There would be a mission scheduled for Saturday, October 30th, but the crew of *Pappy's Pack* was not one of the planes that would go on the mission. Perhaps the paperwork returning Steve to flying status had not reached headquarters yet. It was just as well because with the weather only marginal at Chelveston and poor over the target area, the mission was recalled. This did not really sit well with the crews that were recalled. Not only would they not get credit for a mission, but also they also had an adventure in the sky as each B-17 worked its way back for a safe landing in less-than-comfortable conditions.

The night mission on for the 31st was also canceled because of the foggy weather. The conditions, both local and over the impending target areas on the Continent, continued for the next several days with no missions scheduled by "Pinetree" at High Wycombe, near London, the headquarters for the Eighth Air Force. The head-quarters building looked like a stately old mansion and, until recently, it had been a girls' boarding school.

Even though the weather was barely passable on Wednesday, November 3rd, a mission was on the docket. In fact, the mission called for a maximum effort, meaning that all available planes would be alerted for the raid. The primary target, as stated at the briefing was in Wilhelmshaven, with its German Naval dockyards and installations. There was no secondary target because leading the way on this mission would be the new Pathfinder B-17 bomber equipped with radar, which can peer through the clouds and recognize the target below. The bomber stream would not have to see the target to destroy it. Wilhelmshaven had apparently been chosen because the radar could also distinguish between water and land, making it easier to pick out a specific target.

Fighter escort for the mission would be flying with the four major attacking wings the entire time. In addition to the P-47 thunderbolts, which would number over 300, more than 50 long-range-equipped twin-engine P-38 Lightnings would be accompanying the 500 plus B-17s and B-24s. The mission called for the largest number of American aircraft since the raid of October 14th on Schweinfurt. In addition to somewhat testing how best to use the Pathfinders, the coordination of fighter escort would be undertaken. One group of the P-47s would do the initial escort and then be replaced by another group along the way. Then as the bomber stream entered the Continent, the twin-engine long-range P-38s would move in close and protect the bombers. The P-38s would stay with the bombers even as they exited the Continent and headed for home over the North Sea where once again, the P-47s would become the escort. The 305th Bomb Group had 22 serviceable planes that could fly the mission.

They left Chelveston beginning at 0930 hours and assembled at 8,000 feet, then headed to join the combat wing.

The Carmichael Crew, flying a repaired *Pappy's Pack*, would fly in the formation behind and to the right of the Pathfinder B-17 assigned to lead this element of the mission. They climbed to the assigned altitude of 23,500 feet and flew over the North Sea toward their target. An over-the-water approach to the target meant that they only needed to worry about attacking enemy fighters. The escorts of P-47 fighters were right on time and dashed 3,000 feet above them, crisscrossing over the bomber stream. It certainly was a comfort watching the contrails and knowing that the little friends were about.

The wing entered the Continent just south of Uithuizen and then passed over Appingedam. This route kept them out of the range of Emden's anti-aircraft gun batteries. Finally, a left-hand turn was made toward the IP and the bomb run on Wilhelmshaven's dockyards.

The P-38s had joined the escort and moved in close to the formation. So far, flak was not a problem. However, more than 30 enemy aircraft were looking for ways to disrupt the bomb run. Both FW-190s and ME-109s tried to break through the escort in order to attack the bombers, but they were driven off. Several dogfights were observed. It certainly seemed as though the American P-38s, with their superior firepower, got the best of the action. The Carmichael Crew saw at least four enemy aircraft headed toward the ground. Others had moved away from the action, perhaps waiting until after the bomb run for another attack.

The target was completely cloud covered. A 10/10 cloud cover, as they say. Flak over the target area continued to be light. It was a possibility that many of the anti-aircraft installations were not manned due the unlikely conditions for a raid.

Bombs were dropped by each B-17 as the Pathfinder released its bomb load. It was for Russ Parker, Steve's bombardier, one more time in which he did not care to be just a toggler. He was trained to be a bombardier and he was a good one. Over the plane's intercom, Steve reminded Russ that without the Pathfinder, either they would have had to fly around Germany looking for a secondary target or abort the mission. "We're getting a mission behind us," he said.

As planned, Steve made a hard left-hand turn off the target just after their bomb load was dropped. He aimed *Pappy's Pack* for the coast and the North Sea. P-38s continued to escort the B-17s. The formation exited the Continent between Harlesiel and Neuharlingerseil, where they did not expect that much flak would be fired up at them. In fact, as they neared the coast, no flak was fired from the ground and no enemy fighters could be seen. Once over the North Sea, the closest P-38 to *Pappy's Pack* waggled its wings and a grateful crew waved back. The P-38s headed for home and were replaced by a fresh group made up of P-47s.

The flight back to Chelveston was such that it almost took on the feeling of a practice mission. This was not considered a milk run when it started out, but it finished like one.

The Pathfinder, at least on this mission, proved to be of great value. The escort was superior. All of this, plus light flak and enemy fighters being held at bay, made up for the missions where all hell broke out. This one was easier to survive. The weather had also cleared enough for good landing conditions. *Pappy's Pack* landed at 1546 hours, four engines running. In addition, all of the dispatched 305th B-17s returned home safely.

For Steve, Howie, Bob, and Russ, mission 21 had been completed. Jim McFarland, the top turret gunner and flight engineer also placed this mission in the book as number 21. Eddie Anderson, radio operator, along with Jack Kowalski, left waist gunner, and Joey DeMatteo, tail gunner, had flown two additional missions with other crews early on. Willie Burnett, ball turret gunner turned right waist gunner, was only a couple of missions behind the others. Vincent Campalone, now flying as the ball turret gunner, would ultimately finish his tour of duty with another crew. He had a lot of catching up to do.

It had become a fact that those crews assembled back in the States had a hard time staying together. Crew members killed in action or wounded broke apart the initial crew set-ups.

After interrogation at debriefing, Steve, Howie, and Russ went back to their Quonset hut and took a nap. They would make up for some of the lost sleep. Bob, who had purchased a camera while in London, wanted to take some photos around the base, plus a few of their plane. He would catch up with everyone later.

At the O-Club after evening mess, the four officers of *Pappy's Pack* relaxed at their favorite table. With pints in hand, the conversation initially centered on the day's mission to Wilhelmshaven.

"You know, except for the practice rounds, we didn't fire one gun today," observed Russ.

"Well, with the escort we had, the Thunderbolts and the Lightnings, the bastards couldn't break through to attack us," answered Howie.

"Let's get down to some serious stuff here," said Bob as he took a long drink of his beer and swallowed it in several installments, enjoying every drop. "Where are the peanuts? Are we out?"

The remark brought about a smile to everyone's face. Well, they all did like to munch on peanuts while enjoying a pint.

"Geez, I almost forgot," said Steve as he reached over to a nearby chair and placed a box on the table. "My dad shipped this . . . got it in today's packages. From the rattling, they must be peanuts."

Bob took out his pocketknife and slit open the top of the box. Inside the box were peanuts!

"My knife, so I get the first peanut," said Bob and he took a handful of peanuts.

"Since you are holding a weapon, I won't argue with you, but my dad did ship them to me," replied Steve.

"Okay, here," and Bob handed Steve a single peanut.

"It's best not to argue with the navigator. Most of the time he can find our way home," joined in Howie as he also reached into the box for a handful, giving Steve a single peanut.

"It really is a thankless job, being the pilot and A/C. You have to put up with this," said Russ as he too reached into the box, handing Steve a single peanut.

"Is it my turn now?" kidded Steve.

"Help yourself!" answered Howie.

The evening continued with the men enjoying each other's company. There was no mission on the schedule for tomorrow, so tonight everyone could relax.

However, one upsetting piece of news circulating in the O-Club was that two planes from the neighboring 306th Bomb Group had collided in midair as they started out over the North Sea, and both crews were lost.

There was a mission scheduled for Friday, November 5th. At briefing, they found out that the mission would be a return to Gelsenkirchen. The target this time was the railroad marshaling yards. The previous trip had been a raid on the synthetic oil plant. No one was pleased to fight his way in and out of the heavily fortified flak batteries of the Ruhr Valley. Royal Air Force bomber crews had named the Ruhr "Happy Valley." It was one of the most heavily defended areas in Germany. The August 12th raid at Gelsenkirchen had also been the scene where the 366th Squadron Gerke Crew was shot down and blown from the sky.

The weather once again required that this mission would be one that a Pathfinder B-17 would lead. There was complete cloud cover expected over the target area. The 305th would contribute 18 planes for the raid. *Pappy's Pack* would make the long trip.

Takeoff was again completed in less-than-ideal conditions. The crew of *Pappy's Pack*, as usual, was on the lookout for other aircraft that might stray into their air space during climb out to assembly.

The formation climbed to 25,000 feet as it entered the continent of Europe north of Oostende, Belgium, near Middelburg in the Netherlands, in order to avoid flak areas. The flak would come soon enough as they reached the Ruhr Valley. The P-47 escort fighters flew in and out of the formation with some of the P-47s flying high cover as well. So far, no enemy fighters had come up to fight. At Eindhoven, the escort fighters had to turn back as they had reached their fuel limit. The bombers were on their own. With the weather so poor and the cloud cover so thick, this weather obstacle was working for the formation by keeping the German fighters on the ground.

As the formation of over 170 bombers moved closer to the target area puffs of exploding flak could be seen just ahead. It seemed that the German flak batteries were putting up six shell barrages, hoping a B-17 would fly into one of the bursts. The clouds grew ever thicker. The only way to bomb the marshaling yards today would be with a Pathfinder. The formation turned onto the IP and started the bomb run. As they approached what would have been the target if they could see through the clouds, the Pathfinder B-17 was hit with a huge flak shell burst. The plane looked as though it had at least one engine knocked out and it started to drop out of the formation.

Steve and Howie were too busy flying a close formation to follow the actions of the Pathfinder, so Steve called Russ on the intercom, "Better drop the bomb load when you think we're over the target area. The Pathfinder has been hit and knocked out of formation. Do what's best, Russell."

"Okay, Skipper, I'm on it," answered Russ and he jettisoned the bombs through the cloud cover. "Bombs away, bomb bay doors coming up. Homeward, Skipper," continued Russ.

"Hell of a way to run a war, wish I was in New York. Oh, do I wish I was in New York City and not here!" exclaimed Howie.

"If you were in New York, you'd probably just be sitting on a bar stool, Scotch in hand," said Steve as he pulled away from the target area and headed the plane back across the Continent and toward the safety of England. Then Steve continued, "Howard my boy, I'll make you feel as though you are in New York City. I'll buy you a Scotch at the O-Club tonight!"

Just then, a flak shell exploded just off to the right of the plane. Then another shell exploded just where they had been. "Skipper, I'm not one to worry too much, but somehow through those clouds they are zeroing in on us . . . better shake us around a little," called Joey from the tail gunner's position.

Steve looked over to Howie, who nodded, and they climbed to 27,000 feet and moved a little more to the right as another cluster of shells burst, but well behind them. They were now moving out of range of these particular gunners. P-47s picked up the formation and ferried them home. This trip to the Ruhr had not been hard on the 305th. All of the planes once again returned home to the Chelveston Station. The cloud cover had worked in their favor.

Steve thought to himself as he exited *Pappy's Pack*, that number 22 was now behind him. He was feeling more confident that he would make the 30 missions and return home. In seeing so many B-17 bombers fall from the sky, thoughts of perhaps it might be his time had crossed his mind, but for the sake of the crew, he dare not express anything but positive thoughts. They were counting on him.

Steve also had been thinking that when his missions were completed, he might request some position that could keep himself in England a little longer so that he could spend more time with Maggie. Steve did not want to sign up for more combat missions. You only have so much luck and flying in a war was testing it enough. It was incredible to think of how his path had changed: instead of playing baseball and working to be the Detroit Tigers' catcher, here he was flying a B-17 bomber into war. But then he would have not met the girl who was becoming the love of his life.

Later that evening at the Officer's Club, Steve, Howie, Bob, and Russ once again relaxed at their favorite table. The day's work was over and on this particular day they had survived. Howie related some humorous stories about the country club crowd back home in Glen Cove, Long Island. The stories were told as he held the Scotch whisky that Steve had promised. Steve also enjoyed a Scotch while Bob and Russ had a pint of beer. They all happily munched on peanuts. Howie did make the remark that the supply was getting low. He should have kept the remark to himself. He was elected to obtain, somehow, a new supply. Actually they told Howie to get a large supply and not just some one-pound bag.

The 422nd Squadron was flying one of their night leaflet missions. The squadron would drop the informational leaflets onto the cities of Paris, Amiens and Rouen, and as they flew to exit France, drop leaflets on Caen, located just inside the Normandy coast. The city of Caen was only 28 miles from the small town of Bayeux, on the Cherbourg Peninsula. The famous tapestry of William the Conqueror was displayed in Bayeux and was generally known as "The Bayeux Tapestry."

The raid that was to be flown on November 6th was canceled due to poor local weather with the same conditions existing over the planned target area. Weather also proved to be the main factor in canceling the mission that was scheduled for Sunday, November 7th.

However, it did clear enough during the late afternoon and evening so that the 422nd could fly another night leaflet mission. The mission would be a return trip to Paris.

The November 1943 weather proved to be most frustrating to the planners at Eighth Air Force Headquarters, or Pinetree. It did not permit them to keep continued pressure on the enemy. They would bomb an installation, think that it was out of action and then the weather would not let them bomb again for days on end. The result was that the installations would be repaired and back up and running, which required another visit once the weather permitted. The return visits were often extremely costly, especially when one reflected on the second Schweinfurt mission of October 14th.

Missions continued to be canceled. Those raids initially scheduled for the 8th and 10th were scrubbed, but the weather did clear once again in the late afternoon of the 10th. It cooperated long enough for the 422nd to complete a night leaflet drop over the cities of Paris, Rouen, LeMans and Rennes. The weather closed in once again and the daylight bombing mission that was planned for November 11th was canceled. Two other groups did get off the ground, but they could not climb above the dense clouds as they flew over the North Sea and were recalled. This was very frustrating to the flying crews who simply wanted another mission behind them.

During the lull, Steve had some time with his thoughts. He told his dad in a letter that there were many times he wished he was flying their old Stinson over the Florida landscape. He longed for the peace and quiet of that loud open cockpit, rather than the noise of four Wright Cyclones and the deafening chatter of machine gun fire while the B-17 protected itself.

Steve also answered a letter from Mr. Briggs, owner of the Detroit Tigers. Mr. Briggs stated in his letter how proud he was of his players who were serving in the Armed Forces. Their biggest star, Hank Greenberg, was serving in the Army, and other Tigers serving were Charlie Gehringer, Tommy Bridges, Dick Wakefield and Virgil Trucks. Mr. Briggs tried to keep in touch with all of his players who were away serving their country and Steve was pleased that he had been included. Steve's dad had informed him that the Tigers finished a poor fifth in the American League standings, but they did have a winning season of 78 victories and 76 losses.

In addition to the mail, Steve did manage to reach Maggie by telephone. The call, like most that could even be connected, was not very long. But at least they were able to hear each other's voice, which was really quite important.

The nasty weather once again canceled all thought of a mission for the 12th. Steve, Howie, Bob and Russ spent the better part of the afternoon over in the nearby town of Rushden. They had a pub lunch and a few pints. Later, after evening mess, they trudged over to the Officer's Club and had a few more pints. They did not believe that a mission would be scheduled for the 13th, but sure enough, as they were finishing a second pint, the club closed early because the 305th Bomb Group was alerted.

The 305th also had a new boss: Lieutenant Colonel McGehee was transferred and replaced by Colonel Ernest Lawson.

Saturday, November 13th, had passable weather, just passable. At briefing, they were informed that the mission would be a raid on Bremen, Germany with the target to be bombed, the port area. The flight across the North Sea and entrance onto the Continent was to be the same as the mission to Wilhelmshaven. Once again, the mission would have at the lead a Pathfinder B-17.

From the beginning, the mission seemed to be in trouble. The 16 305th planes were late getting off the ground due to the poor visibility. As the B-17s tried to assemble and prepare to form up for the trip across the North Sea, two major problems occurred that made the mission impossible to complete. Firstly, the bombers could not get rid of the ice, which was building up on their wings. Sufficient icing of the wings and control surfaces could distort their aerodynamic shapes causing loss of lift and control surface effectiveness. In severe cases this could cause the aircraft to become uncontrollable. Secondly, heavy turbulence shook the B-17s violently and bounced them around so much that close formation flying was impossible. Word came that the mission had been recalled. Now the trick would be to land safely back at Chelveston.

"This sure as hell was a waste of time," said Howie from his copilot's seat.

"I guess it falls into the practice mission category," answered Steve as he brought *Pappy's Pack* home to Chelveston. "We get no combat mission credit."

The landing was uneventful, the best kind. Steve then taxied back to the hardstand where Pappy and the ground crew were waiting. They, of course, knew that the planes had been recalled. Their worry was the same as the flying crews: to have the ships all land back at Chelveston safely despite the poor weather conditions.

The weather continued during the 14th and there was no word of sending planes out in the thick fog that seemed to linger over the area. Conditions did begin to improve on the 15th, but not enough over the Continent to warrant a bombing mission. Some of the 305th Bomb Group as well as B-17s from the nearby 306th Bomb Group flew a several-hour practice mission. The crew of *Pappy's Pack*, with their number of combat missions in the book, did not participate in the practice mission. Mostly replacement crews, or rather new replacement crews, flew the mission.

The Officer's Club closed early on the night of the 15th as they were alerted for a combat mission for the 16th. Some bed rest would be needed because of the early wake-up call.

It was difficult to leave the warmth of his covers as Steve was awakened for this mission. It was 0300 hours and the covers felt quite comfortable on a very chilly Tuesday morning. The early rise suggested that a long mission was in store for the aircrews of the 305th.

The smell of coffee brewing and bacon and fresh eggs cooking filled the air of the mess hall as combat crews ate the breakfast, which was reserved for those taking part in the mission of the day.

Steve, Howie, Bob, and Russ spoke in low tones as did just about everyone else. Most of the hushed conversation centered on the questions of where the mission would take them on this day. It could have been that the expected danger that lay ahead made for unusually quiet conversation or it was simply the hour of the morning. Many would agree that it was a combination of both. For a crew like that of *Pappy's Pack*, who had been through this so many times before, it was more the hour, although a couple of the crew felt that their luck was running out. The newer replacement crew members worried the most about the danger that would be before them in a few short hours. Most had a mission or two under their belt, but the fear from all of the stories they had heard often made for a very troubled stomach.

At briefing, the 305th Bomb Group found out that they were in for a long over-the-water mission to Knaben, Norway. Their target would be to bomb a mine in southern Norway that supplied Germany with vital material for the manufacture of steel. The job description for this mission was quite simple: put the mine out of business. There would be simultaneous raids on a hydroelectric plant in Rjukan, plus the ports of Bergen and Trondheim. In total, just under 200 B-17s and B-24s would take part in the long mission. There would be no fighter cover because of the range of the escorts. With so much of the mission being flown over the North Sea, the bombers would be safe while over the sea. Also with so many bombers attacking targets located throughout southern Norway, it was felt that the Luftwaffe would dispatch their fighters in such a manner as to eliminate a concentrated effort by a single group of enemy fighters. The bomber crews hoped that this would turn out to be true.

At the hardstand, Pappy had their B-17 shipshape and ready to go. The engines were warmed up, the fuel tanks topped off, completely full for the long journey and the bomb load was in place. It was estimated that the mission would take more than eight hours of flying time to complete. From indications at the briefing, just a normal amount of ammunition had been loaded aboard.

Steve took the crew aside just before the first flare was fired to give what the crew had come to say was his "fireside chat," referring to what President Roosevelt did back home over the radio. They had come to expect his calm reassuring talk that all would be okay. They were to do what they were trained for and he would do all in his power to get them back from being in harm's way.

Steve knew that some of his crew was becoming a bit jumpy. Several were getting close to completing the required missions and were worrying when their luck would run out. Many a crewman went down on his next-to-last or last mission. It was natural to worry. Steve put up a good front, but he also had the same thoughts.

Finally, after flares were fired from the control tower, engines came to life with a roar, then calmed down during the taxi to the end of the runway. It was time for

Pappy's Pack to fly to war once again. The local weather had cleared enough that assembly was a fairly easy task. The long over-the-water flight to Norway was underway. *Pappy's Pack* would fly the number-two slot in the high group.

In order to keep the bomber stream from scattering because of gathering clouds over the North Sea, the formation climbed higher to 23,000 feet.

"This is turning out to be one long flight," said Howie to Steve as he once again turned the plane back to his pilot after his turn at the controls. Howie then stretched as best he could in his copilot's seat.

"Well, Howard, my boy," Steve replied, "that's one of the reasons why a B-17 has two pilots. We take turns playing like we're flying this machine. Anyway, so far it's been a good flight, plus the engines are running nice and smooth."

Howie started to answer Steve, however, in front of them the lead B-17 was seeming to have problems with their number two engine. Oil was seen running or actually flying off the wing behind the engine. They fired a flare and shut down the number two, which is also the one with the heat exchanger, and feathered it. Then they made a long left-hand turn out of the formation and flew toward the Scottish coast, which would be the closest landfall if an emergency landing were necessary.

Radio silence within the bomber stream was kept. Steve, though, within his ship, stated over the intercom, "Pilot to crew, we'll be taking over the lead." Then, as he eased *Pappy's Pack* into the vacated slot, he continued, "Robert," addressing his navigator, Bob Courtney.

However, before Steve could say anything more, a response came over the intercom, "I'm on it, Skipper, no problem," answered Bob as he assumed the lead navigator role, comprehending exactly what had occurred.

Howie, from his copilot's seat, joined in, "Let's stay alert, we'll be approaching the Norway coast in a few minutes. Enemy aircraft should know by now that they've got visitors."

"Joey, how does it look, everyone in tight enough?" asked Steve to his tail gunner, who had the best view of the formation.

"Looks good, Skipper, everyone moved up a slot and tightened up when we took over the lead," answered Joey.

After three hours and 54 minutes of flying time, the formation flew over the Norwegian coastline. The weather had cleared enough to let them come down to the assigned bombing altitude of 15,000 feet as they headed inland toward their target, which was just outside the city of Knaben.

So far, so good, as no flak had come up to greet their arrival and the Luftwaffe was nowhere to be seen. With at least three other targets being attacked, the initial plan of confusing the enemy was working. For the 305th, the assigned target of the mine, which produced material for manufacturing steel, seemed to be the least protected. Maybe no one expected that a hole dug into a mountain would be a worthwhile target. Perhaps those bombing the hydroelectric plant at Rjukan or the planes assigned the shipping ports as their targets were drawing most of the attention.

While Russ set up the bomb run from the IP, it was hard not to enjoy the scene on the ground below them. There were just scattered clouds and the fjords were things of beauty. With it being mid-November, the hills and mountains were all snow covered. It was almost like bombing a scene on a postcard, but there was a job to be done.

"Bombs away," called Russ. It brought everyone back to the reality of why they were there. "Your plane, Skipper."

Steve banked to the left and made a slow easy turn away from the fire, smoke and the dust that the bombs had kicked up. He made the easy turn so that the integrity of the formation could be kept as they flew back toward the coast on the long over-the-water trip home.

"Let's go home, Robert," said Steve to his navigator.

Bob would use pretty much the same route from the coast of Norway as they did flying to the target. He reasoned that with no enemy action on the way in, it could be the same on the way out. The flight path would carry them between the cities of Kvineesdal, Feda and Haegebostad, plus east of the port city of Flekkefjord. They would actually exit the Norwegian coast flying just east of Farsund.

From the cockpit, Steve and Howie could look to the northwest and see the anti-aircraft fire exploding near the B-17s flying over Flekkefjord and even those at Egersund. Those flying over the port city of Stavanger were also probably catching hell.

From the bombing altitude of 15,000 feet, Steve had the formation climb to 21,000. He felt, as did Bob, that they might even have to climb to 23,000 or 24,000 feet in order to fly above the cloud build-up over the North Sea as they headed home.

Luck was still with them. In the distance German fighters could be seen harassing the B-17 bombers that were leaving the port areas. It was hard to determine at this distance if the Luftwaffe was represented by ME-109s or FW-190s. The fighters did seem to follow that particular formation for miles well out to sea.

As with the flight to Norway, on the way back across the North Sea, Steve would fly the plane for a while, and then Howie would relieve his pilot. They continued this as they flew for England and home.

Finally, after a round trip of eight hours and 53 minutes, *Pappy's Pack* touched the ground at good ole Station 105, Chelveston Air Base. Pappy and the ground crew were at the hardstand as the ship was swung around and brought to a halt after what was a very long day of flying. It was good to be home.

After shutdown, Steve and the other men up front exited the plane from the forward hatch. Pappy was standing by as one by one they left the ship. Steve was the last to leave the plane.

"I heard that you took over the lead," said Pappy to Steve.

"About halfway across the North Sea," answered Steve.

Howie entered the conversation with, "A good mission all around, no shots fired at us from the ground or the air."

Just before the crew boarded the truck that would take them to the debriefing hut, Steve winked and said to Pappy, "Oh, by the way, our boy Lieutenant Courtney found his way to the target and back home!"

Then as they climbed onto the truck, Steve put his hand on Bob's shoulder and said, "One hell of a good job of navigating, Robert, drinks are on me tonight."

"Yeah . . . lead navigator for a day . . . it was fun!" answered a smiling Bob Courtney.

At the debriefing and going into the overall intelligence report, Steve made certain that it known about the job that his navigator and bombardier did. He felt that credit was due them on behalf of the success of the mission.

Later, after evening mess, the tired officers of *Pappy's Pack* gathered at their spot in the O-Club. Steve, as promised, was taking care of the adult beverages. Howie, who had been given the task of replenishing the supply of peanuts, came through. He would not say how he obtained the new supply. They did not come from a package shipped from the States. It seemed that a little deal had been worked out with some of the 305th ground personnel. Things did point to something perhaps cooked up with Pappy and his connections, but Howie would not offer anything other than "peanuts!"

"I'm not going to ask about the peanut supply again," said Steve as he munched and enjoyed his pint of ale. Then after a pause, he continued, "I do want to go on record with Robert and Russell as witnesses to the official appointment of Howard Van Dyke III as our supply officer!"

"Couldn't have made a better choice, Skipper," stated Bob.

"Great appointment. Congratulations, Howie!" offered Russ.

Howie, who was simply taking all of this in from the closest friends he had ever had, said, "Who's buying the next round? No missions are on for tomorrow and remember gentlemen, I'm just the peanut man!" as he held up an empty pint mug.

"He is!" exclaimed Bob and Russ almost simultaneously as they pointed to Steve.

Steve slowly got up from his chair and walked over to the barman, making his request. He was happy to comply. It was an enjoyable evening after a very tiring day. After this pint though, they went back to their quarters and fell into bed. In no time, snoring was the only sound heard.

Bad weather once again became a factor and a night leaflet drop by the 422nd Squadron scheduled for the 17th was scrubbed.

While the weather continued to keep the planes on the ground, it also provided maintenance with the needed time to repair battle damage on some of the B-17s that had just been patched and sent back to war.

Once again, it cleared enough on both the evenings of the 18th and 19th that the 422nd could cross the Channel and fly a leaflet mission. In addition to Paris, Rennes, LeMans, Reims and Amiens, leaflets were dropped on Brussels, The Hague, plus a drop onto Amsterdam. The leaflet mission that was scheduled for the 23rd had to be called off because of weather conditions, both local and over the target cities.

During the lull in action, for some, especially combat crews, it was a boring time. This is not to say that they wanted to fly off to the action of war, but simply to get on with it, complete their assigned missions and go home.

Howie, Steve, Bob, and Russ spent some time in the local towns of Rushden and High Ferrers, enjoying some pub time away from the Chelveston Air Base.

Sometimes during the break in missions, they would take in a movie at the Ritz theatre in Rushden. It was a popular spot for both locals and the men of the 305th. Another nearby town, Irthlingborough, had some very lively pubs, which were frequented by both the locals and 305th personnel.

On Wednesday, November 24th, the weather cleared just enough once again in the late afternoon. The 422nd flew a leaflet mission that night and visited the cities of Brussels, Ghent and Antwerp. Likewise, on the 25th, they flew a mission to Paris and Amiens.

Initially a combat bombing mission was to be scheduled for the 25th, but it was canceled. Word was that something big was on for the 26th, which would call for a maximum effort. What would be the target itself became speculation among both ground and combat crew members.

Even though the O-Club and Enlisted Club would probably close early if the rumor of a major mission for the 26th were true, the clubs were crowded with young men, some still boys, trying to forget the reality of war. So many of their friends had enjoyed a pint of ale or beer and then on the following day, not returned from a mission. Either they were a POW or, perhaps, were killed in action. Life expectancy, as figured out by the men flying the missions, of course, not by headquarters, was now eight to 12 missions before being shot down; that was it! Those who came after May of 1943, the crew of *Pappy's Pack* as an example, had to fly 30 missions and not the popular belief of the earlier number of 25 and home.

Steve, Howie, Bob, and Russ were at the O-Club sitting in their favorite spot, pints and peanuts in hand.

"I heard from someone in the absolute know that the target is Bremen," said Howie as he reached for more peanuts.

"I only hope it's not a visit again to Schweinfurt," answered Steve.

"How good is your contact?" inquired Bob.

"Right on the button this time," answered Howie.

"What about the other times?" asked Russ.

"Other times he's been close," said Howie.

"What the hell does 'close' mean, somewhere on the continent of Europe?" remarked Steve.

"Last call, gentlemen. We're closing early . . . you are on alert for tomorrow," said the barman.

Friday, November 26th, would indeed be a day when a scheduled mission would become a reality. It was a morning that could not be considered cold, but it certainly seemed more than chilly. To those outside it was a nearly clear sky but still quite dark. The clouds were not hanging low. When it was time to go, visibility getting off the ground and form up would not be a problem.

At the briefing hut, when the curtain was pulled back from the map and the route to the target, the ribbon extended across the North Sea to Germany and stopped at Bremen.

Howie did not say anything, but he did lightly poke Steve in the side. Russ and Bob looked over at Howie, who was smiling that knowing smile of someone who was in the know!

They could expect heavy flak and attacking German fighters to contend with on the mission to Bremen.

It was a return trip to Bremen for most of the crew of *Pappy's Pack*. They had bombed targets there on October 8th. It was evident that this mission, a maximum effort raid, would be difficult and equally dangerous.

Once again, *Pappy's Pack* left the Chelveston Air Base and flew toward the European Continent. The planned route "in" would take the 305th over the North Sea with landfall north of the target area between Benseriel and Dornum. The formation would take a slight dogleg to avoid the flak guns at Wilhelmshaven, then drop down to bomb the port area at Bremen.

On the way to the target, cloud cover over the North Sea forced the bomber stream to climb above the clouds in order to keep the formation together and not have them scatter all over the sky. The new altitude brought them up to 28,000 feet. They were flying toward the target with a full cloud cover below them.

Just as the formation crossed onto the mainland from the outer islands, the Luftwaffe greeted them. ME-109s, FW-190s and even ME-110s prepared to bring the battle to the approaching bombers. The 110s shadowed the formation, remaining just outside of the 1.000 yard effective range of the .50 caliber machine guns carried by the B-17s. After achieving their best positions they fired their rockets into the formation, but the B-17s were lucky and none were hit. In the meantime ME-109s were moving far out in front of the formation in order to set up for a four- or five-abreast frontal attack. The strategy was quite simple: kill the B-17 pilot, copilot, navigator, and bombardier! While Jim would also be vulnerable to the head-on attacks, he did have a little more protection up in his turret. Fighter cover from the P-47s had not arrived in time to ward off the initial attacks. With 10/10 cloud cover encountered during the flight over the North Sea, it was difficult for them to locate the bombers.

"Let's be sure of what we're shooting at, don't waste ammo. We might need it on the way out," called Howie over the plane's intercom.

Steve, in the meantime, was quite busy and brought *Pappy's Pack* a little closer to his wingman as the pilots all sought to protect their ships by tightening up the formation. The 305th "combat box formation" was designed to provide the best protection from attacks by enemy aircraft.

Flak was now coming up from the ground and exploding near the formation despite the cloud cover. It was becoming very accurate, perhaps it was radar controlled. Right now, it seemed as though all hell was breaking out as the ME-109s tried to concentrate their firepower on the lead Pathfinder B-17.

The P-47s, which were now at their limit even with the extra fuel drop tanks, tried to drive off the ME-109s frontal attacks and the FW190s that were now attacking the tail section of the B-17s. In addition, several of the P-47s went to work on the rocket-firing ME-110s. The 110s scattered and four were shot down. The sky looked like a group of swarming bees as the battle continued far above the ground.

Suddenly, off to the left, a B-17 was hit with flak and knocked out of formation with one engine on fire. Almost immediately five ME109s came down to finish the job. The doomed big bomber started to roll over on the right wing and fall to earth as the German fighters continued to pound the crippled ship with their firepower. Escaping crewmen could be seen coming out of the burning B-17.

"Count the chutes," called Howie to the crew.

Steve was still much too busy to look around. He was trying to keep *Pappy's Pack* as snug as he could to his wingman without endangering either ship with a midair collision.

Guns were now firing at five ME-109s, which were making a frontal pass at *Pappy's Pack*. The plane shook from the nose twin-50 machine guns that Russ was firing, along with the top turret guns being fired by Jim and the ball turret guns that Vincent blasted away with as the fighters turned over, broke down and away, passing below the bomber after their firing run. Chunks flew off an ME-109, which started to smoke as it flew away to lick its wounds. That German fighter would not fight another day. Vincent watched as the ME-109 pilot ejected from his plane. Seconds later it blew up. Score a kill for Vincent!

In the meantime Joey was hard at work driving off two FW-190s who were trying to creep up on his tail. He fired a long burst, aiming first at one, then the other. The enemy pilots must have figured that it may well be to their advantage to break off and try to attack another ship. This plane was too prepared for them. Willie, at his new position as right waist gunner, and Jack were driving off attacking FW-190s as they tried to come in for a run at the B-17s side.

Finally, the enemy fighters disappeared, but only because the flak was becoming more intense as they reached the IP and started the bomb run. In the meantime, the little friends had to leave due to their fuel supply. The P-47s would have just enough to get home.

"I was kind of busy, but I think most of the crew of the B-17 that went down got out," said Joey over the intercom.

The Pathfinder dropped their bomb load through the clouds and Russ toggled *Pappy's Pack*'s bombs as planned. "Let's get out of here, Skipper . . . bomb bay doors coming up," called Russ.

Just off the bomb run, another B-17 took a direct flak hit and started to fall off toward the ground. The anti-aircraft shell exploded between the inboard engine and the radioman. It took out part of the wing and fire engulfed the right wing. Crewmen started to come out of the burning plane.

"I count eight chutes," called Vincent from the ball turret position where he had a bird's-eye view of the scene below.

"Me too, eight," confirmed Joey as the B-17 continued down and out of sight.

"That ship was from the 365th," said Howie to Steve.

There was not much time for additional conversation because the Luftwaffe came calling once again. The flak explosions became a little lighter as they pulled away from the target area; however, it was heavy behind them as another formation was on their bomb run.

"Here they come," called Willie and he fired a burst of .50 caliber machine gun fire to let the enemy fighter pilots know that they had been spotted.

It was not necessary to call out the enemy approach by the clock numbers as usually would be done, because they were coming in to attack from all directions. Behind a little and to the left of *Pappy's Pack*, a 364th B-17 received a direct flak hit as it flew the exit route, a little south of Oldenburg. The plane started down with nine parachutes seen coming out of the doomed bomber. Then off to the right came a huge explosion. A 366th B-17 had taken a direct hit from the antiaircraft batteries that were located in and around Oldenburg.

"That's *Flying Hobo* . . . Fred Jones' ship," said Howie, shaking his head. "See any chutes?"

"Just two . . . from the rear," called Vincent from the ball turret and after a minute, "only the two." Vincent had a good view of *Flying Hobo*'s wreckage as it dropped into the clouds below.

The flak batteries at Oldenburg were not through yet. Another B-17, this one a 365th plane, was struck and knocked out of formation. In came the ME-109s, six of them to finish off the burning B-17. The alert pilot must have hit the bailout alarm right away after the direct hit, because ten parachutes were seen by Vincent and Joey as the big plane tumbled out of the sky.

The German ground troops would be kept busy rounding up the many American airmen who were destined to become prisoners of war by nightfall.

Enemy fighters continued to attack the B-17s as they fought and battled their way toward the safety of the North Sea, where hopefully the escort P-47s would give a helping hand to fend off the Luftwaffe.

Specks appeared on the horizon. What was left of the now 11-plane group flew as close a formation as possible while they continued to be harassed by a group of ten ME-109s.

The specks grew larger, becoming P-47 American fighter planes, which was a welcome sight.

The meeting point was a little west of Assen, Holland. With the arrival of the little friends, the Luftwaffe called it a day and quickly turned tail. It was a good feeling to have the escort ferry them home. Even though flak shells continued to come up through the cloud cover, the explosions were now much lighter and inaccurate.

Finally, the formation of B-17s left the Europe behind. They passed over Dutch territory at Dokkum, Holwerd, and the outer island town of Hollum. Then it was out over the North Sea and toward England.

There were no enemy planes in sight; just the P-47 little friends flying cover 3,000 feet above the formation.

Back at Chelveston, the ground personnel waited for the returning B-17s, hoping that all of the dispatched Flying Fortresses from the 305th would land safely. Eyes searched the sky looking for the silhouette, which as it became larger would become a B-17.

Finally, the unmistakable sound of B-17 engines could be heard. The returning planes started to join the landing pattern. Flares were fired from B-17s that had wounded aboard. Those planes would land first. An ambulance would race to those planes as they landed in order to get the wounded fliers to the base hospital as soon as possible

Pappy's Pack had received little battle damage from both bullet holes and flak.

They were lucky this time with no wounded aboard and four engines running when they landed. They were the number nine plane to land of the 11 that came back home.

It became evident after a time that five planes were not coming back from the mission. There would be 50 empty beds at Chelveston tonight. The 364th Squadron lost two planes: the George Sartis Crew and Bob Jackman Crew. The Bob Reid and Bob Elliott Crews were lost from the 365th and from the 366th, the Fred Jones Crew. They were the first losses from the 305th since the second Schweinfurt mission of October 14th.

At 1433 hours, Steve brought *Pappy's Pack* to a halt at her hardstand. He and Howie were glad that they were able to bring everyone back safely and in one piece. They could have been just as easily one of the unlucky five. The flak cannot distinguish one plane from another. You are hit or you escape, that's it. As it was, Steve, Howie, Russ, and Bob notched mission number 24 in their belt. They only hoped their collective luck would hold on for six more missions.

The ground crew, under Pappy's direction, once again took charge of the ship to ready her for the next combat mission. Holes in the ole girl needed to be patched and engines once again checked out. Pappy's knowing eyes would go over the plane as though a microscope were inspecting his baby.

Meanwhile, Steve and his crew were at the debriefing hut being interrogated about the specifics of the mission, which included what they saw as the planes of the 305th dropped from the sky.

Afterward, Steve was told to report to headquarters. While there, they asked him if Lieutenant Van Dyke had the leadership and pilot skills to take over the crew of *Pappy's Pack*. The answer, of course, was that the lieutenant was more than capable. At headquarters, they felt the same way and therefore Lieutenant Van Dyke was now the aircraft commander. In addition, Second Lieutenants Robert Courtney, navigator, and Russell Parker, bombardier, would be promoted to first lieutenants.

As for Steve, he was now Captain Carmichael and was being transferred to the 482nd Bombardment Group on a temporary basis. He would be a Pathfinder pilot. It seemed that they had a shortage of qualified pilots for the radar-equipped B-17s, which led bomber formations and found the target under poor weather conditions. The First Bombardment Wing was combing Groups in order to fill specific slots, with experienced pilots being a priority.

When Steve returned to his quarters, he found a note from Howie, telling Steve to catch up with Bob, Russ, and him at the officer's mess hall. They were hungry and had gone over to get a snack.

Steve, after changing from the clothes he wore on the mission, joined what now were his former officers. He entered the mess hall and walked over to their table. On his shoulders, he was wearing his newly appointed captain's bars.

"Will you look at that . . . he's got a pair of railroad tracks on his shoulders!" stated Howie as he pointed to the shiny silver captain's bars.

"Congratulations," said Bob and Russ, almost simultaneously.

"Thank you, let me get a cup of coffee and a donut or two before I join you. I have some news that affects us all," stated Steve.

Bob said, "I'm going to get another cup of coffee . . . anyone else?"

"I'll help you, I want some more donuts too and I know Howie is still hungry from the look on his face," remarked Russ.

Once everyone was settled, Steve opened the conversation with, "Howie, these first lieutenant's bars brought me luck and I'm certain they'll do the same for you."

Howie didn't know what to say. He had hoped for a promotion, but was surprised just the same. Copilots, navigators and bombardiers did not seem to be promoted as rapidly as pilots.

Howie just smiled, looked at the silver single bar of a first lieutenant and reached over to shake hands with Steve. "Thanks, Steve, they're more special because they were yours," he said.

Steve was not through yet. "Russell, Robert, I didn't have enough silver to go around so I picked up a set of first lieutenant's bars for you two as well. I had a second set and decided to divide the new set. You each get one new bar and one of my first lieutenant bars. Congratulations on your promotions. I told them at headquarters that I would like to give you these myself. Tomorrow it will become official."

There were smiles all around. It was an absolutely wonderful scene!

They helped each other place their new rank upon their shoulders. They would pick up another set of silver bars tomorrow to use on other uniforms, but for now, they looked terrific.

Steve then continued the conversation with, "I'll keep this simple. Howie, the crew of *Pappy's Pack* is yours. You are the new aircraft commander. I'm being loaned to the 482nd Group to pilot a Pathfinder ship. It could be permanent; I don't know."

Those words stunned Howie, Russ, and Bob. It was the break-up of a team that had been together since training back in the States. The crew up front in the plane also included top turret gunner–flight engineer Jim McFarland. Very few crews had been able to remain with each other as they had. The integrity of an original crew formation was now almost nonexistent because of casualties. *Pappy's Pack* had lost two gunners, Roger Earp and Ronald Lattamus. Roger was now back stateside still recovering from his combat wounds, while young Ron, the kid from Sterling, Illinois, had been killed.

"I don't know exactly what to say," stated Howie, as he searched for the right words to express his feelings, "I've been quite happy flying in the right seat."

"Well, the bottom line is that they asked me if you could take over the left seat and I said, of course he can, he's well qualified," answered Steve.

"When does all of this take place?" asked Bob.

"It is or will be official tomorrow," answered Steve.

"Do you leave to go over to Alconbury tomorrow as well? Hell, we need time to have a party for you!" responded Howie.

"No, they gave me a pass and a few days before I have to report," stated Steve. "So, after tomorrow's official event, I am off to see Maggie in London. It will be just a short visit, but at least we can be together."

"We'll alert the rest of the crew," said Howie as they all got up from the table and walked toward the door of the mess hall.

"They are the Van Dyke Crew now, Howie. You'll do just fine," said Steve, as he gave a light pat to Howie's shoulder.

Howie turned to Steve and said, "I'm looking for a copilot. Do you want to apply for the job?"

They had a good laugh as they headed back to their quarters to relax a little after another trying day in the air.

It was after evening mess that the four gathered once again at their favorite table in the Officer's Club. Word had quickly gotten around about the promotions and Steve's new assignment. There was an instant party at the O-Club! While the atmosphere was lively, especially since no mission had been scheduled for the next day, it was for the four close friends a somewhat somber time and would probably be the last time they would all be together, at least for a while.

Steve also reassured them that it would only take the beginning of the next mission to relax everyone, especially Howie. He would do well and no one in the crew would experience anything different, just a new voice from the copilot's seat. Steve went on to say that he would waggle his wings to them from his Pathfinder B-17.

Bright and early, the official gathering took place at headquarters. The new copilot was Second Lieutenant Carl Phillips, from Chaska, Minnesota. Chaska was a farming community south of Eden Prairie in the greater Minneapolis–St. Paul area. Carl was a new replacement and the next mission will be his first. He had spent two years at the University of Minnesota and enlisted, as he told the story, before his grades made him eligible for the draft. After the war he was determined to return to the university with a better academic attitude.

Steve, Howie, Russ, Bob, and Carl hitched a ride out to the hardstand where Pappy was working on the plane. Steve and Pappy had a quiet talk while standing under the left wing, while Howie, Russ, and Bob took Carl on a tour of the B-17 known as *Pappy's Pack*.

Inside the plane, it was strange for Howie to be seated in the left pilot's seat while Carl occupied his familiar copilot's seat. They chatted for a few minutes. Bob and Russ were standing just behind the pilots and copilots seats and joined in the conversation.

Howie had arranged a taxi for Steve, which would take him over to the train station in Wellingborough. Steve had been in touch with Maggie and she quickly arranged her working schedule with other nurses, namely Cathy, Emily, and Beth, in order to have some time off to spend with Steve.

Michael, with his old Rolls Royce limousine, picked up Maggie from St. Thomas' Hospital and drove her to King's Cross Train Station to meet Steve.

It was 1500 hours when Steve's train arrived from Wellingborough. The Saturday train schedule was in effect, along with wartime travel, so for Steve it was a slow train trip.

"I can't believe that you're back so soon," said Maggie as she flew into Steve's arms after he stepped from the train's carriage. "You've been promoted again!"

"I'll tell you all about it," answered Steve as he held Maggie tightly. "This is a very short visit, but I'm so happy to see you."

They walked gleefully hand in hand from the train station to Michael's waiting car. Steve and Michael shook hands as both beamed at seeing each other. Michael noticed the captain's bars and congratulated Steve on his promotion. Steve and Maggie climbed in the limousine while Michael placed Steve's bag in the car's boot. As they pulled out into the London traffic, Michael inquired about the other lieutenants and Steve assured Michael that they were all well and looked forward to another London visit.

Michael drove across London and pulled up to the eight-story, majestic Savoy Hotel, located in the Strand. Steve had wanted to stay there ever since everyone enjoyed themselves so much on the earlier airmen and nurses' date at the Savoy's River Restaurant where they dined and danced the night away. With the Savoy being not only a classic hotel, but also an extremely popular one, obtaining a reservation was nearly impossible at this time, unless Michael went to work on the project.

The room that Steve and Maggie had included a sitting room, along with a fairly spacious bedroom. A nice touch, especially in wartime, was the vase of fresh flowers in the room. Ah, the Savoy!

Tea time passed with Maggie and Steve remaining in their room. It was a time for them to be young lovers.

Dinner that evening would be enjoyed in the Savoy's wood-paneled Grill Room. Steve and Maggie both ordered the wild Scottish salmon. Dessert would come from the extensive selection on the sweets trolley. In addition, a little later, they enjoyed a glass of port to accompany some English cheeses.

It was 9:30 when they finally left the Grill Room. Steve and Maggie had thought about going over to the River Restaurant for some dancing, but decided to put that off until the next evening. Instead, they took the lift up to their room, which was located on the sixth floor.

Breakfast the following morning was served in their room. Actually, it was more like a brunch because it was well past the normal breakfast hour. Finally, they emerged from the room and came down to the lobby. A taxi took them to the Victoria and Albert Museum. It was a favorite of Maggie's and she wanted to share it with Steve. They spent a few hours there, enjoying the exhibits, paintings, sculptures, and special collection of miniatures. Steve enjoyed being guided around the vast museum by an enthusiastic Maggie.

When they finally left the Victoria and Albert Museum, Steve and Maggie decided that it would be a good stretch of the legs to walk the mile or so to Harrods for an enjoyable cream tea in the Georgian Room. The walk was not fast paced, but also not slow. It was more like a stroll down Brompton Road.

After tea, a Harrods doorman helped them into a taxi for the ride back to the Savoy. They freshened up and spent some additional time in their room before coming down to the eight o'clock reservation in the Savoy's River Restaurant.

With having Scottish salmon last night, Steve ordered grilled Chateaubriand with pommes soufflés for two. For dessert, they enjoyed Crêpe Suzette. The dancing started at nine and they spent about an hour on the dance floor before retiring once again to their room to enjoy their time as young couples in love do.

There was an early morning call because Steve had to return to Chelveston, pick up his belongings and report to his new assignment at the 482nd Group. Maggie also had to be back at St. Thomas' in order to take her shift.

After breakfast, Michael drove them first to St. Thomas' Hospital. There was not very much time for a long goodbye because Maggie needed to be on duty shortly.

Maggie questioned Steve as to when he thought he would be able to come back to London. "Soon, I hope," was Steve's answer.

From St. Thomas', it was back across the Westminster Bridge, past Big Ben and off to King's Cross Train Station. Michael shook Steve's hand, told him in a fatherly way to take care of himself, then hugged him.

Steve entered King's Cross Train Station, walked over to where he could see the large board that posted the train schedule and checked to determine if the train that passed through Wellingborough was on time. The train actually was already in the station and could be boarded.

Steve bought a newspaper, boarded the train and settled into a first-class carriage. It was not too long before he felt the train starting to move. The only companions in his compartment were an elderly couple who had visited their daughter in Croydon, just outside of London. They had a small farm on the outskirts of Wollaston and watched as the B-17s passed over their home as they make their way to and from the bombing missions. Steve did not speak about anything of a military nature other than the fact that he was a B-17 pilot. The silver wings on his coat showed that, indeed, he was a pilot.

As with all military personnel, Steve gave as few details as he might on behalf of the military, even to a kindly older couple. He kept the conversation on the light side, telling them over a cup of tea and scones how much he enjoyed being in England and that he had become extremely fond of the British people. Steve did not mention one particular British subject who he was more than fond of, although his thoughts drifted that way.

Finally, the train pulled into the Wellingborough Station and as Steve stepped onto the platform from the train, Howie was waiting for him.

"This is a pleasant surprise," said Steve as he and Howie shook hands.

"I was a little worried about you . . . you know, newly transferred soldier . . . not knowing what to do, where to go," answered a smiling First Lieutenant Howard Van Dyke III.

"Any missions yet with your new crew?" inquired Steve.

"Not yet, a little thing called the weather has kept us on the ground," stated Howie.

"How did you get here, steal a Jeep or something?" joked Steve.

"Or something," replied Howie, as in, don't ask! "You know the guy, Richard, who has been bringing us back and forth to Wellingborough when we head for London? Well I hired him because with a few dollars, or rather pounds, he has a way of securing the adequate supply of petrol needed," replied Howie.

"Leave it to you to find someone with, shall we say, proper connections," kidded Steve.

"You know me . . . just a poor ole New York boy trying to cope with the little obstacles thrown in his path," answered Howie, who continued as they left the train station and walked to the waiting car that Howie had hired. "I packed all of your things . . . figured it would save you a little time."

"Thanks, I was going to report to the 482nd and then figure a way to gather up my stuff," was Steve's reply. "Let's get you over to Alconbury. You can buy me some lunch at the mess hall and we'll get you settled," stated Howie. "Hello, Richard, nice to see you again and your companion here," said Steve as he and Richard shook hands.

"Glad to see you again, Captain, but you know me, I'm just a small pawn, drawn in by wicked money," answered Richard with a wink. He then placed Steve's bag in a section of the back seat that was not occupied with Steve's footlocker. "You certainly have accumulated a lot of things there, Captain, the boot is also full!"

"You sound like my father when I came home from college," remarked Steve, remembering when his father wanted to go straight to the dump with the things he accumulated while at the University of Florida.

"We'd better stop at a pub along the way, suggested Steve. "I don't know what to expect with the set-up at the 482nd, especially with the radar-equipped planes. They may not let unassigned group personnel on the base."

"You're probably right . . . a change in plans, Richard," Howie said, then after a few seconds of thought, he continued, "can you find us a good food pub along the way?"

Richard did not answer Howie, but the smile on his face and a nod of the head told them that of course he could find a suitable pub along the road they were driving to the base at Alconbury. It might come down to actually which pub to stop at for a bite and a pint.

The pub chosen was the Horseless Carriage, near Spaldwick. Howie, Steve, and Richard enjoyed a pint or two of English Bitter along with a bowl of hearty vegetable soup, some bread, but no butter, and a ploughman's plate.

After lunch, Richard drove them to the main gate of the 482nd Bombardment Group at Alconbury. Howie and Richard off-loaded Steve's trunk and officer's bag at the gatehouse while Steve presented his orders to the military police sergeant. Steve was asked to stand by. He would be picked up shortly by a Jeep or truck and be driven to his new quarters.

Richard waited on the side as Howie and Steve chatted. It was quite evident that the relationship between the two had grown to more than a pilot and his copilot. They were as close as brothers could be.

It was not very long before a Jeep appeared with two men, a driver plus a major, from the gold leaf on his shoulder. When the Jeep came to a halt, the driver jumped out and walked over to pick up Steve's trunk, placing it upright in the back seat area and then returned to get the officer's bag, which he placed on the floor of the Jeep just in front of the trunk.

In the meantime, the officer walked over to greet Steve and Howie. "I'm Jim Kellner," said the lanky, red-headed major.

"Steve Carmichael and this is Howie Van Dyke," said Steve as he started to salute, but was stopped as Jim reached out to shake hands with both of them.

"Steve, you're assigned to my squadron. Here at the 482nd Group, we have the

812th, 813th and 814th. You'll fly with the 814th Squadron," said Major Kellner.

"Well, Stevie, take care, maybe we can get together on a rainy day of no flying in a nice warm pub over in Rushden," said Howie as he started to shake hands with Steve, but the two close friends ended up in a hug.

"I'll stay in touch. Take care of yourself and *your* crew," answered Steve with a wink, reminding Howie that *Pappy's Pack* was now his charge.

Howie watched and waved as Steve climbed into the back seat of the Jeep. Steve held onto the footlocker trunk as the driver turned the Jeep around quickly and headed toward the main part of the air base. Steve did the best he could to wave and hold onto his cap.

Howie walked back to Richard's waiting car and was quite silent during the drive back to Chelveston. Things would not be the same again for him, Russ, or Bob. They also wanted to come along to see Steve off; however, there was just only so much room in the little English car.

Major Kellner took Steve to a Nissen hut where he helped him get settled in his new quarters. "I'll pick you up at 1700 hours for dinner and introduce you around," the major said. "I'm glad you're over here. We need you."

Steve relaxed a little and with some time on his hands wrote a letter to his dad. He told of being in London once more with Maggie and that he had been transferred to another outfit where they needed some experienced pilots. He did not offer details. In addition, Steve wrote that he was now a captain and that Howie and the rest of his officers were promoted, which pleased him, noting that it took too long for them to be recognized. Steve also wrote a shorter letter, really just a note, to Maggie. The main thing that she would want to read was, "Maggie, I love you!"

Later, at the officer's mess hall, Major Kellner introduced Steve to several other officers. Steve felt a little out of place, trying to remember names and not doing very well. It was not like being back home in the 305th where he knew most of the other flying officers. However, Steve felt that he would not be here too long anyway. He had just six more missions to go for his 30.

While Steve and Howie did not plan on signing up for more missions, they both wanted to wrangle a job that would keep him in England for a while longer. Neither wanted to go back to the States and become an instructor. Maggie and Beth were also in the equation. The two of them had their plans—now to execute them!

Major Kellner, who told Steve to simply call him Jim, stated that they were not alerted for a mission tomorrow, Tuesday, the last day of November. He would meet with him after breakfast mess, take him out to the hardstand, and meet his crew chief and the B-17 he would fly. After that, they would assemble in the day room for introductions to his new crew.

That evening Steve spent some time at the Officer's Club. He figured that it was a good way to meet some of the other officers stationed on the field. He did not plan to stay long. It wasn't the same as being with Howie, Bob, and Russ, arguing over who would supply the next batch of peanuts or who was buying that night. He did miss them. While Steve drank a pint, he talked with several of the officers and found out a little more about the radar-equipped Pathfinder B-17s that he would be flying. One thing that Steve found out was that many of the original Pathfinder crews had been transferred from the 325th Squadron of the 92nd Bomb Group.

Interestingly, a couple of the men who were having a drink with Steve asked if he had flown any combat missions yet. They thought, Steve suspected, that perhaps he had been an instructor pilot who had now just come to fly actual combat missions. The answer, in Steve's best matter-of-fact way, was that he had flown 24, the latest on the Bremen raid of the 26th.

Amazingly, there was an immediate change in attitude toward the newcomer, as the pilots started asking questions to someone who had flown more than twice as many missions as most of them.

Major Kellner had come in a little earlier, but he did not make himself known to those standing by the bar. He stayed in the background listening to the conversations and smiled. He watched in amusement as some of the pilots bragged to Steve about their experiences in the air. The major walked over to Steve a few minutes after he responded to the question about how many missions he had flown to date.

"Captain, I see you've already got a pint . . . may I join you?" asked Major Kellner as he gave Steve a pat on the shoulder.

"Please join us, Major, I'm just getting acquainted with some of these gentlemen. May I order a drink for you?" responded Steve.

"Scotch," answered the major as the barman came over.

While Steve had been told by the major to call him Jim, that personalization would be only for private moments. In a setting where others were present, it would be Major Kellner, out of respect and proper protocol.

After about another 15 minutes, Steve excused himself. It had been a long day and he was tired. Steve went back to his quarters and in no time, he was sound asleep.

Shortly after breakfast, Major Kellner took Steve out to the hardstand to meet his crew chief. As the Jeep pulled up, a master sergeant who Steve thought to himself looked older than dirt, walked over to greet them.

"Hello, Major," said the chief, then looking over Steve for a second, he continued, "Captain."

"Steve, this solid old soul is Master Sergeant Lawrence Freeland. He's been in the service since time began," said Major Kellner as an introduction.

"Glad to know you," said Steve, who was not quite certain how to proceed yet with the old-school crew chief.

"I understand that you came over from the 305th, who was your crew chief?" asked Master Sergeant Freeland.

"Well, we just called him Pappy–" answered Steve, who started to go more into detail, but was stopped in mid-word.

"Master Sergeant Walter O. Creamer . . . best in the business and an old friend. Is he as ornery as ever?" asked Steve's new chief, who also shook his head and smiled.

"I named the plane *Pappy's Pack*, if that gives you an idea of what we think of him," answered Steve.

"Son of a bitch . . . son, you and I are going to get along just fine," responded the Chief. "How many missions do you have behind you?" responded the chief.

"Twenty-four to date," answered Steve. "The last one was the Bremen raid of the 26th. Pappy had some repair work to do as he did on most of the missions. I expect it will be the same here with you."

"Well, it seems as though they try to aim for the ship with the radar under the nose, so you've got to be on your toes," was the chief's reply.

The three spent the next few minutes talking as they looked over the plane. Steve took a few additional minutes and climbed up into the ship to look it over.

A little later, Steve and Major Kellner were off for the crew meeting in the day room. When they entered the room, the men who had already assembled there stood up at attention.

"At ease, gentlemen," said Major Kellner.

They all sat down again, preparing to meet their new skipper.

"Steve, this good-looking lot of men is your new crew," said the Major. "Gentlemen, your new aircraft commander is Captain Steven Carmichael. In case you are wondering, he has flown 24 combat missions, the latest on the 26th over Bremen. The captain comes to us from the 305th, and I feel that we're lucky to have someone of his experience join us." He then nodded to Steve to take over.

"Good morning . . . I'm going to get a cup of coffee and a donut, so fill up and relax while we get acquainted," said Steve.

With that, Major Kellner felt that Steve had things well in hand and he had other duties to perform, so the major made his exit.

"I'll start the introductions, I'm Steve Carmichael and I'll be your new driver," said Steve. He really did not want to go into details at this time. He would find out more about the crew as he came to know them. Steve then motioned to the officer to his left who also had the wings of a pilot on his flight jacket.

"Yes, I'm your copilot, John Williamson," said a blond-haired, fair-skinned second lieutenant. He paused for a moment and then continued, "I've flown four missions."

To his left a sandy-haired second lieutenant smiled and said, "I'm Len Stanton, navigator, and I've flown 11 missions."

Then the other officer in the crew, a first lieutenant spoke, "I'm Tony Pace, Pathfinder bombardier and I have flown 17 missions, eight with a Pathfinder crew. The other fellows are already invited, so I'll invite you to our family restaurant. We have the best Italian food in Scranton, Pennsylvania, Captain."

"Thanks, I'll take you up on that," answered Steve. He now looked over to the enlisted men and started to call on one, but another stood up and said, "Sir, I'm Bill Pannski, your top turret gunner and flight engineer. I've just have three missions in the book, a replacement crewman."

Next, a very young man, really a boy, stood up and said, "Tommy Holiday, sir, ball turret gunner, 14 missions to date. My friends back home call me Doc, after the gun fighter from the old West!"

"Well, Doc, I actually had the great grand nephew of Wyatt Earp in my crew, one hell of a tail gunner, so you have to live up to that reputation," stated Steve.

"I'm radioman," said a staff sergeant who looked like he had been in the service awhile. "My name is Ted Thompson, I've just got seven missions, was an instructor back home."

"Sir, my name is Albert Swift . . . tail gunner. I've flown 19 combat missions," said the cocky-looking staff sergeant.

The next two almost stood up together, "Bob Bradenton, sir, right waist gunner."

Then the last crewman stood and said, "Harvey Bronstein, sir, left waist gunner."

"I'm pleased to meet all of you," stated Steve. "The one important thing for you to know is that I do run a tight ship while we are on a mission. Everyone is trained for his position in the crew and we all need to, well, we must work together as a team in order to be successful. However, please feel free to let me know of any concerns you may have. I take my responsibility as the aircraft commander very seriously, both in the air and on the ground. I'm here to give help if there is a need."

"None of us have really been in a regular crew, Captain, so we welcome the opportunity to join with you and work as a team," stated Steve's copilot, John Williamson.

This sentiment was echoed throughout the room as the men relaxed and got to know each other. They had all come either from different groups as the 482nd was formed or from other 482nd Squadrons and transferred in order to complete this crew. With so many losses, crews always seemed to have at least one new crew member on each mission.

Steve closed out the meeting, thanking each of them for their support and telling them that it was his pleasure to have a solid crew such as this flying with him.

He then went over to Major Kellner's office for some additional indoctrination, as instructed. Steve reported that he was quite pleased with his crew and felt that they would do just fine together as a combat team.

The major and Steve went for lunch at the officer's mess and then returned to the office to continue Steve's education about the 482nd and piloting a Pathfinder B-17.

This will be an exciting adventure! Steve thought to himself. However, as Steve left the office to go back to his quarters to freshen up a little before supper, the danger of this situation became clear: it was his ship that would be leading the formations and be the one that enemy fighters and flak gunners would give top priority for destruction.

At evening mess, Steve sat with John Williamson, Les Stanton, and Tony Pace. It was here that he started to become more familiar with his copilot, navigator, and bombardier. They were anxious to learn more about Steve, so he told them about his background and hopes for a baseball career, as well as working with his dad on their cattle ranch in Central Florida.

Tony talked about growing up in the Scranton–Wilkes-Barre, Pennsylvania area. Many of his relatives had worked in the coal mines and one uncle was a line supervisor at the Mack Truck factory. His family actually lived just outside of Scranton, in the town of Clarks Summit. Tony's grandfather had operated the restaurant, with his father naturally going into the family business.

Les Stanton hailed from Detroit, Michigan, so he was quite interested to hear that Steve had signed a contract to play in the Detroit Tigers organization. He, like those throughout Michigan and even the folks across the Detroit River in Windsor,

Ontario, Canada, had grown up as Tigers fans. His family, like many of the residents of Detroit, was involved with the auto industry in one way or another. Les went on to say that he actually had relatives who worked in each of Detroit's big three: Chrysler, Ford, and General Motors. It was not quite fun when all of the family got together for summer picnics and the arguments would start over who built the best cars and trucks.

John Williamson, Steve's new copilot, hailed from Baton Rouge, Louisiana. He had attended the local university, Louisiana State, and intended to complete his studies after the war. His father worked for Standard Oil and his parents family had come to Baton Rouge from the little pulp mill town of Bogalusa for the job with the oil company. Bogalusa, located near the Pearl River, was not too far from the Mississippi state border.

After the evening meal, they all adjourned to the O-Club for a couple of pints. They were not there very long when it was announced that the club would be closing early; they were on alert for a mission tomorrow, the first day of December.

Steve enjoyed the company and conversation while it lasted. He hoped that there would be more evenings like this with John, Les, and Tony. After "last call," the four left the Officer's Club and headed to their quarters for some sack time. Tomorrow would come soon enough and most likely result in a long day of flying.

Steve and his crew were awakened at 0500 hours. Breakfast would be served at 0600 and the briefing for today's mission was scheduled for 0700 hours.

Steve was eager to fly his first mission as the pilot of a Pathfinder B-17, but he was also somewhat nervous. This particular day would certainly be different as he flew with an unfamiliar crew. Steve's concerns and hopes were that they would perform well under battle conditions. He had trained and worked with the crew members of *Pappy's Pack* and knew exactly how each reacted under the strain of the running air battles and flak barrages sent up by the anti-aircraft batteries. The hope was that these men would do as well under those conditions.

The briefing on this overcast Wednesday morning revealed that the mission for this first day in December would be to the Cologne, Dusseldorf area of Germany. The actual cities that would be targeted were Solingen and nearby Leverkusen. The Pathfinder B-17 would lead several elements to both targets and bomb several heavy manufacturing factories in both cities. In addition, the crews at the briefing were told that they could expect a long day in the air with close to eight hours of total flying time. The good news was that there would be meaningful escort for the entire time over enemy territory. Both P-38 and P-47 fighters with long-range fuel drop tanks would accompany them. As the B-17s withdraw from the Continent, British Spitfires would join in to help ferry the bombers home to their bases in England.

The mission route would take them across the North Sea, entering the Continent at the port of Knokke-Heist, Belgium, above Oostende. From there the formations would fly north of Antwerp to avoid the flak batteries stationed there, then continue over Netherlands territory at Valkenburg, fly to Julich, Germany, and finally turn north and fly to the IP for bombing Leverkusen, the target assigned to Steve and his Pathfinder crew.

After dropping the bomb load, the flight path toward home would have them turn left away from the target area, fly north of Cologne (Köln on the German maps) to avoid as much flak as possible. Then they would fly west to Aachen, located on the German-Netherlands border, enter Belgium just above Liege, fly north of Brussels and finally exit the Continent between Dunkerque and Calais.

"Captain, we certainly will be taking a traveler's dream trip: England, Belgium, Holland and Germany," said Steve's copilot, John Williamson.

"Yes, all from a bird's-eye view and we're being paid to go!" joked Steve.

After briefing and settling a few last-minute details, the flight crews were driven to their respective hardstands.

Master Sergeant Freeland and his ground crew were waiting as the truck pulled up. Steve and the crew jumped from the truck and walked to their waiting Flying Fortress. The master sergeant and his men had already been at the hardstand for more than an hour making certain that the ship was ready to go.

"Good morning, Captain," was the greeting from Master Sergeant Freeland.

"Good morning," was Steve's reply. Then looking at the number on the plane, 42-3489, Steve continued, "We'll have to give this ship a name. Think of one while we fly the mission. I don't like flying a B-17 without a name."

"That we'll do, she's been a base unit plane up to now," came Master Sergeant Freeland's reply. "The plane is listed as a B-17 G model, came to us in mid-August. Quite frankly she looks like a refitted F model to me."

While at the hardstand and before they boarded the plane, Steve gave his usual "fireside chat" talk to what was his new crew. It served its purpose, especially right now with a crew that was new to him. After saying "let's all relax and do the job we are trained for," each of the men went about completing their preflight tasks.

Steve and John went about the preflight procedures. Steve wanted to be certain that his new copilot was on top of his job in the cockpit.

Finally, at 0818 hours, flares were fired from the control tower and B-17 engines came to life. The familiar, unmistakable sound of B-17 motors echoed throughout the peaceful countryside. Leaving their hardstands and lining up on the taxiway, the big bombers waddled their way to the end of the runway and the takeoff position. Each B-17 struggled from the additional weight of bombs, ammunition, and extra fuel as they tried to become airborne before they were out of runway.

The formation and assembly occurred without incident as Steve's Pathfinder B-17 slid into the lead position of the bomber stream. His old 305th Bomb Group was one of those in the formation.

From his pilot's seat, Steve was on the lookout for the B-17s that had a large "G" painted in the triangle on the vertical stabilizer. He was also looking for one particular ship, a B-17 with the nose art name of *Pappy's Pack*. It wasn't too long before Steve spotted Howie's plane. Steve gently eased his wings a bit, rocking them in recognition. Howie did the same. Radio silence had to be maintained.

With the bombers starting out over the North Sea, the escort fighters, both P-47 and twin-engine P-38s, joined the formation. They met as they crossed where it seemed that the English Channel and the North Sea met. Soon the European coast was entered exactly where they were supposed to be, a little north of Knokke-Heist. Some flak started coming up from the ground batteries, but so far, it was light and inaccurate. At least for now the exploding shells were off to the right of the bomber stream. They were likewise exploding at a lower altitude than the 25,000-foot level that they were currently flying. So far, luck was with them.

The P-38s were flying high cover, with the P-47s working their way in and out of the formation as well as flying both sides and below. Specks appeared on the horizon, which, as they came closer, became German ME-109s. So far, they were keeping their distance, looking over the situation and seeing if there was a spot at which they could launch an attack on the B-17s. The frontal attack plus the rear attack was the favorite on the B-17s as well as the four-engine B-24s.

With the lead ship as a target, a frontal attack was attempted. ME-109s flew well out in front of the formation, then turned and five abreast made for the lead Pathfinder B-17, which was Steve's ship.

"ME-109s coming in at 12 o'clock!" called John from his copilot's seat.

"I'm on them," stated Bill Pannski in the top turret. He opened fire sending a stream of .50 caliber machine gun tracers out toward the attacking German fighters, even though they were still out of range. It would let the German pilots know that he was alert.

Tommy Holiday, in the ball turret, moved his machine guns around to fire at the German fighters in case they broke down and away, which was a favorite maneuver.

The ME-109s opened fire , but broke off the attack early as four P-47s came charging to the rescue and drove them off. None of the ME-109s came close enough for Doc Holiday to get in a burst. He was actually disappointed and stated that over the plane's intercom system.

"Everyone okay?" asked Steve, knowing that at least a couple of the machine gun bullets from the German fighters had hit the plane.

Each station checked in. One bullet had penetrated the nose of the B-17 and lodged in the padding behind the navigator and bombardier's compartment. Some other bullets had ripped into the right wing, but it appeared that no real damage had occurred. Flak was now becoming heavier and more accurate as shells started to explode within the formation. So far, none of the planes had received a direct hit; however, the showers of dirty, black shell fragments were hitting the ships and ripping into their fuselages. Flak shrapnel can cause casualties within a plane if the hot, flying pieces were to hit a crew member. Flak jackets helped as did the fact that some of the crew, usually the radio operator and waist gunners, as well as the tail gunner, often brought aboard an extra flak jacket and placed it under their feet for added protection from the deadly shrapnel.

The formation had crossed the Netherlands and now the bomber stream was flying over Germany. They flew on through the dense flak as they approached Julich and prepared to turn onto the IP and the bomb run.

"Looks like 10/10 cloud cover . . . that plus the smoke they're putting up . . . your plane, Tony," said Steve to his Pathfinder bombardier. The time was 1222 hours, or 22 minutes past noon.

"I've got her . . . right on it," answered Tony as he took over the control and path of the plane preparing for the bomb drop. As a Pathfinder B-17 bombardier,

Tony had the equipment in this radar fitted ship that allowed him to peer through clouds and smoke to "see" the terrain below. He dropped the bomb load and all of the other B-17s in the formation toggled their bombs on the Pathfinder's signal. Flashes of exploding bombs could be seen through the 10/10 cover.

"Bombs away . . . your plane, Captain. Bomb bay doors coming up," called Tony to Steve.

The plane, now much lighter with the bomb load gone, started to surge upward as Steve once again took over the controls. He followed the flight plan and made a left-hand turn away from the target area. Flak shells continued to explode around them. They were now flying north of Cologne and heading west toward Aachen, which is still in Germany. The plan was not to fly directly over Aachen or the city of Maastricht, Holland, which lay about 15 miles west, but to skirt those flak batteries and enter Belgium just above Liege as the formation made its way back to the coast.

So far, the fighter escort had been able to keep the Luftwaffe at bay. They tried several times to infiltrate the formation but were driven off by the P-47s. The high-cover twin-engine P-38s also had not permitted the FW-190s or ME-109s to climb above the formation and then dive onto the B-17s as they continued to fly toward the coast and exit the Continent.

Flak bursts started to appear once again as the formation flew near Aachen. The flight plan showed that flak would be more intense around the center of Aachen and not at the plane's current position. Some mobile flak batteries, which could be relocated by trucks, lorries, or rail cars, must have been what were shooting up at them right now as they prepared to cross the German–Dutch border. The exploding flak shells were becoming deadly accurate at their altitude. This was not good. Steve looked over at his copilot and could see that John was clearly frightened at what was happening.

"Better shake us around a little, Captain," called Al Swift from his tail gunner's position.

Steve started to move the ship to the left and to climb 500 feet, but it seemed that no matter what he did, shells continued to explode near his plane. Other B-17s were going through the same barrage of cannon fire from the ground.

Suddenly Steve's lead plane bounced violently upward as a loud explosion became a fireball on the right wing. The B-17 started to roll to the right, almost turning over. Quick action by Steve brought the big bomber back to a level position, at least briefly.

"Give me a damage report," called Steve over the plane's intercom.

The right wing was on fire and John activated the fire extinguishers, but they had little effect and the fire was spreading out of control.

"Captain, I think we've lost her. That wing looks pretty bad," reported John as he watched from his copilot's position, where he could clearly see the damage.

The explosion had knocked out both engines on the right wing and they were now falling out of the formation. They simply could not keep up. Almost immediately six ME-109s were boring in for a kill. It seemed that Luftwaffe machine gun and cannon fire was coming from every direction. They were making a frontal pass and at the same time a pass at the tail gunner's position. Then additional ME109s were firing at the side of the crippled B-17.

It seemed that only seconds had passed and it really was not that much longer, perhaps just a minute, two, or maybe three when the right wing became completely engulfed in flames. It was now a hopeless situation. Steve could not believe that he had lost the aircraft. To him this was unthinkable!

The gunners in the B-17 fought back, trying to drive away the attacking ME-109s. They continued to shoot at the swarming enemy fighters. It was a fierce battle and two of the ME-109s started to smoke from their engine compartment.

Up front, from the pilot's seat, a now angry Steve Carmichael called out through the plane's intercom system, "Okay, men . . . time to go . . . get out of here NOW!" and the bail-out alarm was sounded.

Everyone started to leave their position and head for an exit. Just as the two waist gunners were about to leave their posts, a flash of cannon fire hit the side of the burning B-17, ripping into the plane and instantly killing Bob Bradenton and Harvey Bronstein. Ted Thompson, the radio operator, had just left his position and saw both men hit and spun around with cannon fire slamming them to the floor of the plane. He knelt down to check on Bob and Harvey as Tommy Holiday was climbing out of the ball turret. Al Swift had just come forward around the tail wheel well from his tail gunner position. Al had already kicked open the rear door and released it. He was preparing to leave the ship, but looked forward to where Tommy had joined Ted in trying to look after the two waist gunners. Ted slowly shook his head. Both Bob and Harvey were indeed dead. Al then jumped from the crippled B-17 with Ted and Tommy soon following.

It was quite evident to Steve that they all must leave the plane before it exploded. He had seen this happen all too often to other B-17s. "John, it's time for you to leave the plane, do it right now," urged Steve. "I'll be right behind you. Make sure that everyone up front has left the ship." Then Steve saw that Bill Pannski was still there, just behind the controls, not knowing how he could but wanting to help Steve in some way. Steve smiled at his top turret gunner–engineer and pointed to the nose hatch area, "I'll see you on the ground, Bill."

Steve radioed in the clear that his ship was lost and for the deputy lead to take over. At this point, both the navigator and bombardier, Les Stanton and Tony Pace, crawled out from the nose, gave a wave to Steve and then dropped out of the nose hatch, just behind Bill Pannski.

An exasperated Steve Carmichael set the plane up so that he could now leave the ship. This was his 25th mission and Steve felt he was well over the hump, so to speak, and could complete his 30-mission tour. However, he was now in a situation that had gone well past his control. He could not do anything to correct it. It was frustrating for someone so confident in his flying skills.

In the meantime, *Pappy's Pack* saw that Steve's plane took a direct exploding flak hit and was knocked out of formation. It was a horror that was almost too much to take. A half-dozen ME-109s raced in and nearly ripped the ship in half and they were not able to do anything about it. They were shocked. How could this have happened to Steve?

"Take over for a minute," stated Howie to his copilot, Carl Phillips.

Howie half stood up trying to peer out of his B-17s windscreen to see what was happening to Steve's plane.

"Count the parachutes!" shouted an excited Howie over the intercom.

"I counted three from the rear and four from the front," called Russ Parker from his bombardier's position in the nose of *Pappy's Pack*.

With Steve's lead plane still in front of them, although it appeared to be down to 12,000 or 13,000 feet at this point, Russ had a good view of what was unfolding.

"I confirm that," said Jack Kowalski from his left waist gunner's position.

By now, four P-47s were attacking the German ME-109s and driving them off Steve's B-17 as two other P-47s followed the smoking enemy planes to finish the job.

Steve's ship was now down to less than 5,000 feet. The entire wing was burning away from the plane. The situation was becoming desperate. Steve may have waited too long to get out! Concern was growing from the crew of *Pappy's Pack* about their old Skipper.

"Stevie . . . get the hell out of there," yelled Howie over the radio frequency that Steve was tuned, figuring that Steve would know that it was Howie.

Howie was hoping that Steve was perhaps one of those who had already left the burning plane. With four of the five men up front parachuting from the plane, one was unaccounted for in the B-17. And with just three leaving the plane from the rear, two were unaccounted for in the ship. Five crewmen were located in that section of the plane.

Howie knew that two were still in that section and probably dead from the fierce attack. That the plane Steve was flying might explode at any minute was uppermost in the mind of the *Pappy's Pack* crew.

With Steve's crippled B-17 dropping closer and closer to the ground, inside Steve became caught by centrifugal force as the plane now started to go into a spin. He fought and struggled his way toward the forward hatch. In a final throe to save itself, the B-17 tried to level herself once more. This sudden moment, just seconds long, freed Steve and he quickly completed the journey to the hatch, patted the old girl for letting him escape and dropped through the hatch, now free of the plane.

Steve did not pull the ripcord on his parachute right away, even though the ground was coming up to meet him quickly. He wanted to be certain that he had cleared the burning aircraft. Finally, at what seemed to be a little less than 2,000 feet, he pulled the ripcord and the canopy opened above him with a jolt. The plane was almost out of his sight when it hit the ground and exploded in a huge fireball.

"Howie," called an excited Joey DeMatteo, the tail gunner of *Pappy's Pack* who at this moment did not speak in military protocol, "one more parachute just came out of the front hatch!"

"Well, at least he's over Dutch territory and not in the middle of Aachen," answered Howie in a broken voice. Nevertheless, Howie could not imagine that Steve might be a prisoner of war. Son of a bitch, he thought to himself.

Howie took the controls back from Carl. He still had the job of bringing *Pappy's Pack* and her crew back to Chelveston. Howie forced himself to keep his mind on the task at hand, even though most of his thoughts really were of Steve. Howie was worrying about Steve's safety as he parachuted into a strange and dangerous territory. It was enemy territory and the German Army on the ground would be looking to capture the American aviator at the end of that parachute.

Ground Crew of *Pappy's Pack*

High Wycombe Eighth Air Force Headquarters (Pinetree)

Pappy's Pack on the Bomb Run

High Flying B-17 Formation Contrails

CHAPTER SIX

Steve watched the B-17 formation fly out of sight. Then he looked over the countryside as he floated nearer to the ground. The area appeared quite rural. There were mostly what looked like small farms and orchards. So far, he saw no German soldiers or their trucks in the area he was about to land. Steve figured that at least 15 or 20 miles now separated him from the rest of his crew. As the ground now came up in a hurry, Steve was descending into an apple orchard. The parachute hit off one tree, catching on some of the limbs, which slowed his fall. Steve was lucky; this was his first real parachute test. They did practice back in training, but that was a very long time ago. With the parachute still stuck in some of the branches, Steve landed without a huge jolt, although he bounced along the ground for several more feet. He slid out of the parachute harness and then gave a hard tug, which brought both his parachute and about a dozen small branches down on him as he lay on the ground.

Steve quickly freed himself from under the parachute and started to fold it up into a large ball. He was now looking around in order to figure out his next move. With this being December 1st, the cold, damp afternoon air plus his recent experience caused him to shiver.

Suddenly Steve spotted an elderly man walking toward him. "American airman, come now." Old Man, as Steve would call him, motioned for Steve to follow him. Steve fell in line behind Old Man, who was obviously a local farmer or perhaps the owner of this apple orchard. Old Man motioned once again to Steve and took the parachute from him. It was held as though it were a prize. Steve figured that the parachute material would be put to good use.

At the edge of the orchard, there was a small farmhouse and likewise a small barn. "You can get rest in here," said Old Man. "You will be safe from the Boche . . . the Germans, but now, you come into house. You can drink warm tea."

"Where am I? What is this town . . . city?" inquired Steve.

"Village of Margraten," was the answer.

Margraten, thought Steve, as he tried to keep up with Old Man. *This means that I'm seven or eight miles west of Aachen, Germany, and seven or eight miles east of Maastricht. I'm in the Netherlands . . . what luck!*

"Come quickly," said Old Man as he opened the door to the farmhouse. The door opened into the kitchen and Steve was rushed inside where it was warm.

"I thank you very much for helping me," said Steve as he stood before a large iron stove, which served as a cook-stove and a way to heat the room. He rubbed his hands together to warm them.

"Mother will give you some warm tea," said Old Man.

Steve turned to see a very pleasant-looking, round-faced, gray-haired grand-mother come into the kitchen. She patted Steve on the shoulder as a welcome and then pumped some water into a large kettle. The kettle was placed onto the wood-burning stove. She then went to the cupboard for the teapot and a tin of tea.

Old Man motioned for Steve to sit down at a chair by the table. He spoke some Dutch to Mother and she set the table with cups and plates, then placed a loaf of bread and cheese on the table. She smiled and left the room to continue what she had been doing before the airman dropped in on them.

"I speak good English, but Mother does not," said Old Man.

"You do speak very good English and I do not speak Dutch," replied Steve as he sat down at the table.

Old Man cut slices of bread and wedges of cheese. "I am sorry that the bread is not as white as you like, but we do not get very good flour anymore," said Old Man as he placed wedges of cheese on a plate and handed it to Steve, motioning for him to help himself to the bread. "We bake the bread ourselves these days." Old Man continued, "Are you alone?"

"I was part of a bomber crew," answered Steve as he took a sip of tea. "We were shot down and most of the men bailed out of the burning plane just east of Aachen. I am the airplane's pilot and was the last man to leave the B-17. For a while I was trapped inside, but managed . . . was able to escape the burning plane." Steve tried to speak words that Old Man would understand.

"You are lucky," stated Old Man as he placed more cheese on Steve's plate. "There are just a few German soldiers in this town. Most of them are stationed in Maastricht or in Aachen."

Mother reappeared, poured Steve another cup of tea and once again patted him on the shoulder as her way of welcoming him.

Steve smiled and took her hand, holding it for just a moment. Mother under-stood this.

"I can't thank you enough," said Steve as he held the teacup to warm his hands. "I know that you are taking a big chance just helping me and to come into your home is very dangerous for you."

Old Man held up his hand and said, "We will not let the Germans have you.

You will be safe and we do some work on you." Old Man stopped for a moment as he thought about his English and shook his head figuring that Steve understood what he said.

"I understand," said Steve as he smiled at Old Man and Mother.

"You will eat here for supper and then you must go to the barn to sleep for the night," stated Old Man as he motioned for Mother to clear the table of any evidence that someone else had been there. "I am sorry, but you cannot sleep the night in the house; it will be too dangerous for all of us."

"If the Germans do find me in the barn," explained Steve to Old Man, "I will tell them that I had just looked for a place to get out of the cold and that the people in the house do not know that I am here."

"This is good, you are an intelligent airman," answered Old Man, satisfied that Steve understood the situation.

"Is there any way possible to know about my crew?" asked Steve.

"It would be very dangerous to ask questions," answered Old Man. "While most of us just want the Germans to go back across the border and stay there, some people have made out well by helping them. It is hard at times to know who to trust, but I will inquire about the big plane that flew so low over our village. Maybe I can find out the story of the plane."

"I understand the problems it could cause you," stated Steve as he took the last sip of tea and handed the cup to Mother. "Do not ask any questions that will place you in danger. I am thankful for the help you are giving me."

"Both Mother and myself are happy to keep you from the Germans. We will be careful," said Old Man as he stood up from the table. Then he spoke to Mother in Dutch and she smiled at Steve.

Mother said something to Steve, but while he did not understand what she was saying, he did understand that she spoke with genuine sincerity.

Steve did not reply, but he smiled at Mother and squeezed her hand.

Old Man then motioned for Steve to follow him. He had Steve retire to one of the two bedrooms. The young airman looked very tired to him and with supper still a couple of hours away, rest would be what he needed right now. After supper, when it was dark, Steve would be moved to the barn where he would spend the night.

As Steve lay on the bed, he thought how appreciative he was of what was being done for him. He was so lucky to have been rescued by Old Man, rather than falling into the hands of German soldiers. Steve's thoughts were also of his crew and their fate. With them bailing out of the burning B-17 near Aachen, they were probably in the custody of the Germans. It was not too long, though, when exhaustion took over and Steve was sound asleep.

In the meantime, Howie brought *Pappy's Pack* back to her hardstand at Chelveston. He and his copilot Carl Phillips went through the shutdown procedure for the B-17 and in a few minutes, they slid out of the nose hatch and dropped to the ground. The rest of the crew had already left the plane and were standing near the front of the war-weary bomber. The ground crew, at Pappy's direction, was already at work servicing the plane. Pappy was impatiently waiting for Howie to emerge from the ship.

"The boys already told me the news about Steve," said Pappy as his eyes met Howie's. "They said that they saw him finally leave the plane." The worried look on Pappy's face told the rest of the story. While he was a tough old crew chief, Pappy had become extremely fond of the young man from Florida.

"We're pretty certain that Steve was able to get out and that he came down in Holland and not Germany," said Howie. "I don't know if that makes any real difference, but the Dutch people are very decent and no harm should come to him, at least that is what we hope."

Then Howie gathered his crew together before they jumped onto the truck, which would take them to the debriefing. "Look, before we board the truck, we are all concerned about Steve . . . Captain Carmichael," said Howie. "As best we all know, he got out of the plane before it hit the ground and exploded. He came down east of Maastricht in what I believe is farmland. If he was able to evade the Germans, then perhaps the Dutch people will take care of him. Let's hope that luck is with him."

As the crew boarded the truck and headed for the debriefing, they spoke among themselves, the only subject being discussed was that of Steve's fate.

Later after evening mess, Howie, Russ, Bob, and Carl gathered at the Officer's Club.

Howie had written a letter to Steve's dad, Ray, and wanted input from the others. Carl, being the junior officer of the crew, did the honors in bringing the pints of beer to the familiar corner table, while the others looked over the letter.

"It's fine, Howie. You've spent time with Steve's father, so to me what you've said is right," stated Russ.

Bob nodded his head in agreement.

"I've got to reach Maggie tomorrow," stated Howie as he shook his head, still in disbelief that Steve had been shot down. "I thought about phoning the hospital now and trying to reach her, but it will be tough enough for her to take, so at least I'll let her sleep tonight."

"Maybe you should reach Elizabeth first," reasoned Bob. "Either she can break the news to Maggie or at least be with her when you call."

"Good idea," answered Howie. He then sat back in his chair, took a small sip of his beer, and tried to think of the proper words to tell Maggie.

Back in Margraten, Holland, Steve sat at the dinner table and ate alone. While Old Man sat near and Mother was in the kitchen as well, Old Man told Steve that he and Mother had already finished supper while Steve was still asleep. It was best that way, for if they had a visitor, hopefully not one wearing a German uniform, Old Man would simply take Steve's place at the table and say that he had been attending to things on the property and now was having his supper. Steve would be hidden in the root cellar until it was clear that all was okay. Old Man also told Steve to relax, as they usually did not have anyone come to call after dark. After eating supper, with no moon and the night quite dark, Steve was guided to the barn.

Old Man lit a lantern after they had closed the barn door. "I have already fed the animals, so they should be quiet," he said as he pointed out a large draft horse and a cow to Steve. "We use the horse for the orchard and the cow for milk. We do not have feed for any others. I sold the pig before the Germans came calling and took half of my apples. They would have taken the pig for themselves like they did to other farmers in the region. That is the way it is for now. The cats may sleep with you to keep warm."

"I'll be fine . . . thank you once again," stated Steve, as he was shown the ladder that would take him up to the hayloft. "I don't know how to repay you for your kindness."

"I will be back for you just before dawn, while it is still dark," said Old Man. "Then you will come back into the house for the day. If necessary, you can hide in the attic. It is small, but no one can really get to it. The entrance is hidden and you must know how to unseal it from behind a chest in the bedroom where a ladder takes you up . . . a secret room, you can say," and Old Man laughed.

Steve climbed the ladder in the barn after Old Man left, blanket in hand, that Mother had given to him, and settled in the hay. It was pitch black and Steve was glad that he still had his small flashlight. He was careful with the light even though there were no windows up in the loft, just a closed door through which the hay is pitched up into the loft.

This was very different from his warm bed back in England but he would make the best of the situation. At least he was in friendly hands and not sleeping in the company of German soldiers, or worse. Steve pulled some hay over to make a comfortable and warm place to sleep. He then fixed the blanket like a sleeping bag. In no time at all, there were two visitors who planned to bunk in with Steve. The cats had come up the ladder and were quite curious about their roommate. As Steve pulled the blanket over himself, the cats settled in, one by his side and one gently walked up onto his chest and found a comfortable spot. The only other sounds beside the cats purring were those of the animals moving around in their stalls down below the loft, and Steve fell into a deep sleep.

It was morning, very early in the morning. The sun had not come up yet and it was still quite dark. A light snow was falling as Old Man quietly opened the barn door just enough to squeeze in. He then lit a small lantern and kept the flame low so that not much light was visible, but enough to see by. This was his barn and Old Man did not need much light because he knew exactly where everything was. The animals moved around in their stable area, figuring that it was feeding time, but they would have to wait a little longer. Right now, Old Man wanted to bring Steve into the house before it was light.

He climbed up the ladder and almost in a loud whisper called out to Steve, "Airman, it is now time to come to the house while it is still dark and no people can see you."

"Okay, just give me a moment," answered Steve. "I'll move the hay back so that it looks like no one was here."

"No, you come now," was Old Man's reply. "I will take care of the hay when I come back to the barn . . . come now."

Steve eased the one cat off his chest, patted the one next to him and crawled to the ladder. He didn't want to light his flashlight, which might upset Old Man, and crouched to avoid hitting his head on one of the crossbeams near the top of the small barn.

Old Man came down the ladder, followed by Steve. The dim light of the lantern was bright enough for Steve to see and he followed Old Man to the barn door. The light was extinguished and the door opened wide enough for them to exit the barn. Steve went out first and Old Man quickly followed, closing the door behind him. They went rapidly through the light snow toward the kitchen door. Steve wanted to say something, especially about the foot tracks in the snow, but figured he would wait until they were inside the kitchen. He was ushered into the kitchen. A blanket had been placed just inside the door, which covered the entrance, so no light could be seen from the outside. The dim light from the kitchen lantern was turned to high and the kitchen was now illuminated.

"We must not let the light be seen from the outside when we come in or out," said Old Man. "It makes for fewer questions about unusual movement around the property."

"I understand and, as I said yesterday, I appreciate the help you are giving me," answered Steve. "I know that I have placed you kind folks in danger."

"You are welcome here," said Mother as she placed the kettle on the wood-burning stove.

"Thank you, Mother," answered Steve, with a wide smile on his face, knowing that Old Man had taught her to say that last night.

Steve could still not believe his good fortune. He also worried about the fate of his crew members. Steve was still not certain how many of the crew had actually escaped the burning B-17. He was so busy up front trying to save the plane that he did not know that, in fact, the two waist gunners had been killed by the attacking ME-109s.

"Sit down, have eggs and bread. We have enough and it is all right for you to eat much," said Old Man to Steve as he helped Mother by brewing the tea.

Steve sat down and ate his breakfast alone. Old Man once again explained that this was best because no one should come to the house and count that three people were eating when the house had just two people living there. He and Mother would eat later, after the beginning of the day chores were completed.

Steve, of course, understood. As Steve ate, Old Man, cup of tea in hand, explained that Steve must stay in the house during the daytime. If someone came to the house, then Steve must go to the hidden room upstairs and remain very quiet. Later in the day, if the snow stopped, then Old Man would venture into Margraten and see if anyone saw the American bomber fly overhead and explode. He would also contact some trusted friends that might be able to help Steve more than he and Mother could.

Just after the chores were completed, Old Man came back into the house from the barn. Mother had reset the table for two. She was prepared to serve their breakfast when Old Man motioned to Steve to follow him. He opened a small closet, moved a box that contained spare work boots and foul-weather gear, then reached down, pulled up a trap door and pointed for Steve to go down into the hidden root cellar.

"I saw an army truck going to the farm that is down the road," said Old Man in a quiet voice just above a whisper. "They will come here and could be looking for you. This root cellar is where Mother and I keep special things from the German soldiers. They have looked into the other root cellar and taken things, but they do not know that I have outfoxed them with this special place."

"What about my footsteps from the barn to the kitchen door?" asked Steve.

"Do not worry; the snow falling has covered up those tracks," answered Old Man.

"I will be fine and very quiet," reassured Steve.

Old Man patted Steve on the shoulder then replaced the trap door and box. He closed the closet, went back to the table, and started eating. He looked over to Mother and smiled. She understood and ate breakfast as though nothing was out of the normal routine.

The sound of a truck engine in the yard let Old Man know that there soon would be a rap on the door. While the truck engine continued running, a lone young German soldier came to the door and gently knocked.

Old Man patted Mother on the hand and went to the door. He opened the door to find the young German officer standing there.

"Guten Morgen," said Old Man.

In German, the officer began, "I have come to ask you some questions."

"Come in out of the cold. Would you like a cup of tea?" asked Old Man.

"No, but I thank you. Did you see an American bomber fly low over the area yesterday?" was the initial question from the German officer.

"Yes, I did," answered Old Man. "It was very low and in a few minutes, I heard a loud explosion. I felt that it had crashed and hoped that it did not hit any houses."

"It crashed in a field and exploded, then burned," stated the German officer. "No one could get to the plane to see if anyone was in it because the fire was too hot. But when the fire was put out, there were the remains of two or maybe three American airmen, it was hard to tell."

"At least no one on the ground was injured according to what you said . . . this is good," stated Old Man as he tried to show that he was not partial to the Americans.

"I have orders to check the area," stated the officer. "We do know that seven of the crew members were captured. Perhaps the others died in the wreckage or the Luftwaffe killed them up in the air. Did you see anyone escape from the plane?"

"I was trimming some branches from my fruit trees to get them ready for the spring," said Old Man in a reassuring voice. "We also use the wood in our cook-stove. It happened so fast, a large plane on fire and flying so low. I saw no people escape the plane."

"I will have to look through your house and I will have to look through your barn. These are my orders," stated the German officer.

"I understand," answered Old Man, who thought for a moment and added, "Should I show you around?"

"Yes, this will be good," was the answer.

Old Man showed the young German officer through the house, then put on his coat and walked with him to the barn. Mother took a peek of what was going on through the kitchen window, but was careful not to be seen.

Everything seemed to be in order because the German officer climbed back into the waiting truck and was off down the lane and onto the road. Soon the truck was out of sight.

Old Man closed the barn door tightly and walked back into the house. He then went quickly to the closet, opened the door, moved the box and pulled open the trap door to the secret root cellar.

"It is now safe, come back to the kitchen," said Old Man to Steve. "You should drink some tea to warm you."

Mother had a proud look on her face as she poured Steve a cup of tea. She and Old Man had kept him safe and themselves as well.

"I must tell you that seven of the men in your bomber have been captured," said Old Man to Steve. "This is what the German officer told me. He also said that at least two and maybe three men were in the burned wreckage. I am sorry to tell you this bad news."

Steve thought for a moment. He knew that the two who were killed must have been in the rear of the plane, but whom? Steve was certain that everyone up front was able to escape. He also figured that if seven had been captured and were now prisoners of war and if the Germans thought that, three had been in the wreckage, then perhaps they would stop looking for him since all ten members of the crew were accounted for. Steve said this to Old Man, telling him that a B-17 had a 10-man crew and that it seems that the Germans might think that he was among the dead.

Old Man smiled. If the Germans thought that Steve was indeed dead, then they would relax and not search anymore for him. This would make it easier to move him around under the unsuspecting German noses.

Back in Chelveston, while there was no snow, still the weather had closed in and there would be no bombing missions on this day. Howie managed to get through to St. Thomas' Hospital in London by telephone. He was able to reach Elizabeth and explain the situation about Steve and that he would like her to be with Maggie when he broke the news. Elizabeth understood and stated that Maggie was on her floor today and that she would bring Maggie to the telephone.

"Howie, is everything all right?" questioned Maggie in an almost broken voice.

"I'll say this straight out, Maggie . . . Steve has been shot down," stated Howie. "We are pretty certain that he was the last one to bail out of the burning plane and did so over the Netherlands." He did not mean to be blunt, but figured that it was best.

"Do you think that he is okay?" asked Maggie in the steadiest voice that she could manage. "Was he captured by the Germans?"

"We figured that he parachuted down east of Maastricht, which is farmland and apple orchards, so maybe he was taken in by a Dutch farmer," answered Howie reassuringly. "At least that is what we all hope."

Word of Steve being shot down spread quickly on the floor that Maggie and Elizabeth were working on at St. Thomas' Hospital. In a short time, Maggie, with Elizabeth at her side, was joined by Catherine Wilks and Emily Graham. They tried to comfort Maggie, who was now crying softly and looking up at them wanting to say something, but not knowing what to say.

Elizabeth took the telephone from Maggie and started to speak with Howie, but she was interrupted when Maggie said something to her in a quiet voice.

"Howie, Maggie just asked me if Steve's dad is aware of the situation?" relayed Elizabeth.

"Not really . . . it takes a few days for the telegram to reach him," answered Howie. "In the meantime, I have written a V-Mail letter to him and told Mr. Carmichael that I would follow-up with a longer letter and continue to write as I found out more information. The War Department will send a Western Union telegram. I really don't know the timetable, but figure, as I've said, a few days to a week."

"We'll take care of things here with Maggie, but keep us informed as well," responded Elizabeth. "When are you coming to London?"

"Soon, I hope. As you know, it's hard to tell," answered Howie as he and Elizabeth said goodbye.

Weather once again continued to keep the daylight bombing raids from flying to European targets. The night leaflet dropping missions, however, did continue. The 422nd Squadron did not require quite as good weather in order to complete their missions. A leaflet mission to the cities of Bremen, Harburg and Oldenburg was carried out on the 2nd of December, plus on the 4th, night leaflet missions were flown to the Paris area, along with a mission to LaRochelle.

Back in Margraten, Holland, Steve was about to spend his second night sleeping in the barn. The two cats, who now must have figured that Steve had become their bunkmate, would once again join him. The day was spent in the house with Mother. There was not much for him to do since he had to keep out of sight. Steve did manage to have Mother sit down while he cleaned up the luncheon dishes and pots. Old Man came in and out of the house several times, as he tended to the animals and gathered up some of the cut wood for the stove. He wanted things to look quite normal. In addition, Old Man left the orchard for a couple of hours during the late afternoon. He returned just as night started to fall. It would be another dark, moonless night.

In the kitchen, they ate dinner, this time with all three eating together, since Old Man did not figure that anyone would venture out in the night to visit them. They freely talked throughout the meal. He informed Steve that during the next morning a friend would come to visit them. The visitor would come into the house and not to the barn and perhaps he could be of important help to Steve. At least he would be able to move Steve from their house and help him to maybe get back to England. It was a risk all around, but it was better than staying here, where eventually it would become dangerous for everyone. After the evening meal and with it now quite dark, Old Man once again guided Steve to the barn for what might become the last time. Thoughts of how lucky he was to have parachuted into the orchard of these kind people ran through his mind as Steve drifted off to sleep, one cat at his side and the other cat quite comfortable resting on his chest.

Once more, as it became morning, but was still quite dark, Old Man opened the barn door then quickly closed it. He climbed the ladder to the hayloft and called to Steve in a voice just above a whisper. It was time to wake up and come into the house before it became light. Old Man then went down the ladder to wait for his barn guest. Steve carefully eased the cat off his chest and used his small flashlight to find the opening where the ladder was. He did not use the light continuously, but also wanted to be certain that he found the hole before it found him.

They closed the barn door and quickly made for the house. Mother had already set the table for Steve. As before, since it was becoming daylight, they would eat separately so as not to arouse any suspicion in the event that unfriendly people came to call, such as German soldiers.

Steve enjoyed his breakfast of fresh eggs and toasted bread. Old Man and Mother joined Steve as they all had morning tea. They explained that coffee was hard to come by, so the beverage they now had in the house was tea.

As they enjoyed another cup of tea, Old Man said, "In a short time we will have the visitor. We do not use names as you have found out; it is better that way and it is much safer for everyone involved. I hope you have understood that, my friend."

"I certainly do," answered Steve as he spoke slowly enough for the words to be understood by Old Man. "However, at some time in the future I want to thank you in a more proper way than to say just thank you. You are the kindest folks I have met and I know that you have and are risking your lives for me. I will never forget you."

"To help you is our pleasure," answered Old Man. "You are doing your best to help us be free once again and you are from so far away. You have risked your lives for us and many of your comrades have died trying to help us."

Mother listened as Old Man spoke to her in Dutch and explained what both he and Steve had just said. She walked over to Steve and gave him a hug.

Steve smiled and had to look away as a tear came to his eye.

Old Man continued to speak, but in English to Steve, "The visitor will ask you some questions. He must be satisfied that you are the American aviator who you say you are. He is a kind man, but you must understand that he needs to be careful. You will probably be handed over to many different groups of people and the safety of them and their families are most important. One rotten apple will spoil the barrel. The Germans know that there are Dutch people who have helped both the British and American aviators plus the Jewish people escape. They try hard to find out who is helping. They would torture to find out who is helping and kill them and their families. Do you understand?"

"Yes, I completely understand," said Steve as he took a sip of his tea.

"I must go back to my chores and I will come back into house when our friend comes to call," said Old Man as he put on his coat and ventured outside.

Steve helped Mother clean up after breakfast and then went about his chore, which was to wait for the visitor.

A little more than an hour passed and it was just past ten o'clock when Mother motioned to Steve that they had company. Steve was trying to figure out if he should go to the hidden root cellar, the hidden room upstairs or simply stay still when Mother, who had peeked out of the kitchen window, turned to Steve and smiled, it was okay.

The kitchen door opened and in came Old Man followed by a huge man. The man was well over Steve's six-foot-one-inch, 185-pound frame.

Steve figured that the man must be at least six foot six, maybe six seven and he looked like he was close to 300 pounds, maybe more. He stuck out his hand to shake hands with Steve. Steve felt like a child holding onto a grown-up's hand.

"Where are you from, my friend?" asked Big Man.

"I am from Florida . . . a small cattle town in Central Florida near Orlando by the name of Kissimmee where my dad and I have a cattle ranch," answered Steve. "I graduated from the University of Florida in May 1942. I have been flying since being a little boy and after college, I joined the Army Air Corps. I am a captain and pilot of a B-17 bomber."

"Why don't you two go out to the barn for some work and stay there for maybe 10 minutes or so," said Big Man to Steve's hosts, speaking in Dutch to them.

Old Man and Mother immediately put on coats and left the house for the barn.

Steve looked puzzled and Big Man smiled and held up a hand to Steve, so as to say "wait a minute, we need to talk."

After they left the house, Big Man continued, "I need to ask you some more questions and it is better for them if they don't know this information right now. Sometimes it is better not to know, because if you are asked questions and do not know the answer, then better for you . . . understand?"

"Yes, I do," answered Steve. "I also want to protect these fine people who have been so kind to me."

"What is your name, Captain? And let me see your dog tag so that I can make certain of all the information," questioned Big Man.

"My name is Steven W. Carmichael," answered Steve. "Can you read the tag or should I tell you the number?"

"Let me see," Big Man said as he leaned over to read the number.

"What else do you need to know and should I ask the questions that are on my mind or is it best to wait?" questioned Steve.

Big Man laughed heartily. "It is best to wait. I like you, young man," said Big Man and he stood up, with Steve also quickly standing up. They shook hands and Big Man put his hand on Steve's shoulder, "You will be helped."

It was just a moment or two later when the kitchen door opened and Old Man with Mother came back into the house. They were carrying more than a dozen eggs in a box.

Big Man said something that Steve did not understand because it was spoken in Dutch. He then gave a slight wave to Steve and left the house, box in hand with the eggs, his reason for coming to the house in the first place, for anyone watching.

After he was on his way Old Man, who had taken off his coat and hung it back on a hook, turned to Steve and said, "He will be back here after it is dark. You will leave with him to begin your journey."

"Once again, I must thank you for all of the help that you have given to me," said Steve as Old Man motioned for him to sit down. "I feel so lucky that I have not fallen into the hands of the Germans and become a prisoner like the rest of the crew members. It is because of you that I am still free."

"I feel cold and some hot tea will warm us," said Old Man as he pumped some water into the kettle and set it on the cook-stove. He then gave Steve a fatherly pat on the shoulder. He understood the young man's gratitude.

Mother, in the meantime, put two large spoonfuls of loose tea into the teapot. She placed the pot on the table at the end that was closest to the stove, and reached into the cupboard for three large cups.

"It will be a long day for you, the waiting time," said Old Man in his best English.

"Yes, I know," answered Steve, knowing that his place for the day would be in the house and out of sight. "I wish that I could help you outside as you prune the apple trees, but I would not want to get you into trouble if anyone saw me and asked questions."

"You must also go upstairs to the small hidden room and rest on the bed up there," stated Old Man. You will be able to sleep and not be disturbed in the event we have a visitor. Tonight, you may travel and not receive any rest as you travel."

Mother quietly poured the tea. Having used fresh eggs, a little honey and some flour, she had baked a cake. Mother cut large pieces of cake for the two of them while they talked. She also poured tea for herself, cut a small piece of cake and sat down at the table. She did understand a little of the English, but not most of the words. She understood, however, that Steve would be moving on when night fell.

After they had finished the tea and cake, Steve was shown to the little hidden room, which was part of the attic in the house. The tiny room contained a chair, small desk, small square of an old rug that may have been cut from a larger rug that had seen its days as a downstairs rug, plus an old iron bed that had been made up for a guest, if the need occurred. In this case, Steve was the guest in need. There was also a very small oval-shaped window, which was almost hidden by the house eaves. A sharp eye from the outside might wonder about the window. However, from the outside, it was not conspicuous enough to draw attention. On the inside, the window, even though quite small, gave a big view of the countryside. The attic was high enough to overlook a large section of the orchard and the road leading to it, as well as the barn and farmyard of the property.

Steve could peek out of the window without being seen. It would at least make for a not-so-boring day as he waited for the next step of what he figured would be a long, roundabout journey back to England. His thoughts wandered from his crew who were not as fortunate as he was to his old crew back in Chelveston to Maggie and what she must be going through and, of course, his dad and what he would go through after the dreaded Western Union telegram.

The day itself went slowly. Steve tried to be as quiet as possible when he moved around in the little room. He would look out of the attic window for a while and gaze over the countryside, however, on this cold December day there was not much activity. Steve thought that on the far road, there might be some military trucks traveling along, but none was seen. He spotted three books on the small desk, but could not understand any of the words since they were not in English. He smiled to himself that there were not even pictures to tell him a little of what the books might be about. Finally, Steve stretched out on the bed, even though he did not feel tired. In a short time, he had fallen asleep.

"American, it is now time to eat supper," said Old Man as he gently shook Steve.

"Come down the steps as quickly as you can."

Steve awoke, surprised that he had fallen asleep, gathered himself together, straightened the bed, just smoothing it out since he had slept on top of the covers, and carefully walked down the steep, very narrow, steps through the back of the closet and into the kitchen.

Old Man patted Steve on the shoulder, then went into the closet and pulled the panel at the back of the closet shut. He then rearranged some of the things to make it look normal. He stepped back into the kitchen and turned around to face the closet. Satisfied that it did not reveal anything other than just a storage closet, Old Man closed the closet door. He shook his head to Steve and Mother as if to say that all was well.

Mother had set the table for three, as Old Man had requested. They would eat together for this last meal. When it was late and very dark, Steve would be leaving them, so this supper, they would all enjoy together. As an evening beverage, Old Man produced three large bottles of beer. To be sure, Steve enjoyed the good Dutch beer!

It was close to half past eight when the quiet rap on the door broke the conversation that Steve and Old Man were having after dinner as they enjoyed a glass of cognac, which Old Man had saved for special occasions.

Old Man opened the door and Big Man quickly stepped inside. Without saying a word, Big Man was poured a glass of cognac. He shook his head in agreement at a welcome drink from the cold night.

"I have brought you a warm coat," said Big Man to Steve. He then sat down at the kitchen table to enjoy the cognac before the journey with Steve began.

Steve did not say anything. Anyway, he was not certain of what to say at this time.

Big Man finally said, "We will discuss the journey after we have left the house. It is best if these people do not know of our plans. It is safer for them this way."

"I understand," answered Steve, smiling at Old Man.

"This drink was good . . . makes me warm . . . it is now time to go." Big Man stood up, finished his cognac and placed the glass on the table.

Steve, Old Man and Mother also stood up. Steve put the oversized coat on over his flight jacket and turned to hug Mother. She held him close and tightly. Steve also shook hands and hugged Old Man. Old Man, as did Steve, wiped a tear away.

"When this thing is over, you come for a real visit," said Old Man.

"I will do that for certain. Take care of each other," stated Steve as he and Big Man quickly left the kitchen door, just after Old Man had dimmed the lantern so that almost no light would show to the outside when the door was opened.

"We will walk through the apple orchard so we will not be seen on the road," said Big Man as he set a quick pace. "Also, you can call me Horst. I am not afraid of using my name!"

Steve did not answer. The pace that they were setting almost made it difficult for him to talk anyway. Steve thought of himself as being in pretty good shape, but he was having trouble keeping up with Horst, who had a wide stride when he walked. Steve was almost taking two steps for every one that Horst took.

In the distance, dogs were heard barking. They were not barking at Steve and Horst, but at something that was bothering them near their home. The noise masked Steve and Horst's movements as they walked across the snow-covered apple orchard.

"We can take a stop for resting," stated Horst as he and Steve came to the edge of the orchard.

Steve was glad for the rest, brief as it might be. He smiled to himself that perhaps Horst was not using the best English grammar, but he certainly made himself understood in English far better than Steve could attempt in Dutch.

"Is it best that I don't ask questions?" Steve asked as he propped himself against the trunk of an apple tree.

"We will take this road for a few miles," answered Horst. "There should be no traffic using the road until the morning. By then, my friend, we will be at my house and you can rest until the next part of your journey is arranged. This is our immediate plan."

Steve did not answer, but nodded his head in comprehending what was to take place. He was grateful that total strangers would give him this much help.

Horst motioned to Steve that it was time to move on. There was a lot of ground to cover before dawn. The two started to walk down the road side by side. A road sign near an intersection of two roads pointed to the town of Eijsden. They walked toward that town which was located near the Dutch–Belgium border.

"We must keep our conversation very low and we must listen carefully to hear if any motor machines are coming," stated Horst in a voice just above a whisper. "If one hears a machine, we must quickly get low in the ditch near the road and remain very still until it passes. We must also be quiet so as not to alarm the dogs. It is better that they do not bark and wake people who are sleeping. The less that see us, the better for now."

Steve was then instructed to walk in Horst's footprints. Horst noticed that the two walking side by side was clearing out too much snow along the road. By having Steve walk in Horst's footprints, he figured that anyone who might be watching that morning would think that a single person, probably a local, had been making the journey.

The two continued walking down roads, across fields and back onto other country roads. It was evident that Horst knew exactly where he was going. A light snow had started falling, which did not completely cover their tracks, but did cover up the individual shoe prints. It would be harder to decipher what the prints meant thanks to the fresh snow.

At close to five in the morning, just as they were on the edge of Eijsden, Horst made a right turn onto a lane that led to a small, two-story brick house. The snow was now coming down very hard, which seemed to please Horst, who thought that the heavy snow would soon completely cover their tracks.

With the morning light starting to brighten the horizon, Steve could clearly see the outline of the house. In addition, there was a small brick building to the left of the house, which to Steve looked more like a large shed rather than a small barn.

Horst motioned to Steve and the two quickly went to the back of the house, entering it through a back door that opened into the kitchen.

"I live here alone," stated Horst to Steve, noticing that he was looking around, expecting to see someone else in the house.

"Can I help do anything?" asked Steve.

"Go into the formal room and build a fire . . . in the fireplace!" said a laughing Horst, knowing that he had made a joke.

Steve also laughed. It was a relaxing laugh, as one would do around a friend, especially knowing the overall situation. Steve felt safe with Horst. Here he was, far from Chelveston and the 305th Bomb Group, which he thought of as home, right now feeling safe behind enemy lines on the Dutch–Belgium border. A crazy situation, he thought!

"I will make a fire in the stove and cook us some breakfast," stated Horst. "I am hungry and you should be too." He then put some wood into the cook-stove and lit a match, placing it under the tinder wood. The fire would warm the kitchen as well as cook their breakfast.

Steve walked into the front room of the house, which served as the living room, or as Horst had said, the formal room. There was comfortable furniture and paintings on the wall in what was an attractive, formal yet inviting room. A prominent feature was two old but quite sturdy-looking rocking chairs that sat close to the fireplace, one on either side. The rocking chairs seemed to be the most used furniture in the room.

Steve walked over to the fireplace, moved the fire screen to the side and knelt down to place wood onto the grate. He felt he would have a better fire if he moved some of the ashes to the side, so picked up the fire stoker and spread the ashes around under the grate and to each side. Satisfied, Steve placed wood on the grate using the smaller logs and dry sticks, then lit a match, holding it long enough for the kindling wood to catch fire. In no time at all, he was placing larger logs on the now blazing fire. It was good to start a fire with such dry seasoned wood. Steve then replaced the fire screen so that no sparks would shower into the room. He gave a broad smile and shook his head in satisfaction as he looked at the fire and warmed himself.

Horst entered the room and walked over to the fireplace, twisting his hands as to warm them. "You have a good fire," he said. "Now, come into the kitchen. I hope you like coffee. I like to have coffee in the morning. I kept six of the eggs I got from the orchard farmer. I gave the others to a friend, the place I visited while waiting for the darkness and to come for you. We can have the eggs and I have some good ham. I can also make toast bread. It will be a good breakfast for us." He then motioned to Steve to sit down at the kitchen table.

The room smelled of fresh-brewed coffee. Horst had brewed the coffee in a large, very old, faded blue-enameled steel coffee pot. He poured the steaming hot coffee into two large mugs. While Steve normally liked to add cream to his coffee, there was no such luxury on this cold morning. He took a taste of the coffee and smiled in appreciation to Horst, but thought to himself as to whether he should chew or drink the extremely strong brew!

Horst, in the meantime, took a sip of his coffee, nodded his head in approval and exclaimed, "Just right!"

Soon three fried eggs and a large slice of ham were placed in front of Steve. Horst had cooked them in a large, black, iron frying pan, cooking all six eggs and two slices of ham at the same time. A metal, upright, stove-top toaster, which held four slices of the freshly cut bread at one time, nicely toasted the bread. Horst turned the bread once and both sides looked perfect. Steve remembered that they had used the same type of toaster on the ranch when he was a little boy, before the purchase of an electric toaster. One of his jobs had been to turn the toast for Lillian.

After breakfast, which had been eaten mostly in silence, Horst pumped some fresh water into a kettle, heated it on the stove and washed the breakfast dishes and pan. Steve offered to help, but Horst motioned for him to just sit and enjoy a second mug of coffee. The second mug actually tasted pretty good to Steve. He found that it did not take very long to get used to something, especially when it was all that was available.

Horst patted Steve on the shoulder and said, "Even though you have had two mugs of coffee, I think you will sleep for a few hours. Let's go upstairs and rest."

Steve got up from the table, stretched and then waited for a moment as Horst placed a large, sturdy slat of wood into the holders, which were on either side of the kitchen door. The door looked to Steve to be very solid and what Horst did would certainly make it difficult for anyone to enter the house. He had noticed the same thing when he was in the foyer of the formal room, that a barricade was already on the front door, which is why they came in by way of the kitchen door.

Steve followed Horst through the formal room and into the foyer where they walked up the staircase to the second floor. Steve noticed that there were two smaller bedrooms, plus one larger bedroom. There was also a small, closed door that Steve figured led to an attic. Horst showed Steve to one of the small bedrooms, which was used for overnight guests.

"You can relax and enjoy a good sleep," stated Horst. "We are in an area that is not of importance to the military. I understand that the Germans think you perished in the crash of your plane. They have, I believe, accounted for all 10 men of the bomber crew. I am very sorry for your comrades, but this also lets you be a very lucky man, my friend. The Germans think you are dead and they do not look for you. We can move you around easier because of this."

"I cannot tell you how much I appreciate what you are doing for me," answered Steve. "You and the older folks are due much more than what I can offer."

"If we can get you all of the way back to your American comrades in England, then that will be our thanks," responded Horst. "It will be a victory for all of us."

Steve undressed down to his shorts. He placed the "bunny suit," his long johns, on the chair next to the dresser and climbed into the quite comfortable bed. Steve then pulled the heavy quilt over himself. While some of the heat generated from downstairs was beginning to reach the upstairs, the warmth of the quilt sure felt good. In no time, two mugs of coffee and all, Steve was in a deep sleep.

Back at the 305th Bomb Group Headquarters in Chelveston, they were alerted for a daylight bombing mission. The date was Sunday, December 5, 1943. The targets lay in southwestern France and the port city of LaRochelle.

The greater overall plan called for other groups to keep the Luftwaffe busy and essentially out of the air, by bombing their airdrome at St. Jean D'Angely. That city lay around 50 miles southeast of the 305th target at LaRochelle. The B-17s flying to St. Jean D'Angely would be involved in a low-level mission, which was not to their liking, but was designed to destroy the airdrome and the German fighter planes stationed there.

For Howie and the officers of *Pappy's Pack*, they reminisced at the plane's hard-stand about 305th missions and that LaRochelle would be their 26th trip over enemy territory.

More often than not, crews did not stay together for very long. That was a fact of the war. In addition, the earlier days of flying 25 missions, as did the crew of the *Memphis Belle*, were gone. Thirty was now the requirement because so many crews were lost and replacements were slow to come.

The takeoff for the mission to LaRochelle was normal, as was forming up. This would be a long flight, which would carry them over water and included flying through a portion of heavily fortified southeastern France, just west of Rennes. As the flight started across France, heavy cloud cover could be seen far out in front of the formation. The groups that were to bomb the airdrome at St. Jean D'Angely, were forced to look for other targets because of 10/10 cloud cover over their target. The 305th continued toward their initial target of LaRochelle following its lead Pathfinder B-17. The formation dropped their bomb load as the Pathfinder released their bombs.

Because of the heavy cloud cover, no Luftwaffe fighters came up to meet the B-17s. In addition, the sky was free of anti-aircraft flak explosions. *Pappy's Pack* flew back to their base at Chelveston, landing after the eight-hour and twelve-minute round trip. It had been a very long mission, but one in which no guns fired a shot, except the initial rounds fired as practice to be certain that the guns were all in working order. A tired crew went to debriefing. It seemed that the English weather was once again going to keep the planes grounded for a few days. Perhaps a trip to London could be worked out if the missions were canceled.

Steve, in the meantime, found out that he would be spending several days at the home of Horst in Eijsden. Steve felt quite safe with Horst, but still, he was well behind enemy lines. Horst told Steve that exactly how he might get back to England would be a matter of very careful planning. Horst also explained that other British and American airmen had made it back to England using several different routes so that the Germans could not determine if one or the other route would be used. In addition, changes could be made along the way because of circumstances that might determine it necessary. Horst mentioned that a very well-organized group, the Dutch–Paris Underground, would look after him. He would be in safe hands.

On most days, as Steve waited for the day that he would move on, Horst would leave the house after breakfast and not return until after dark. Steve was instructed to stay inside and to maintain a simple fire in the cook-stove, adding just small amounts of wood, enough to keep the kitchen warm, but not enough to alert a passerby who might see fresh smoke coming from the chimney. A fire in the fireplace would be built after Horst came back to the house.

Steve tried to keep himself busy and not bored while waiting for Horst to come home. He invented some crossword puzzles and, in addition, used a small piece of wood to carve the shape of what looked to be a shark or perhaps a dolphin. Steve figured that both the carving and puzzles could easily and quickly be disposed of in the cook-stove fire, if the need arose. They would burn right away.

A few days had passed with no word about the next phase of Steve's journey. Horst preached that Steve must be patient and he understood this, but the waiting was difficult. Finally, one evening after dinner as Horst and Steve sat in the formal room rocking chairs before a warm, roaring fire, Horst brought up the subject.

"Let me pour you some more Calvados," said Horst as he freshened Steve's glass and refilled his own. "You seem to like it. Then we will speak of your future."

"This is good, but I thought it was cognac," answered Steve as he bent a little forward in his rocking chair, very interested, of course, in the next step of his journey.

Horst handed the bottle of Pere Magloire VSOP Calvados to Steve. "Calvados is an apple brandy from France and is from the region of Normandy," stated Horst. "It is traditional in that part of France. Since you might be visiting that region, I wish you to be acquainted with it. They make good goat cheese too," and he gave out a hearty laugh.

"Am I to leave soon?" questioned Steve, who did not ask more about the goat cheese.

"Well, you will travel in two, maybe three, days at the most," was Horst's reply. "Arrangements are being made for your clothing. You will be able to keep your warm underwear, my friend, but soon you will take on the look of a local working man. We will disguise you. You must not shave for a while because we want you to grow a beard, not too messy, but one that makes you belong to us and not the look of an American pilot. But for now, my friend, we will not place any more wood on the fire because I am tired and soon it will be time to sleep."

CHAPTER SEVEN

I n Kissimmee, Florida, half a world away, Steve's dad came out onto the porch of the ranch house as an olive-drab 1942 four-door Army Ford drove into the farmyard. Three uniformed Army men emerged from the car. Ray Carmichael recognized one of the men as Sergeant McConnell, the recruiting sergeant from Orlando. With him was a major. The third man, who was the driver, stayed by the car.

"Gentlemen, come into the house," said Ray and his voice cracked a little. "I see you have a telegram for me." "Mr. Carmichael, we don't believe that Steve's been killed," said Sergeant McConnell in his best reassuring tone. Ray asked them to sit down; then, he quietly opened the envelope containing the dreaded telegram.

Lillian, who had been in the kitchen, came to the doorway of the living room. She said nothing, but the look on her face spoke volumes.

Ray's mouth and jaw tightened as he prepared to read the telegram, which at the top in large printed words stated Western Union. The telegram showed that it had come from the government, Washington, D.C., the date and time stamp showed *Orlando, 10 December 1943, 8:44 a.m.* Also listed was the address of the ranch. Then came the body of the telegram, and Ray carefully read each word:

> *The Secretary Of War Desires Me To Express His Deep Regret That Your Son Captain Steven W Carmichael Has Been Reported Missing In Action Since One December 1943 In The European Area If Further Details Or Other Information Are Received You Will Be Promptly Notified.*
>
> *– The General Adjutant*

Ray sat back in his chair, took a deep breath and asked, "What's next? Where do we go from here?"

The major spoke first. "Your son was the pilot of a Pathfinder B-17," he said. "He was on loan to that special group from the 305th Bomb Group. It was his 25th mission, we understand. His ship was hit by flak, anti-aircraft fire. The wing, I'm not sure which one, became engulfed in flames and then the plane was fired upon by German fighters. Several crewmen bailed out and were captured by the Germans, east of the city of Aachen, Germany. The city is located on the German–Dutch border. Your son and two other crew members are missing. The plane crashed in Holland, near Maastricht. It is possible that as the aircraft commander, he was the last to leave the plane and could be in Holland, but this is, of course, speculation. We have no other word right now."

Lillian, who had been listening, started to cry softly.

Ray got up from his chair and went over to her. "If there's a way for him to escape, he'll do it," said Ray. "Do us a favor and put on some coffee for these gentlemen." Then he gave Lillian a hug, knowing that her concern was almost as strong as his.

"I agree with you, Mr. Carmichael," said Sergeant McConnell as he tried to bring some cheer into the conversation. "Steve must surely be in Holland and in hiding. The Underground looks to help American fliers when they can."

"The last letter that I received from Steve said that he's now a captain and had a special assignment," Ray said. "This boy is one hell of a flier and I'm sure he is alive. I feel it!" He then motioned for the men to come into the dining room for coffee and some coffee cake that Lillian had baked yesterday.

There was some lighter conversation while they talked at the dining room table. The major Ray now called Major Carter. He may have said his name when they first came into the house, but Ray didn't hear it because when he received the telegram, names were not what he was paying attention to. Major Carter promised, as they left the ranch house, to obtain as much additional information as he could and to keep an open dialogue with Sergeant McConnell and Ray.

They shook hands by the Army car after Ray walked out with them and thanked them, especially Sergeant McConnell, for coming out to break the news in person. The men had already climbed into the car when down the lane came the rural delivery mailman.

"Hello, Ray, got some mail and one from overseas . . . one of those V-Mail letters," said the mailman as he handled a small bundle of mail to Ray.

"Go inside and have some fresh coffee," said Ray. "Lillian also has some coffee cake. I'll be there in a few minutes."

Ray then put the bundle of mail on the steps of the porch and started to open the V-Mail, which to his surprise was from First Lieutenant Howard Van Dyke.

By this time, both Sergeant McConnell and Major Carter had gotten back out of the car and were standing next to Ray as he opened the V-Mail from Howie. The words were heartwarming; Howie saw Steve's plane go down and was certain that he saw Steve leave the burning ship over Dutch territory. Ray continued to read that the area was farmland and not a city. Howie, it seemed by his letter, felt that there was a good chance that Steve could evade the Germans. If nothing else, it gave Ray hope.

As the Army car drove back down the lane, Ray walked back into the ranch house to share the letter from Howie with Lillian.

Back in Chelveston, England, at the 305th Bomb Group, Howie had hoped to obtain a three-day pass to London. He wanted to see Elizabeth and spend time with Maggie as he tried to keep her spirits up with more than a telephone call. The trip to London was not to be. The 305th had other plans, which would include Howie and the crew of *Pappy's Pack*. A mission, which would be Howie's 27th, needed to be flown. It called for a maximum effort, which meant that all available aircraft would be at the ready. The target was designated as Emden, Germany. For *Pappy's Pack*, it would be a return trip to the heavily fortified coastal area port city. Missions number 15 and 16 on September 27th and October 2nd had been raids on Emden. The mission flight path called for the long trip over the North Sea. With this being an all-out effort, close to 600 B-17s and B-24 heavy bombers would participate in the raid. They would meet up with just under 400 escort American and British fighters, who would work to protect the bomber stream from the Luftwaffe. The sky would be filled with Allied planes.

After the long, over-the-water trip, the target was approached. The Germans, knowing that the bomber stream was headed toward Emden, covered the target area with a heavy, dense smoke screen. The target was, for the most part, obscured. Small peeks through the cover permitted bombing. This was not intended to be a Pathfinder mission, but to be bombed through visual sightings. Even though a fair amount of bombs fell harmlessly out of the designated target area, most did find their mark and brought heavy damage to the docks, harbor area and rail junction. The hope for each of the participating planes was that enough damage through the maximum effort had been accomplished, so that a return trip would be put off for quite a while.

Pappy's Pack had fared well under the circumstances. During the debriefing interrogation, the crew of *Pappy's Pack* reported that while flak had been lighter than expected, at least for their group it had been pretty accurate at their flight level. Four small holes had ripped into the ship's skin. Two pieces of flak about the size of a prune had hit just behind Eddie Anderson's head in the radio compartment, making it a bit drafty, according to Eddie. He did also mention that he just about jumped out of his skin when he saw how close the holes were from his noggin! The experience was close enough to where Eddie thought he might have needed a change of underwear. The other two holes were above Joey DeMatteo's tail gunner position. They did not pose a problem and Joey said that he was unaware that the flak had hit the ship until they were on the ground. Flak explosions were going on all around them with tremendous noise, plus showers of flak particles and dust were being sprayed all over the sky.

The 305th was very lucky on this Tuesday because they had all planes return home. The fighter escort had kept the enemy at bay. Other groups in the long formation had not fared as well as the 305th. In the action above Emden, 22 ships had been lost to direct flak hits and German fighters. This included mostly B-17s, but three B-24s had also been shot down.

After the mission, a day of "catch up" would take place before the next mission occurred. Howie was able to reach Elizabeth by telephone, but it took four attempts before he was able to speak with her at St. Thomas' Hospital in London. They managed a short conversation while Elizabeth was on duty. Elizabeth stated that Margaret, or Maggie, had secured permission to visit her parents in Sandown, on the Isle of Wight. Normally no one had been permitted to enter or leave the Isle of Wight, the island that lay just six short miles off the coast and the huge Portsmouth Naval Base. However, through a family friend who was a councilman for the Isle of Wight, a special grant had been obtained. Margaret would return to London and her duty at St. Thomas' Hospital just after Boxing Day, the 26th of December.

Steve remained with Horst in Eijsden. Horst informed him that while he thought that Steve would be moving on to the next phase of his journey in just a couple of days, the exact date could not be confirmed. Sometimes circumstances changed arrangements. In Steve's case, which took very careful planning, a snag had occurred, which meant putting off his departure from Horst's house. A British Lancaster bomber had been shot down near Liege, Belgium. Since Liege was the place where Steve coincidentally would go next, plans were placed on hold.

The Lancaster had crash-landed after a direct hit by flak. The big four-engine British bomber became engulfed in flames, which lit up the night sky. The crew managed to escape the burning plane and most were captured as they touched the ground, still in their parachutes. However, it was reported later in the night, that two of the British aviators were still at large. With the German Army searching the Liege area for the missing airmen, it was not, of course, safe to move Steve from Horst's home.

Horst, it seemed, was just as glad that Steve would be his guest a little while longer. He had become fond of his American visitor. That night they relaxed before the warmth of the roaring fire in the formal room fireplace. To hear the conversation, you might think that they were lifelong friends. Horst had also secured two more bottles of Pere Magloire VSOP Calvados through a business friend who was able to travel in parts of the Netherlands, Belgium and France. The friend was also much more than just a businessman. This particular man could, through special papers, travel fairly freely. The man had helped Jews escape the inevitable, as well as British and American airmen who found themselves deep behind the lines in enemy-controlled territory. The identity of the individual was not to be spoken about and Horst did not know if Steve would eventually meet him personally or be passed along through a network of people who would remain strangers.

Several more days passed before Horst came home one evening with news that clothing for Steve had been obtained and that he would move to the outskirts of Liege in two nights or two days. It was still to be determined if the move would be made in broad daylight or deep into the night.

As the two sat in the formal room before the warmth of the fireplace on the cold December evening, glass of Calvados in hand after a hearty dinner of large pork chops, Horst opened the conversation with, "The beard is growing nicely on your face. It will help disguise you."

"It certainly feels strange," answered Steve. "I wish I had a photograph so that my father could see how I look."

"You will have the photograph," stated Horst and he gave a hearty laugh. "Tomorrow, we will take your picture so that it can be applied to your papers. You will be dressed in your new clothes and look like a Dutchman."

"This sounds just fine," said Steve. "Will I have a different name on the papers?" asked Steve.

"Of course, both names will be changed and you will use them . . . remember them in the event that you are stopped for inspection," replied Horst.

Steve took a sip of his Calvados and changed the subject for the moment. "Those pork chops were outstanding, delicious. I enjoyed them so much, but I do not like to take special food from you. I know how hard it is to come by."

"It is not a problem," was the answer from Horst. "Let us just say that I have some special contacts. I help many and they like to return the favor. One day, when you return to see me, I will explain."

"I will ask no more questions," stated Steve.

"Well, you can ask all of your questions," replied Horst. "I just may not be able to give you an answer for all of them."

"I understand," said Steve with Horst nodding his head.

"Now you and I will make a trade," said Horst as he reached into his vest pocket and pulled out a well-worn pocket watch.

"A trade, my American watch for a Dutch-looking pocket watch," said Steve, as he completely understood why such a trade needed to be done.

"This is a nice timepiece," said Horst as he accepted Steve's wristwatch. "What brand do you call it in America?"

"It's a Hamilton," replied Steve. "My dad gave it to me when I graduated from high school. The Hamilton Watch Company is from Lancaster, Pennsylvania."

"You and I can trade back after this damn war is concluded," said Horst. "I will hide it in a safe place in this house. I must warn you, though, I will not be winding the timepiece every day," as he let out a large belly laugh at the joke he just made. He then refilled Steve's glass and, after a short pause, handed his glass to Steve to hold while Horst placed another log on the fire and stoked them to bring out more flame.

They sat before the fire, neither saying anymore, but just enjoying each other's company and the warmth of the flames. It was about a half hour later when Horst and Steve decided that they were both tired and it was time to head upstairs to get a night's sleep.

The following day just after noon, a loud knock on the back door brought an old lady who had a well-worn hemp bag with her, from which she produced a camera. Horst placed a blanket over a cabinet so that when the photo was made, no one could trace the picture to Horst's kitchen. Steve had changed into the clothes Horst provided the night before and looked nothing like an American airman. His beard was somewhat neat, but not so neat that he looked groomed. Horst also provided Steve with a fisherman-type beret. Satisfied that Steve looked the way Horst wanted him to, the picture was taken. Then, just as she had come, the old lady was gone. Papers would be produced and Steve would be provided with a new identification.

Horst took down the blanket and said to Steve, "Now, let me tell you the name you must learn. It will be you until you reach England. Your name is Paul Reens. We have decided that you are not Dutch, my friend, but from Vise, Belgium. Vise is the first town you will pass through as you travel toward Leige. It is on the frontier of the Netherlands and Belgium."

"Paul Reens, okay . . . it will not be a difficult name to remember . . . Paul Reens," answered Steve as he slowly shook his head up and down. Steve also thought about all of the trouble people were going through in order to keep him safely out of German hands.

Horst, in a firm voice, said to Steve, "Traveling will be a little easier if you are perhaps a truck driver's helper. This way, even with papers from Belgium, you could have a reason to be in France. Also, my friend, it is best if while you are with the truck that you act and look like a deaf mute. This way you and the driver will be much safer. He will do the talking if you are stopped by the Germans for an inspection. They usually will not bother a poor, simple-acting person. But remember, the German soldiers are not stupid. You must completely fool them. Otherwise, it will not be good for you or the driver. They may well shoot you right then. This is not your Hollywood."

"I understand," answered Steve. He knew this was serious business.

"Your papers will be here tonight and your journey will begin very early in the morning," stated Horst. "You might be in Liege tomorrow night or maybe some other place. I am not to know anymore about where you are or where you are going. That way I can never give any information about you if I am confronted."

"Well, my friend, Horst, there is no way that I can thank you enough, except to give you one million thanks, but one day I will show you my great appreciation for everything you have done for me," stated Steve.

"As I have told you before, no thank you is required, but I do want you to keep your promise to visit me sometime in the future," answered Horst.

It was much later in the evening, after Horst and Steve had finished supper and were enjoying a glass of Calvados in front of an inviting fire in the formal room's fireplace, that their conversation was interrupted by four fairly loud knocks at the back door.

Horst told Steve to stay where he was. There was no reason to hide because the four knocks at the back door were expected. Horst then got up from his rocking chair and answered the door. He was there for only a few short minutes. Muffled conversation could be heard, but since it was in Dutch, Steve did not understand what was said.

After speaking with the visitor, Horst came back into the formal room with Steve's papers. Steve was now officially Paul Reens from Vise, Belgium. Steve did not see the visitor. Horst explained that while the visitor would have liked to meet Steve, it was best for all concerned if that did not happen.

Horst reviewed the papers with Steve. Not satisfied that the papers looked as they should from the standpoint of wear, Horst took some coffee grounds and roughed up the papers with them. He also folded them and put them into his pocket, and he even stepped on them with his shoes. Horst also had Steve rehearse how to present the papers and how to act if he was stopped by a German soldier or by the Gestapo at a checkpoint. Finally, it was off to bed. The early morning departure would come soon enough.

Steve slept quite soundly despite the anticipation of the next stage of his escape to England. It could have been the Calvados or his confidence in Horst. He had even produced a map of the Netherlands, Belgium and France to impress the distance that must be conquered. The realizations of the difficulties that lay ahead were quite evident. Horst said that he knew very well that Steve was an intelligent man and that all emotions must be controlled. Horst went on to say that, Steve was to worry just one day at a time, it was easier on the nerves that way.

A gentle shaking brought Steve out of a deep sleep. He was to dress and come down to the kitchen for some breakfast. Steve noted as Horst left the bedroom that in slightly pulling the curtain back and looking through the window, outside, it was still dark.

As Horst descended the stairs, he called back to Steve, "Just push your hair back, do not comb it. You will be wearing the fisherman's cap and, of course, do not shave. You will look like hell and this is good." The thought of it let Horst laugh aloud.

"Terrific," said Steve under his breath, but he also had to smile as he looked into the bedroom mirror.

In just a few minutes, Steve came down to the kitchen. Horst motioned for him to take a seat at the table and poured him coffee. Horst then placed a dish in front of Steve that contained a hearty breakfast of three eggs, cheese and two large slices of dark bread.

"This will fill you up," said Horst as he placed his plate on the table and poured himself a second cup of coffee. "You may not eat again until supper as a regular meal, but I will give you something to share with the driver as you journey on your way today." He looked at Steve's coffee mug, saw that it was still half full and started to place the coffee pot back onto the cook-stove, however, he stopped and came back to the table and filled Steve's cup. "I top it off, as you Americans say!" said Horst.

Horst then sat down and joined Steve for breakfast. There was no conversation as the two ate, but in looking across at the big man seated on the other side of the table, Steve's thoughts were of how fortunate he had been to come into contact with Horst.

That thought and breakfast ended as the sound of a truck engine broke the silence. Horst looked up, then got up from the table, coffee cup in hand, and pulled back the dark curtain to peer out of the kitchen window.

"It is time to go," Horst said. "Finish up while I go outside and talk to the driver. Bring that sack with you when you come outside," as he pointed to a large hemp-type sack at the end of the table.

Steve finished his coffee, got up from the kitchen table and put on the coat and fisherman's cap that was supplied to him by the Underground friends. Once outside, Steve walked over to Horst and gave the big man a bear hug. It was hard for Steve to say anything as he tried to say goodbye to Horst.

"We will meet again," said Horst as he walked Steve toward the passenger's door of the truck.

The truck was piled high with hay, which had been stored in a barn. The truck was old and much of the original paint either was worn or had just rusted away. The engine had a sound something like the old 1931 Ford that Steve's dad, Ray, had refused to sell because, for some reason, Ray considered it a good luck truck. This engine had that same whistle to it. Well, it was running!

Horst stopped Steve and said, "You have your papers. Remember what we spoke about, my friend. The driver knows that your name is Paul. He also knows to do all of the talking at checkpoints. You are not to ask him his name or anything else. This is for the protection of both of you. He will drive you, and only on this day will you be with him. He will take you to a safe house for tonight and from that house, you may leave soon or perhaps later. It will be determined by each group as you journey on to your destination. Okay, my friend, good luck." Horst then opened the passenger side door of the truck, shook hands with Steve, said something to the driver in Dutch and closed the door.

The driver nodded and answered Horst in understanding. He then smiled and nodded his head to Steve. Steve smiled back but did not say anything. The truck then started out of Horst's long driveway and onto the road toward Steve's new hometown of Vise, Belgium, as Paul Reens.

The drive through the countryside to Vise was uneventful. Neither Steve, now Paul, nor the driver said anything. It was a silent drive, except for the whistle of the truck engine. However, as they approached the Netherlands–Belgium frontier, a checkpoint came into sight.

Steve tensed up in seeing that several German soldiers, rifles at the ready, manned the border crossing between the Netherlands and Belgium. The driver reached over and patted Steve on the leg.

"It will be okay, no Gestapo here," said the driver. "Remember, I talk."

With the truck coming to a halt, the driver lowered his window and spoke a greeting to the approaching German soldier. The soldier said something to the driver. Steve, of course, did not understand what was being said, but saw that the driver was handing his papers to the soldier. The soldier then stood up onto the running board of the truck in order to get a look at Steve. He said something, but Steve continued to look out of the front window of the truck. The soldier then said something else to the driver, who answered then motioned to Steve that the soldier wanted to see his papers. Steve shook his head, reached into his coat pocket, and produced the papers for the waiting soldier. The papers had a well-worn look about them. The German soldier then took both sets of papers into the border hut for inspection. In the meantime, three other German soldiers came toward the truck with pitchforks. They stabbed well into the pile of hay from both sides of the truck to be certain that no one was hiding in the hay. The soldiers then went into the hut. It was just a few minutes, but to Steve it seemed like an eternity. Finally, the soldier who had taken the papers returned and gave both sets to the driver. The border gate was lifted and a soldier motioned for them to proceed.

It was clear that Steve was relieved to be leaving the border area and the checkpoint. The driver, of course, had to smile and note that Steve was now a little more relaxed.

"Everything okay. You did okay," said the driver as they made their way through the town of Vise.

The building that stood out to Steve as they drove through the town was the Hotel De Ville, which had a classic look to it and seemed very inviting. The somewhat scary thing, as they continued to drive on the narrow the streets of Vise, was that there were a good number of German soldiers walking about, and probably some of the German officers were living at the hotel. In addition, it was interesting for Steve to see the River Meuse from the riverbank. It was not too long ago that he and his crew had flown over the river and saw it from 31,000 feet in a Boeing B-17 bomber.

After leaving Vise, the driver continued along the river road toward the town of Herstal, which was on the outskirts of Liege. With Liege being a fairly large city and one that would certainly be a stronghold for German soldiers, Steve wondered if this would be their stopping point for the day or would they try to go around? Horst said to worry one day at a time. It seemed to Steve that to worry one town at a time was more accurate.

As they continued riding in the truck loaded with hay, the driver informed Steve that fairly soon they would be crossing a bridge over the River Meuse in order to drive through the town of Herstal. There surely would be another checkpoint at the bridge, so they would need to follow exactly as they did at the last checkpoint and all would work out all right.

With the bridge in sight, Steve took a deep breath and slowly let it out. It was just about the same thing he would do to relax himself when he was back at college and in the batter's box facing a tough baseball pitcher. This situation, as it unfolded, would need him to be relaxed enough to once again pull off his new identity.

Steve noted, as the truck was being brought to a halt at the checkpoint, that there was an island in the middle of the River Meuse, which was off to his right. He looked at what seemed to be a hidden military installation and made a mental note. The initial routine was pretty much the same as the Netherlands–Belgium frontier checkpoint. A soldier came to the driver's side of the truck, requested both men's papers and then disappeared into a small concrete blockhouse that served as the checkpoint headquarters. In the meantime, four soldiers poked their rifle-fixed bayonets into the hay. Unlike the more country setting of the last checkpoint, these soldiers did not have pitchforks.

The soldier who seemed to be in charge returned to the truck with the papers. He then spoke something to Steve, who pretended not to hear and continued to stare out of the front windshield with a blank look on his face.

The four German soldiers who had poked into the hay now gathered at the cab of the truck, two on each side with their rifles at the ready. Steve was about to be pulled out of the truck when the driver intervened and explained about his helper's medical condition.

The driver was then ordered out of the truck and taken into the blockhouse. The soldier in charge and two others went with the driver while the two soldiers stayed by the truck to guard Steve. One soldier had moved to the other side of the truck in case Steve tried to escape through the driver's door. While his heart was pounding, Steve worked hard to play his role.

Inside the blockhouse, an officer who was sitting behind a desk confronted the driver. The papers were handed to the officer and he looked them over once again, this time scrutinizing them slowly. The driver simply stood quietly and had a quizzical look on his face. After all, they only had some animal feed on the truck. Finally, the officer spoke and asked why would the driver have a handicapped man as his helper. The answer the driver gave, which seemed to satisfy the officer, was that the boy's father was the owner of the truck and wanted his son to feel that he was worth something.

Satisfied, the officer gave the papers back to the driver. The driver walked to the truck, climbed in and started the engine. He did not look at Steve, but simply put the truck in gear and waited for the barrier post to be lifted so that they could proceed. All of the motions were noted by the soldier in charge of the four guards. He was keeping an eye on the driver to see if he spoke to Steve. In a couple of minutes, he raised his right hand telling the guards that it was all right to lift the gate. The truck started out very slowly and crossed over the bridge.

After they were out of sight of the checkpoint, the driver said to Steve, "You did okay again . . . good."

Steve just nodded his head. He quietly thought to himself that the past half an hour almost called for a change of underwear. Here he was, well behind enemy lines, seeing German ground troops everywhere and so far having to pass through two well-guarded army checkpoints. It certainly was a test for keeping his nerves under control.

Driving through Herstal, a relatively small town, presented no additional problems. Steve keenly observed his surroundings, in hopes of relaying some intelligence when he returned to England. In Herstal, the Cathedral of St. Paul was a noted landmark. It was a beautiful and quite important church for the people of this area and Steve hoped it would not be damaged by the war. What did surprise Steve was seeing armed German soldiers walking the streets and that the locals simply went about their daily routine. They looked to be unaffected by the occupation. Perhaps the soldiers did not want to unnecessarily interfere with the lives of the Belgian citizens, which would have made occupation quite difficult.

It was not long before they entered the city of Liege. The driver kept the truck at a slow and steady city street pace. For now, they drew no particular attention, which is exactly how it was planned.

Steve noticed that there was another island in the River Meuse as they continued the trek through Liege and the island also contained what looked like a military installation. As they drove past the Liege train station , there were a good number of soldiers around. Here, a truck loaded with hay was drawing some attention and Steve was not so sure that they would make it through Liege without being stopped for another inspection. A truck full of hay is not the usual vehicle that would be traveling the city streets, but so far, so good. Steve would wave at the soldier who was taking a second look at the truck and most waved back.

Then, just as the driver turned a corner, a German vehicle about the size of an American Jeep pulled in front of the truck and motioned for the driver to bring the truck to a halt. Three of the four soldiers got out of the vehicle. One asked to see their papers while the second and third soldiers stood by each side of the truck with their rifles in hand. The rifles were not pointed at the driver or Steve, but the soldiers certainly seemed ready in case there was trouble. The papers were presented to the officer, who remained in the vehicle. The soldier returned to speak with the driver, wanting to know why a truck loaded with hay was being shipped so far from Vise. The answer that satisfied them was that a relative lived near the town of Saint-Nicolas and that both the hay and the deaf mute were being delivered. The truck owner wanted to have his boy work on the farm and become useful.

The German Jeep moved on and so did the truck. The driver once again had fooled an inspecting group of soldiers. They continued driving slowly, proceeding through the streets of Liege, and were now headed toward the small but very crowded city of Saint-Nicolas.

The driver, who continued to look straight out of the windshield and not at all at Steve, quietly, just above a whisper, informed Steve that they would stop at a small farm near Saint-Nicolas. It would be a safe house. The hay would be off-loaded there so that the truck would not be spotted driving around the countryside and create suspicion with the Germans. Cover integrity must be maintained for the Underground and the people who risked their lives for the cause.

The truck approached a dirt lane located on the right side of a two-lane paved road. Grass was growing in the middle of the dirt lane. The tires had to travel in deep ruts on the road, which would make for a rough ride. The driver slowed the truck to a crawl and leaned forward, as far as he could to peer out over the steering wheel and out through the windshield to be certain that nothing appeared out of the normal routine on the farm. Everything looked okay as the turn onto the lane was made. The truck proceeded down the lane slowly and instead of coming to a halt in front of the house, the driver drove straight to the barn. This would look more normal in case someone was spying on the farm's activity.

The driver climbed down from the truck, as did Steve. Both walked toward the back of the truck. They started to loosen the ropes that held the hay in place on the truck bed. A man came out of the back door of the house and walked over to greet them. He spoke only to the driver. He motioned to them and they all walked into the barn.

"May I see your papers?" the farmer asked Steve in relatively good English.

Steve presented the papers, which contained his photo and the name Paul Reens, but he did not speak.

The papers were quickly but thoroughly examined. The farmer handed them back to Steve and reached out to shake hands with Steve. "You are welcome here and we thank you as an American airman for your service fighting the Germans. We will try hard to help you escape the Gestapo and get you to your final destination."

"I thank all of you people for your help, it is greatly appreciated," answered Steve.

The farmer smiled, nodded his head and then said, "We will take the hay from the truck and place it in the barn. This should be done without conversation. Then we all will go into my house."

The three, pitchforks in hand, quickly off-loaded the truck, placing the hay up in the loft above the barn where it would be kept dry. Steve, to the surprise of the other men, worked with very good precision and actually moved more hay bales than the others. Ever since he was a little boy, Steve handled hay on the ranch in Florida. Steve was enjoying himself and it showed.

When they were finished, the driver parked the truck and the three walked at a normal pace to the back door of the farmhouse. Steve and the driver followed the farmer into the large farm kitchen. A good-sized table was in the middle of the room, which to Steve seemed like it would be used to feed the farm workers. The large cook-stove, like the one in Horst's home, also served to warm the kitchen. It felt good for Steve to get out of the cold, gray December afternoon and into a cozy, warm room.

The farmer motioned for the two to sit down at the table. He took three mugs out of the cupboard and poured fresh coffee. The farmer also placed some bread and cheese on the table.

"Later we can have some wine with supper, but for now the coffee will warm us," said the farmer as he sat down and joined Steve and the driver.

"The coffee tastes very good, nice and strong," said Steve as he took a sip from his mug.

The driver was not so sure about it being that strong, but he did not complain.

"We shall not speak of anything about you until the man who drove you here has left," said the farmer. "This is for his protection as well as yours. When we have finished with the coffee, I will walk him out to the truck and he will be gone. I do not know how long you will be here, but it must not be long. That is all I can say right now."

A short time later, the farmer wrapped up some cheese and bread for the driver. He also gave him a bottle of beer for the trip home. Then the driver and Steve shook hands. Steve thanked the driver, and then the farmer walked him out to the truck. In no time, the truck was back up the lane and out of sight. The farmer then came back into the house.

He and Steve went into a sitting room where there was a small fire in the fireplace. The farmer placed a couple of logs on the fire, stoked it and sat down on a chair near Steve.

"I have sent my wife to be with her sister for two days," said the farmer. "This way she will not see you and cannot speak of you in the event that the Germans come to the farm. You will be here tonight and then you will move on to the next safe house. We must keep a step ahead of the people who are on the alert to track down our visitors. On one of your stops you may have to stay more than a few days, but we will do our best to take care of you."

Steve expressed his gratitude. "You are welcome, my new friend," answered the farmer, as he spoke in his best English. "I wish you could stay for a few days. You are a good, strong worker."

The two continued their conversation for more than an hour. Then, as the farmer saw that Steve became tired, he took him to a small, sparsely furnished bedroom on the second floor of the farmhouse. He suggested that with the supper being perhaps two hours from now, some good rest was necessary. The farmer went on to say that he would come up for Steve when the supper was ready to be served.

Left alone in the small bedroom, Steve walked over to the window and peered out over the countryside. It took on a slightly different look when viewed from the second story of the farmhouse. Then, Steve dropped onto the bed, quite exhausted, and in no time he was sound asleep.

The farmer softly knocked on the door and then opened it. Steve looked over to the farmer who had just entered the room then quickly sat up.

"It is okay, come down for supper," reassured the farmer.

Steve came down the steps, but paused before taking the final two steps as the outline of two men came into focus. He was surprised to see others in the kitchen and did not know what to expect.

The farmer, seeing that Steve was a little uneasy and suspicious, quickly introduced the two men, not by name, but that they were friends who would help him continue his journey.

Now, more relaxed, the four enjoyed the evening meal along with some very delicious Belgian beer the new friends brought. They talked well into the night, with most questions centering around the topic of what was it like to live in America and were all Americans rich as they have heard?

Steve did his best to speak about how America was put together; that it consisted of 48 individual states, which formed the United States of America. He further explained that just about each individual state was perhaps the size of certain European countries. For example, New York State was near the size of Germany; the Netherlands was about the size of New Jersey; and that England, Scotland and Wales were not quite as large as the state of California. The state he was from, Florida, might just be almost the size of Italy.

Steve also pointed out that to the north of the United States was Canada and that with Mexico, they combined to make up North America. He thought about explaining how Alaska, Hawaii and Puerto Rico figured into all of this, but determined that might be better for another time. Steve loved geography, but it was getting quite late and those territories along with Central and South America would have to wait.

Just before dawn, Steve was awakened by a gentle knock on his bedroom door. The farmer told Steve that he was to get ready as quickly as possible. There would be a hearty breakfast and then Steve would leave and be in the care of the two men.

It did not take long for Steve to be ready. He washed his face in the bowl of water on the dresser and then carefully left the house for the short trip to the outhouse.

Breakfast was indeed a hearty meal. The farmer had prepared fresh eggs with pork bacon, which to Steve was known as English or Canadian bacon rather than American bacon. In addition, there was some hot porridge and very strong coffee. The bread slices were cut from a large loaf. While the bread had a good fresh taste, the color was almost gray and did not look as appetizing as the bread back home. The taste of the bread improved with some delicious apple jelly.

After the morning feast, Steve and the farmer shook hands. They also gave each other a meaningful bear hug as both men said goodbye. They wished each other good luck and then Steve climbed into the truck with the two men, taking the middle seat position. He would now continue as the man who could not speak or hear. The two men said that if they were stopped, he could mumble a bit, but not in words, just soft sounds. The truck was smaller than the one Steve had arrived in. There was no cargo, just an empty truck bed behind the cab.

The story they were using was that they were on the way to the city of Dinant for work. The route would take them through the narrow country roads so perhaps they would not see or be confronted by the military. The route they were taking to Dinant also allowed them to avoid most known German checkpoints, at least that was the plan.

Steve took note of the town names as they passed through the villages of Jemeppe and Floree. On the road, which passed through Spontin, they stopped for a short time at the statue marked Natoye-Sacre Coeur. Local residents were placing fresh flowers at the base of the statue. The two men said something that Steve did not understand and then blessed themselves with the sign of the cross. Steve stood silently near the men and when they were finished, Steve simply gave a slight bow and crossed himself as he had seen the others do. Even though there were other people there, no one seemed to look or acknowledge each other. Perhaps war does this!

They continued on driving through the town of Thynes. Then, finally, in the late afternoon, Steve spotted the sign that stated that they were in the city of Dinant, a very old town located on the River Meuse.

Entering the city of Dinant, two prominent features stood out. Above the city center on a cliff, which seemed to be about 100 meters high, stood what looked to Steve to be an old citadel. Below on the river level stood a magnificent example of an old church.

There had been very little conversation during the truck ride. Every once in a while one of the men would say something to the other, but in a language that Steve did not understand. They had not spoken to Steve. He figured that perhaps they did not want him to get into the habit of talking, since he was told not to speak. In addition, Steve understood that those working in and for the Underground really, for the most part, did not want to be remembered by those they helped. It was better that way and they could continue to help if operations were anonymous and kept low key.

The drive from the farm was quite uneventful. By taking the old, narrow, local roads the trip was a little longer; however, what they wanted is what occurred. They ran into no checkpoints or German soldiers.

Finally, the driver turned to Steve and spoke. They had just driven up a narrow street, almost an alley behind the church.

"The fifth house from the cathedral is where you will knock softly four times on the back door," stated the driver. "They are expecting four knocks and no more or no less. They will answer the door and you will go in very quickly. We will stop the truck just long enough for you to get out. We wish you good luck—no more talk."

The truck stopped at the third house. Quickly, the passenger door opened and

Steve slid past the man sitting by the door. The man gave Steve a pat on the shoulder as he left the truck and Steve gave a fast handshake of thanks. The truck then continued down the narrow street, turned a corner and was gone. There was complete silence, no noise at all, except the distant sound of a dog barking. It was a strange feeling.

Steve looked around, counted the houses and noticed that the fifth house, if this was the correct one, was much narrower than the ones on either side. The fifth house almost had the look of being squeezed in between two already existing houses. It also was at least three stories high, maybe four.

Steve walked swiftly to the fifth house and gently knocked on the back door four times. In just a moment, but to Steve it seemed a lifetime, the door opened. An older lady motioned for him to enter the house with haste.

"Welcome . . . come with me," said the thin, frail-looking, white-haired woman.

"Thank you," answered Steve as he quickly stepped inside.

The old woman did not say anything more, but led Steve through the basement and to a staircase, which brought them up to the first living level. The lady then took Steve into what was obviously the formal living room.

"Good evening," said a tall, stately man who appeared to be in his late 50s or perhaps he was past 60. A large hand was extended and Steve reached to shake hands.

"Thank you for your help," stated Steve as he felt a genuine welcome through the firm handshake.

"Let's relax with a drink," said the man in a soft voice as he gestured for Steve to follow him. "Come into my sitting room where I keep my whisky."

They walked from the formal living room to a room that to Steve seemed to be a combination of what he knew as a den and office. It reminded him of his dad's den at home. There was a solid-looking, old, wooden desk with a large, comfortable chair behind it, plus two older-looking leather chairs that Steve would call overstuffed chairs. The room itself had a warm feel about it. Books lined the shelves against the far wall.

"We will have some supper in a little while, but for now we can enjoy a whisky," Steve's host said. "I have saved a few bottles from the years before the war when I was a businessman who traveled to London and up as far as Scotland. A favorite town in Scotland where I did business was Oban. They have a distillery there, which is located below a cliff of what looks like the beginning of a Roman Theater on that hill. The whisky, you Americans spell it with an 'e,' whiskey, is quite aged. Sit there." The man pointed to one of the leather chairs for Steve to settle in.

Steve sat down. He was weary.

The man poured two meaningful glasses of Scotch whisky, handed one to Steve and sat down in the other leather chair. He saw that Steve was admiring the leather chairs.

"I bought these chairs at a London auction house and had them shipped here . . . in 1937, I think," said the man as he relaxed in his chair and raised his glass to Steve. "It is hard to go to one of those auctions and not be caught up in the atmosphere. The chairs to me seemed that they would complement my sitting room and the more I saw them here, the more I knew that a good purchase had been made."

"They certainly are comfortable," stated Steve as he also raised his glass in salute and took a sip of the Scotch whisky. It was a small sip of what is called "neat," without the ice, that Americans usually associate with American whiskey.

"My name is Henri," said the host as he took another sip. "As far as I am concerned, you are Paul Reens and we will leave it at that."

The old lady came into the room after first knocking on the open door. She brought some cheese and bread to accompany the drinks and conversation.

"It will be easier for you to call my sister Mother," said Henri as Steve stood up at the presence of a woman entering the room. Henri was pleased to see that Steve had the manners and good taste to stand as a lady came into the room.

"I am pleased to meet you," said Steve now that a formal introduction was made. He was uncertain exactly who the lady was that answered the door.

The old lady, now Mother, smiled, took hold of Steve's outstretched hand, squeezed it and left the room.

Steve then turned his attention to Henri and brought the conversation to the historical nature of the city of Dinant. "This seems to be a city with quite a history," he said. "I noticed the fort on the top of the hill, plus what looks to be a very old church."

"Yes, the Citadel was first built in the 11th century," Henri began. "A new section was added in the mid-16th century. Then the French burned and destroyed the Citadel in 1703. This happens in war, you know. What you see now is the modern Citadel, which was rebuilt in 1820 during the occupation of the Dutch. After this war is over, wars always end sometime, you must come back to Dinant and climb the 408 steps that are carved into the rocks. There is a beautiful view of the river and valley from the top. The city itself dates back to the seventh century. That is when official settlements began here. Now, we have a population of perhaps 10,000. The church is what we call the Cathedral of Notre Dame. It dates to the early 12th century, the 1100s. Think about that, my boy, this was close to 400 years before Columbus sailed his ships to America." With that statement, Henri took another sip of his Scotch whisky and reached for some cheese from the table between their two leather chairs.

"Wow. You are right, in America, we do not understand all of the history that has taken place around the world well before our country was discovered by the explorers. I also see that you have a large library. The book cases are full," said Steve as he glanced toward the bookshelves.

"Many of the books are in English," answered Henri. "Several are actually American books. Ernest Hemingway is a favorite author. And as a man, he is quite the adventurer. I like that about him. You are welcome to read any of the books while you are here. Speaking of that, you will be perhaps with us for a week, maybe more. It must be completely safe for all concerned before you are moved to your next destination."

"I understand and you have my sincere gratitude," stated Steve.

"We have a comfortable room for you and you will be safe here in the house," stated Henri. "One day I will show you the area as a traveling visitor, but for now, you must remain in the house. Often, when we have visitors, you must also remain out of sight. We think that they are all friends, but people do talk, even when they do not know that some things should be kept quiet. The bedroom that will be yours is on the top floor. It has a small window, which looks out on the street below and the river. You must be careful not to be seen if you look out. This is very important."

Steve shook his head in complete understanding, then remarked, "I noticed that a lot of the towns we drove through today looked to also be a lesson in history," as he took another small sip of Scotch and ate the bread and cheese.

"A town near here, Engis, is a very historical village," answered Henri. "In 1829, they found several skulls and bones of Neanderthal Man. So yes there are many history lessons in this area." He thought for a moment and then continued, "This city of Dinant is famous for one of the men born here. Adolphe Sax . . . you know of him . . . of course you know of him!"

"I don't think so," answered Steve as he searched his mind.

"Adolphe Sax, inventor of the—" started Henri and Steve joined in with the word, "saxophone!"

Steve had to smile and repeated, "Well, I'll be darned, the saxophone!"

"Ah, but the city has seen some very sad times," remarked Henri.

"In 1914, during the Great War, devastation came when the German Imperial Troops executed 674 inhabitants. My two uncles and one cousin were of those killed. To be sure, the Germans are not liked here in Dinant."

"I'm not too fond of them myself, fighting against them in this war," stated Steve as he slowly shook his head in almost disbelief as to why so many citizens would be murdered.

"Are you an aviator?" asked Henri.

"Yes, a pilot of the B-17 bomber," answered Steve. "I was shot down on my 25th bombing mission. At least two of my crew were killed and I believe that the Germans captured the others. I almost did not make it out of my burning aircraft. But, here I am, in your care." He then thought for a minute about the fate of his crewmen.

They talked for a little while longer with Steve telling Henri that his Scottish ancestral home was, in fact, Oban. Steve told Henri that he had flown over the city after he crossed the Atlantic Ocean and had flown low enough to see Dunollie Castle, probably scaring the local population. They also spoke about London, a favorite city of Henri's, and of the restaurants in London, some of which Steve had dined in, while in the city on military leave.

There was much to talk about, but it could wait, and after a while, Henri took Steve up three flights of steps to the top floor. There Henri showed Steve to a bedroom that was in what most would consider an attic. There were two dormer windows that looked out onto the street below, plus the River Muese and the shoreline on the other side of the river as Henri had stated. Once again, Henri cautioned Steve. These were dangerous times and no one must suspect that a person could be hiding in the house.

Steve would take all of the necessary precautions, which had to be addressed and adhered to for the safety of everyone. He was not about to do something stupid! He had, with the help of so many people in the Underground, come a long way from the day he was shot down. Still, there was a long and dangerous road that lay ahead before he would see England again.

Henri told Steve to sit on the edge of the bed, and while he stood, told Steve that there had been a break in security at the farm.

The Germans had been given a note telling them that perhaps they could find an American aviator staying there as a worker. When the German truck came to the farm, they found nothing; all signs of the American visitor had been erased. The farmer stated that he did not understand why the Germans had come to the farm, but that he indeed needed some help, so if they came across someone looking to work and a place to stay, send him to him. He gave the soldiers two large bushels of apples. Then satisfied that the note meant nothing, the officer in charge crumbled the paper and threw it on the ground after having searched the house plus the outbuildings. Finally, they drove back down the lane. The farmer then picked up the note and placed the crumpled paper in his pocket. The farmer would check signatures when he paid his help to try to determine if any of the writing matched the note. He must find out where the leak was and take care of things. The truck that took Steve had left the farm just one hour before the German soldiers arrived. It was a close call!

As Steve listened to Henri speak, it became apparent that Henri was much more than just informed about what was going on. Henri was probably a very important individual within the Underground. How, or why else, would Henri know so much about what had taken place just hours ago? Steve understood further why Henri was making certain that he be cautious.

Henri and Steve went back down to the sitting room, but were there just a short time when Mother announced that supper was ready. While they ate, Henri told Steve that he would become acquainted with some local specialties that Mother made. He went on to say that the flamiche is a favorite and a local version of quiche. In addition there was the couque, one of Europe's hard biscuits, which is like a cookie, honey sweetened and impressed with a special mold before baking. In fact, Steve could help Mother make them tomorrow to have with some afternoon tea. They would try to keep him busy and not bored while he waited for the next part of his journey.

Back in Chelveston, England, the 305th Bombardment Group continued to fly their assigned missions as weather permitted.

Howie and the crew of *Pappy's Pack* flew a mission to Bremen on December 16th. For Howie, Bob, and Russ, plus top turret gunner–flight engineer Jim McFarland, number 28 was now in the completed missions books. While no one on the ship was injured, the plane did sustain battle damage from both fighters and flak. Over 600 B-17s and B-24 flew the bombing raid on behalf of the Eighth Air Force.

The damage to *Pappy's Pack* consisted of a flak hole in the nose Plexiglas that made for a drafty ride home, plus more than 30 little tears in the skin of the plane due to close flak explosions. In addition, 11 much larger holes had been ripped through the fuselage by machine and cannon fire from attacking fighters. The most severe damage was just behind Eddie Anderson in the radio room. Cannon fire had come in on an angle, which ripped a large hole in the side and exited through the roof of the B-17. It was an extremely close call, not more than eight or nine inches from his head as it traveled through the roof and left the plane.

The narrow escape for Eddie marked his 30th mission. In addition, Joey DeMatteo, the right waist gunner turned tail gunner, and Jack Kowalski, the left waist gunner, also marked this as their 30th mission and a ticket home.

All three men told Howie that they would stay on and request permission to fly two additional missions, knowing that Howie, Bob, Russ, and Jim needed two more to complete their 30. Howie, however, thanked them but said that they had done their job and he did not want them to be exposed for two more missions. To make it to 30, under these extreme circumstances, was quite enough.

With Howie losing three very valuable crew members, this became the topic of conversation at the Officer's Club that evening. It was Thursday night, December 16th, 1943, a cold windy night, in which the fire in the fireplace certainly felt good. On this night, the 422nd Squadron flew a night leaflet mission to Hannover, Brussels, and Lille.

It had been 16 days since Steve was shot down. Even with him gone, Howie would not accept the thought that Steve had been captured or killed and had an empty chair placed at their table each time they came to the O-Club. In Steve's honor, Howie made certain that peanuts were at the table. You can call it superstition, but Howie maintained that little tradition. Howie's copilot, Carl Phillips, the young second lieutenant, sat on the other side of what would be Steve's chair.

"When do we get the word on replacements?" asked Bob.

"Good question. Answer . . . I don't know," replied Howie as he reached for a handful of peanuts. "But I do know that we have a three-day pass, so London, here we come!"

"When were you going to tell us?" questioned Bob.

"I just did . . . figured the news would go well if you had a pint in your hand," was Howie's reply.

"Okay, when does this little holiday start?" asked Russ.

"Well, it could have started tomorrow, but I asked if it could be put off a day so that we can take Eddie, Jack, and Joey out for a farewell dinner," said Howie. "They will be out of here in a couple of days. I figure that's the least we can do for them."

"Couldn't agree more," stated Russ.

Bob nodded his head.

Carl, who had a long way to go, thought it was a great idea; he would certainly chip in for the dinner and drinks.

Howie explained that he would take care of things and give half of the bill to Steve when he saw him, after all he was their first aircraft commander.

Howie went on to explain that just after he received word about the three-day pass, he telephoned their friend and driver Richard for the ride to Wellingbourgh's train station. All would come off in a day or so. It looked as though no one would be flying for a couple of days anyway, because a weather front would keep the planes on the ground. There was also the slight problem of patching ole *Pappy's Pack* once more, plus the number two engine had to be shut down just before they landed. It would need some looking into.

"Well, I hope that Catherine can make some time for me," stated Russ.

"I know, short notice, hope Emily can find some free time as well," added Bob, who paused for a moment, then continued, "I know that you'll see Elizabeth," as he nodded to Howie, "what about Maggie, ah Margaret?"

"She is back home . . . got special permission to return to the Isle of Wight," said Howie. "They have wartime restrictions, you know. Elizabeth said that Maggie will be visiting with her parents until the day after Christmas . . . Boxing Day."

"What about him?" kidded Russ as he looked over to Carl.

"I've already asked Elizabeth if she can find a nurse for an ugly ole kid who happens to be a flyboy," answered Howie.

"What about the Stafford Hotel? Can we get a couple of rooms?" questioned Bob.

"It's taken care of and Michael will meet our train as usual," was the reply from Howie.

"Well, as Howie said, London . . . here we come!" said Russ.

Across the Atlantic Ocean in Kissimmee, Florida, Steve's father, Ray, had no further information. Howie had mailed him a detailed letter in addition to the V-Mail. In the letter, Howie told Ray that he was quite certain that Steve was the last crewman to bail out of the burning ship. The Dutch were well known for helping American and British aviators, so he felt that Steve might well be in very good hands. Howie went on to say that he would stay in touch and not to get down. He knew Steve would come through okay. Ray nonetheless continued to worry about his son. He would worry until he had word that Steve was safe again.

For Steve, his worry was for his dad, whom he figured was not getting very much information. With using the name of Paul Reens, for now, Steven Carmichael did not exist. Steve wished that he could spend just five minutes with his dad to reassure him that he was being well cared for by people from the Netherlands and Belgium whom he had never met before.

Steve's stay in Dinant, Belgium, lasted for several days more than had been anticipated. The leak within the organization had now been found. Henri told Steve that it was not one of the farmer's workers, but a person who lived nearby and had been drinking with one of the workers. The worker helped the farmer determine who in particular was the problem. Apparently, the Germans paid for the information. Some way, best we do not know how, the problem was resolved. In addition, the worker involved learned a lesson of being careful whom he spoke to, along with the subject matter.

Henri informed Steve that arrangements were being made to move him on to the next safe house. Although Steve had become very much attached to Henri and Mother, he was also anxious to move closer to British soil.

With Christmas just a day away, Henri wanted Steve to spend Christmas Day with him and Mother. One day more or less would not spoil the overall plan, and the extra day would make certain that the plan of movement was carried out properly. This was not the time to rush things, especially as the next stopping point would be in France, which would require a border crossing. In addition, quite frankly,

Henri wanted to keep Steve around for another day and did not want him spending this particular holiday with strangers.

During the evening they had an enjoyable Christmas dinner that included roasted goose, a small one, but still a Christmas goose. Mother did not ask Henri how he obtained such a rare prize during these wartime days. She knew that her brother had, let us just say, many connections and was content to leave it to that.

Henri and Steve continued their discussions, which included curing the world of its ills, with a glass of Oban Single Malt Scotch Whisky in hand. Relaxing in Henri's study was a favorite comfortable place to be for Steve. He stated that one day he would duplicate a study like this in his own home. Steve told Henri all about the cattle ranch in Kissimmee, Florida. He said that one day he intended to build a house on the ranch near his dad's place, with it just a "hollering" distance away.

Steve, on this Christmas Day, 1943, thought about his dad and that it would not be a happy one for him. He knew that his dad would be wondering if his son was still alive. The report in the telegram would have simply stated that he was "missing in action." Steve, of course, did not know that Howie and his former crew had watched his plane go down and that they thought they saw one last person escape from the B-17, and would write this information to Ray Carmichael. Steve took a glance at the old wall clock in Henri's study. It read 2100 hours, or nine o'clock in the evening. He counted back six hours, determined that it was three o'clock in the afternoon in Central Florida, and wondered what his dad was doing right now. The not knowing was difficult for both father and son, however, at this point, more for the father.

The journey, as it had come to be known, would continue early the next morning, Sunday, the 26th day of December. Steve was told that the dangerous part would be in crossing from Belgium to France.

The Dutch–Paris Underground, a very important group of dedicated men and women worked hard at the risk of their own lives and had already saved hundreds of people from capture or death, mostly one individual at a time. They would continue to secure safety for the American aviator now in their charge.

It was a little after four o'clock on Sunday morning when Henri gave Steve a gentle shake to awaken him. "It is time to go, my boy," said Henri in a soft voice.

"I'm awake . . . okay," answered the still sleepy Steve.

Henri left the bedroom and went back down the stairs.

Steve quickly dressed in the clothes that Henri had laid out for him the night before. They were his size and, while a little worn, were better than the ones he came with. Steve during his stay had worn some other actually more comfortable clothes that Henri provided, but these clothes would more likely represent the person who Steve was supposed to be. He then came down the stairs and into the kitchen as the smell of fresh-brewed coffee gave a scent that anyone could follow. Henri was already sitting at the table, cup of coffee in hand. He motioned for Steve to sit down. Mother immediately placed a plate of fried eggs, a thick slice of ham, and three slices of toasted bread in front of him. Henri held up the fourth slice of toast to show Steve that he had it. Henri then spread some apple jelly on his toast and passed the jar of homemade jelly to Steve.

Steve did not take long to eat the breakfast. He knew that timing was important and that this was not the time to linger over a meal.

After breakfast, Steve said his goodbye to Mother in the kitchen. There were tears in the eyes of Mother as she held Steve close and worried for his safety.

Henri then motioned for Steve to follow him down to the basement. As they stood near the basement door, which led to the alley behind the house, Steve tried to say the words of thanks to Henri. It was hard not to choke up and words were not coming forth as he left behind a man who so generously had opened up his home and heart.

"I understand . . . words are not important," said Henri. The handshake then became a hug.

Henri opened the back door just a crack. On hearing the sound of an approaching vehicle, he gave two short blinks from the flashlight he held in his hand. The vehicle, which only had its dim lights on, flashed them off, then quickly back on.

"It is now that you must leave," said Henri as he motioned for Steve to step outside. "Go quickly to the open car door."

Steve started to walk briskly, then stopped a second to look back, but saw that Henri had already closed the basement door. The passenger's door of the car was flung open. It surprised Steve because, rather than the usual car door that he was accustomed to, this one opened from the front, which reminded him of a 1934 Ford that his dad once owned. Steve quickly got into the car and softly closed the door so that not too much noise would be made. He did not say anything to the driver, but both he and the driver nodded a hello.

The car moved down the alley and onto the main street. It crossed the bridge and then followed the River Meuse for a short distance. It then turned to the west toward the town of Gerin. Snow was now falling. While at this point it was not a hard snow, the flakes were large and the driver had to turn on the windscreen's lone wiper. The driver had still not uttered a word, but was concentrating on driving in the dark with just the dim headlights on and now, having to contend with the falling snow.

"We are now making the final turn for Gerin," said the driver in surprisingly good English. "It is snowing, a poor day to travel, but also a very good day to travel because most everyone, including any German soldiers that may be in the area, will want to stay inside and keep warm."

"I did not realize that you spoke English," said Steve as he also peered out to what was now becoming a wind-driven snowstorm.

"I learned English in school while my father worked in London. I was schooled in London for almost a year."

Steve did not continue the conversation. He did not know if he should speak or let the driver concentrate on driving. He would let the driver dictate when they should converse.

"We will not exchange names right now," said the driver as they drove through the quiet farming community, the small village of Gerin. "Later I will let you know the plan we will try to carry out."

The car slid a few times as the driver continued to negotiate the narrow, snow-covered road. Traction and control of the car was becoming more difficult as the snow fell at a more rapid rate. The snow was now perhaps four or five inches deep.

Steve continued to be silent. He did not want to distract the driver who had all he could do to just to stay on the road and not slide off into a field.

Finally, after a long silence, the road, which had been a series of winding curves probably from ancient farmland boundary lines, straightened out, the driver began, "From Gerin, we are driving toward Philippeville. We will continue to use roads that are best known to just the local residents. The driving is a little more dangerous because of this weather, but that's to our advantage. I have papers that show this car is belonging to France. When we are ready to cross into France from Belgium, we will make the change of the license plate. I know a way into France that will not be patrolled, even in good weather," continued the driver with a proud look on his face.

"I understand . . . very good thinking," said Steve. "The driving certainly is an adventure and you are doing very well."

The driver turned his head toward Steve for just a second and smiled. He agreed with that statement.

By now, it was daylight and while the driving continued to be hazardous, the headlights of the car were turned off and visibility became much better.

As they continued to drive on toward Philippeville, they passed just southeast of the town of Florennes. The driver pointed out the top turret of their famous château. He also told of the history behind the landmark.

Steve was interested and would like to have seen more of the château. Then something caught his eye. There looked to be a Luftwaffe air base not very far away. He spotted ME-109s parked on an airfield.

There were soldiers cleaning snow from their wings. The airfield was almost completely hidden by a small forest. He motioned to the driver and pointed to the German aircraft. This was a major find.

"We cannot change speeds for one second, even though we are not traveling very fast," said the driver. "We must not give the hint that we are interested in those airplanes."

Steve nodded his head, but tried to count the number of planes near the airstrip.

In a short time, they drove through a much larger forest. Then they entered the outskirts of Philippeville. In keeping to the plan of using more narrow country roads, the driver worked his way south of Philippeville, then drove through the small village of Neuville and toward the city of Chimay. After Chimay, their test would be crossing the Belgium–French frontier.

They had not quite arrived at the town of Chimay when the driver made a left turn off the road onto a long lane, which went to a farmhouse that was partly hidden by old trees that were quite close together. During the time when leaves were on the trees, one could not even see that there was a house. Now, with the snow still falling, the tree branches held snow and while you could see that there was a house, the trees blocked a view of any activity that might be going on. The driver continued around to the back of the house and drove into a small barn, which actually could be considered a large shed. The back door of the house opened and two men came out and walked into the shed to greet the driver. The driver motioned for Steve to get out of the car; all was clear.

"We will have something to eat here and the car will be filled with petrol. This is where the car will become French," said the driver to Steve as he shook hands with the two men.

"This young man is our charge," said the driver to the two men.

"You are welcome," said one of the men in his best English.

"Thank you for your help," answered Steve.

While the driver, Steve and one of the men entered the house through the back door and into the kitchen, the other stayed behind to put petrol into the tank of the car. He also would change the license plate to one that showed the auto was from France. The plate was quite rusty and the numbers could be hardly read, just as it was devised. In a short time, he joined the three who were already sitting at the kitchen table eating a bowl of hot potato soup with some bread and cheese. There were also two bottles of red wine.

Steve did not say anything, but listened as the three men conversed. He could not understand anyway. Steve now thought that he should have taken French in high school rather than Spanish. The soup was hot, the bread good and crusty, the cheese was delicious, plus the wine was most enjoyable and he was still out of German hands, so he figured things were quite all right. He was among friends.

"Once we are in France, then you and I will become more personable," the driver told Steve. "I shall have a name change back to my real name. I come from a little town in Normandy called Valognes. It looks as though I will be in your company as we both try to go to England. These men have told me that the Germans want me for an activity, which we shall not speak of, that I did in Belgium. It is better that I continue on to England rather than be captured by the Germans. They have certain ways, which can make you give information that could hurt other operations. I must also flee France before the Germans catch me. I am also on a list of people who are to be arrested by the Gestapo. It seems that perhaps when we reach England you, my friend, will have to look after me."

"Now the auto is ready and we must be on our way," the driver said to Steve. "We cannot stay here too long; let's go," he added, as he got up from his chair, said something in French to the two men and shook hands with them.

Steve also shook hands and thanked them in English, and added a "merci" in French as well. He followed them out to the barn and got into the car. Soon they were back onto the road and on their way to the town of Hirson, France.

The road was still snow covered, although the snow had all but stopped falling. They drove through Chimay. The driver pointed out the Chimay Castle that he said was also known as Le Château de Chimay. They continued past the old post office. A short time later the driver pointed out a Trappist monastery, Scourmont Abbey, explained that, it was famous for being the Chimay Brewery. The town of 7,000 people enjoyed having the brewery in Chimay.

Continuing along and being lucky so far, with no German patrols on the snow-covered road, they crossed the Oise River and took the back road route to avoid as best they could any control points, which might stop them and ask for papers of identification.

"The crossing into France is going to be a little difficult and what you Americans call tricky," said the driver as he winked at Steve. "We now drive toward the city of Macquenoise, but not through the town. We will use some roads which are known only to the locals. It will lead us to a little-used road and part of the Forest de Saint Michel. I just hope this auto will not get stuck in the snow, otherwise it will be embarrassing to be shot because of a stuck car."

"I agree, we don't want to be embarrassed," answered Steve.

The driver laughed, but Steve just smiled nervously. This was not quite a laughing matter.

They continued for a little less than hour when the driver turned off the road and onto what Steve thought was a snow-covered field. Not very much conversation occurred during that time. Steve thought it was best to keep quiet and let the driver concentrate on keeping the car on the road. There had already been a couple of lurches toward the side of the road and once they almost drove completely off of it. The temperature had dropped a few more degrees and now the road had become somewhat icy in spots.

"Don't worry, I know where I am going," said the driver, seeing that Steve had a quizzical look on his face. "We will cross this field where the ground is hard and then we will come to the old logging road that will carry us through the forest and into France without anyone knowing. The wind should blow the snow and cover up our tracks."

As they drove on, Steve's mind wandered. He thought of Chelveston and his buddies back there at the 305th. Steve figured that by now, they probably would have flown the required 30 missions and been on their way home before being reassigned. Then, he soberly thought of his last crew and that those who were not killed were in prisoner of war camps.

"When all this is over and we are safely in England, I know of a great little restaurant in London which serves some very good French wines," Steve told the driver. "I shall personally take you to the Ebury Wine Bar and Restaurant. We can enjoy it with some good Scottish steaks!"

"Okay, my friend, but no English beer. We Frenchmen do not care for that stuff which looks like it has pond life floating on it," answered the driver.

I never thought of it as having pond life, he thought to himself. *Quite frankly I enjoy the British Bitter. Oh well, he is a Frenchman and entitled to his thoughts on beer and wine. Come to think of it, I have never heard of a French Beer.*

The car slowed to almost a halt as the driver came to what he thought was the junction for which he was looking. He brought the car to a stop and got out, motioning for Steve to stay put. The driver walked up what looked to be nothing more than a trail. He was gone for a few minutes and had actually walked out of Steve's sight. When he returned, he slowly shook his head up and down and curled his lip as one would in being proud of finding the needle in the haystack. This was the right junction. The driver then made a left turn onto the trail and slowly drove forward at just above the speed of a crawl. The trail, or perhaps a lane, did not have too much snow covering it. The tall trees of the forest had collected the snow so that it did not reach the ground below. There was no one in sight, not even the sign of an animal.

It was more than an hour later that the driver once again stopped the car and motioned for Steve to stay in the auto as he walked forward down the narrow road. The slow speed in which they had been traveling kept the car's engine noise just above a whisper. They had not even disturbed any of the birds that were high in the trees. Steve knew how important it was that no one would suspect them in the forest, as the two worked to sneak into France without being observed.

Soon the driver returned. "We are in luck," he told Steve. "I don't see anything out there. We can continue on our way. I think that I can now say to you, welcome to France, my friend!"

They drove out of the forest and onto another one of the country roads. The town they were headed for, or more properly, the town they would now skirt around, was Hirson.

"This is an area of strategic railroad intersections," stated the driver. "Several railroad lines pass through Hirson. With some of the disruption of rail service through what we call creative work, is actually one of the reasons why I must continue on to England with you."

"I remember hearing about a bombing raid that our twin-engine B-25s carried out in this area with the rail junction being the primary target," said Steve, as he also kept a keen eye out for any traffic that might be on the road, both front and back.

"Yes, I was not very far away when the first bombs dropped from those planes," said the driver. "The ones that dropped in the beginning were not on the rail-yards, but hit a house across the road from where I was hiding. The house had been taken from the people who lived there by the German soldiers and they used it as a head-quarters for the rail junction activity. Through some good luck, the bomb blew hell out of the house. We all had to dive for cover because bricks, glass, roofing and even bodies were thrown up in the air and against the house I was in. The next bombs exploded and did good damage to the rail-yard plus a locomotive and some boxcars. We reported that information to our friends to be passed along. We also reported later that the Germans had the rail service repaired in just a few days."

"Hitting the house was more than likely dumb luck, especially from 15,000 or 18,000 feet," stated Steve.

"We had to vacate the house we were in very quickly because the German soldiers knew that information had been given so that the rail yard could become a target," added the driver. "They were searching all of the houses looking for us as we took leave and scattered for the time being. They searched the house we used for spying on them and then took it as a new headquarters."

While they continued driving the narrow country roads, Steve could see activity in the rail junction. They were about a half mile away but could clearly see that steam locomotives were moving both boxcars and the open gondola cars through the yard. Once again, the driver pointed out that they must not change speeds. So far, no one on this cold December afternoon was paying any attention to them.

A light snow started to fall once again. The snowflakes were the large, dry type and not a wet snowfall. Actually, it was quite beautiful seeing the large snowflakes fall onto the windscreen of the car.

As they approached an intersection, which had just one road entering it from the right, a large German Army truck appeared on the side road that could well lead to a military installation tucked away in the wooded area. The driver slowed the car to a crawl in order to let the military truck enter the road.

"I hope he turns left and drives toward Hirson," said Steve.

"Yes, he is going to turn in the direction of Hirson. Wave to him as he passes us, wave!" answered the driver.

Both the driver and Steve waved to the German Army driver of the truck. They were relieved to see the driver and his helper who was in the passenger's seat wave back.

"Don't look back, don't cause any suspicion; I can see them in the mirror," said the driver. "It must be hauling freight or just an empty truck because I do not see any soldiers behind the cover in the back."

They continued driving at speeds between 20 and 30 miles per hour. It was the best speed they could do under the conditions of both the weather and the narrow, slippery, winding back roads.

Soon they passed through the village of Buire, then Origny-en-Thierache. It was becoming dark as they passed through the village of La Bouteille on the way to the city of Vervins where they would spend the night in a safe house.

It was completely dark as they entered Vervins. Near the historical Villa Bourgeoise, the beautiful four-story landmark in Vervins, a figure stepped into the road waving his arms in order to bring the auto to a stop. With it now becoming completely nightfall and because of the dim, blacked-out headlights, they almost struck the man before the car could be brought to a halt. The driver reached for a pistol, which Steve did not know he had. Then he recognized the man and handed the pistol to Steve, motioning for him to keep it handy but hidden. The man stepped onto the car's running board and pointed for the driver to pull into a small area just off the road. The man then jumped off the running board as the driver opened the car door and stepped out. He motioned for Steve to stay put, but to be at the ready, if needed. Steve held the pistol below the seat level so that the gun could not be seen. He wished that he had his pistol from his survival kit, but at the time he had all he could do to escape his burning B-17 with his life. The pistol at that particular time had not been the first thing on his mind.

The two men spoke quickly but quietly in French, both using their arms to gesture. After a few minutes, the driver shook his head and got back into the car. Before one could look twice, the other man had disappeared.

Steve had a look of concern as he handed the pistol back to the driver. The driver pulled back onto the road and continued driving.

"We cannot stop here in Vervins," said the driver. "The place where we were to stay is being watched. It seems that the Gestapo has some information about the house being used by the Underground, so it must be suspended from use for now, maybe longer. The house is under constant surveillance and we cannot even go near it, otherwise the people who own it could be arrested. Some Frenchmen value money more than their freedom. However, this is not true with most Frenchmen. We will some day soon have our country back, with the help, of course, of you Americans and the British. That man has been out there hiding in the cold for more than two hours waiting to warn us."

"We are lucky that you have such good friends," remarked Steve.

"This is true. You know we all try to work together as one," answered the driver.

"What is the plan now?" questioned Steve.

"We have enough petrol and will continue on to the village of Sains-Richaumont," answered the driver. "There we can rest. This has been a long day, my friend."

With it now being quite dark on this moonless night, the driver took the most direct route toward Sains-Richaumont. At the junction in the road, if the driver did not know where he was going and had kept driving straight ahead, they would have gone to the city of Guise, but he made a left turn and continued on to just the outskirts of Sains-Richaumont. Then the driver made a right-hand turn onto a very narrow one-vehicle lane. He slowed the car to a crawl and waited for a signal to proceed, but ready to turn the car around, using part of the frozen, snow-covered field in the event an escape might be necessary. Finally, from an area near the house, two flashes of light from a lantern let them continue to the house. A man dressed in farm clothes directed them to drive behind the house and into the section of the barn where the farm implements were being stored for the winter. The engine was shut down and the farmer quickly closed the barn door.

The farmer came over to the car as the driver got out. They spoke to each other in French and both seemed glad to see one another. Steve got out of the passenger's side and before closing the car door, stretched. It had been a long, treacherous drive and he was glad for the break. After the farmer and the driver had greeted each other, the farmer came around to Steve's side of the car. Steve put his hand out to shake hands and the farmer took Steve's hand in both of his.

"Bienvenue, welcome," said the farmer and he gave Steve the traditional French welcome with the kiss on both sides of his face.

Steve smiled and started to say something to which the farmer seemed quite interested in, but the driver interrupted Steve.

"He does not speak English, but I will tell him that you are saying that you are grateful for his help and hospitality," stated the driver. "We will go to the house where his wife has prepared a meal and we can sleep in the extra bedroom."

They entered the house through the back door. Then, through what Steve would call a mud room, they entered the kitchen. A short, round woman greeted them with a smile and gestured for them to sit at the kitchen table. She did not speak, although her lips seemed to move. Perhaps she was speaking softly or was telling herself what to do next.

As they sat down, large bowls of a vegetable–potato soup were placed in front of Steve and the driver. A loaf of bread was also set on the table. Then the farmer placed three wine glasses on the table and filled them with a very dark red wine. He raised his glass in salute and the three men took a drink. The wine was quite strong and tasted good. The driver especially appreciated the wine to the delight of the farmer who proudly said that he made it himself. There was plenty and the farmer poured the wine freely.

Throughout the meal, there was continuous conversation. The driver did the interpreting between French and English. With Steve being the first American he had met, the farmer was most interested in America and life there. He had read that the French people had given a very large statue to America and did they still have it? Steve explained that it was the most famous statue in America and that Americans called it the Statue of Liberty. It welcomed people to America from its own island in New York Harbor. Steve went on to say that the Americans cherished this most special statue. This seemed to make the farmer very proud.

As they finished the soup, the lady of the house placed an old wooden tray that held a large block of cheese on the table. The driver explained to Steve that the cheese was made here on the small farm and might have a strong taste that he was not used to, but it was very good. More wine was poured and everyone enjoyed the cheese. The farmer had placed a fourth wine glass on the table just as the cheese was being served so that his wife could relax and join them.

At the end of the night, Steve and the driver were taken to the spare bedroom, which was located in the house's attic. Two narrow but comfortable beds were in the sparsely furnished, small room. There seemed to be several layers of blankets on each bed, so they both would certainly be warm during this cold night.

As they climbed into their beds the driver said to Steve, "We will be here for two or three days. I am not certain of how we will move on to our next stop. The farmer has no petrol so it must be brought in or we leave the auto and proceed in a different way. Good night, my friend."

Steve certainly understood. Whatever they planned would be fine with him. He had placed his trust in all of the wonderful people who had helped him along the way and they all had taken his safety quite seriously. He simply answered, "And a very good night to you, my friend, and I thank you."

In just a few minutes, two very tired young men were fast asleep, probably with the aid of some very good homemade wine!

Across the Channel in England, maintenance crews were working through the night to ready the 305th Bomb Group B-17s for the December 30th mission to Ludwigshaven, Germany. It was a mission in which the Van Dyke Crew would not participate. Howie, copilot Carl Phillips, navigator Bob Courtney, bombadier Russ Parker and several other crewmen had come down with very bad head colds, with fevers and flu-like symptoms. With the plane not going on this mission, Pappy and the ground crew performed some of the maintenance items on their list that they had been waiting to catch up on.

This would have been mission number 30 for Howie, Bob, Russ and top turret gunner–flight engineer Jim McFarland. Flying their last combat mission would have to be placed in abeyance.

Mission number 29 for the men of *Pappy's Pack* had been flown on Christmas Eve, Friday, December 24th. The raid had been to bomb what was considered an important military installation in the northwest of France. The target was a German rocket-launching site for the V-2 rockets aimed for London.

The group had good escort support throughout the mission. Both P-47s and the twin-engine P-38s kept the Luftwaffe away from the bomber stream. The flak, however, was another story. It was fired up from the ground installations in a barrage of four shells at the correct altitude. Exploding shells sent deadly black shrapnel throughout the formation, showering the skin of the B-17s and ripping holes in the bombers.

Pappy's Pack crew member Willie Burnett was severely wounded after being hit by exploding flak, some the size of a prune. Willie had been wounded before when he was the ball turret gunner and had spent more than a week in the base hospital. When Willie returned to the crew, he did not want to climb down into the ball turret again. He was then assigned to the right waist gunner position, with newcomer Vincent Campalone going into the ball turret.

Pieces of the exploding anti-aircraft flak shell ripped into the skin of *Pappy's Pack* and through the open waist gunner position. Flak particles hit Willie in the face, arm, and chest. It just missed new crew member Howard Cox, who had joined the crew after Jack Kowalski completed his 30 missions. Willie had his flak jacket on, which most certainly saved his life. Howard Cox moved Willie from the waist to just outside of the radio room, and new radioman Kenny Davis applied first aid. While there was a lot of blood on his face from cuts and small shrapnel particles lodged in his skin, his eyes were spared from injury. Willie was lucky from that standpoint. A piece of shrapnel took away a portion of his upper left arm and although it had not hit an artery, his condition was indeed serious. Despite protesting that he wanted to go back to his position, Willie was made comfortable and told to stay exactly where he was by copilot Carl Phillips, whom Howie had sent back to check on Willie.

Once back over the Channel, Howie applied additional power and flew a direct line to Chelveston. Flares were fired, notifying the airfield that wounded were aboard from *Pappy's Pack* as the B-17 lined up on the final approach. The ambulance met the plane and Willie was immediately taken to the base hospital. He had completed 26 missions and would be ticketed for a stateside hospital stay. Just before they closed the ambulance door, Howie climbed in for the ride to the hospital. Carl could handle the debriefing session. During the ride, they had a talk, with Howie telling Willie that he had performed his job and had done it well each time they went into battle. "Just like Wyatt," when the first tail gunner had to go back to the States for hospital treatment, "it is now time for you to go home." Howie went on to tell him that they would surely make an aerial gunnery instructor out of him. Finally, as they took Willie into the operating room, Howie told him that he and the crew would see him before he left for the States.

With a tear in his eye, Willie said, "Thanks, Skipper, your coming to the hospital means a lot to me."

Howie, now quite exhausted himself and still in flying gear, wondered how he would get back to his quarters when Pappy walked into the hospital.

"One of yours is one of mine; how is the boy?" asked Pappy.

Howie explained the situation to Pappy and climbed in his Jeep for the ride back to the 366th.

Pappy and Howie discussed the new crew members, including Kenny Davis, the radioman from Gainesville, Florida. He knew of Steve from his days as a base-ball player at the University of Florida, in Gainesville. His quick first-aid work had perhaps saved Willie's life as they flew the last part of the mission home. Kenny took the place of Eddie Anderson, who, like Jack Kowalski and Joey DeMatteo, had completed his 30 missions. Howard Cox had also joined the crew as the left waist gunner. Howard was from the community of Green Tree, Pennsylvania, near Pittsburgh. Another new crewman was Marc Siegel at the ball turret. Marc was scheduled to be the new tail gunner, but Howie wanted someone back there with more experience, so Vincent Campalone moved from the ball to the tail. Marc was from Falls Church, Virginia, just outside of Washington, D.C. Now for his 30th and final mission, Howie would need a new right waist gunner. Just four of the original crew would be on his last mission. It was not supposed to work out that way. When they left the States, they were told that crews would train together, fight together and come home together.

A mission was also on for Friday, December 31st, the last day of 1943, but with most of the crew of *Pappy's Pack* still sick, they would miss out once again. This mission was scheduled to bomb the Château Bernard Airfield in the Bordeaux region of France.

There was celebrating the New Year at the Officer's Club, but the officers of *Pappy's Pack* stopped in just for a short visit. They really did not feel jubilant, so celebrating the beginning of 1944 would have to wait.

The following day, New Year's Day, brought the new crew member to replace Willie. He was John Lowery from Valdosta, Georgia, just above the Florida–Georgia border. John would be the right waist gunner. He had actually flown seven missions, but with three different crews.

Weather played a little part in the early days of 1944 and for the first few days, no missions were scheduled. When one was scheduled for the 3rd of January, it was eventually canceled due to weather conditions.

On January 4th, a cold but clear Tuesday, *Pappy's Pack* was scheduled to take Howie on his final combat mission. At the early morning briefing, the curtain was pulled back to that the mission for the day would be a return to Kiel, Germany. Kiel was an important port city with a huge submarine base.

"What the hell kind of aircraft commander are you?" whispered Bob Courtney, *Pappy's Pack* navigator. "This is our 30th mission and we're taking a ride to Kiel. I always heard that the final mission was supposed to be a milk run."

"I guess no one in the Eighth Air Force gives a damn if it's our first or last," answered Howie, softly but loud enough to be heard by some of the other crews sitting near. "Besides, think of it as a nice, relaxing, over-the-water, sight-seeing ride. The beautiful waves below, that sort of thing."

From the stage, the Kiel mission briefing continued. The route in and out of the target area——the submarine pens at Kiel——would be an over-the-water flight. The raid would entail an 850-mile round trip. Furthermore, escort fighters would be with them the entire time over enemy territory. There would be P-47s, P-38s, and the new P-51 Mustangs to accompany the B-17 and B-24 heavy bombers. In total, over 500 bombers would participate in the mission to Kiel.

For Howie, this marked his first return to Kiel since he had been Steve's copilot on the July 29th mission with the original Carmichael Crew. That raid was just their second combat mission and they were still an innocent group of young men. Oh, how six more months of additional combat could change one's life!

At the hardstand, Pappy was waiting for the crew to arrive. The ship was warmed up and ready to go. Pappy met with Howie as Carl did the walk-around preflight with one of the ground crew. Pappy also made it a point to speak with Bob, Russ, and Jim, the other crewmen who were flying number 30. While many of the men who knew Pappy thought he was a tough old bird, Howie knew exactly who he really was, especially at times like this. The fatherly way in which he felt toward and cared for these youngsters came through in a big way.

It was not too long before the first flares were fired and the sound of B-17 Wright Cyclone engines filled the air. It was an unmistakable sound; once you heard it, you knew that a B-17 was around. All was normal as *Pappy's Pack* left the hardstand, taxied and took off. The climb and form-up also went well. Finally, the turn to course was made that would start the long over-the-water flight to Kiel.

More often than not, at this time of the year the target area in and around Kiel was cloud covered. In addition, the Germans would deploy a smokescreen from the ground in order to obscure the view that the bombardier would otherwise have. For that reason, a Pathfinder B-17 would accompany them on this mission.

While the formation flew this long, over-the-water North Sea trip, it was more relaxing than flying a long mission over German-controlled land area. There were no enemy fighters to attack them and they would not have to dodge the deadly flak, at least not until they reached land in northern Germany.

A flight like this called for some very meaningful work on the part of the navigator, especially with *Pappy's Pack* in the lead ship position of the low element. Bob Courtney had some help as his partner in the nose of the ship, bombardier Russ Parker, worked with him. The two had shared that cramped space in a B-17 for 29 previous missions and had become much more than just friends. They had planned to become partners and purchase a small winery with some extra planting land for vineyards in the Sonoma or Napa Valley just above San Francisco after the war. Vineyards and producing wine was a good investment for the pay that they were not spending.

Finally, landfall came into view as they flew over the German Frisian Islands. Light and inaccurate flak came up from the area of Wittdun, Nebel, as they passed the outer islands and approached the mainland just south of Bredstedt. Cloud cover, as expected, was quite heavy and may have accounted for the light flak. Those flak batteries must not have been equipped with the radar-directed anti-aircraft guns, which surrounded the key cities.

The formation crossed the coast not far from the border of Denmark. Flensburg, Germany, just south of the Danish border, was the secondary target. So far, so good; the Luftwaffe fighters had not come up yet to oppose the bomber stream. The only fighters in sight were the little friends that had flown with them using long-range drop tanks.

The formation made a hard right turn, flying west of Schleswig and Rendsburg, then a left turn north of Lubeck Bay, and finally another left turn as they came north to Preetz and the IP for the bomb run on Kiel's submarine pens. With a heavy smoke screen and almost complete cloud cover, there was an unusual break in the clouds revealing a short glimpse of the ground. The Pathfinder B-17 took over the bomb run and everyone would simply toggle their bombs when the Pathfinder unloaded its cargo.

By now, the flak was coming up to greet them. It was heavy and relatively accurate at their altitude of 25,000 feet above Kiel. *Pappy's Pack* bounced from the nearby flak explosions. Shrapnel pounded the side of their airplane and sounded like rain on a tin roof; a heavy rain! Four small holes appeared just behind the radio room. Carl ducked as a large flash and explosion occurred in front and a little to the right of their plane. A shower of hot flak pelted the side window on the copilot's side as well as the right wing. The engines continued to run, although Carl had a worried look on his face as he glanced at the two engines on his side of the aircraft.

With bombs away, the formation made a turn to the left off from the target; the job now was to get out of Germany in one piece and to the relative safety of the North Sea for the flight home. They flew between Schieswig and Rendsburg in order to encounter as little flak as possible, and the Luftwaffe showed up. The American escort fighters dropped their now all-but-exhausted wing fuel tanks and prepared to fight the German ME-210s and ME-110s. The German fighters tried to reach the bombers, but the P-51 Mustangs kept them away. P-38s were flying top cover as they also protected the bombers. The P-47s helped the other groups. It seemed that at least on this day the Luftwaffe was not as aggressive as usual. They did not drive home their attacks. They were, quite frankly, outnumbered by the American fighters.

The last city that *Pappy's Pack* flew over before reaching the North Sea was Busum. Some very light flak came up but it was inaccurate and not at their flight level. Locals, with perhaps military supervision, were probably manning the flak battery. No matter, *Pappy's Pack* had survived and was on the way back to Chelveston.

"Howie, the number four engine is starting to smoke and run rough," said Carl.

"The oil pressure is dropping. We've got a problem with it," reported Jim as he looked over the instruments.

"Feather it for now . . . we may have to restart it later," answered Howie as power was increased on the other three engines in order to stay with the formation.

"That damned flak hit it while we were over the target," said Carl as he looked out of his side window.

All the while they kept an eye on the three working engines, especially the number three, hoping that while it had also sustained some flak damage, it would not quit on them. So far, on the flight back to Chelveston all of the engine instruments read normally.

"We're not going to make Pappy very happy with three beat-up engines and one shot out by flak," said Carl.

"The ole girl is bringing us home, that's what is important," answered Howie, who then added, "hell, I'll just blame the whole thing on you!"

"Thanks," was all Carl could answer.

"I'm innocent, just a poor ole enlisted man following orders!" chimed in Jim.

That made Howie and Carl laugh as they started the turn inland, which would take them back to Chelveston.

"Let's slow them down a bit, make sure that the three engines are all working when we need them," said Howie.

After a few minutes of flying time, when they were nearing the base, over the plane's intercom Bob Courtney spoke up, "Howie, buzz the tower! Russ and I voted."

"I've got three engines and one of them could quit on us at any time," answered Howie.

"Howie, are you a pilot or not? Stevie would have buzzed the tower . . . do it for him!" said Russ.

"Since you put it that way . . . hang on!" stated Howie.

Having slowed down, they were the last B-17 to enter the pattern to land that day. The control tower was still full of those counting the returning B-17s and *Pappy's Pack* would make it official that all planes returned from today's mission. Ground crews had scattered as each one of their B-17s landed and worked their way to the hardstands they occupied.

As Howie lined up on final approach, the landing gear came back up and the power was poured on to the three running engines. *Pappy's Pack* flew the length of the runway a little off center and buzzed the control tower to the delight of, well, some!

Then he went around again and turned onto the final approach for the last time as a B-17 combat pilot. While he had been asked, Howie did not sign up for five more missions. Howie, Bob, Russ, and Jim each had agreed that surviving 30 missions was just about a miracle in itself under the circumstances. You only have so much luck—no sense pushing it. They knew of several crews who had been lost while on their last mission.

After landing, Howie taxied to the hardstand, eased *Pappy's Pack* around and then shut down the three operating engines. Carl and Howie completed the checklist. Howie told Carl to go along ahead of him; he was going to just sit in the plane for a few more minutes. In the meantime, Jim, Russ, Bob, and Carl left the ship from the front hatch while Vincent, Howard, Marc, Kenny, and new crewman John Lowery left by the rear door.

Pappy, along with his ground crew, took charge of *Pappy's Pack* to mend her wounds. He could easily see that the old girl had been through a lot today. While Howie was buzzing the field, Pappy stood at the hardstand, arms folded, tight-lipped, but also quietly proud of the boys who flew his airplane. She had brought the crew home once again.

Howie spent a good 10 minutes sitting in his pilot's seat unwinding and taking in all that had happened since he left Glen Cove, Long Island. He thought about Steve and how much he enjoyed his company, let alone flying with him from the right copilot's seat. They had formed a great partnership. Howie had learned so much about flying and commanding a crew from Steve. He eased himself out of the seat, made his way down to the forward hatch, and dropped to the ground. No one said anything to Howie, who patted ole *Pappy's Pack*, turned his head away so that no one could see his face and wiped a tear from his eyes.

It was now time to board the waiting truck and head to the debriefing hut. Howie, before climbing aboard the truck, stopped to speak with Pappy. He did not have to report on the battle damage or the operation of the engines as Carl had already done that. Pappy understood and simply gave Howie a fatherly hug. Neither said anything; there would be time for that later.

At the debriefing, Howie was about to be given hell for buzzing the control tower. It was simply against the rules, last mission or not. "We do not need a bunch of hot-rod cowboys flying these damn planes!"

Howie waited for an opening to explain, "We had landing gear problems and had to go around, sir, and as aircraft commander I made that decision. Rather than take the chance of a belly landing or worse, cart-wheeling, it was better to bring the gear back up and be certain that it was actually down and locked. How we got near the tower was simply the pulling of the engines, after all, we had lost one."

"You said all that with a straight face. I imagine that your copilot will confirm all of this?" replied the group commander.

"And so will my engineer; we all fought the problem," added Howie.

One of the other officers, a lieutenant from headquarters joined in where he should have kept quiet, asking, "Then why were the officers in the nose waving as you flew by the tower?"

"They are right over here, why don't you ask them. I believe it was not waving but fright at the thought of a crash landing," answered Howie in a sober tone.

"That won't be necessary, Lieutenant," stated the group commander, who gave Howie a wink. "As the aircraft commander, you did what you thought was right!"

With this being number 30, Howie was given a free pass and nothing more would be said.

On the evening of January 4th, a bitter-cold Tuesday night, Howie had obtained permission to take his crew off base and into Rushden for dinner at the Four Lions Pub. This was an opportunity to have his officers and enlisted men relax together without rank getting in the way. There was also an empty seat, for Steve, as Howie said, "just in case he walks through the door." A good time was had by all and some had a hard time remembering how they got back to base that night!

There was a mission scheduled for the next morning. *Pappy's Pack* would not fly on this day. There would be a major crew change, plus their aircraft was not available, so Howie's former crew would sit this one out. Pappy and his ground crew were in the meantime working on the ship, getting the B-17 ready to get back into action.

On Wednesday, January 5, 1944, the 305th mission would be a follow-up raid on Kiel. Back-to-back days flying to and from Kiel would call for another very long day of flying for the B-17s and their fighter escort pilots, in their cramped cockpits.

For the crew of *Pappy's Pack*, the news that Second Lieutenant Carl Phillips would move from the right seat to the pilot's left seat came as no surprise. He would need four replacements to complete his crew. Carl would be flying with a new copilot, navigator, bombardier and top turret gunner–flight engineer. With the recent departure of Eddie Anderson, Jack Kowalski and Joey DeMatteo, plus the loss of wounded Willie Burnett, the Phillips Crew would certainly be one of replacements.

His hope was to assemble a crew quickly and maybe fly a practice mission or two before taking them into battle.

Howie was hoping to land a ground job and stay over in England for a little longer. He asked that he not be sent back to the States right away. Howie also still had the feeling that Steve was alive and evading capture. Others had done exactly that with the help of the Underground and returned by way of the Pyrenees Mountains into Spain and then back to England from Gibraltar. The request for Howie to stay in England was under consideration.

In Florida, Ray Carmichael did not have a Merry 1943 Christmas or a Happy 1944 New Year. He had no further news or word on Steve. Howie had written to Ray that he also had not heard anything more and tried to cheer Ray up; no news was actually good news. If Steve had been captured, then word would have come from the International Red Cross that he was indeed a POW. Howie went on to say that, he felt strongly Steve was, in fact, working his way back to England through the Underground and that any day now there would be word from Spain that Steve was there and would then be shipped back to the United Kingdom.

In the meantime, Steve had indeed spent a few additional days at the small farm just outside of the village of Sains-Richaumont, France. This included New Year's Eve and New Year's Day 1944. There had been the coming and going of a few selected people who brought food and wine for the extra guests. There was even a small party held on New Year's Eve. No one seemed to be concerned about a visit from German soldiers, or as the locals called them, "the Boche." They were not stationed in this particular area at this time.

On Thursday morning, the 6th of January, an old truck pulled into the farmyard. The truck had a load of hay, which had a dirty look to it, as though the hay had been out in the weather. To Steve, the truck, which had as much rust on it as paint, looked to be from the early 1930s.

"It looks as if our transportation has arrived," said the driver to Steve, as they both looked out of the kitchen window, cup of tea in hand.

"Well, it looks to be a good day for traveling, bright and clear," answered Steve. "I just hope that on such a nice day we don't get stopped."

"We will keep to country roads, some paved and some not, drive slow and act like farmers delivering hay," stated the driver.

Two men got out of the truck and came into the warm kitchen. They were all introduced, but not by name. Steve reached out and shook hands with each of them.

"Don't ever shake hands in public, my friend. They will surely know that you are not who you are supposed to be," reminded the driver. "Just stand back and do nothing."

The two men spoke at length to the driver and farmer. There was hand gesturing, but Steve could not make out exactly what was being said. Knowing French would certainly have come in handy during the past month. Lucky for him, some of his new friends spoke pretty good English.

After things looked to be settled, one of the men left the kitchen for the farmyard. He walked to the barn and opened the door where the implements were stored, started the auto, backed it out of the barn and drove up the lane and out of sight.

Steve looked over toward the driver as if to ask a question, but said nothing, figuring that they all knew what they were doing.

"The car must not be on this farm," stated the driver. "They do not own a car, so finding one in the barn could be very dangerous for this family. You never know when the Boche could inspect the property. They often come off the main road to see if they can confiscate some food, eggs, chickens, pigs or wine for themselves. The farmer told me that he has a large root cellar out behind the barn, which is hidden and has four beehives around it. In the cellar, he keeps his main supply of food and wine. The German soldiers showed up one day looking around for what they could take, but would not go near the bees. In case they come while you and I are here, we will also be hidden in the root cellar, hopefully protected by the bees."

The farmer, along with one of the men that brought the hay truck spoke with Steve's driver for several minutes. Steve sat back down at the kitchen table. The farmer's wife pumped some fresh water for the kettle and made another pot of tea. They all joined Steve for one more cup.

"We will leave here in a short while," the driver told Steve. "I will be driving the hay truck because I know the exact roads which to take to keep us safe. You will sit in the middle between this man and me. If we do meet up with anyone, anyone at all, just nod your head. Do not speak even one word. I will do all of the talking. Even this man will not speak. If I tap your leg one time, nod as in yes. If I tap your leg two times, then slowly nod no. Local people will be using the roads we travel on and the poor condition of the hay we will say is for the barn floor and not for animal feed. With the beard you have, you look much like one of us. Keep your beret just like you have it and things should be "okay", as you Americans say. Remember, I must not be caught the same as you must not be caught, my friend." He then turned to the other man and shook his head as a statement of Steve's understanding the situation, which he certainly did.

As they were preparing to leave the house, the farmer handed the man who would occupy the passenger's seat a sack with some food for the trip. He also gave him two bottles of wine, not the wine he made, but bottles that had been brought to the house. This way the wine bottles could not be traced back to this farmer.

Steve shook hands with the farmer in the kitchen, but the farmer gave the more traditional kiss on both cheeks to Steve. Steve then gave a hug to the farmer's wife. The farmer watched as the three travelers got into the hay truck and started up the lane. A last wave from the farmer came just before he went into the barn to do his daily work.

The driver slowly eased up the lane and made a left turn onto the country road, which had been paved at one time, but now was mostly dirt. This road would take them to an important junction. At the junction the driver turned left and headed toward the town of Crecy-Sur-Serre, or Crecy, as it was now more commonly known. As they passed through, Steve noticed an old brick clock tower. It must have an interesting history, he thought. Steve also wished that this were a trip in which he could explore these old towns and villages. Crecy served this particular farming region, and from what the driver said, had perhaps 1,500 inhabitants.

The driver broke the silence in the truck cab once again by telling Steve that

Laon was a city that they would avoid for good reason. As a rail junction, it had a concentration of German soldiers. There had been some sabotage carried out on the rails and every vehicle that passed through the area was subject to a complete inspection. They would instead drive toward the city of Chavy. This would mark a more meaningful turn toward the west, as up to now, they had been traveling on a southwest course.

As they drove, Steve also thought of his journey to date. He had come a long way from when he was able to escape his burning B-17 and descended into an apple orchard in Margraten, Holland. Steve likewise recognized that he had incredible assistance and could not have stayed free from capture without the help of so many people. Nevertheless, he also thought of the many dangerous miles that lay ahead before he possibly made it back to the safety of England.

They drove through the little village of Chavy without anyone taking notice. No soldiers had been seen. Luck continued to travel with them.

Eventually they came to Chauny and drove along the narrow road by the canal. As they drove the canal road, a German truck was spotted parked on the side of the canal, with several German soldiers standing nearby. Apparently, they had stopped to take a break. Some were smoking while others conversed.

Steve was jolted out of a nap. While they were not driving fast, the sudden slow-down of the truck woke him, and seeing the German soldiers just 30 meters away snapped him to attention.

"Quiet now," said the driver. He made the slow turn to get around the parked truck, which in addition to the soldiers on the ground had what looked to be a half dozen soldiers sitting in the back of the truck. "Give them a wave, but not a generous one. Just acknowledge them," continued the driver.

Steve followed what the driver told him with the same type of cordial wave. In the passenger's seat of Steve's truck, the man gave a nod of his head and just below the window level and out of sight, gave a "finger salute."

The German soldiers, all very young-looking men, waved back and did not pay any particular attention to the beat-up old truck hauling hay.

"We did okay. Good," said the driver, who continued driving slowly along the canal road before heading toward the village of Abbecourt.

They continued, driving south of Dampcourt and then to the small town of Appilly before reaching the historic French town of Noyon. In Noyon, they drove slowly past the Hotel de Ville where German soldiers could be seen walking around the town. Perhaps the soldiers had taken over the hotel as quarters or as a headquarters, as two soldiers were stationed on either side of the main entrance. The truck drove at a crawl so that pieces of hay would not fall into the street and draw attention. So far, they had not gotten more than a glimpse.

As they approached the Gothic cathedral with the beautiful but silent bells sitting on top, the driver turned toward Steve and quietly said, "You must be glad that we are not making this journey by bicycle. That could be tough on both of our nerves, my friend."

"I agree with you," answered Steve. "I am not a very good bike rider. I grew up on a cattle ranch, and we only traveled by truck or horseback. Sometimes we would fly in an old airplane that my father purchased years ago. So, yes, I am glad that we aren't bicycling."

The driver translated what had been said to the other passenger, who nodded his head yes and smiled to Steve.

"If you have a cattle ranch, then you are a cowboy . . . right?" asked the driver. "Do you live in Texas? I know of one of your cowboys, Gene Autry. His horse is Champ. I know about this!"

When the driver translated this in French to the passenger, Steve picked up the English words "cowboy" and "Texas." The man was very impressed.

Steve figured that it was best to "just let it alone." An explanation where he was from would be much too difficult, especially with the language barrier.

There was a sense of relief when they took the right turn that brought them across the canal to the other side. Closer in toward Noyon there were German checkpoints, but out here, nothing. It was a strange but welcome sight not to see a checkpoint at the canal crossing. Did the three looked so scroungy and unimportant that they were not worth the German soldier's time? Either way, they would take it!

At a little past noon, the driver found an old logging road on the right, which was partly covered by thick brush. He drove very slowly onto the rutted, narrow lane, far enough so that the truck was hidden from view before stopping. The man in the passenger's seat went back to the opening they had made with the truck and fixed some of the downed brush so that no one could tell that it had been disturbed.

"We can rest and have some food and wine," said the driver to Steve.

When the passenger man returned, he opened the sack that contained three small loaves of bread, cheese and three apples, plus the wine. The driver opened the wine bottles. The dark red wine, perhaps Burgundy, Steve thought, was poured into small glasses that were supplied by the farmer. This was an odd place to have a picnic. However, the three vagabonds were enjoying each other's company.

At this point, they were between the villages of Larbroye and Suzoy. In the distance, the sound of anti-aircraft cannon fire could be heard. It was coming from the north, probably from Laon. Overhead and north of their position, they could see specks, which to Steve's trained eye was a bomber stream of B-17s, perhaps on a mission to bomb Laon or Reims. Steve imagined he was up there with the airmen, flying deeply into harm's way with a sky filled with deadly exploding flak.

"It is time to proceed," said the driver to Steve. "We must leave this area and get away from German troop activity. They will become more curious about machines on the road."

The driver then spoke in French to the other man who immediately walked up the dirt lane to the area where they had turned off the road.

The truck motor was started. Steve took his place in the middle of the long seat as the driver slowly eased up the lane to where the other man motioned that all was clear. He then jumped into the truck and soon they were back on the road that would take them toward the village of Evricourt. They stayed to the dirt back roads as they drove around Evricourt. The road took them past fields that had been plowed last fall and through the small village of Piemont and on toward the town of Lassigny.

"You are getting to see the country and not the big city," laughed the driver, who thought for a moment then added, "We are not very far from Paris. Maybe we should take a detour and drive this old truck there, right through the streets of Paris."

The passenger did not understand what the driver was laughing about until he translated what was said to Steve. He just shook his head and rolled his eyes.

Steve answered with a smile as he said, "I've seen Paris from a little over 30,000 feet above . . . think I'll wait to see it from the ground."

The driver continued to do well in keeping to the narrow, often-unpaved country roads known just to the locals. There were very few signs to direct anyone and the roads were so remote that the German military would only use them in an emergency. In fact, most of the signs had been removed by the Underground or were pointed in the wrong direction to throw off anyone unfamiliar. Their route could not even be traced on a map.

The hope, of course, was if anyone did see them as they drive along, it would seem that some rustic farmers were in the truck for a local delivery. As long the travelers kept to themselves, no one would suspect that they were on a mission to guide an American aviator to his freedom.

They were now driving through the town of Lassigny and on toward Gury. Once again, there had not been any incidents that would alarm or bring attention to the slow-moving, loaded hay truck. The truck, old as it was, continued to chug along. The truck had not been pushed hard and the engine did not break down, which from the beginning was a worry for the driver. Luck continued to accompany them on the journey.

Outside of Gury, a forest could be seen set back beyond a field and a large lake appeared on their left, where the driver spotted a horse-drawn cart near the lake. The horse was eating some grass and the cart moved with him as the horse grazed along. A man stood on the lake bank, fishing pole in hand, and seemed quite intent on catching his supper. The driver pulled the hay truck off the road and brought it to a halt near the horse cart. The fisherman quickly put his fishing pole down and walked briskly to his cart. He and the driver greeted each other while Steve and the passenger stayed in the truck. Moving fast, the driver and fisherman took three cans filled with petrol from the cart and poured the gasoline into the truck's petrol tank. Just as quickly, they parted company, each returning to his position in the truck or on the lake. Steve thought that a racing car pit crew would have been impressed. The truck engine started and they once again drove onto the road that would eventually take them to the town of Ressons.

Finally a town started to come into view. "This is the town of Ressons-Sur-Matz," said the driver to Steve as they entered what looked to be a fair-sized town. "The locals just refer to it as Ressons. In this area, there are some small farms with their cozy houses, a nice village," continued the driver.

"Will we be stopping here?" asked Steve.

"Yes. Listen to the name of the street which you should forget I told you—Rue du Jeu de Paume," stated the driver, who knew that the long name would impress his aviator friend.

Steve just smiled—*whatever happened to names like Elm Street?*—as the driver turned up a lane that had grass growing up the middle. The farmhouse came into view, typical of those he had seen all along the journey. There were two outbuildings, a barn and a large shed, which, Steve figured, doubled as a workshop. He did not ask any questions, figuring that all would become known in a short time.

The driver spoke to the man in the passenger's seat in French. The driver brought the truck to a halt. He looked toward the house, received a nod of the head from someone standing in the doorway. The driver then tapped Steve on the shoulder, motioning for him to get out of the truck on the driver's side. Steve quickly and quietly followed orders, and as he and the driver walked toward the house. The other man moved from the passenger's seat to behind the steering wheel and the engine, which continued to run, was placed in gear. The truck was then turned around, driven out of the farmyard and up the lane. It was all completed so quickly that Steve had no time to say goodbye.

The driver saw Steve turn as if to say something or to wave, "I will tell him goodbye someday," said the driver to Steve. "But for now, it is not important, he understands."

As the two entered the farmhouse through the back door entrance, Steve noticed that the inside of the house also had a familiar look about it. The cozy, warm kitchen made him feel quite comfortable.

The driver and the owner of the property spoke French for a few minutes. The owner looked Steve over, smiled and reached his hand toward Steve. It was an American instead of a French greeting. "Welcome, American aviator," said the man. "We shall not exchange real names, but you can call me William. This is easy for an American to remember."

Steve shook hands, noticing that the large hand he was shaking was that of a man who knew hard work. It was rough and his grip strong.

William, as he would be known, motioned for them to sit down at the kitchen table. He then produced three glasses and a bottle of cognac. The cognac would take the chill from the travelers.

The driver spoke once again to William in French. William nodded and then in English, the driver said to Steve, "This man is very much our friend. The Germans took his son several months ago to work in some kind of a factory, but he does not know if his son is still in France, in the Netherlands, or perhaps Germany. His wife died three years ago and he operates this small farm by himself. He said that his personal needs are not great and that we are welcome to stay here for a few days or longer if that is necessary. The German soldiers do not bother with him. They know how much he hates them and that he would be willing to die himself as long as he killed some of the German soldiers. They do not travel up his lane, considering him a crazy, crotchety old man."

Steve looked over at William after the driver had spoken, smiled and simply raised his cognac glass in salute. He would have liked to say something, but with the language barrier, the salute said volumes.

William acknowledged Steve's salute, smiled, nodded his head approvingly and took a sip of the cognac, tasting it for a moment and then nodded his head. The cognac was good.

The driver told Steve that they would be sleeping inside the house and not in the barn. William was not concerned that it might be more dangerous in the house and it would be much warmer than a cold barn. William had enough food for everyone. In addition, and just as important, there was plenty of wine and cognac! Under all of these favorable circumstances, the driver kidded that this would be a good place to sit out the war. He gave Steve a wink.

Pleased that he was in safe hands, Steve still asked, "Is our transportation coming back? How long do we expect to be here?"

"We will be using some other means of transportation," answered the driver. "You see, the truck filled with hay might have been noticed because it is a long way from its base town. It could start to be dangerous to continue with that particular truck. We do not want to raise suspicion. My friend, you have come a long way, but there is still much traveling to do. Where we are going, it will become even more dangerous. There will be more and more soldiers on alert as we move closer to the coast. Our traveling may also be delayed from time to time, as plans are made and changed. Remember, I also must leave with you, so caution must be taken each step of our path to England. The Germans often take young men such as us for use in factories or concentration camp work. Since we are both young and perhaps a little suspicious, we do not want to bring any real attention to us. Our friends are already planning the next part of our journey. We will know together when the time is right."

Back at the 305th Bomb Group Headquarters in Chelveston, Bob Courtney, Russ Parker, and Jim McFarland prepared to leave for the United States. Their orders had come through and the three would soon be on their way back to the States. The combat tour of 30 missions was over. They were lucky! The odds were beaten and they were going home. To be sure, they had earned their pay while flying the dangerous sky above occupied Europe. After a well-earned leave to visit with family and friends, a reassignment would be in order on behalf of the next phase of their service, most probably as advanced instructors.

There, of course, would be a party or two before they began the trip back home. Whether the party was in Chelveston, Rushden, or over in Higham Ferrers, the main qualification for the party centered around a public house—a good ole fashion "pub"!

They had been warned by Howie that stateside would certainly seem tame compared to what they had gone through the past eight months, which may well be the welcome case. Each officer had matured greatly in the last eight months. A combat war would most certainly do that.

For Howie, who hosted most of the pub gatherings, his request was granted to be reassigned within the Eighth Air Force as an officer working on the operational team at High Wycombe. This was meaningful for First Lieutenant Howard Van Dyke. He would remain in England in a non-flying position.

High Wycombe was the Eighth Air Force Headquarters, located about 25 miles west of London. Before becoming the Eighth Headquarters, it was the Wycombe

Abbey Girls School. It also had a grand life as a stately country manor house, located near the Chiltern Hills. The property was quite park-like, with extremely old trees marking the landscape.

Lieutenant General Jimmy Doolittle, of the famous Tokyo Raid, took command of the Mighty Eighth Air Force on January 6, 1944. He was replacing a well-respected General Ira Eaker, who was promoted and assigned to command all Allied Air Forces, including the 15th Air Force, which was now operating from Italy.

Howie was really pleased with the new assignment. He would help in the planning of missions rather than flying them. His experience as a combat B-17 pilot would serve him well in this new position on the operational team. The team itself had, at any one time, more than 100 officers devoted to planning all of the important aspects of the bombing raids with targets in France, the Netherlands, Belgium, Poland, and Germany. Howie had flown to many of the targeted areas and his first-hand knowledge would be quite valuable. An extra benefit for Howie was the fact that being assigned so close to London would enable him to see more of Elizabeth! He also kept the thought alive in his mind that the Germans had not captured Steve. His hope was that somehow Steve, rescued by the Underground, would soon resurface in England.

At the small farm just outside Ressons, France, Steve settled in as best he could until the time was right for the move to the next location. It was difficult waiting. However, Steve understood that timing, as in many situations, was the key to the success of an operation. This one was no different, but then it was quite different as many individuals put their very lives on the line for him. Each location brought Steve closer to a trip across the Channel and landing safely in England.

From what the driver told Steve and from his own observations, he felt safe with his host. It also became apparent that more German troops would be encountered as they moved closer to the coast. The one thing, which was always in their favor, was that the French were opposed to having the dreaded German SS troops on their soil. There were, of course, those who cooperated with the enemy for their own well-being and profit. Many of these people were identified and as those in the Underground would state, "They would have to stand for their actions at some time in the future. Nothing would be forgotten!"

While having some afternoon tea in the farmhouse, the driver kidded Steve once again, that the two of them should take the train to Paris for the weekend. After all, Paris was less than 140 kilometers to the south and he would show Steve a good time. However, the weekend of January 7th would be spent holed up and trying to stay warm in Ressons.

On Saturday evening, the 8th, a visitor came to the farmhouse at six o'clock or, as they say, 1800 hours. Even though it was dark, the visitor did not try to hide the fact that he came for dinner. He had a small sack of food and two bottles of wine with him. The visitor parked his bicycle near the back door, but in plain sight. To anyone who was on the lookout for something suspicious, nothing would be found here.

Once inside, although names were not exchanged, the visitor warmly greeted Steve. He spoke fairly good English, which pleased Steve. He would now be included in the majority of the conversation. What was being said or taking place, of course, would be explained to the man known as William.

William said something to the driver and the visitor that made their eyes light up. It was explained to Steve, that in his honor, William was bringing out a bottle of Scotch whisky that he had acquired long ago as payment for something or other, he could not remember.

Supper could wait a little while as everyone became more acquainted over the glass of whisky. Smiling to himself as he raised his glass to his hosts, Steve thought that Howie would enjoy what was taking place around the old wooden kitchen table. Howie enjoyed Scotch and good conversation, plus he spoke quite good French.

"I was also an aviator," said the visitor to Steve.

"Really . . . did you fly in the First World War?" asked Steve.

"Yes, it was called the Great War to us," answered the visitor as he shared a proud past. "I flew with the French, of course. This is how I came to speak English. I knew your Captain Eddie Rickenbacker. He was a fine man and a great flier that shot down many German airplanes . . . I believe 26."

"All Americans know of Eddie Rickenbacker," said Steve.

"I also shot down the Hun. It was just two, but as you can see, I am still here!" The visitor let out a loud laugh. He stroked his beard, remembering a time of long ago.

"I am very impressed," said Steve, who paused a moment and then continued, "as I understand it, you had to be a very good aviator just to survive!"

"This is just as true today, my friend," commented the visitor as he reached once again for his glass, raised it in salute to Steve and took a sip. "It is such a different war, the airplanes and machines of this war are modern, but then the hell of it all is really always the same."

"I must salute all of you," answered Steve. "The help you are giving to me is surely not the first time you have aided a flier. The danger you place yourself in is most appreciated and to me. You and all of your friends are the true heroes."

"My friend, I am glad that you understand the full situation," explained the visitor. "We have had to explain the danger to some of the fliers, both American and British that if found out, we would be tortured for information and then executed."

"The mercy would come in the form of a bullet after the terrible torture," joined in the driver.

It was explained in French to William what had been just said as he placed the supper on the table.

"Ah, but enough of this, we now eat," stated the visitor. "You know I was about your age when I first flew an aeroplane. That was in 1914 and what a thrill to look down at the countryside and see what the birds saw all along. It was amazing. They did not need me anymore after the Armistice, which was in November of 1918. I was 28 years old, came home to Ressons and started a business." He then took a sip of wine that was served with dinner, nodded approval and then asked, "Did you learn to fly in the military?"

"I learned as a boy of 11 years old," answered Steve. "My dad bought an old mail airplane. It was built during the First World War, but the war was over before it saw any combat, so it became a mail plane, which for many years carried the mail from city to city. No one knew how to fly the plane and most of our neighbors thought that my dad had lost his mind, but he hired a man who lived in Orlando to teach us. Our instructor was a pilot who was in the war, but I do not know anything about the time he was in the service. At first, I had a difficult time reaching the pedals. I soloed when I was 12 years old.

We still own and fly the old bi-wing plane. She is slow, but fun to fly and, as an airplane, quite forgiving to her pilot."

"They tell me that you are a pilot who flies the B-17 bomber. Having four engines must keep you quite busy?" questioned the visitor.

"The B-17 is a dream to fly," responded Steve. "You have a copilot and the help of an engineer, so it is not as hard as one might think, after training, of course. You are, though, kept quite busy as you said. All is well until the sting of the combat battle brings on almost unbearable tension, especially if the plane is severely damaged to the point where you have lost her and she will not fly anymore. The really tough part is when you realize that there is nothing you or your training can do to save the plane. You have lost the plane and your crewmates. They either have been killed or will become prisoners of war. I was lucky enough to have parachute-landed in a place where there were no German soldiers and was taken in by a kind, old farmer."

Everyone was silent for a moment as the reality of what this young man experienced was brought to light, especially his thoughts on losing his crew and plane.

The driver reached for the wine bottle, filled everyone's glass again and said, "I raise my glass to you and we all salute you, my friend." They all toasted Steve, who was a little embarrassed by revealing his deep thoughts. He smiled with humble appreciation.

With the main meal finished, William brought out some cheese, biscuits, and a bottle of cognac. Dinner dishes were cleared from the table and placed in the kitchen sink, next to the water pump handle for cleaning at a later time.

"Okay, my young friend," the visitor said to Steve, pausing for a second as a glass of cognac was placed before him. "We have a plan, crazy as it may sound, to take you toward your next destination."

Steve already had a sip of cognac and nibbled on a biscuit and small wedge of cheese. He placed his glass back onto the table so that he could digest every word about the next phase of his journey.

"Do you think that you can drive a big bus?" questioned the visitor.

"On our ranch in Florida, I've driven the tractor, my small truck and also the fairly large truck that we own, but I've never driven a bus," answered Steve. "I will say this, if it has gears to shift, then I believe that I can drive it."

The visitor laughed at Steve's remark. "This is good," he said. "With the beard you have and the clothes you are wearing, you look much like a local. We will get you a driver's cap to make you look official. I will need your papers so that a driver's permit can be made. We will also change the place you come from so that it will not bring on any suspicion."

Steve handed over his papers confirming that he was Paul Reens.

The visitor looked them over and placed them in his coat pocket. He told Steve, or rather Paul Reens, that he would return the following night with the correct papers, showing that Paul Reens was now from Valognes, in Normandy. The driver was from this same small city. The driver would teach Steve, Paul, all about the area around Valognes and Huberville. The one big obstacle was that Steve did not speak French. He, of course, had picked up some of the words and could now understand some French, but really, not that much.

As both languages, French for William and English for Steve continued, William said to the visitor that while Steve would be driving the bus, he would not be considered as the primary driver, but a relief or driver in training. This way the man they all called the driver could be the number one operator of the bus and that way he could do all of the talking, if it became necessary.

The visitor nodded his head in agreement, as did the driver. This part of the conversation had been spoken in French, but Steve saw that, whatever the plan, it had been modified to everyone's satisfaction.

It was then that the visitor explained the overall plan to Steve. The fact that he was not to speak a word was quite understood, especially if a German soldier was present. Steve was also instructed that a nod of the head would be all right, but just a small nod as dictated by the eyes of the driver.

Steve agreed and thanked them. "Thanks for sticking your necks out for me."

The "sticking your neck out" comment was at first questioned, but accepted as American slang with a laugh all around.

The visitor prepared to leave, but not before alerting Steve to be ready to move in two days. The plan for the bus trip would be explained tomorrow night when he returned with the proper papers. He then left the house and pedaled his way back up the lane.

William refilled the glasses with cognac and the three walked into the formal room to relax before the warm fireplace. Between the wine and cognac, a good night's sleep was assured.

The following day, William went about his chores in his normal routine. A few vehicles, including two German trucks that carried soldiers, could be seen on the main road, but none came down William's lane. Inside the house, Steve and the driver talked a good deal about the Normandy area and especially Valognes, plus the hamlet of Huberville. Steve was also told of nearby towns of St. Mere Eglise and Bayeux, where the famous tapestry was kept. In addition, a game of chess was played. Neither Steve nor the driver was very good. They were passable, but not good. Then William joined in and both men learned how to lose gracefully.

That evening the visitor returned with what certainly looked to be proper and quite official papers for Steve—Paul Reens. He also had a worn bus driver cap for Steve and likewise one for the driver. He reviewed a plan, which would have the bus originate in Ressons in the early morning at about seven. This was to be a regularly scheduled bus that would pick up and transport passengers along the way. The "real driver" of the bus would be aboard and sit in the front seat as the instructor. Next to him would be the man Steve referred to as the driver, with Steve doing the actual driving. This way, instructions could be conveyed without causing any particular suspicion. Because Steve was the driver of the bus, in the event of an inspection, the German soldiers would be looking at the passengers and checking their papers for anyone whom they might want to detain. With Steve, as the driver quietly just sitting and waiting for the inspection to be over, he would not be one who would even have his papers checked. This was the hope of the plan. From Ressons, the route would be to Maignelay-Montigny, but not to Montdidier, where a tough German checkpoint existed. The route instead would travel through the villages of Ansauvillers, Bonvillers, Beauvoir and on to Breteuil.

While Steve looked at the map of the trip to be taken, he noted that Breteuil was less than 30 kilometers from Amiens. He had been there on August 31st on a bombing raid. Just above Amiens, perhaps another 40 kilometers north, was where the boys of the Abbeville Fighter Squadron of the Luftwaffe were stationed. No, he did not want to meet them, when asked. He already had at 30,000 feet and they were not friendly.

Steve was also told that at Breteuil it would be determined if he should continue as the driver, or if it looked to be dangerous in the event that the Germans were catching on, then other arrangements would go into effect.

Dinner with wine, plus the after-dinner cognac, made for a good night's sleep. Steve, although concerned about the so-called crazy plan, had confidence that he was safe. He actually was looking forward to driving the old bus partway across France.

Morning came early as William gently awakened his American visitor. It was just past five o'clock. A breakfast of strong black coffee and freshly baked biscuits, along with apple jelly was waiting at the kitchen table as the driver and Steve sat down to enjoy their last moments with William, who had been such a kind host.

An hour later, the man whom Steve knew as the visitor, came down the lane in a car, which Steve imagined was from the late 20s or early 30s.

A quick French goodbye was said to William. Steve also shook his hand and gave him a hug. William closed the door to the kitchen and gave a last look from the window as the car disappeared back up the lane and turned left onto Rue du Jeu de Paume. William would continue to worry for the safety of the young American flier.

In just a few minutes, the car arrived at the garage where the bus was parked. Actually, there were two buses parked behind the garage. Both of them looked to Steve as though they belonged in a transportation museum and not in active service. The two looked like they might be from the early 30s, very early 30s. It was quite obvious that they had seen a lot of road wear, although when the garage mechanic went to start the engine of the one to be used this morning, it sprang to life with relative ease and its hum was steady and solid.

The garage mechanic, who was part of the local resistance, took Steve by the arm and motioned to Steve's companion, the driver, to accompany him onto the bus. Also present was the actual bus operator who would sit in a front seat near Steve and act as the tutor.

The garage mechanic had Steve sit in the driver's seat and spoke in a voice just above a whisper, explaining how to work the bus door and exactly how the four gears of the bus shifted. He also showed Steve how to start, driving slowly, easing the braking so as not to jolt the passengers and cause suspicion. While all of this was spoken in French, it was translated in English to Steve. He looked over to his instructor with a smile of confidence; he understood what had to be done.

Steve drove the old black bus from the garage to the bus depot, which was actu-ally at the railroad station. Steve thought to himself that this would certainly be an interesting tale to tell his dad and Howie.

At the bus depot, there were six people waiting to board the bus. A low-rank-ing German soldier checked the papers of those about to board the early morning bus. The soldier did not come onto the bus himself but simply gave a greeting of a head nod to Steve as he sat behind the large steering wheel. Steve gave a faint smile and nodded back. At exactly seven o'clock, Steve closed the bus door and eased the bus away from the depot. He drove slowly through Ressons and toward the road to Maignelay-Montigny.

So far, to the regular passengers, the trip was quite normal. Steve caught on quickly and drove the bus almost like a veteran driver. He double clutched and moved through the gears smoothly. Steve was not taking anything for granted though. He was paying attention to everything he was doing so that it all looked routine. The real bus driver was now more relaxed and believed that Steve might actually pull off this far-fetched charade.

Steve was alerted as they drove along to slow down and stop by the side of the road at a dirt lane, which led to a farmhouse. The bus was brought to a halt by the lane and two people boarded the bus, a man and woman. They looked puzzled in seeing the regular driver sitting in the front passenger's seat with a stranger sitting behind the steering wheel. The real driver simply greeted them and stated in French that the young man was a driver in training. The man said something to Steve, while the lady, obviously his wife, smiled at Steve who smiled back and tipped his driver's cap. Steve's partner, whom he called the driver, acted as a passenger and sat near Steve just in case someone started a conversation with Steve in French. He did not know exactly what he would do, but perhaps he could swing the conversation to himself and away from Steve.

One old but well-dressed man left the bus in Maignelay-Montigny, as did the man and his wife. There was a much older lady waiting for them. At this stop, two older gentlemen boarded the bus. They were together and took seats next to each other, halfway towards the back of the bus. It was the most comfortable place to ride, because directly over the wheels one could feel every bump in the road. There were no soldiers present at this stop, which let a more-relaxed Steve pull away from the town square and proceed on the route.

Steve brought the bus to a confident halt at each designated stop, picking up and discharging passengers. It was not until he pulled into the railroad station in Breteuil that all of his passengers left the bus. Steve thought that perhaps those who looked like businessmen departing would then take the train to the nearest larger city, Amiens, while others might be visiting relatives or friends in Breteuil. As each passenger left the bus, a German soldier checked their papers. Four additional sol-diers stood near, rifles at the ready, as each passenger presented their documents. All seemed to be in order and the passengers were permitted to walk toward the train station or to wherever they were going.

The soldier who had been checking the papers and seemed to be in charge was not an officer. He climbed aboard the bus. The regular driver greeted the soldier in German and explained that he had two drivers in training in order to replace two others who could no longer handle the big bus. One of the older men would continue to work as a mechanic in the bus barn, but the other had a heart attack and died. All of this was explained in a calm, matter-of-fact way and the German soldier did not question further. The soldier was offered papers by the real driver, but he simply gave a wave of his hand and left the bus. The five soldiers walked away from the bus and toward the railroad station, perhaps to get warm inside the terminal.

Now passenger-free, Steve and his partner congratulated the real driver with his convincing act. With Steve behind the steering wheel, Steve's partner still in the passenger's seat and the real driver standing in the aisle, the conversation shifted to the next portion of the journey. Should there be a continuation to Beauvais with all three or should the real driver take over driving and leave the two who were still trying to evade capture exit the bus in another part of Breteuil, in an area where a safe house existed?

Just then, a woman who was nicely dressed walked from the train terminal toward the bus. She was carrying a small valise.

In French, she said to Steve, "This is the coach to Beauvais, yes?"

"Yes, you are correct, madam," answered the real driver. He went on to explain that the man actually driving was a bus driver in training.

"Then we should continue the journey as soon as possible," stated the woman in good clear English, smiling at Steve.

Steve did not know what to do so he did nothing. For all he knew, the woman could be a plant, and if he answered in English to her that would end his attempt to continue evading capture.

Steve's partner spoke French to the woman. They conversed for just a short few minutes, but to Steve it seemed like a lifetime.

The real driver, who was just now catching on to what was taking place through the conversation in French, was becoming angry that English had been used. If anyone had overheard, and there were a few people standing around not too far from the bus, then someone could have reported this to one of the soldiers and endangered everyone. He was also glad that Steve had kept his mouth shut.

The woman, aware now that she could have made a serious blunder, apologized to everyone saying that she did not think. She only wanted the American to feel at home and now realized that the danger could have been catastrophic. The valise the women carried had food and money, which she was told to deliver to them and to ride the coach to Beauvais.

Things now settled down. The real driver explained that they did not need food just now and that they had brought their own, but perhaps when they reached Beauvais they would have some. The money was placed in a box under a floorboard to the driver's left. His feet would cover that space and no one would notice anything out of the ordinary. It would be there for safekeeping. The valise was placed in the overhead bin above a seat five rows from the front of the bus, which is where they sat the woman who was obviously with the resistance, but still had a lot to learn. The incident would be reported so that she could be more properly trained, but in the meantime, she was simply told to sit and be completely quiet. The real driver explained to Steve and his partner that to have left her at the depot in Breteuil might have caused suspicion, so it was better to have her on the bus. The real driver also had a laugh when the lady referred to the bus as a coach. "This old hardworking piece of machinery," he stated, "is simply a bus and not a more sophisticated coach!"

As they were about to leave two men came on board the bus, tickets in hand, then two more men and a lady. They also took their seats after presenting their tickets; however, before Steve could close the door and pull away from the depot, the soldiers returned to check the papers of the new passengers. This time, although the same group of German soldiers who had greeted the bus came back, an officer was now with them. The soldier who had come aboard before checked the passenger documents while the officer stood in the front of the bus and carefully looked everyone over.

"You cannot be too careful these days," said the officer to Steve in French.

Steve glanced over toward the real driver. He gave a slow nod to Steve, who in turn slowly shook his head in agreement with the officer.

Finally satisfied that all was well, the officer and soldier walked off the bus. The officer gave a wave to proceed.

With a look of relief on his face, Steve fashioned a small smile to his companions as he closed the bus door and started driving to the road that would take them to Beauvais.

Having armed German soldiers within an arm's length was certainly unsettling on the nerves. Steve wondered if anyone else could hear his heart pounding. At least being the driver of the bus made him concentrate on the task at hand instead of the prospect of encountering more German soldiers. Moving closer to the Normandy coast and the boat, which could take him once again to British soil, was becoming a dangerous cat-and-mouse game, however, this certainly was not a game!

The 28-mile trip from Breteuil to Beauvais was, as they say, uneventful, which was fine with Steve. The real driver made a motion to Steve about halfway through the trip to see if he was becoming tired from driving. Steve could relax and the real driver would take over for the balance of the drive to their destination. Steve shook his head no. He continued the trip from behind the steering wheel. Actually, he was fatigued, but the adrenaline rush kept him alert.

When they arrived in Beauvais and Steve brought the bus to a stop next to the railroad station, German soldiers were once again present. This time two soldiers were stationed at the rear emergency door with four more plus an officer at the front door of the bus. As each passenger, including the lady who sat in row five, got off the bus, they and their papers were examined. A soldier standing near the officer who was inspecting everyone politely took the valise from the lady. He held it while her papers were scrutinized. She played her part well. She explained that she was in Beauvais to help her sister care for their elderly father. Their father was now having great difficulty in remembering things. Cleared to go on her way, she walked toward the town center, valise in hand. The lady did not look back.

One of the male passengers had a nervous look on his face as his papers were being inspected. The officer did not say anything while the man was on the bus, but as he stepped off, they took him in hand, escorting him to an office they were using in the railroad terminal for further questioning. The man broke free and started to run away toward the railroad tracks. He refused orders to halt and was shot by two of the soldiers. He had been hit twice in back. Stumbling, he fell to the ground just before the tracks. The soldiers retrieved his limp body and dragged it toward a boxcar sitting on a side rail, where they dumped the body inside. A lone soldier stood guard over the dead man who was on the wanted list of the Gestapo.

Steve was stunned. He could not believe that this could happen.

It brought home even more how he needed to be careful and play his part as best he could. What had just occurred was real. This was not Hollywood. A man was shot dead!

After the atmosphere had calmed, the real driver explained to the officer that the bus must be driven to the garage in order to refuel for the return trip. The schedule, he explained, called for the bus to be back at this parking place at the train station in two hours.

The officer thought for a moment, then said in fluent French, "Because of the recent problem we encountered, it is best if I check the papers of the bus employees, just to be certain everyone is who they say they are."

The real driver showed his first and motioned for Steve—Paul Reens—to go next. Steve's papers had a somewhat worn look, including the photo of him in the same bus driver's cap, which satisfied the officer much to Steve's relief. But the officer also gave a careful look at Steve's bearded face. Next, the man who Steve called the driver presented his papers to the German officer. The photo was not as clear as it could have been. The officer took a very long time in examining the papers and questioned him about their condition. The answer given was simply that he had them for more than three years and once they had gotten wet while German soldiers were inspecting them during a rainstorm. He had dried them as best he could. This satisfied the officer and the bus was released to obtain the needed fuel for the return trip.

Steve pulled the bus away from the parking space at the train station and followed the real driver's directions to what they called the bus barn. In truth, it was just a simple garage. There were no other buses parked there and, in fact, just a single auto was there.

"We say goodbye," said the real driver to his two wards as the bus came to a halt in the garage parking area.

Steve, still behind the steering wheel, smiled and gave a "Fist Salute" to the real driver. They had made yet another dangerous part of his journey with help from the brave Underground resistance fighters.

As they left the bus and entered the garage, two men met Steve and his companions. Some words were spoken in French. The real driver then came over and bid Steve farewell. He was proud to have known him, even for just a short time. Then he left the garage to supervise the refueling of the bus.

Steve and his now lone companion followed the two men out a back door in the garage. It was near dusk and the four men walked a few blocks, then entered the back door of a house.

"You will both rest here for the night," said one of the men.

"We have already begun working on the next segment of your journey," said the other man in his best English. "Though we won't know when you will depart until the plan goes into effect."

Steve's companion, who he simply referred to as his driver, was in deep conversation with the other man. They were speaking in French. The man who was conversing with Steve looked over toward the two every once in a while as he picked up parts of what the plan could be.

Everyone was now feeling more relaxed in this small safe house, which was located in a more industrial part of Beauvais. The house inside and out was nondescript. It was quite plain with no woman's touch. Perhaps, though, this house was perfect for what was needed on behalf of the work being conducted.

"We have changed the route that you are to take because of some German troop build-up. Additional inspection stops are making things more difficult. It is important to remain flexible," said the man who spoke English.

"Is that the reason why we are to stay here until further notice?" asked Steve.

"No, you two will be here tonight and all day tomorrow and part of that night," the man replied. "Then in the very early morning, you will be made a helper on a truck that will carry milk to a fromage factory or cheese factory to you in English. The factory is in Orbec. Each of you will be in a different truck. I will be with you and my friend will bring him, as he motioned toward Steve's companion. We will also drive separate routes to arrive at the same destination. This is not for safety, but to make a stop for additional milk."

He then started to explain in French to Steve's companion, but was interrupted as it became clear that the companion spoke English and understood what had been said.

The man who only spoke French prepared dinner. It was not fancy: some hearty soup with lots of potatoes, leeks, carrots and a small amount of ham. A large loaf of bread accompanied the soup. It was filling and tasted good, especially on the cold January night. The red wine was plentiful.

After dinner, as they sat and chatted, a bottle of Calvados was placed on the kitchen table along with a large chunk of cheese. The Calvados bottle had no label on it and Steve surmised that a nearby farmer had produced the apple brandy. It was good, warm going down and after a couple of glasses, Steve was quite ready for a good night's sleep.

The following day was uneventful. One could say that it was boring, but when so many are working to help you, that word boring is set aside and you cope with what is at hand. With the two men away during the day, Steve and his companion spent most of it talking and playing chess with the old set that was on a table in the parlor. They enjoyed the game. One would win a game and lose the next, often not knowing exactly, as an expert would, which move eventually cost them the game.

That evening was spent much like the previous one. They all turned in early. They would have to leave the house at four o'clock in the morning, then walk to the garage where the bus had refueled and drive the dairy trucks to Orbec.

Knowing that Steve had done well driving the bus made things a little easier for the overall plan. Steve would not be a passenger, but the driver of the dairy truck. Having Steve behind the steering wheel would let the Frenchman become the "helper" and therefore less suspicion would occur as the "helper" could then handle all of the paperwork and conversation with authorities, should the need arise.

At a little past 0430 hours, Steve drove out of the garage yard and slowly proceeded from Beauvais toward the village of Auneuil. He took notice of the stately old Cathedral de Beauvais. The outline of the cathedral could be seen even in the darkness. They also drove past what looked to be a very old timbered hotel, which Steve's helper pointed out as the Hotel du Lion d' or Beauvais. In conversation, Steve was told about a statue to Jeanne Laisne or Jeanne Fourquet, "Jeanne Hachette," with her swinging an axe. The French heroine was born in 1456.

So far, as they drove on, they had not encountered any German soldiers who were paying attention to them. Perhaps it was too early in the morning or maybe the truck, which often took this route, was looked upon as simply routine.

The drive to and through Auneuil was made rather quickly with no delays, especially because of the weather. It was a clear, brisk morning. The village of Auneuil had beautiful old mansions, one of which was pointed out to Steve, La Maison Boulenger.

From Auneuil they proceeded to Gisors. It was now completely daylight. On the road, a truck filled with German soldiers, followed by another truck that had a cover hiding whatever was in it, came into view.

"Slow down a little and just give a wave," said Steve's helper. "That should satisfy the bastards."

Steve did as he was told and the drivers of the military trucks waved back and continued down the road.

As they entered Gisors, Steve took notice and remarked that the town had an old, medieval look to it. A good assessment, he was informed that the old castle fortress was called Château de Gisors.

From Gisors, they drove to the town of Les Andelys. It was a town on the River Seine, 20 miles northeast of Evreux, the largest town in the immediate area. As they entered Les Andelys, Steve, who was all eyes in viewing these historical towns and villages they were passing through, took notice of an old residence he figured was a medieval castle, which stood out on a hill that overlooked the town and River Seine.

"The Château Gaillard . . . and you are correct, it is what you would call a medieval castle," said Steve's helper.

"There are some really beautiful houses in this town," said Steve as he pointed to a white Tudor house with turrets on the second floor that overlooked the road they were traveling. "I studied architecture at the university before I joined the Air Corps." In addition, the house overlooked the river with quite a beautiful view.

Steve's helper enjoyed the enthusiasm that Steve showed as they drove past landmarks, which he had taken for granted, having driven in the area for years.

The reality of what was the here and now came sharply into focus as they approached Le Pont, a bridge that would take them across the River Seine. A German inspection was stationed at the bridge. They were the fourth truck in line. Two soldiers approached their truck, one on each side. While the soldiers did not come but within several feet from the truck door, it was clear that no one would be able to make a clean escape should they try to flee. They did not point their rifles toward the truck, but it was apparent that they were ready to take action if necessary.

"Give me your papers," stated Steve's helper. "I will get out and present them when it is our turn. Just stay where you are and ease the truck forward. Two more trucks are now behind us. This is good. The Germans do not expect things to be amiss in this area. I believe this inspection is just more of a formality. Don't run over any soldiers or we will catch hell." This playful warning eased the tension a little.

Steve kept the truck at a crawl as they approached the border-type inspection hut. The gate was down in order to halt each vehicle that desired to cross the river. When they reached the spot where the officer in charge put up his hand to stop, Steve's helper got out of the passenger's side of the truck and walked over to the officer. In the meantime, three other soldiers stood near the cab of the truck. Two had rifles, and the other had a machine gun. Steve gave a slight smile, but it was not returned. They were all business.

The officer looked over the papers, including the truck manifest of cargo, then walked around to the driver's side. He motioned for Steve to open the truck window so that he could get a good look at him to make certain that the photo and man before him matched. Absent from Steve's papers was the bus driver permit. The permit was removed the night before when his papers were checked by his host.

Satisfied, the officer gave a nod of his head to Steve and handed the papers back to Steve's helper. He rejoined Steve in the truck cab. Steve acknowledged the officer's nod with one of his own, hardly believing that he, as an American airman, was actually just a few feet from a German officer. The gate was lifted and they drove across the bridge over the River Seine.

After they crossed the bridge and were out of sight of the inspection hut, the helper told Steve that the next town, Evreux, was one in which they would stay on the western side of the river. Evreux was an old city that interested Steve; it had a cathedral and two older churches, plus an old Roman wall. However, just east of the city, almost to Fauville, was a Luftwaffe air base. The helper went on to explain to Steve that it had actually been an airfield since the 1920s, when it was a civil aerodrome. The concrete runway had been constructed in the 1930s and, with the fall of France, the Luftwaffe took over. They flew the Messerschmitt 109s and Junkers 88s from the base. Also of late, the Focke-Wulf 190s had been spotted flying from this airfield.

Steve's helper was impressed when Steve told him that his bombardment group had bombed this field on August 24th. There were several airfields hit, with the one near Evreux included in the raid on that day. In addition, Steve stated that he had visited Amiens and Romilly-Sur-Seine from more than 25,000 feet above.

The route they now drove took them away from the center of Evreux. It was better to be safe. They took a country road to Sacquenville, a small village. It did not take long. The town's old church stood out and could be viewed from the entire countryside. By going this way, it was a much less traveled path, which would also evade unnecessary questions by the German military.

Just outside of Sacquenville, Steve brought the truck to a halt and they changed drivers. Steve could now relax in the passenger's seat. From here, the truck was driven through the little villages of Claville and LeCoudray. Then it was on to the town of Conehes. As they expected, on this back-country route, they did not encounter any military forces.

With several stops along the way, after passing through Conehes, the next stop was at a dairy farm near the village of La Neuve-Lyre. Here, they picked up additional milk. Steve helped load the large containers onto the truck, but as instructed, he kept to himself and did not offer to speak. There was no reason to bring the unassuming dairy farmer into the mix of things. After Steve finished the loading, he returned to the passenger's side of the truck and climbed into the cabin, settling in his seat. In just a short time, they were back on the road toward the next town, which was Broglie.

"We do not have far to go now," the helper turned driver said to Steve.

"I'm glad you are driving," answered Steve. "It is starting to get dark and some of these roads are a challenge."

In a little over nine kilometers, they entered the town of Orbec. They drove through the narrow streets, which were lined with shops and old timber houses. A beautiful, older-looking church stood out, even in the coming darkness.

"We shall be stopping at the cheese factory, what we call La Fromagerie, in just a few minutes," said his driver friend. "Stay in the truck until I come for you. This way we keep everything quiet and safe for all of us."

"I understand," answered Steve, as the truck left the roadway and came to a stop behind the main building of La Fromagerie.

As instructed, Steve stayed in the truck cab. He was also on the alert in the event that all did not go as planned. Someone could have found out that an American aviator and a wanted Underground resistance fighter were to meet up with others from the resistance and given this information to the authorities for a cash reward.

A few minutes passed and then Steve became a little concerned. *Should I leave the truck cab, wait on the ground and be ready to run away before I'm captured?*

Those fears disappeared as the driver of the truck opened a side door to the factory and waved for Steve to come into the plant.

Once inside, Steve was introduced to a very large man who was perhaps in his mid-60s. He had messy white hair, possibly from having just taken off a cap. In addition, he had a full, snowy white beard. Steve chuckled to himself as though he had met Santa Claus!

While the man did not speak English very well, he could be completely understood. He spoke his English slowly, working to pick the right words. Steve pointed out, when the man apologized for not speaking better English, that his English was much better than Steve's French. This pleased his new acquaintance and they were fast friends.

"I leave you, my friend, in good hands," said Steve's helper, driver and partner for the day. "Maybe someday you will return to France, and we will break bread and drink good wine."

"My thanks are little payment for all the help you have given me," stated Steve as the two bid goodbye.

"We must leave now . . . quickly," said the white-haired man.

Steve looked back just before he followed the white-haired man out of a door on the darkened side of the factory. A wave of the hand and yet another individual who had risked his life for Steve was gone.

They walked briskly for several minutes through some darkened streets to what seemed like the main street of Orbec. A sign on the side of a building read *Rue Grande,* from what Steve could make out in the increasing darkness, which had not yet turned to night.

Steve followed the white-haired man into an old timbered house. It actually looked as though it was leaning a little. Once inside, the man whom Steve had come to know simply as the driver got up from a chair and walked over to greet Steve.

"We have been awaiting your arrival my friend," he said. "We arrived at La Fromagerie a little more than an hour ago. Before we go on with this conversation, it is now safe for me to formally introduce myself. My name is Albert Leterrier and this dear old friend with the flowing beard is Andre Le Cacheux."

"It is a pleasure to call you something other than the driver . . . and, Andre, thank you for taking in a poor ole refugee," answered Steve.

"It is not important that you divulge your real American name," stated the driver, now Albert. "You can tell me this after we leave France. To us you are Paul Reens and this is all anyone needs to know. We still have a long dangerous journey ahead of us."

"I understand," answered Steve. "To be here an hour before me, you must have taken a more direct route with your dairy truck."

"That we did," answered Albert. "From Beauvais, we drove to Gournay-en-Bray to Rouen and then down to Bernay before coming to Orbec. We made three stops along the way for pick-up and here we are. Back at Bernay, which is an old timber and plaster house town, much like Orbec, the Boche stopped us for a full inspection. Bernay is on the direct main railroad line from Paris to Cherbourg, so the Germans are very careful about who you might be."

"It is time to eat," said Andre, as he motioned for Steve and Albert to come into the kitchen for supper.

Another man who had been cooking acknowledged Albert and Steve, but he did not say anything. He just kept on cooking the supper.

Andre sat down at the end of the large kitchen table and, with a sweep of his hand, motioned for Steve and Albert to join him. They took chairs across from each other, leaving the other end chair for the man who was cooking.

Andre poured each one a generous glass of rouge-red wine and toasted his dinner companions, who in turn toasted him and the man slaving over the cook-stove.

Dinner was placed on the table, first a hearty soup of potatoes, carrots and onions. A traditional large loaf of bread accompanied the soup. Andre actually had butter for the bread. It was something Steve had almost forgotten existed; oh, did it taste good!

The man who was cooking joined them and sat down. He said something in French and smiled at Steve and Albert. Albert explained to Steve that the cook hoped they were enjoying the meal. Steve gave the thumbs-up sign, which pleased the cook.

After the soup course was finished, the cook got up to remove the bowls from the table. Steve started to get up and help clear the table, but the cook motioned for him to just sit and relax. He would handle things. In the meantime, Andre poured more wine.

The cook went back to work. He was humming a tune to himself. You could not make out a song or even a real tune, but he was self-satisfied and happy.

The following course was quite special—*Poisson*—fish, fresh that day from the historic port city of Honfleur. Each man received a plate with a whole fish on it. The fish had been cooked in old cast-iron frying pans on the large wood-burning cook-stove. The stove also served to heat the kitchen and other nearby rooms. To Steve, the flat fish resembled what he knew as flounder; however, it was thicker and larger.

"The *Poisson*, to you in English, fish, is in your honor," explained Andre in his best English. "You would call this kind 'sole.' The harbor town of Honfleur is one that artist painters come to create beautiful works. You must return someday and visit like a tourist."

"Thank you . . . wow, I had to come to France to taste the best fish I've ever eaten!" proclaimed Steve after taking his first bite of the fresh catch. The cook was appreciative of Steve's compliment.

After supper, Andre told Steve and Albert to follow him into the parlor. He asked if they would like cognac or some Calvados. Albert said that he would appreciate some Calvados and Steve agreed. If Steve had been in another part of France, then perhaps he would have requested the cognac, but here in Normandy, Calvados was King!

While they enjoyed the Calvados, the local apple brandy of the region, and the warmth of the fireplace, Andre spoke of the next part of the journey. It was more for the benefit of Steve, since Albert was from Normandy.

"You came about 200 kilometers today, maybe 124 miles to you Americans," said Andre. "It was a long and dangerous journey. The build-up of the German Army continues in this region and it is becoming more dangerous every day. Where you are going, you must outfox the fox. The one important thing in your favor is that Albert is from this part of France. We are trying to get you to a safe house in Balleroy. This village is about 135 kilometers from here, maybe 83 miles as I calculate. The plan, which Albert may change as you go along, is to travel through Livarot, St. Pierre, Potigny, going around and away from Falaise, the historic old town where William the Conqueror was born. But, my young friend, this is also where a very large German Army build-up is taking place."

Then turning to Albert, Andre continued, "So from Potigny, Albert, with you knowing the area as well as anyone, what do you think of going through the village of Thury-Harcourt and staying away from Caen for the same reasons as Falaise?"

"I agree with you," replied Albert. "The village of Aunay-Sur-Odon is the home of some of my relatives. We could stay there if getting to Balleroy proves to be difficult. There are perhaps 30 kilometers between the two villages."

Steve listened to each word that was said by Andre and Albert. He also followed along with Albert as he pointed out each village on the map, which was spread out on the floor in front of the fireplace.

Having finished his work in the kitchen, the cook joined the men as the conversation continued. He poured himself a glass of cognac and sat down in a chair before the fireplace. The cook sat for just a moment or so before setting his glass down. He then got up from his chair and stoked the fire, adding two more logs. He listened, but did not join in the conversation that was spoken mostly in English. The cook could deduce what was being said in English, but he did not speak it very well and so did not try to join in.

Steve simply followed along as the conversation switched between French and English. He was amazed at how much reconnaissance had gone into the overall planning, not to mention the knowledge amassed by these Underground resistance fighters.

Steve had much admiration for people who put everything on the line for their country and the freedom they brought to those they helped escape the German occupation.

Later that evening, Steve and Albert were taken to a small bedroom on the third floor. It was furnished in a hodgepodge manner: there were two single beds with different headboards, plus an old kitchen chair and a small chest of drawers. That was all the room contained. There was also a door that Steve thought might be a closet; however, after opening the door, he saw steps that led up to a tight, low-ceiling attic. It might serve as a hiding place if needed.

Albert and Steve had a good night's sleep. They were quite tired. Between the wine and Calvados, it was not difficult to fall asleep. Extra warm blankets were supplied, since no heat rose to the third floor.

The following morning brought a heavy rainstorm and strong winds. The sound of the pounding rain on the roof woke both Steve and Albert. They had not been awake for too long and were in quiet conversation when a knock on the door told them that they had company. Andre poked his head in and told them to dress and come down to the kitchen for some breakfast.

As Steve and Albert entered the kitchen, the cook motioned for them to sit down at the table. They took the same places where they sat the night before. The cook handed each a mug of strong black coffee. On the table were some freshly baked croissants, confiture, or apple jelly to Steve, plus cheese, or as Albert would call it, fromage. In addition, the cook had secured a good-sized slice of jambon, or ham, for the four of them. It was a good hearty breakfast under the circumstances; a special treat.

Andre came into the kitchen a few minutes later. He was wet and obviously had been outside. He hung up his coat and sat down at the end of the table, his usual place. The cook handed Andre a mug of coffee. He held the mug between his hands to warm them before taking a sip of the coffee.

"It is miserable outside, raining very hard and windy. This is the best news we could have," said Andre with a bright smile on his face. He paused a moment and took another sip of coffee, then continued, "Ah, with the weather so bad it is perfect for you to continue your journey. The Boche will not be out patrolling. Those bastards will be trying to keep dry and not mess up their uniforms. I have arranged for a small, old truck. It has hay in the back truck bed, not too much, but enough for a poor farmer. The hay will have a partial cover, just enough to cover the hay but not large enough to show that we are trying to hide anything. We have used this system before and it has worked. Albert, you and your friend will be on your own. You know the route and the roads as well as anyone. We also do not want to risk any of the locals, if you know what I mean." The statement was in English for Steve's benefit.

"I have been in a situation before where we used a truck with hay and it worked just fine," stated Steve.

"This is good," answered Andre to Steve.

"I understand the situation. How far should I take the truck?" questioned Albert.

"As far as you believe is safe," answered Andre. "We will have the truck returned to its owner in good time when you no longer need it."

Steve did not say anything more. He just listened, figuring that whatever the plan was fine with him.

"When you do reach Valognes, do not go to the home of your parents," stated Andre. "They will come to see you before you leave France. We are arranging a safe place for you to stay. I will tell you as you are leaving here."

"When do we leave?" asked Albert.

"You will depart within the hour," answered Andre. "It looks as though this weather will keep up all day, so drive carefully but not too fast. It is best to blend in with everything that is normal."

Albert did not say anything else, and nodded his head in understanding. He surely did not want to have Steve or himself stand out. Driving the old truck through these conditions would be bold enough. Albert then looked over to Steve and gave a reassuring smile, then rolled his eyes.

It was about 20 minutes later when Andre motioned to the cook that he would be leaving. He signaled for Steve and Albert to follow him. From the kitchen they entered a small pantry closet. A panel in the back that held a mop and broom in place was removed. The three then entered a very small hidden storage room in the adjacent building. They were no sooner in the room when the cook replaced the panel behind them. Andre waited, torchlight in hand, until the panel was securely in place before he turned the torchlight on. They were in total darkness for a moment or two. Each man stood completely still. Andre turned on the light for just a second, holding it low and toward the back panel so that the light itself could barely be seen. He motioned to Steve and Albert to continue to stand still and be very quiet. Andre opened a peephole in the wall near the door. He listened for any kind of sound and gave a long look into the warehouse. Satisfied, Andre turned on the torchlight and opened the storage room door. The three then walked into the small warehouse. The warehouse contained some old machine parts. There was also a workbench against one wall. Sitting in the middle of the warehouse was the old truck. The hay and small cover were already in place and well secured.

Andre saw the look on Steve's face and that Albert was slowly shaking his head and laughing. "It does run well, my friends, and this is what you can depend on," stated Andre. "It looks like this for a purpose."

Albert gave Andre a slap on the back and a hug and said his thanks and goodbye.

He then opened the truck door, looked everything over, shook his head once more and said, "Yes, this is fine, my friend."

Steve shook hands with Andre, gave him a solid hug and got into the passenger's side after thanking him for his hospitality.

Andre opened one of the two large warehouse doors after Albert had started the engine and gave the thumbs-up signal.

The truck was no sooner out of the door when Andre closed it. He quickly retraced his steps and in no time was back in the house having a cup of coffee with the cook. Two more friends had passed through this safe house. Andre was very proud to be of help.

In the meantime, as they drove on, Steve looked over to Albert and received a smile that all was well. They were now on the road outside of Orbec driving at a moderate speed.

"This is as fast as we should travel. If we are too hard on this old truck, which has to be from the 1920s, we will soon be walking. The old girl has seen some rough times," said Albert with a laugh.

"Is Livarot the town we are headed for?" asked Steve.

"Yes . . . it is about 22 kilometers . . . maybe less than 14 miles," answered Albert as he reached up and wiped some condensation from inside the windshield. "Then we will pass through the village of St. Pierre, after which we will travel some back roads mainly used by the farmers, so that we can avoid Falaise and advance to Potigny."

The rain continued coming down hard. Several times Albert drove around water that had built up on the roadway. If he hit a water puddle that was too deep, it could splash up toward the engine and stall it. The one thing Albert was glad of on the old truck was that an electric windshield wiper had been installed to replace the old one which you had to turn by hand every once in a while to clear away the rain water and see out of the front window. There was only one wiper. It was on the driver's side, and it was enough for the driver to see the road ahead. Steve pulled the canvas a little tighter, which covered the window opening on his side. The wind-driven rain was sweeping around in all directions and getting him wet. Albert did not secure his side canvas, but let it remain loose so that he could pull it aside occasionally to look out of the driver's side window. His left arm was getting wet, but as he said before, it was better than walking.

Before they entered Livarot, almost a half hour had passed. Albert pointed out the Livarot cheese factory where the Fromagerie makes the famous Livarot cheese. This is the alternate place they would have gone with the dairy truck if things were too difficult at Orbec; that is, the presence of the German Army.

"Each Fromagerie makes the best you know," remarked Albert as they continued for the next ten kilometers to the village of Saint Pierre. "Everyone is proud of the cheese they produce."

As they entered the village of Saint Pierre, Albert pointed out an old Abbey with its stately church.

"This is a very old village. I will give you a history lesson since you are so interested in these things, my friend," said Albert. The Abbey dates from the year 1012.

It was partially destroyed, but rebuilt by William the Conqueror's Aunt, Countess Lesceline. It was completely restored by the 16th century. In this old village we will also drive pass an 11th century market hall."

"It is amazing to someone from the United States to see real history," said Steve as they drove past the 11th century market hall and he tried to imagine what was taking place here in that time. "Before I came to England, I studied English and European history, but to actually see the castles, churches, and buildings in person is a great experience. Before crossing the Atlantic Ocean all I saw was the Hollywood version of history . . . Errol Flynn as Robin Hood . . . Douglas Fairbanks, if you know what I mean."

From Saint Pierre, they drove some 20 kilometers, maybe a little more, using the back-country roads toward Potigny as they worked to keep themselves east and away from Falaise. Luck continued to be on their side because the rain and wind whipped around as before. Andre had been correct. So far, the weather was keeping most people inside, including the German soldiers.

In driving through Potigny on Rue General Leclerc, Albert pointed out an impressive church, which had a stone wall around it. Steve was impressed with the architecture of the church and its wall.

The heavy rainstorm continued as they drove through the village of Thury-Harcourt. As they prepared to cross the Orone River, an army outpost was spotted near the Pont, or bridge.

"What do you want to do?" Steve asked of Albert.

"Here, show them my papers and your papers," stated Albert as he handed Steve his papers. "Hold them up so that they can see we have them. Do not offer to hand them out in the rain. I will bring us to a stop by their hut. Look, the barrier is not even down. I do not believe that the soldier who is in the hut wants to come out in this weather to inspect our credentials." He then brought the old truck to a complete stop.

Steve did as Albert had instructed and held up the two sets of documents so that the soldier inside the inspection hut could see them.

Steve could see that actually two soldiers were inside; one giving a wave to proceed. Apparently, the two men in an old beat-up truck did not look like a threat to the mighty German Army!

Albert drove across the bridge over the Orone River and then continued toward the village of Aunay-Sur-Oden. The drive, which was now on a main road, would cover 14 kilometers. Even though they were driving on a better roadway, a paved road, Albert kept the speed of the truck the same as before. The "old timer" had continued to perform and there was no reason to push their luck.

Aunay-Sur-Oden was a small village. It was also the home of an uncle of Albert's, his father's brother. Albert drove through the village and to the small farm that his uncle owned. He pulled into the farmyard and brought the truck to a halt. He told Steve to stay in the truck until he called him into the house, just to be certain.

Albert climbed out of the truck and made a dash through the rain toward the back door of the farmhouse. The door was already open as he approached it, and Albert disappeared inside.

In just a couple of minutes, the back door opened again and Albert gave a wave for Steve to come into the house.

"Welcome," the uncle said to Steve in English.

"Thank you," is all that Steve could say before the uncle smiled and motioned for Steve to sit down at the kitchen table. It was a little past noon and Albert's relatives were preparing to have lunch. Two additional individuals having lunch with them was not a problem. They had enough food for everyone.

"We will be speaking French because my uncle and aunt do not speak very much English. It is not because we don't want you to join in on the conversation," said Albert to Steve.

"No problem . . . I understand," answered Steve, who smiled and shook his head toward Albert's relatives to show that their speaking French was fine with him.

Bowls of hot soup along with some freshly baked bread tasted especially good on this chilly, rainy day. Throughout the meal, a steady conversation was going on between Albert and his uncle. Albert's aunt mostly listened and every once in a while she would add to the conversation. Albert would stop the conversation at times and as a courtesy include Steve by telling him what was being said.

During one of these times, Albert told Steve that the safe house in Balleroy was being watched. While the Germans had no proof, they thought that the owners of the house might be part of the resistance. The word was that the house was being scrutinized for activity. In knowing this type of information, it seemed as though Albert was not the only one in his family who was working with the Underground.

"My friend, it is best that we spend this afternoon and tonight here with my aunt and uncle," stated Albert. "If there would be any suspicion, I am here for the reason to help my poor old aunt and uncle. I will just bring out one of the other identification papers to show that I am not Albert Laterrier, but some other relation and we will simply hide you from sight. The most efficient plan for you and I will be completed during the time we are here which could include a couple more days. To be sure, since we have come this far . . . we, as you say in the American movies, will stay on the lam." Albert then laughed at his own joke.

When he had finished his lunch, Albert left the kitchen table, went out the back door toward the "work side" of the animal barn and opened the large door. Then he quickly started the truck and drove it inside, shut the engine down, closed the barn door behind him and returned to the kitchen. He had not taken his coat off yet, and after some conversation, Albert went back outside and handed in some firewood to his uncle. Albert then came back inside, took off his coat, hung it on a hook and accepted the hot cup of tea that his aunt handed him.

The three men retired to the parlor to relax by the warm fireplace. Albert's uncle was very interested in hearing about America and, through Albert, asked many questions. Steve answered as best he could. He did know a little about New York City and Washington, D.C., and he was somewhat familiar with Boston and its great history. He did not know Al Capone, nor did he know too much about Chicago, except what he had learned from his crew members who were from that area. Steve also said that so far when asked the question about movie stars, he did not know any personally; however, he did meet cowboy star Gene Autry one time when his show came through Orlando. Steve went on to say that Bob Hope did a USO tour show in England that he attended and once he had been to a dance in which the Glenn Miller Orchestra played, plus on another USO Show he got a chance to shake hands with Roy Acuff and Ernest Tubb from the Grand Ole Opry of Nashville, Tennessee.

With the wide-ranging conversation still going on, Albert's aunt came into the parlor with some cheese and a loaf of freshly baked, hard-crusted bread. Albert's uncle smiled at her hospitality seeing that she had brought three glasses as well. He got up from his chair, left the room for a moment and returned with a chilled bottle of just-opened Chenin Blanc. Steve was told that the wine came from the Loire Valley, which was south and east of where they were, near Orleans, the one in France and not America! The wine and cheese were very good, but Steve really savored the bread and could have made a meal of it alone.

They talked the afternoon away. When Steve explained the size of each of the United States, Albert's uncle had a hard time comprehending the mass of land that made up North America, including the size of their neighbor to the north, Canada. Steve had gone through this explanation before as his hosts asked questions about his native country. Like many Europeans, they were surprised at the size of each state, which was often the same size as many European countries.

That evening at supper, another man who was part of the resistance joined them. He brought news from Underground sources that perhaps it would be best if an additional day was spent at Albert's relatives' house.

Late that night, just outside of Carentan, a town in which the main railroad lines passes through between Cherbourg and Paris, an explosion would take out all of the rails for maybe 100 meters. It was best not to be in that area for a few days, especially tomorrow when the Boche would be out in force looking for those responsible for the damage. Even two men traveling in an old truck could be in for extra questioning.

Steve wanted to know if he could go along and help. This looked like an adventure in which he would like to participate. Steve was thanked for his support and spirit, but told that this night had been planned for several weeks and that each person involved would be doing a specific job. Steve was also told that there was a planned escape from the immediate area just before the explosion so that no one could be caught. To be caught would endanger far too many individuals and their families.

Steve, of course, understood. He was also quite impressed to know that these were not just random attacks, but done with complete professionalism by otherwise normal, everyday citizens who placed themselves in great danger in order to do their part to be free from those who were occupying and ruling their country.

After supper, the evening continued in the parlor with Calvados and cheese, plus more of the crusty bread. Plans were, it seemed to Steve, changing. The man, along with Albert and his uncle were deep in conversation, with Albert once again stopping the conversation in order to translate for Steve. They had a map laid out on the table and everyone, including Steve, was hovered over it. There was much pointing and sometimes disagreement, not loud disagreement, just points of view for the overall safety of Albert and Steve. They were all pulling their oars in the same direction, so to speak, but had different ideas of how to arrive at the departure area.

It now seemed that the best route to Valognes would be to go six kilometers to Villers-Bocage, where, if it became necessary, they could hide in the old church with high walls around it. From there, Albert and Steve would then continue for an additional 13 kilometers to the village of Caumont-L' Evente'. This route would keep them east of the town of Caen and, for the most part, out of harm's way with the German troops who were stationed in and around the important canal linking the river port. Caen was likewise the capital of Lower Normandy and therefore a very busy town. The trek would then take them on to Balleroy with its famous château, Kasteel Van Balleroy Normandie. It was mentioned that staying away from the safe house in Balleroy, which was being watched, was essential, but no one had to tell Albert twice about that.

Albert also said that he would be using mostly the back-country roads where coming upon German soldiers would be at a minimum. It would likewise keep them west of St. Lo, a German stronghold. Since they would now completely avoid the town of Carentan, Albert made mention of the roads he would now travel on, driving just north of Periers. This would keep him east of both Carentan and Sainte-Mere-Eglise. German soldiers were now filling the town of Sainte-Mere-Eglise. This route, although driving on roads that took many turns, would eventually lead directly to their goal of Valognes. Along the way, they would pass through the villages of Saint-Jores and Orglandes where they would not expect to encounter any problems.

It seemed to Steve that everyone was coming to an agreement about the route to be taken. Heads were nodding in the affirmative and when Albert's uncle got up to refill the glasses, there were smiles all around. The glasses were raised in salute!

"It is set, we are all in agreement. We will be in Valognes in two days," said Albert to Steve.

"Two days. You know I've lost all track of days and dates. Those things used to be so important. What is the date today?" asked Steve.

"Tomorrow will be Friday," replied Albert. "The date is January 14th and the year, of course, is 1944. You have been strong and have done well, my friend," said Albert.

"The year and the month I know, but I had lost track of the day and date," said Steve, who paused for a moment, then continued, "I was shot down on a Wednesday, the first day of December. It has now been 45 days since I went missing in action with no good news to report to my worrying father."

"Hopefully within a week he will hear the good news that you are safely back in England!" answered Albert.

Albert's uncle said something in French as the man got up to leave. Steve and Albert stood up to say goodbye and to thank the man for his help. It was his honor to be of help, the man replied, in French, which was translated to Steve by Albert.

Albert also told Steve that their trusty old truck would quietly be refueled sometime during the night.

Soon it was time for everyone to go to sleep. It had been a long day. Steve had a room to himself in the attic. Although it was small, it was quite comfortable. In addition to the old handmade wooden bed, there was a night table with three draw-ers and a straight-back chair. These also looked to have been handmade, by either Albert's uncle or some other local. The bed had several blankets, layered for warmth. It looked inviting as Steve climbed in under the covers and, in no time at all, a very tired young man was sound asleep.

In the morning, a knock on the door awakened Steve from a deep, sound sleep.

"Come on, lazy man, it is time for breakfast," said Albert in a cheerful voice as he placed a pitcher of warm water, a bowl and towel on the night table. "We will be leaving today."

Steve opened his eyes and climbed from beneath the warm covers. He washed his face and toweled off with the small towel that was set beside the bowl.

In a few minutes, Steve joined Albert and his aunt and uncle in the kitchen for breakfast. In addition to the baked bread, there was apple jelly and fresh eggs, plus coffee. Albert was sent to the barn by his aunt to move the hens aside and collect eggs for breakfast while the bread was baking. While in the barn, Albert also checked on the truck and found that, indeed, it was refueled as everyone in the house slept.

There was lively conversation at breakfast. Albert's uncle wanted to review the route one more time. He also reminded Albert that they must stay away from Carpioquet and Marcelet. The Luftwaffe had an air base between the two villages to protect their interests in and around Caen. Any hint of vehicle movement near those villages would certainly attraction attention. They would be searched and possibly detained. Albert reassured his uncle that he would take extreme caution and not drive in an area that could cause alarm.

It was now a little past eight o'clock in the morning and time to go. Albert was saying goodbye to his aunt and uncle. It was an affectionate goodbye that could have lasted for a couple of years, maybe more.

Albert's aunt handed him a sack of food and a bottle of wine for the trip. Steve, who was standing near, did his best to thank them for their kindness. He had, over the past month, picked up a few French words, enough that his hosts understood that he was grateful for their help.

Albert's uncle went out to the barn with Steve and Albert. He opened the barn door just enough so that the truck could drive out. He then closed the door and gave a clasp of the hands as to say good luck. Albert, with Steve in the passenger's seat, eased up the lane and turned right onto the road, which would take them to Villers-Bocage, six kilometers away.

It was just starting to snow on this cold Friday morning. The snow was mostly flurries and was not going to make driving difficult. The road to Villers-Bocage was paved. However, most of the roads to be traveled on today would be the unpaved, less-used kind. It was safer that way.

Before Albert and Steve drove into the village, Steve spotted what looked to be an ancient stone tower sitting in the middle of a field. He questioned Albert about the tower.

"I believe it is from the Roman times and there was not always an agriculture field there," answered Albert. He wished he could tell Steve more about the tower. To him it had always been there and he really did not know its complete history.

It was quiet, no one in sight, as Albert and Steve drove past the old village church with the high stone wall around it. From Villers-Bocage, they continued toward the village of Caumont-L' Evente, which lay 13 kilometers ahead.

The snow, which had gone from flurries to a light snow, continued. It was heavy enough to cover the fields, but not the roadway. Albert maintained a slow and steady pace. He wanted anyone who saw them to think that they were nothing more than a couple of men hauling some hay for their animals.

The tall church steeple stood out over the countryside as Albert and Steve entered the village of Caumonte-L' Evente. They drove through the small village and continued for another 14 kilometers to the town of Balleroy. While they saw the famous château, Kasteel Van Balleroy Normandie, it was all too clear that people, other than French citizens, occupied the château. Albert joked that, at some other time, he would show Steve the beauty of the famous Balleroy landmark! Right now the German Army was using the château as a headquarters.

The little truck continued to chug along. It ran much better than it looked. Those who designated this particular truck for the job it was performing here in Normandy knew exactly what they were doing: poor old farmers just trying to get along with a vehicle that looked like it could barely run.

As Albert and Steve continued the trip, it was now that Albert's knowledge of the old farm roads became important in order to evade those dressed in German uniforms. There were no road signs to point the way. In leaving Balleroy, Albert drove across country, using these roads as he kept a heading, which would have him drive above and west of St. Lo. He also stayed east of Bayeux, pointing out to Steve that in addition to being the home of the masterpiece Bayeux Tapestry, or Tapisserie de la Mathilde, Bayeux was a very pretty town with water running through it, a spillway and old mill, plus the 12th century Notre Dame Cathedral. One day he would take Steve through the area as a tourist and show him all of "Normandie."

Albert avoided the village of St-Clair-Sur l'Elle. He did drive through the small village of Saint-Jores, where to Steve the main landmark seemed to be an ancient stone church. There were also the vast fields and dairy farms in the area. They continued, unnoticed it seemed, as they passed through the tiny villages of Pretot-Sainte-Suzanne, Les Moitiers-en-Bacptois, Etienville, Urville, Hemevez, Lieusaint and Les Fontaines.

It was near dark by this time. Even though they had only traveled about 100 kilometers, or about 62 miles. Driving on the narrow back roads, zigzagging around farm boundaries, meant a slow speed. Extra time was also needed to traverse the unpaved roadways. The weather, which had improved little, also kept Albert on the alert so that he did not end up in a farmer's field.

As they prepared to drive into Valognes, Albert pointed out old ruins that were from Roman times. They also drove past a very old Gothic church. Albert said that the church actually dated from the 14th century and that the Gothic dome was added in 1612. He also told Steve that it was the only Gothic dome in all of France. It was obvious that Albert was proud of his church. One of Steve's thoughts as Albert was telling him about the church was that in America, the Pilgrims did not arrive until 1621! The dome had been there for nine years before the Pilgrims set foot on Plymouth Rock in what is now Cape Cod in the state known as Massachusetts—amazing!

"The city is crawling with German soldiers," said Steve as he peered out of the truck's side window.

"They are being billeted in many homes throughout Valognes," stated Albert as he kept his eyes on the road. "The town has a great history and was formally known as Norman Versailles because of the great number of chateaus and manor houses in and around the town. I love this area." After a pause, he continued. "Do not look at them. It is evening and many of the soldiers are off duty, so let them remain that way."

Steve sank a little lower in his seat and looked straight forward. So far, no one had bothered to do any more than glance at the old beat-up truck with a few bales of hay in the truck bed.

"Are we going to stay in Valognes?" asked Steve.

"No, there are far too many houses being occupied by German soldiers," answered Albert. "Those that were safe houses are really not anymore. We are very close to reaching our goal so must be careful, my friend. My mother, father, and little sister live in a house near the edge of town, but I will not stop to see them. It might draw attention to them, having visitors and questions could be asked. Some people, sorry to say, Frenchmen, will pass information to the Boche in order to gain favors from our enemy. We will stay at a manor near here in the village of Huberville, with a silent 'H.' My parents will be brought to this house to say goodbye to me."

Albert now reached the end of Valognes and turned onto a rural road. They drove slowly for a while on this narrow roadway. Darkness was now almost upon them and it was beginning to become difficult to see and stay on the roadway. They dared not turn on any truck lights. They continued at a slow pace so that they did not wind up driving into a ditch. Albert, in knowing this particular road, was driving purely on instinct.

"Do you want me to walk out in front of the truck?" asked Steve.

"I think I'm okay . . . just a little further. Ah, here is the lane," answered Albert as he made a right turn and negotiated up the driveway to a manor house.

"We are here . . . just about your last stop before England," said Albert as he and Steve got out of the truck. "Let us hope that our host is my friend and that this is still a safe house."

The door to the manor house opened and then quickly closed so that just a minimum of light was seen from the outside. A young man about Steve and Albert's age stepped out to greet them. Another much older man also came out of the house. He nodded to Albert and Steve, then went over to the truck, started the engine and drove it behind the house and into an outbuilding that was about the size of a small barn. The young man motioned for Albert and Steve to follow him on foot to the small barn. The hay had already been removed from the truck bed and placed on the second floor of the barn by the time the other three arrived. With a hand jack, each wheel was taken off the truck and soon the old truck was sitting on concrete blocks. A cover was then placed over the entire truck and its bed. Some dirt and bits of fallen hay were scattered on top of the cover, and in a short time, it appeared as though the truck was just rusting away in the barn. The wheels with tires still on them were handed up to the second floor. They would be stored in the rear of the building. Some dirt and a light sprinkle of hay made them look as though they had been there for some time.

It was too dangerous to drive the truck back to the owner at this time and perhaps for some time. The young man and the older one, satisfied that everything was in order, left the barn. Not a word was spoken. The older man walked away and disappeared out of sight as he crossed a field.

Albert and Steve followed the young man toward the manor and entered through the rear door.

"Bonsoir, and to you, my new American friend, good evening," said the young man. He then handed Steve and Albert a glass of apple brandy, Calvados, and continued, "Bienvenue . . . welcome . . . this will warm you and then we will have some supper. I am very glad that you are here."

"You speak very good English, so I will say thank you for your hospitality and for helping me," said Steve as he raised his glass to the young man.

"You are more than welcome, my new American friend. The interesting thing is that we do all of this right under the nose of the Boche," said the young man. "I will tell you that it is best if you and I do not exchange names. I have known your companion for many years and we share the same beliefs, plus we have also shared many dangers together, but for the safety of you and me, this is for the best. I hope you understand that I am not being rude."

"I completely understand," answered Steve.

While Albert and Steve warmed themselves before the fireplace in the parlor, sipping their brandy, the young man spoke of the area, which was rich in history and has magnificent manor homes with quite varied architecture.

"This area, where Huberville manor houses are located, is a very dark-at-night countryside," stated the young man. "There is also thick cover for hiding throughout the region. Not far away is a beautiful manor known as Le Manoir d' Huberville. It has actually been featured on old post cards for the tourist of years past. The manor has a wonderful family of farmers who work the land. In the front yard, by the road, is a statue of Jeanne d' Arc . . . or to our American friend, Saint Joan of Arc. The statue sits upon an old Roman Column from the ruins located not far away. She was canonized in 1920, but the statue was placed there in the late 1800s while the owner was a bishop of France, Monseigneur Le Nordez, actually the bishop of Dijon. It is a good replica of the national monument to her at Vaucoueurs, in the north of France. The manor has a tower and from the tower, and even the bedroom windows on the upper floors, you have a perfect view of the English Channel as well as the beach known as La Madeleine. Well, my friend, it is now also occupied by German soldiers. They are sleeping on the upper floors, so the enemy is all around us."

He refilled their glasses, then sat down and continued, "Another nearby manor is called Anneville. You passed it on the way here. It is by the crossroads at the bottom of the hill when you came from Valognes; quite near to the little church. While the German soldiers are not billeted in the main part of the house, they are living in the secondary part near the large main gateway. Anneville is a magnificent place with barns, stables and secondary houses.

"Ah . . . but enough of that for now. You must be hungry!" the young man continued. "Come into the kitchen with me and we will prepare supper. My parents are away, on purpose, visiting my mother's brother for a few days."

This lanky young man, who seemed so informed, was a very active member in the French Underground. He and his group had already helped many individuals that were either escaping capture or who were being passed on to another group of the Underground, which was also known as "the Maquis." He and Albert had participated in espionage and the destruction of those things that, as Albert described, "Annoyed the invaders who did not belong on French soil."

After they entered the kitchen, the young man reached into the wine rack and took out two bottles of Bordeaux. He opened both and poured everyone a generous glass.

"Very good . . . rich, dark-red color . . . good solid tannin," said Albert and he took his first sip and held it for a moment in his mouth before swallowing. He shook his head, noting that this was good wine, and then took another sip.

"It is some of my father's best wine and is to be enjoyed. You both must understand one thing which is that I can boil water and place pasta in it for nine, ten minutes, so guess what we are having for supper," stated the young man with a laugh.

Steve had the job of slicing the fresh country bread that the young man purchased earlier in the day. While he was doing that, Albert told Steve that he and the young man would be conversing in their native French about some of the plans and not think them rude.

While eating the quite good-tasting pasta, for which the young man had made up a sauce using olive oil, garlic and sea salt, not a tomato-based sauce. The conversation, now spoken in English for Steve's benefit, centered on the next phase of the plan. They talked specifically about how things would be set up for the cross-channel journey to England.

The young man unfolded a small map of the area that appeared to Steve as being handmade. As he spread out the map, the young man explained, "We feel that the best route to the port of Saint Vaast la Hougue, which is where you will sail from, is to go cross-country, then join the old Roman road that links Valognes with our destination. We will have you stay away from the villages of Belaunay and Hameau Malherbe. There is no need to alert anyone there of your presence."

"One place where we must be very careful is getting too near the Château de Montaigu la Brisette," the young man went on to explain. "The Germans are setting up a V-1 launching pad in the field across from the château. There is an artificial lake on the other side of the château. This is the side we will travel on since there is good cover and no one will know that we are passing by. The 'Doodle Bugs' are aimed for London. We have plans to disrupt their activity, so we do not want to be detected in that area. We have made London aware of the facility and they know of our plan with the launching pad. We also will work to disrupt the trains that carry the flying bombs."

The young man got up from the kitchen table and opened another bottle of wine. While he was pouring the wine, Albert continued the conversation: "Beyond the château is where we will meet up with the old Roman road. Then we will pass through a village called Piedechou with an intersection know as Le Pied du Chou, which silly as it might seem to an American, means 'the cabbage stalk.' We then enter Bois du Rabey . . . the Rabey Woods. There are many good hiding places in case we are being followed. When we exit the woods, if it was daylight, you can see the Channel. It is a wonderful view, although we won't be able to enjoy it, at least on this trip," laughed Albert, as he took a sip of wine.

The young man then continued, "The town is Quettehou. There is a very old and quite famous stone church on the top of the hill. You will hide in this place and make certain that all is safe. You will be like the celebrated 'Black Prince.' During the Hundred Years War between the French and British, he was hidden there before escaping, so you will be in good company . . . even if many years later! From the bell tower you could survey the entire countryside and the bay from which you will depart France. The church grounds also contain a cemetery. The priest will not be around when you visit his church. The church will be left unlocked for our use. It is best for his safety that he knows nothing."

"It seems as though major planning has been done," stated Steve as he tried to take in all that was said and follow the route on the map.

"You are correct about that," answered the young man. "There are many people who have been working for your safe return that you will never meet. They supply information, provide transportation, food, wine and even Calvados for the best comfort and security we can give to you."

"I do have one concern, as I think about this, that we need to review," stated Albert, in English, as he reached for the bottle, poured more wine. "The port of Saint Vaast la Hougue . . . it may be far too fortified with German soldiers and patrol boats. There is also the island of Tatihou. It has a garrison occupying the old Napoleon fort and they have searchlights. I believe it could be much too dangerous for everyone if we try to sneak pass all of these obstacles."

Steve just listened as Albert and the young man continued to work out the details. They were speaking English for his benefit.

"What other plan would you suggest?" questioned the young man. "You know these areas as well as I do."

"From Quettehou we could travel the short distance to Morsalines," answered Albert, hoping that the young man would agree. "There are fields that lead to the bay's edge. With the sailing boat waiting off shore in the deeper water, we could row a small boat out to it. By doing this, it would place us below the fort at the point of the hook of land. We would also not be in the view of the soldiers stationed at the fort on Tatihou."

"Where you would be . . . is the area of the mussel and oyster beds," answered the young man.

"I know, that is why I did not suggest Le Rivage, because of the shallow water," answered Albert. "We could only leave at the high tide anyway, so the beds should not be disturbed."

"I think you are right," stated the young man. "This is a better plan. I will take care of the details tomorrow. The high tide we are looking for will occur at about three or four in the morning. We should plan for the departure to be tomorrow night. There is no moon and that will help shield you from view."

Steve listened carefully to each word as it was being spoken. He was holding in the excitement of finally realizing his dream of safely returning to England. Through these amazing people, so far, he had evaded the enemy for almost 47 days.

The rest of the evening was enjoyed in a more relaxed atmosphere. The three sat before a warm fire and talked mostly about the United States. Both the young man and Albert were curious about Steve's life before he joined the military. With Steve and his father having a cattle ranch, they considered him a real cowboy! Steve thought that they might have seen too many American movies. He would have fun telling this story to his dad. The conversation continued to be broad: from radio programs to Hollywood movies to the Grand Canyon and Niagara Falls. Steve said that he had viewed both landmarks, but not from the ground. He flew over them while flying the B-17 bomber on training flights.

Finally, well after midnight, the three were ready for a good night's sleep. Both Steve and Albert shared a bedroom on the second floor of the château, down the hallway from the young man. He would wake them when breakfast was ready.

Steve felt refreshed when he awoke the following morning. He was alone in the room. Steve quickly dressed, washed his face in the bowl left for him, and came downstairs to the kitchen. Albert had risen quietly, leaving Steve to sleep a little longer. He came down to help the young man start breakfast. A fire in the cook-stove was well on the way to brew the coffee and warm the kitchen.

At breakfast, which consisted of croissants, apple confiture, *yaourt,* or yogurt to Steve, plus rich strong coffee, the young man said he would be away for a good part of the day. He would show them a secret room in the cellar in which to hide, should the occasion present itself. He also told Steve and Albert to fix up the bedroom they had slept in so that it looked as though no one had been in the room. They were instructed not to go near any windows. There was a possibility that someone could be using binoculars to track movement in and around the château.

The young man left the house on a bicycle. Albert and Steve kept out of sight during the day, just as they were told to do. The young man left some food for them to eat at lunchtime. He also had told them to use the library for reading or to play chess. Albert and Steve did a little of each. The young man's father had several books with English print, including two written by Ernest Hemingway, *The Sun Also Rises* and *A Farewell To Arms*. These were pointed out to Steve just before the young man left on his bicycle.

It was late in the afternoon when the young man returned to the château. He had a sack of food and a loaf of bread with him. This made his time away from the house seem normal. He placed the bicycle in the small barn. While there, he took an extra few minutes to look at the old truck and its cover. Some additional dust had settled on it and he was quite satisfied that the truck gave the impression as though it had been there for some time and not just a couple of days.

Once in the house, the young man emptied the sack, placed the bread on the kitchen counter by the cupboard and said, "Everything is set for tonight. A man will come to the château and you will leave around 2200 hours. He will guide you on foot through the route we discussed last night. Just outside of the main part of Quettehou, you will be hidden in the church until it is two o'clock in the morning. It is then that you will take to the fields, and at three o'clock, you will be rowed out to the waiting sailboat. By that time, there is a full high tide and you should be able to slip away unnoticed. The boat captain thinks that the trip from here to the Isle of Wight, in England, should take perhaps 30 hours."

The young man, with the help of Albert and Steve, cooked supper. It was a second night of pasta, made the same way as before and served with the fresh, crusty bread. No one seemed to mind the repeat. The wine was good, and in the relaxed atmosphere as friends, they enjoyed each other's company. The conversation was light and did not center on their departure later that night. The plans had already been made. It was now time to successfully execute those plans. It was not time to worry . . . yet!

A light rain had started to fall. While it was a moonless night, the rain and heavy cloud cover made it seem even darker on this particular night.

"I expected the rain," stated the young man as he pulled back a curtain at the kitchen window just enough to peer out and see that all was well. "We have secured two naval storm slickers for you to wear over your coats. They are both black so will not stand out, and they will at least keep you a little dryer than just having your coats. The weather will also wash away any tracks you make."

At 2100 hours, there was a quiet knock on the back door. The man who would guide Steve and Albert came into the kitchen. Albert knew the man and they exchanged greetings. While Albert was a local, many things changed almost daily, especially the movement of German soldiers. Even though Albert was quite familiar with the route they were going to take and had helped with the planning, he was grateful to have the guide lead them through the night, where avoiding some areas would be best.

The young man then asked Steve to join him in the family library. They would relax by the fireplace for a little while. It was for the safety of all that Albert's family did not meet him. "You cannot speak about things you do not know about," said the young man as he poured Steve a glass of Calvados.

While Steve sat, glass of Calvados in hand, his thoughts were of his dad who still did not have additional information of his son's whereabouts. He also thought of Maggie and that if luck stayed with him, they would soon be together.

The guide had gone to the rear door and opened it, once he determined that all was safe within the house. Albert's mother, father and little sister came into the kitchen. It was a warm reunion. The guide left the kitchen and joined the young man and Steve in the library. Albert took his family into the parlor for their last goodbye. It was a sad time for them.

In about 45 minutes, the guide left the library and joined Albert's family in the parlor. It would soon be time for them to leave. The guide went back to the kitchen door, opened it and said something to a man who had been waiting outside. All was safe and Albert's family prepared to leave. There were tears all around, but all knew that for now it was best for Albert to flee France and go to England where he would join General De Gaulle and enlist with the Free French Army. The man, who had been waiting outside in the darkness, then escorted Albert's family out into the night and home.

The guide and Albert then joined the young man and Steve for a farewell drink in the library, where the young man accepted thanks and wished Steve and Albert good luck on the last phase of their journey. There was no time for a long goodbye. After the glass of Calvados to warm them, Steve's second, the guide, Albert, and Steve left the château through the back door.

The rain was not coming down as hard as before; it was just a mist now. The three quickly walked from the château to an open field behind the barn. It was so dark that after walking just a few feet into the field, they were out of sight.

The pace slowed as the three came near enough to the Château de Montaigu la Brisette that they could see the long, rectangular artificial lake that was behind the château.

"We must be very quiet . . . no talking and quiet steps so that we are not spotted," whispered the guide in English.

"I'd sure like to see that launching pad for the flying bombs, but I guess that would place us too close," whispered Steve.

"You could shake hands with the guards and I'm certain that they would let you see exactly what is going on just before they shoot you," answered Albert, who got a tug on the arm by the guide to be quiet.

The pace they were walking picked up once again as they came onto the old Roman road. Being on the roadway made for much faster walking, but Steve, who was not used to walking this fast for a long period, was falling a bit behind.

Albert motioned to the guide that they needed to slow down a little, quietly saying that they were making good time and would simply spend less waiting time at the Eglise, or to Steve, the church.

It was near midnight when they approached the village of Piedechou with great caution. A dog was heard barking, but it was from a farm or château some distance away.

"With the light rain still falling and the night cold enough to bring on a chill, I believe that everyone is nicely tucked away for the evening," said Albert to the guide.

"I agree," answered the guide. "We can continue on this road."

They went through the village without a problem. The dog was still barking, but no other dogs were answering back.

The three slowed down considerably as they neared the intersection known as Le Pied du Chou. There could be German soldiers stationed at the intersection. The guide told Albert and Steve to stay where they were. He would ease up to the intersection and check it out. The guide kept low to the ground as he got nearer for a better look.

In a few minutes, he was back. "There is a small German Army vehicle where the roads meet," stated the guide. "It seems to me that there are four soldiers in the vehicle. I think they are all asleep and keeping dry from the rain. It is best if we leave the road, take to the woods and go around them. I know a path through the woods and we can then return to the road."

As they walked through the woods, Albert stepped on a twig in the pathway.

The sound of the snap as the twig broke was like that of a gunshot on this otherwise silent night, or rather it sounded that loud to the guide. Albert and Steve stopped at once. They all stood still listening to any movement that would indicate that others heard the tree branch break. They waited for maybe two minutes. Nothing; no one seemed to be alerted. It was all right to proceed.

"If we get caught and they ask who wants to be shot first, you raise your hand," whispered Steve to Albert as he tried to break the tension.

"Okay, I'll volunteer," joked Albert.

The three continued on the wooded path for some distance. Eventually the path crossed a road that led to the intersection. They were perhaps 600 meters away from Le Pied du Chou. Even though the misty rain continued to fall on this extremely dark night, the guide insisted that they cross the road and continue on the wooded path by crossing one at a time, keeping low to the ground so that if seen, the low figure could be mistaken for an animal. The guide would go first to be certain that it was safe.

The three came out of the woods into a small clearing by the side of the road. Once again, they stayed still and quiet, listening for any sound, which would let them know that humans and not just animals were nearby.

The guide motioned that he was crossing the road. Steve and Albert waited. As the guide instructed them to do, he kept low to the ground, bent over, as he quickly crossed to the other side. Albert went next and Steve followed. Perhaps they did not need to be this cautious, but why get careless especially when they were so close to their goal?

The guide brought them back onto the Roman road after a few hundred additional meters on the wooded path. Any vehicles approaching from either direction could be heard first and then seen. If that happened, they would drop into the ditch alongside of the road and hide until the vehicle passed. At this time of night, or rather very early in the morning, only military vehicles would be on the road.

Finally, they arrived at the church, which was located on the outskirts of Quettehou at the intersection of Rue du Stade and Rue Saint-Vigor. The guide checked his wristwatch and it was now 10 minutes past one o'clock. The light rain continued to fall. While the wetness of the rain was uncomfortable, the presence of rain was a comfort. It was quiet, and because of the hour and bad weather, no one was about.

"You two stay here in the church cemetery," whispered the guide. "I will come back for you." He then crept forward to have a closer look at the church in order to make certain that all was completely safe.

Steve and Albert knelt down behind some of the taller tombstones and waited quietly for the guide to return.

In a few minutes the guide returned as he had gone, creeping close to the ground. "We can go into the Eglise," said the guide. "Follow me and stay very low to the ground. No one should know that we are here."

Albert and Steve followed and the three entered the Eglise. Even though the church was not heated, it felt good to be out of the misty, miserable night. It was warm enough inside the church that they took off the storm slickers and their coats.

Both Steve and Albert also had heavy sweaters on. The storm slickers, for the most part, had kept them dry; just their pants and shoes were wet.

The guide locked the church door. "We will exit through another door near the back," he said. "It will be safer not to leave by the same door we came in. Here, have some bread and wine. It was brought here for you. It is best if you have a full stomach when you are on the boat. The priest also left some fromage . . . good cheese."

"Does the parish priest live near here?" asked Steve.

"Yes and I imagine he is asleep," the guide responded. "This way, he does not know anything and won't be viewed by the Germans as part of the resistance. It is safer for him and he can continue to help us this way. Now it is time for you to rest because we will leave here in less than one hour." He picked up one of the three uncorked bottles of wine and drank from the bottle.

Steve ate some more cheese and passed it on to Albert who was enjoying the wine. Albert handed Steve a bottle of wine and some more bread.

They both tried to rest, but it was hard to do as anxious as they were to get on with the journey. Still, with time seemingly crawling by, Steve picked out a church pew and lay down using his coat as a pillow. He rested, but did not sleep.

About 45 minutes later, the guide checked his wristwatch and said, "Let us prepare to leave. Take the wine bottles and everything else that would show that we were here and I will discard them later."

The guide then quietly and very slowly opened a door at the rear of the church. It seemed that he stood at the opening for two or three minutes, listening. The light rain continued and the night was still quite dark. The guide motioned for Albert and Steve to follow him outside and to stay low to the ground once again. They crept amongst the grave tombstones in the church cemetery and onto a narrow road that would take them through the village of Hameau du Pont and then across fields to the beach near Morsalines.

The rest at the church did Steve some good. He was now able to maintain the quick pace. Even though his legs felt a little sore, he could put that behind him, knowing the purpose of the walk, which frankly, was more like a forced march.

It began to rain harder as they approached the village of Hameau du Pont. The sound of their walking could not be heard above the sound of rain as it fell onto house roofs and the road. As he looked around to be certain that all was still safe, the guide was pleased that the weather had kept even the dogs of the area under cover, rather than alerting their presence by barking.

Once they passed through the village, they turned onto a very narrow dirt road that ended at the sea. No words were spoken, but the guide did slow the pace as they moved closer to the shoreline.

"You stay here . . . if all is well I shall come back for you," said the guide in a voice just above a whisper. "Otherwise go back to the safe house." He then left Albert and Steve as he made his way further down the narrow lane.

Albert and Steve waited by the side of the lane near some tall grass. They could move quickly into the tall grass and lie down so they would not be seen, if that became necessary.

In a few minutes, a figure appeared out of the darkness. It was the guide. He did not speak but gave a wave to follow him. Steve and Albert quickly fell in line behind him as he took them down the lane to the beach area.

There was a small rowboat, not more than eight feet long, lying in the grass near the beach area. The rowboat had a few inches of water in it from the rain. The guide tipped the boat to its side to let the water drain away, after handing the oars to Albert for him to hold. Then the guide motioned to Steve to pick up the back end of the rowboat as he picked up the front. They walked the little boat to the water's edge, then three or four feet into the water so that the boat was floating. Albert followed them into the shallow water. The guide then motioned for Steve to sit in the stern and for Albert to sit on the floor at the bow. He then got in, sat on the center seat and placed the oars in the oarlocks. Keeping the oars at a very shallow depth, he rowed the boat gently away from the shore.

The bay was calm. The wind was not very strong so the wave action was minimal and no water was shipped into the boat. The tide was still coming in, but the water was deep enough for them to row without disturbing the oyster beds which were farmed by local fishermen. If it were a few hours earlier, there would not have been enough water to float a toy boat.

The rain once again slowed to a misty drizzle. They could now see for perhaps 50 meters. The three and their small rowboat were now a good distance from shore, but there was no waiting sailboat to be seen. The guide gave a low whistle. There was no reply. He rowed on further and once again gave the whistle. This time a return whistle came from out in front and to the right. Soon the outline of a boat came into view.

Steve strained to see the boat, which he thought, would be a fancy sailboat. He had been told that they would be using a sailboat for the trip to England. As they drew near and worked their way to the side of the sailboat, Steve was shocked to see a boat that looked to be only around 24 feet long. It was not a sailboat, but a fishing boat, which happened to have a sail. It certainly was a humble vessel. One might consider it as an old scow of a fishing boat; a sailboat of sorts!

The man on board the fishing boat held the little rowboat still as Albert and Steve climbed aboard. Steve looked around and wondered how this boat could possibly travel the length of more than 200 kilometers through the Channel and safely get them to England. It would be a trip to tell his children, if he lived to have any.

The guide held his finger to his mouth as in be quiet and say nothing. He just waved and quickly rowed away into the darkness toward the shore.

It was, in a way, an empty feeling for Steve. There were so many people from the Dutch–Paris Underground that had risked their lives in order to help a lone downed American airman escape capture from the occupying Germans. He would forever have fond memories and be grateful to them and the unseen individuals who he would never meet. Steve vowed that after this war was over, he would return to more properly thank these wonderful people. He was reminded by Albert that helping him remain free was their reward.

The captain of the fishing boat did not say anything to Steve and Albert. He just went about the task of rowing his boat quietly into deeper water. It was too soon to raise the sail. He would do this when they were a little farther out to sea. Mother

Nature was helping some. The wind had picked up slightly and was moving them along, making rowing much easier.

Albert and Steve remained quiet. They sat on the floor, near the small cabin in the bow. The captain had them sit on the floor so that they were out of sight from anyone who might be counting heads.

The rain had now slowed to a very light drizzle, really just a mist. Boat engines could be heard in the distance. Through the mist, a searchlight was seen going on and off, lighting portions of the area. It had to be a German patrol boat making its rounds.

In his best English the captain said, "Go into the cabin, lie down and pull the extra sail over you. I do not have to tell you to be quiet."

Albert and Steve did not answer, but quickly and quietly followed the captain's instructions.

The captain stopped rowing, placed the oars into the boat and raised the single sail. It was something he had done before. He knew from experience that if he were under sail and not rowing, the patrol boat, which at some point was going to spot him, would not directly pull alongside and board the small fishing boat, but instead would just look him over. This is what had happened before on his almost daily fishing trips. He hoped that the same would be true on this occasion, especially with the cargo he carried. If they did board his boat, it certainly would be dangerous for everyone. There would be danger enough with the long, open-water trip across the Channel to England.

The initial problem would soon be resolved. The engines of the German patrol boat grew louder as though they were coming directly toward the fishing boat. Their location was near the last point of land known as La Hougue, the hook of land where his architect, Vauban, built one of Napoleon's forts.

The wind had picked up a little more as the boat sailed just beyond the point. The wave action was also building now one to two feet high. While the patrol boat was not going very fast, it was going faster than they were sailing. Out of the darkness, the searchlight of the patrol boat scanned past them, stopped and returned to illuminate the fishing boat under sail. The mast and sail stood out in the darkness.

"Be careful and do not move around," whispered the captain.

He really did not need to say anything because both Steve and Albert understood what was happening.

The German patrol boat kept the searchlight on the fishing boat as it drew nearer. The light looked them over bow to stern. Two men were seen on the deck with machine guns in hand.

The fishing boat captain, who was in the stern on the tiller, waved as he had done in the past. The German patrol boat slowed to the speed of the fishing sailboat. It was now running alongside. They were perhaps 10 to 12 feet away and those on board the patrol boat, machine guns at the ready, were making certain that all seemed normal on the old work boat before releasing it.

"Do you have fresh fish?" asked someone on board the patrol boat. He was speaking French, but not very good French.

"No, I have just stinky bait," was the answer. "I am on my way to catch fish. See me when I return and I shall be happy to share my catch."

In less than a minute, a wave came from the patrol boat as it moved away and continued on its rounds. The searchlight was turned off and the sound of engines faded in the distance.

The captain steered the boat away from the point and was now in open sea. He waited for perhaps five minutes before he said anything to Steve and Albert. The waves seemed to be growing a little higher, but now that they were back in complete darkness, it was hard to judge the height of the waves.

"It is okay now . . . come out of the cabin and get some fresh air," said the captain. "I hope you do not suffer from Mal-de-Mer, or to you, my new American friend, sea sickness."

"I'm all right for now, but who knows," answered Steve.

Albert did not answer. One could tell, though, that he was not a sailor and that his stomach was churning with the waves.

The wind had picked up enough that the force of it on the sail had the boat heeling a little as it reached for the next wave. They were now moving at a faster pace as the boat pitched forward. Soon, water sprayed over the bow, but it had not come into the cockpit.

The captain was holding the tiller under his armpit and seemed to be completely enjoying the challenge that was unfolding as the wind continued to blow harder and the waves grew in height. The hours passed as they sailed along.

The rain had mercifully stopped as the first signs of daylight began to emerge from the east. For this little fishing boat under sail in the Channel, the waves now looked like mountains. Some spray from the sea had soaked the bottom of the boat. Albert and Steve used the small buckets issued by the captain to bail out the water.

The skill of the captain was keeping the boat headed in the right direction and afloat. To navigate, there was a small compass. In addition, the captain was doing his best to determine wind drift and, to be sure, by simple dead reckoning. With his charts, the captain had plotted a course that he hoped would take them directly to England's Isle of Wight. The captain's charts had been carefully memorized, and now the course was embedded in his head.

"It is time that we introduce ourselves," announced the captain in English, for Steve's benefit. "We are far enough out to sea now that no one should interfere with our little adventure. I am Roger LeMelland. This fine vessel is also my wife. We are one and she has made me a good living. Now, we sail to England and I shall join with De Gaulle and the Free French. I am 51 years old, but still strong as an ox."

"Albert Leterrier is my name," said Albert, who was now feeling a bit seasick or at least, one who wished he were on dry land. "I have worked with the Resistance for more than three years. The Gestapo has tried to catch me and they came very close several times. Like you, Captain LeMelland, I will join with the Free French."

"My name, whom everyone has known me, for more than one month has been Paul Reens," Steve said. "My real name is Steven Carmichael and I hold the rank of captain in the American Air Corps. I am a B-17 bomber pilot."

"Okay, Captain Carmichael, once we arrive on the shores of England, you are in charge!" asserted Roger.

"I am very sorry," said Albert as he leaned over the side and emptied his stomach.

Steve was not quite at the point of being seasick, but he did not feel his best either. Maybe the bouncing around in a B-17 under flak fire had conditioned him, at least a little. However, they still had a long way to go.

"I am hungry," stated Roger. "In the cabin, there is a sack of food and some wine. Bring it out for us to eat. Albert, you need to fill your stomach, and Captain Carmichael, you must keep your stomach full so that you do not become ill."

"I'll get it," said Steve. He went into the cabin up forward and searched for the sack. He found it under a spare sail and brought it and two bottles of red wine back to the cockpit.

"Please, just call me Steve," he said as he handed the sack to Roger.

"Okay, Steve . . . here is the opener, you are the wine sommelier," said Roger as he continued to hold the tiller under his armpit which gave him two free hands to open the sack of food. The sack contained cheese, four loaves of bread, and quite a few hard-boiled eggs, at least a dozen.

Steve opened the wine bottles and sat the bottles into a makeshift rack, which Roger had fashioned to hold them. It may have been his own invention for when he was fishing alone. It certainly worked; there would be no tipping over of wine bottles. Steve poured wine into what looked to be coffee mugs, handing one to Roger and Albert. Steve also ate a hard-boiled egg, placing it between two slices of bread he cut from the loaf. He also had some cheese he cut from the large cheese wheel.

Roger declined when Steve offered to cut bread and cheese for him. He had two free hands and was used to doing for himself as a fisherman.

Albert forced himself to eat and drink, which brought some color back to his cheeks.

The weather, though not raining now, continued to be windy, Roger estimated around 15 knots. The sea now had rolling waves of maybe six or seven feet. Whitecaps were visible all around them. The sky was dark with storm clouds. It was, Roger told them, "Just another day in the Channel."

They continued to sail on. Steve, who was not used to sailing in open water, felt uncomfortable in not seeing any land. It was different when you did not see land for just a short while, when flying a B-17 at 25,000 feet and had four Wright Cyclone engines running smoothly, because either the coast of Europe or the coast of England would come into sight as you flew the bombing missions. This bobbing around like a cork in a 24-foot fishing boat with a stick in the air called a mast with a sail on it made him, let's just say, uncomfortable. England was still quite a long way, but Steve tried to tell himself that he was closer than he had been in more than a month and a half. In addition, Roger certainly seemed to know what he was doing, so maybe the worry was just for worry's sake.

Albert looked brighter now that he had something to eat and was getting used to the routine. The routine, of course, was bobbing around like a cork in the Channel, which certainly felt like open ocean.

The long day was coming to a close. They had been sailing since approximately

3:30 in the morning. A check of the clock on Roger's chain showed that it was close to 1700 hours, or five o'clock. They were now about 14 hours away from the French coast. Roger estimated that they would see land in 10 to 12 hours. They had traveled more than half way, Roger thought.

Just before dark, the sound of airplane engines were heard. Specks were seen several miles to the left, off their port side. They seemed to be heading toward England. Everyone on board grew a bit apprehensive. Were they Allied or Luftwaffe planes? Their boat was on a heading in the direction of England, which would not go unnoticed by the Germans. They could certainly shoot them out of the water. One of the planes must have spotted them because it peeled off for a better look-see. Steve could not quite make out the plane yet, although the distant silhouette told him that it was either a German ME-109 or British Spitfire. The closer it came the plane took the shape of the Spit, with the white-blue-red circle on the wings confirming its identity.

Albert and Steve waved. The Spitfire came around for another pass and waggled his wings, then flew back to join his formation. The uncomfortable feeling became a little more comfortable for Steve.

"If you ever wondered what the middle of the Channel looked like, gentlemen, this is it," joked Roger as he tried to lighten things up a little.

"To be very honest, I never wondered . . . not at all," answered Albert. "Get me to dry land! How about you, Paul, I mean, Steve?"

"I've seen the middle of the Channel and remember where we are going they refer to it as the English Channel," responded Steve, who paused for a moment. "Yes, I have seen it and the middle of the North Sea close to 50 times, as I flew to and from bombing missions. I must say though that I have never been able to reach out and touch it! I find the actual texture much like that of ocean water . . . wet and salty."

They all had a good laugh. The situation, as the little boat continued bobbing its way toward England, was too serious to do anything else as a second night of complete darkness was upon them. The waves were no higher nor were they any lower. To Steve and Albert the waves were high enough, actually far too high for either of them. They would prefer the calm of a lake. However, Roger was enjoying every minute that the wave action challenge presented.

There was no rain, although each of them was quite wet from the wave's spray as it drenched the boat on what seemed to be every seventh or eighth wave. The storm slickers kept them dry from the waist to the head, but their pants and shoes were soaked with water. Both Albert and Steve continually used the little buckets to keep the water in the cockpit at a minimum, but still it sloshed around their shoes. The low clouds prevented any view of stars, making the night seem even darker. Every so often, Roger would flash his torchlight toward the compass to make certain that their course remained reasonably steady.

"Reach in the cabin and bring me some food and wine. I'm getting hungry," said Roger.

Steve motioned to Albert to stay seated. Steve then went forward to the cabin and fetched a second food sack. Like the other sack, it had hard-boiled eggs, cheese and two extra loaves of bread. Steve also brought two more bottles of wine back for

Roger, Albert, and himself. Steve handed the sack to Albert while he opened one of the two bottles of wine. Roger, still with the tiller under his armpit, munched away at a hard-boiled egg. Steve was amazed how Roger could handle the boat's tiller, peel the shell from the egg, slice the bread and make a sandwich as a normal activity. Then, as a fisherman, perhaps all of this was normal.

"I saw a couple of bottles of cognac in the cabin. When do you want a little to warm you?" asked Steve as he poured more of the red wine for Albert and Roger.

"Later tonight, when we are all much colder than we are right now," was Roger's answer.

Hours passed as they sailed on. The bright spot was that with each minute they were getting closer to England. The old boat was doing well. It certainly was not one of those fancy racing sailboats that ran the course of the America's Cup, like Sir Thomas Lipton's *Shamrock,* but they were on a heading for the same Isle of Wight that in 1851, hosted the first Cup Race, which eventually became known as the America's Cup Race.

Suddenly a rogue wave hit the boat! She rolled over hard to starboard, sail and mast splashing into the sea. Roger quickly reacted and brought the boat back to where she was, just heeling slightly. They had been close to capsizing. From his seat at the tiller, Roger let out enough sail so that just a little luffing took place. In the darkness it was hard to tell where that wave came from. He thought about reefing the sail, but the wind, which had died down to about eight knots, did not call for that. Wave action in this darkness was difficult to judge, and that particular wave certainly got everyone's attention.

While all three men were extremely tired, both Albert and Steve forced themselves to stay awake to talk with Roger in order to make certain that he did not fall asleep at the boat's tiller. They had asked Roger a couple of times if he needed a break, because either one could spell him for a while, but Roger insisted that he was all right. It was also doubtful that any of the three could fall asleep. With being cold, wet, and anxious, plus the adrenaline that was flowing, the three men were completely awake!

The time at sea continued. While the Channel crossing between Dover and Calais was about 26 miles, the crossing between the Cherbourg Peninsula and the Isle of Wight–Portsmouth area was about 100 miles. No matter, this was a long trip in a small sailing vessel.

A check of Roger's clock showed that it was 0435 hours. In an hour or so, the sky would start to brighten, as daylight would happily be exchanged for the very dark night.

They had now been at sea for a little more than 24 hours. The compass showed that for the most part they had been on or near the plotted course. Roger thought that he had accounted for wind and current drift, as best he could bring that variable into the overall equation. The hull speed of the old fishing boat under sail could also be a factor. Maybe they were not moving as fast as they thought. No matter, as Roger pointed out, they would run into land eventually. If it was soon, it would be England; later could be America!

With his spirits still running high, Roger called out, "It is now time for cognac and some bread, if there is any that is not soaked with salt water. See if there are any more eggs and fromage . . . I am hungry . . . oh, what a breakfast!"

Steve went back into the cabin and handed out what remained in the second sack to Albert. There was also one bottle of wine left, along with two bottles of cognac. Steve had packed the bread so that it was protected.

Cognac was poured for Roger, and Albert and Steve shared the last bottle of wine. They might join Roger for some cognac later. Steve and Albert each had an egg and gave Roger the last two. There was plenty of fromage, so the three shared the cheese and the bread as they sailed on through the early morning.

A light fog had developed and along with it a slight mist. It made everything seem damp. The sky was getting brighter off their starboard side. The break of dawn was not far away. The wind had died down to what Roger thought was less than five knots. They were not moving very fast. The waves were now no more than one foot.

"This is good," said Roger as he scanned the horizon, then continued, "There is a rock formation on the western side of the Isle of Wight called the Needles. They extend out to sea and I was afraid if we were too far west, then we could run into those rocks. The slower speed will let us come upon the land like professionals," and he gave a hearty laugh.

"I think I see land off the bow," called Albert as he strained to look through the fog and mist.

Both Steve and Roger stood up to see if there was indeed land ahead of them. Neither did, although Roger thought that they might be just a few miles off the coast.

"I'm glad that it is now light," said Roger with a wink of the eye to Steve. "I did not tell you because you might worry, but I was concerned that if we were in a shipping lane we might just get run over by a warship. It would not even know if they had crushed us."

The remark made Albert put both hands to his face. He had not thought of that kind of danger.

A check of the time showed that it was now 0730 hours. They had been under sail for 28 hours. The fog was lifting and actual sunlight was peeking through the clouds. It was a brisk morning for one to be out on the water. The three were now being fortified with both the sunshine and cognac. However, they were still cold and quite wet.

"I could really go for a good hot cup of coffee right now," said Steve.

"It is not yet time to break the boat up for firewood, maybe later," answered Roger.

In the distance, land finally came into view, about an hour's sail away. A look at the chart that Roger had Steve retrieve from the cabin showed that the outline of the coast indicated it was England's Isle of Wight. Roger pointed to the chart and then to the distant land and stated that it looked to be St. Catherine's Point.

"We must be careful now . . . Steve, I need you to go up to the bow and stay there," stated Roger. "You must keep on the lookout for mines, which are sure to have been planted for security of these waters. Albert, you need to keep an eye out on the port side. I will look for them on the starboard side. It is best if we do not explode since we've come this far."

Steve did not say anything, what was there to say. He just worked his way to the bow and planted himself so that he had a good view.

"We must also take caution when we land the boat. There could be land mines planted on the beaches," continued Roger.

"Are you going to land at St. Catherine's Point?" asked Steve from the bow.

"No, I don't think so," answered Roger. "I do not know if many people live around there. I think it is best if we try to work out way around to the town they call Ventnor."

Albert, in the meantime, was looking hard at the sea for mines. This was a worry that he had not counted on.

"My girlfriend's parents live on the Isle of Wight, in the town of Sandown," said Steve. "This island is restricted and people cannot easily travel to and from the mainland, even though Portsmouth Harbor is just six miles away."

"I see Sandown on this old chart of mine," said Roger. "First from here comes Ventnor, then Shanklin, Sandown and the large bay."

As they sailed closer to the Isle of Wight, but were still more than three miles away, off their starboard bow a boat was spotted that would intercept them before they reached land. The boat was traveling at a high speed.

"Looks like we'll have company in a few minutes," stated Steve as he pointed out the launch that was approaching.

"Captain Carmichael, remember you are the one in charge," said Roger. "We do not want them to tell us to go home . . . De Gaulle . . . the Free French Army . . . we are not spies."

"Don't worry, you are now in my care and I'll make certain that you are treated well," answered Steve.

The outline of the approaching boat showed that it was a British patrol boat. Steve had seen this type of boat before. It was like those that picked up downed airmen that had crash-landed in the sea. The boat slowed as it approached the sailboat so that its wake would not disturb the small boat too much. It maneuvered into position about 20 feet away and eased along at a very slow speed.

A sailor with a bullhorn called out, "Lower your sail. Who are you? What is your purpose to be in this area of restricted waters?"

Steve, who was still up forward in the bow of the boat, cupped his hands to his mouth and called back, "I am Captain Steven Carmichael, a B-17 pilot of the United States Army Air Corps. I was shot down on December 1st over Aachen, Germany, and these people are part of those who have helped me escape capture. They are here to join General De Gaulle and the Free French Army."

"Hold on a minute, Yank," responded the sailor. "We've got to check things out on the radio . . . be back in a minute with instructions."

In the meantime, Roger lowered the sail and the fishing boat drifted on the now calm sea. The patrol boat came to just about a halt as it continued to maneuver slowly, keeping the same distance from the fishing boat that was no longer under sail.

Just a minute or so later, the sailor called back on the bullhorn, "We are going to throw you a line. Tie it onto your bow. You all look as though you could use a hot cup of tea. We will maneuver closer and take you on board our boat. A seaman will work your tiller as we tow you into port."

The patrol boat eased around so that its stern was just in front of the fishing boat. A line was tossed the short distance to Steve. He caught it and while still on his knees so that he did not fall overboard, tied the line to a cleat at the bow.

"Is this okay?" called Steve to the seaman aboard the patrol boat. "Yes, that's just fine," was the answer. "We can make adjustments when our man is on your boat. Leave it as is for now."

The line from the stern of the patrol boat to the fishing boat had a lot of slack in it to permit maneuvering. A seaman on the patrol boat held the line above the water so that it would not become entangled in their propellers. The patrol boat then maneuvered to the side of the fishing boat. With bumpers out on the starboard side, it eased next to the fishing boat. Albert, Roger, and then Steve were helped aboard the patrol boat. As they were being guided to the warmth of the wheelhouse and cabin, two seamen boarded the little boat, which had brought them safely to freedom. One seaman went forward to the bow so that the towline could be properly adjusted, while the other went to the stern to operate the tiller that Roger had so skillfully held for more than 29 hours.

"Welcome aboard, I am Lieutenant Bruce Ellis," stated the skipper of the British patrol boat.

"Thank you, my name is Steven Carmichael. I am a captain in the American Army Air Corps, a B-17 pilot who had the misfortune of having my plane shot down on December 1st. These gentlemen are both French and have been of great assistance in keeping me from falling into enemy hands. They will be joining with De Gaulle and the Free French Army. This is Albert Leterrier. Albert has seen me through a great deal in the last few weeks and this man is Roger LeMelland. Roger is the captain of the sailing vessel that brought us here from the Cherbourg Peninsula. It was quite an adventure and one which I would not choose to do again."

"My Lord, some quite good navigating, I'd say," stated Lieutenant Ellis.

A seaman handed Steve, Albert, and Roger mugs of steaming, hot tea. Another seaman brought blankets into the wheelhouse and draped a blanket around each man's shoulders. It certainly felt good to be warm once again.

Steve raised his tea mug to Albert and Roger. He did not say anything. The smile on each man's face spoke volumes. Steve actually shivered a little as he sipped the hot tea. He didn't realize how cold he had been.

"Do you gentlemen speak English?" asked Lieutenant Ellis to Albert and Roger.

Steve broke in before they could answer. "They speak English much better than I do French," he said on their behalf.

"This is good because my French is also quite limited," responded Lieutenant Ellis as he invited the three men to join him in the main cabin of the launch. This way they could all sit down and relax while they chatted and drank their tea. Lieutenant Ellis then went on to say, "We knew that you might show up, but we didn't quite know where. An RAF Spitfire that was returning from a sortie reported that a relatively small sailboat looked to be heading for the U.K., perhaps from France."

"That was us all right," responded Steve. "We saw the Spit break off from the formation and check us out. By the way, where are we headed?"

"We are making our way to the base in Bembridge, here on the Isle of Wight," answered Lieutenant Ellis. "With the slow speed we are making because of the tow-line, it will be more than an hour before we land."

Steve, while sitting on a bench near the launch's galley, looked toward Roger with a nod of his head, then spoke to Lieutenant Ellis, "Captain LeMelland did an outstanding job of navigating in order to have us sail across the Channel and damned near bump into St. Catherine's Point. It was quite a trip, I can tell you. If you hadn't caught up with us, we were going to try and land at the town of Ventnor."

"I cannot commend you enough, Captain LeMelland, on your navigating and dead-reckoning skill," stated Lieutenant Ellis as he raised his tea mug in salute. "You also had to take into consideration wind and current . . . bloody amazing. But to be sure, you must also be congratulated for sailing that little boat across that much open water, and the past few days have not been the best of weather conditions."

"Tell me about it," said Steve. "Albert and I slowly gained our sea legs while Roger simply sailed along." He paused for a moment to sip some tea then continued, "We might just draft him into the Air Force as a navigator!"

"Well, perhaps the Royal Navy may well enlist him for his seamanship as well as his navigation skills," countered Lieutenant Ellis as they all had a good laugh.

"The problem is, my friends, I do not have the skill with your instruments. What I know is in my head," answered Roger. He then peered out of a porthole and questioned, "Is this Ventnor we are passing?"

"Yes, Ventnor and Ventnor Bay, then around the next point you will see the Isle of Wight towns of Shanklin and Sandown," said Lieutenant Ellis. "They share Sandown Bay. You are welcome to join me in the wheelhouse or perhaps you would like to continue and rest here."

"I would like to see from the wheelhouse," answered Roger in his best English.

"I think perhaps a rest here would be better for me," stated Albert, who still did not feel that well.

"I'll join you in the wheelhouse," said Steve.

Lieutenant Ellis called aside one of his crew, spoke quietly to him, and then turned to Albert and said, "This man will show you to a bunk where you will be more comfortable."

Once in the now crowded wheelhouse, Lieutenant Ellis had Steve and Roger sit on the high bench, which would give them a good view of the Isle of Wight's eastern coast.

"Our commanding officer is Commander Christopher Hulbert," said Lieutenant Ellis. "He is a veteran of the Great War and enlisted once again to help our country in their time of need. He will be meeting us when we arrive at Bembridge. There will not be a brass band to meet you, but there will be brass there to give you a hearty welcome. Commander Hulbert will arrange for some clothes for you to wear. To me, you all need a change of clothes, no offense intended. I am sure that someone will come over from Portsmouth representing the American Forces, but that may be later in the day."

"I would like to stay on the Isle of Wight for a day or so if that can be arranged," said Steve.

"A little tour of the Isle . . . it is quite an interesting place," said Lieutenant Ellis. "I am from the other side of the island, a town called Yarmouth. It was a great yachting area before the war. Then there is also the town of Cowes, an important sailing and yachting city with a great history. As a boy we learned that what you call the America's Cup Sailing Race took place there in, I believe 1851. We usually don't speak about the outcome of the race." He then pointed out the pier at Sandown and continued, "The middle of the pier has been removed so that if a German spy tried to land at the end of the pier and gain access to Sandown, he would not be able to continue on into the town. In addition, the bay has been mined and the beach barricaded with concrete blocks at each beach entrance, plus barbed wire, to act as a blockade against an invasion by the Germans."

"Well, the real reason why I'd like to spend a day or so would be to meet my lady friend's parents," said Steve as he in particular took in the view of Sandown from Sandown Bay. "They live in Sandown."

"Very interesting . . . I'll speak to Commander Hulbert," stated Lieutenant Ellis. "I am sure that he could arrange the meeting with her parents for you." With a wink of the eye to Steve, he continued, "I believe that you would also want to be certain that what you could now call your wards, are properly looked after before you leave for the mainland."

"Thank you, good lead to follow! You won't be a lieutenant for very long, my friend," kidded Steve.

The launch was now passing Culver Cliff with a view of Culver Downs above it. Then they eased through Whitecliff Bay with the fishing sailboat nicely trailing behind. The seaman on board the little vessel actually looked as though they were having a good time, which they were!

Finally, after rounding the point at Foreland, the launch, with the little boat in tow, headed toward and into Bembridge Harbor, or in the British way, Bembridge Harbour. It was now past 10 o'clock on this mixed sun and overcast morning. To Steve and his companions though, the sun was shining as bright as could be! The date of Steve's return to England was Wednesday, January 19, 1944.

With the sea rescue launch secure at the dock and the fishing boat tied up, it was time to step back onto dry land—English soil.

There were several British military officers standing on the dock that looked to be representing at least two branches of the British Forces, the Navy and Army. Steve was anxious to meet with them, but the most important thing on his mind right now was to somehow, get word to his dad that he was safe.

"Let me escort you off of the launch," Lieutenant Ellis said quietly to Steve. "That way I can do the introductions."

Steve did not answer but nodded his head. He then motioned for Albert and Roger to follow along with him. They all got in step behind the lieutenant as he stepped off the launch and onto the dock. Then the four walked over to the waiting officers.

In the meantime, the crew of the launch went about their duties, plus they made certain that the sailboat was completely secure. In addition, they also did a check of the contents on board the sailboat just to be certain that there were no explosives. This was nothing special, just routine.

Lieutenant Ellis, standing in front of the British officers, gave the British salute to his superiors while Steve drew to attention and gave the American salute.

The lieutenant then stated, "Sirs, this is Captain Steven Carmichael of the American Air Corps." Then before the lieutenant or Steve could say anything else in introducing Roger and Albert, Commander Hulbert interrupted them.

"Welcome back, young man," he said. "I'm glad that you've been returned to us safely," as he gave a hearty handshake to Steve. The commander looked toward Roger and Albert and said, "Introduce me to your companions. From what I heard through the transmission on the patrol boat, they should be congratulated for bringing you back to England."

Steve, in trying to be as formal as possible before the British Naval officer said, "Sir, this gentleman is Captain Roger LeMelland. His navigation and seamanship skill across all of that open water is what enabled us to survive and reach England. My other companion and friend is Albert Leterrier. Albert's skill as a member of the French Underground is what kept me out of enemy hands, with quite frankly, the enemy all around us all of the time. They both intend to join the Free French Forces here in England."

"I'm pleased to welcome you to England, gentlemen," stated Commander Hulbert. "Do not worry about the sailors with rifles. It was just a normal precaution that I am sure you all understand. The Isle of Wight has fairly easy access to the mainland and we are always on the lookout for those who might want to slip in one way or another."

Commander Hulbert then introduced the other officers. The armed sailors were excused and the commander called Lieutenant Ellis aside, telling him to take Steve, Roger and Albert to the barracks so they could have a warm shower, shave and receive fresh clothing before joining the commander for lunch.

"Sir, before we leave the dock area," started Steve.

"The American Air Corps have already been informed of your arrival," said Commander Hulbert as he anticipated Steve's question. "The wheels are spinning at the High Wycombe Eighth Air Force Headquarters so that your absent-without-leave status is brought up to date. Tomorrow you will have an escort, or more likely a nanny to look after you so that you do not give away any military secrets, especially to those of the newspaper and radio press when they catch up with you. My boy, you have created paperwork."

"One more thing, sir . . . letting my dad in Florida know that his son is alive and safely back in England," added Steve.

"I will see to it that they are informed of your immediate wishes and concerns," said the commander as he softly patted Steve's shoulder. "We will talk more at lunch, Captain."

"Thank you, sir," was Steve's reply.

Lieutenant Ellis then had his three wards follow him to a nearby barracks. To be sure, the hot shower felt good! Steve actually stayed under the hot water longer than normal. With a pair of scissors provided by the lieutenant, Steve did his best to cut off most of the beard he had grown. He cut to the point where he could shave off the rest, and now looked much more like military.

Photos had been taken by the British Navy of the three men as they stepped onto the dock from the patrol launch, and some of their fishing sail boat. Steve was going to ask for a copy to show his dad how he looked with a full, untidy beard.

A mixture of clothes was brought to the barracks for the three refugee travelers. Underwear, black socks, plus British Navy regulation black shoes were there to try on. In addition, seaman's pants that had flared legs and a buttoned flap in the front were provided. A dark blue shirt and naval sweater completed the makeshift wardrobe.

Steve looked in the mirror and pronounced himself "completely out of uniform!" Right now, though, he could have cared less. He was warm, clean-shaven and the clothes fit pretty well. The last piece of clothing issued was a British Naval peacoat.

Lunch was held at the officer's mess. It was a very relaxed atmosphere. The hot meal tasted as good as Steve had ever eaten. Then circumstances made the luncheon taste better than perhaps it really was. No matter, it was good and everyone had his fill.

While at lunch, Steve mentioned that he would like to meet Margaret Steele's parents who lived in nearby Sandown. Their names were Edward and Ruth Steele. They lived on Station Avenue, but Steve could not remember the house number.

Commander Hulbert would see to it. In addition, the commander explained that while Steve was free to leave the base and the Isle of Wight when it came time to rejoin his Air Force Group, Roger and Albert would have to stay behind and, for the time being, would be confined to the base. He was sorry, however, through security rules, they needed to be restricted to a barracks general area during the day and there would be a guard on duty during the night. This would be in force until they were completely checked out and approved to join the Free French Forces. Then someone from the Free French would collect them. Commander Hulbert went on to state that they were not being treated as prisoners, but as guests while their unusual situation was clarified. Both Roger and Albert understood and were simply pleased that they were being treated so well.

After lunch, along with Lieutenant Ellis, Commander Hulbert escorted Steve to a large Quonset hut building where an interrogation would take place. Inside, at one end of the building, tables were set up in a semi-circle. A small table and chair was set before the semi-circle. At the semi-circle tables sat uniformed British officers and a American Naval officer. No other branch of the American armed forces was present. There was what looked to be a stenographer settling down at a separate table, preparing to take down what was said by Steve.

First, Commander Christopher Hulbert, for the record, introduced himself and stated the purpose for the meeting. He then introduced Steve to the assembled group of officers. There were individuals representing the British RAF, Army, Navy and Coastal Command. Commander Hulbert then asked the American Naval officer, a lieutenant commander who had made the six-mile trip from Portsmouth, to introduce himself.

Steve thanked the assembled group for their hospitality and was sorry to be out of a proper uniform. The group of officers had a hearty laugh. Steve then went on to say that, he would answer their questions as best as his memory would allow at this time, and that he intended to put pen to paper to recreate a day-by-day event log which might serve others who might find themselves behind enemy lines.

Questions were asked about each phase of Steve's 50-day ordeal. He did his best to answer each question and elaborate on how his plane was destroyed. Steve stated that most of his crew bailed out east of Aachen, Germany, and that he was able to finally, escape the burning B-17 bomber west of Aachen, over the Netherlands. Steve further stated that he knew at least two crew members were killed, through a report provided by the Dutch Underground. He also said that the Germans thought there might be three bodies in the plane's wreckage. The ship was badly burned after it exploded on the ground. This fact had given him some breathing room; there was not a meaningful hunt for him. Steve went on to use a long pointer as he stepped over to a large map and showed as best he could the route taken and areas that either the Dutch Underground or the French Underground avoided. Some questions were asked again with a different twist to help Steve jog his memory on individual events. At one point, Steve asked Commander Hulbert for a transcript copy of what he had said. He wanted to review it and add things as they came to mind, knowing that when he met with American Intelligence, many of the same questions would be repeated. Commander Hulbert said he would provide the transcript.

Commander Hulbert concluded the meeting just before supper. The only break during the afternoon of interrogation came at tea time. It was not a proper "cream tea." At this particular setting, a mug of tea, along with scones and strawberry jam were served.

Handshakes and a welcome back were offered, as everyone congratulated Steve on his successful escape while they filed out of the Quonset hut. It was a very tiring event, but Steve was glad to provide as much information as possible. Perhaps it would help another downed flier evade capture in the future.

Commander Hulbert told Steve that he would have dinner and would stay the night at his quarters. He was welcome to stay longer as arrangements were made for a meeting with the Steele family. The American Naval lieutenant commander was invited to stay for dinner, but he excused himself stating that he needed to get back to Portsmouth. It was just as well, because Commander Hulbert could see that Steve was a tired young man. After a relaxing Scotch whisky, plus dinner with wine, his guest needed some sleep.

CHAPTER EIGHT

A light knock on the door to one of two spare bedrooms in Commander Hulbert's quarters and a "good morning, Captain!" woke Steve from the most restful night's sleep he had in almost two months.

Steve quickly dressed and joined Commander Hulbert at his breakfast table. The setting of the table was located in a corner from which there was a clear view of the base pier area. The commander, believing that his young guest might be hungry, had arranged for a full English breakfast. He was correct because Steve ate, as they say, as if it was his last meal.

While the commander and Steve were enjoying a second mug of tea, they had a relaxed conversation about each other's lives before the war. Steve, of course, spoke of his dad and the cattle ranch they had in Central Florida, his learning to fly an airplane and the sports career he hoped to have when the war was over.

Commander Hulbert stated that he served during the First World War and had remained in the British Naval Reserve. He spent the time between wars as a tea merchant, tea taster and blender of tea. The commander went on to say that, he was actually in Ceylon working at a tea plantation or as some say a tea garden, when in 1939 the war broke out with Germany. He was recalled to active duty in early 1940.

After breakfast, the commander went to his office and Steve received permission to visit with Albert and Roger. The commander told Steve that an officer from the Eighth Air Force Headquarters at High Wycombe was on his way from London by train to Portsmouth Harbor, and he should arrive in early afternoon. A launch would pick him up in Portsmouth Harbor and bring him to the Isle of Wight at Ryde Pier. The commander had arranged for a car to meet the launch and bring him to the base at Bembridge. The officer would bring a proper uniform for Steve.

Steve then made his way over to the barracks where Albert and Roger were staying. Their breakfast was in the cafeteria-like mess hall. They told Steve that such a large variety of food was unusual for them. They certainly had their fill. Albert and Roger also assured Steve that they were being well treated by the British. Albert went on to say that the Free French Army had been notified of their presence and perhaps within a week they would meet with a representative. They continued having a relaxing chat as though they had known each other for a long time. The time together was interrupted when a seaman informed Steve that he needed to accompany him to Commander Hulbert's office.

Steve gave a light knock and then walked into Commander Hulbert's office. To his great surprise, there stood First Lieutenant Howard Barclay Van Dyke III.

"It's about time you showed up, Stevie ole boy," said Howie as he grabbed hold of Steve and gave him a solid bear hug.

Steve, at first, did not say anything. The emotion was too much. He just returned Howie's hug with one of his own. Steve also had to fight the tears that filled his eyes at seeing his best friend.

"Man, am I glad to see you," stated Steve as he wiped his eyes. "I thought your tour was over and that you'd be back stateside."

"After you were shot down I completed my 30 missions, then talked my way into a job at High Wycombe rather than go home," replied Howie. "I just had the feeling that you weren't captured and wanted to stick around to welcome you home . . . so here I am!"

"I tell you that being shot down is one hell of a mess," stated Steve, who by now was all smiles at seeing Howie. "I wouldn't want to make a habit of it."

"Does my dad—" started Steve, but before he could finish the sentence, Howie interrupted.

"Your dad will receive a telegram today stating that you are well and back in England," stated Howie. "When you write to him, the facts surrounding your escape are classified, so no details until you are back on the ranch in Kissimmee with him sharing a beer."

"Why don't you two go over to my quarters?" said the commander. "Captain, you can get into the proper uniform that your friend brought, and we can all meet for lunch. Lieutenant, you will be staying the night, so will take the other spare bedroom."

"Thank you, Commander," answered Steve as he and Howie started to leave the office.

"Oh . . . by the way, Lieutenant, the captain is needed here on the Isle of Wight for at least another day, maybe two," stated the commander with a wink of the eye to Steve. "There is some business in Sandown which must be addressed."

"Yes, sir . . . much appreciated," was Steve's reply as he and Howie left the commander's office and walked toward his quarters.

"What was that all about?" questioned Howie.

"A meeting with Maggie's parents has been arranged. Does she know I'm back in England?" asked Steve as they reached the commander's quarters and entered the building.

"I left a message with Emily Graham," said Howie as they sat down at the table where Steve had breakfast. "I couldn't reach Maggie, Cathy or Elizabeth at their place or St. Thomas' Hospital. Emily will tell Maggie that you're okay."

During the next hour, Steve and Howie talked nonstop. Howie said that Bob Courtney and Russ Parker were back home and instructing, as were the rest of the crew. Carl Phillips was still flying *Pappy's Pack* and had a close call between flak and fighters, but managed to make it back to Chelveston on three engines with an American fighter escort of P-47s that came to his rescue. Howie also told Steve that he saw his B-17 Pathfinder get hit and knocked out of formation. He went on to say that at least six ME-109s came in to finish the job. Howie's crew had counted the parachutes, especially the ones coming from the front of the plane, and they breathed a sigh of relief when finally the fifth came from up front, figuring that it was him. With the escape from the burning ship over Dutch territory, Howie said that he felt Steve had a chance to keep from being captured by the Germans.

Steve talked about parachuting into an apple orchard in Margraten. He went on to say how fortunate he was to fall into friendly hands that were not afraid to help a downed American airman. The conversation continued until Commander Hulbert came in and said it was time to go over and have some lunch at the mess hall. Steve had not changed into his uniform yet, but the commander said not to worry, he could make himself proper looking for supper.

While at lunch, Commander Hulbert told Steve that arrangements had been made for the Steele family to join him on the base at the commander's quarters for lunch tomorrow. In addition, the commander went on to say that before leaving the base for the mainland, perhaps a quick visit could be made at the family home in Sandown. The immediate concern, of course, was security. The old usage of "we'll see" was stated.

After lunch, Steve took Howie over to the barracks to meet Roger and Albert. Howie, to be sure, was very impressed to meet individuals who were active in the Underground movement. The danger they placed themselves in to help others gave him an understanding of the struggles and lengths people would go to in order to be free. Howie spoke fairly good French, which made the conversation easy and relaxed for Roger and Albert. Steve was able to get a feeling for what was being said. He had picked up many words and those who had helped him also gave Steve some lessons in the French language.

At 1530 hours, Commander Hulbert sent a seaman to the barracks to ask the four men to join him for afternoon tea. The tea, served with freshly made scones and strawberry jam, was held at the commander's quarters. It was the first time in the couple of days that Commander Hulbert could take some time to meet with Roger and Albert in a less formal atmosphere.

The afternoon tea extended into what Howie would call the cocktail hour. It was obvious that everyone, including the Commander, enjoyed the lively conversation that ranged from the pre-war activities of Roger and Albert to Steve and Howie's lives in the United States. Commander Hulbert also gave them an education into the world of tea as seen from the expert tea taster that the Naval Reserve officer was before the war.

From time to time Commander Hulbert would leave the living room where they had all settled after tea, to meet with an officer or seaman in the small office he maintained in his quarters. He would return and join in the ongoing conversation. The commander had, between the two world wars, traveled often to France and for a short while he had been "across the Pond," as they say, working on a tea-related project in Canada back in 1937.

Commander Hulbert further stated, "I have also visited the New York area with the Thomas J. Lipton Tea Company—Lipton Tea with their tea packing plant in Hoboken, New Jersey. The Lipton plant was near the other Hoboken giant, Maxwell House Coffee. Maxwell House had a large sign that could be seen from across the Hudson River in New York City showing that their coffee was 'Good To The Last Drop!'"

A little later, the five men settled back at the table for dinner, that is after they all had enjoyed a cocktail or two. The commander, Steve and Howie had Scotch whisky. Howie pointed out that in America they add an "e" . . . whiskey! No matter, they enjoyed the continued conversation and their adult beverage. Roger and Albert had red wine. Somehow the commander produced a very good French Bordeaux telling them, "Don't ask questions!"

One of the questions Steve did ask of the commander, while they ate dinner was the story behind what looked to be a windmill up on the hill. "In fact, it is called the Bembridge Windmill and dates from the 1700s. It is the sole remaining windmill on the Isle of Wight and still has the original wooden machinery inside. The windmill has four floors and there is an outstanding view from the top floor. The coastal command operates it right now," stated the commander.

After dinner and some cognac, Roger and Albert departed for their barracks while the commander, Steve and Howie also decided to call it a night. Howie would bunk in the other spare bedroom, next to Steve's room. Before retiring for the night though, Commander Hulbert kidded Steve that he had yet to see him dressed as an American officer. Steve joked back that he was quite comfortable in his makeshift uniform, but promised to look more official at breakfast. With everyone tired from the long day, before long they were sound asleep.

The following morning, Friday, January 21st, 1944 saw a dense fog roll in from the sea. The morning also had a chill to it, not really cold, but what could be called a wet, bone chill that went right through you.

The commander had been over to his office quite early and had felt what Mother Nature had in store, at least until the fog hopefully would burn off as the day progressed. Commander Hulbert then returned to his quarters in order to have breakfast with his guests.

When Steve came down the stairs with Howie for breakfast he was dressed in his proper officer's uniform, silver captain's bars on his shoulders and battle ribbons on his chest. Howie had brought Steve's full uniform when he came to the Isle of Wight.

"Well look at you . . . I'm impressed," stated Commander Hulbert as he stood up from the table and looked Steve over.

"It feels good to be back in uniform, but at the same time it feels a little strange," answered Steve.

"I know the feeling . . . same as me when I went from tea merchant back to naval officer," stated the commander. "Come, sit down you two. I've already had one mug of tea."

"Smells like freshly brewed coffee," said Steve as he and Howie took their places at the breakfast table.

"A surprise for our young American captain, I secured some coffee," stated Commander Hulbert as he motioned for a seaman to serve the coffee to Steve and Howie.

Breakfast was enjoyable: full English and quite filling. The conversation was lively as the commander had Steve and Howie tell him about how they met and became as close as brothers. The commander said that they were lucky because not many people get to choose their relatives.

Steve and Howie also spoke of the tough, more difficult times, like losing a friend named First Lieutenant Wright Gerke, seeing his plane go down and not being able to do anything to help.

Commander Hulbert understood. He lost a very good friend during the First World War and likewise, being on another ship, could do nothing to save his friend.

As they finished breakfast, the commander told Steve to come over to his regular office. He had the transcript of the meeting for Steve to review and make adjustments or additions. There would also be a copy for Lieutenant Van Dyke so that he could read along and possibly joggle the captain's memory whereupon more information could be extracted about his recent escape. A final copy would be supplied to all present at the interrogation meeting, except the American Naval lieutenant commander. Steve, Howie, and or their superiors at High Wycombe would determine who should receive the report on the American side.

Steve mentioned that he would not add the names of those who had helped him. He purposely omitted specific names during the initial interrogation so as not to compromise particular individuals working for the Underground in the Netherlands, Belgium and France. By omitting them for the official record, keeping them anonymous and safe, as safe as one could be who placed their life in harm's way in order to help others, they could continue the work they did so effectively. At High Wycombe, there might well be an unofficial mention of names, if we could somehow help those people.

The commander understood and had no problem with Steve's statement. He said that, Steve and Howie could use the conference room and would not be disturbed until 1100 hours. That was the time that the Steele family would be arriving. The commander said that transportation would be supplied for them. He understood that the names were Edward and Ruth Steele in case Steve's memory was foggy on that point, to which Steve just smiled.

Once in the conference room Steve started to read what he had said at the meeting on the morning he, Albert and Roger were rescued off St. Catherine's Point. Howie read his copy and from time to time shook his head in disbelief at what Steve went through once on the ground in the Netherlands.

"Man, you sure as hell went through a lot and I'm just on the first couple of pages," said Howie as he put the papers down for a moment and looked over at Steve. "You were, my friend, one lucky guy."

"I'm more than aware of the luck factor," answered Steve as he slowly shook his head. "But I'm also aware that I lost a crew, at least two which I know are dead. Those who are alive are in a Stalag someplace in Germany . . . prisoners."

"Understand one thing, Stevie ole boy, you took a direct flak hit," said Howie in a stern voice. "There is not a damned thing you could do about that one solid fact. The plane was lost . . . gone and no fault of yours. You were simply the pilot and being in the Pathfinder, sitting out there in front of us all."

Steve shook his head and smiled weakly, almost in defeat. What Howie said was true, but his being spared while his crew was not did not make it all right in his mind. It was something he had to live with.

"By the way," said Steve as he thought for a moment, "To have all of this make complete sense, write down what you saw. That way the report will have a more detailed look about it."

"Okay," was Howie's reply, and he went to work writing down his thoughts from just before Steve's plane was hit by anti-aircraft fire to counting parachutes east of Aachen, Germany, to when his crew reported seeing a final chute come out of the B-17 Pathfinder's front, just west of Aachen, over Holland.

At a little past 11 o'clock, or 1100 hours military time, there was a knock on the conference room door and Commander Hulbert peeked in.

"May we come in, Captain?" asked Commander Hulbert, who paused for a moment, then continued, "there is a young lady here who wants to introduce you to her parents!"

The door was opened fully. In no time Maggie was in Steve's arms! She squeezed him tightly, tears streaming down her face. Steve and Maggie kissed, looked at each other and one again held on to each other like they would never again let go. Steve wiped the tears from Maggie's cheek with a handkerchief Howie handed him. The emotion of the moment was overwhelming.

Commander Hulbert stood aside, observing what was obvious: these two young people were indeed in love. He simply smiled at the wonderful scene.

Finally, Maggie, or Margaret to her parents, turned to her mother and father and said, "Mommy and Daddy, this is Steve Carmichael . . . the man I've told you about."

"I'm pleased to meet you, Mr. and Mrs. Steele," said Steve as he shook hands with Edward Steele and gave a hug to Ruth.

"Well, we've certainly heard a lot about you, Captain, and we're so pleased that you've made it back to England safely. Margaret can now stop worrying where you are and if you are all right," said Mr. Steele.

"Why don't we all go over to my quarters and enjoy a relaxing lunch?" suggested Commander Hulbert as he motioned for everyone to follow him. "You can stay there for the afternoon and I'll join you for dinner."

As they walked over to the commander's quarters, Steve and Maggie hand in hand, Steve asked Maggie, "How did you get here?"

"I came with Howie," said Maggie as she squeezed Steve's hand as they walked. "When he found out that you were safe on the Isle of Wight, he volunteered, as only Howie can do, to be the man to bring you back to headquarters at High Wycombe. He came to the hospital and told them that I was needed on the Isle . . . a family problem. Howie had me in such a state, wondering who was ill or what situation had occurred that I needed to leave right away. As we left the hospital in an official car for Victoria Train Station, Howie told me that all was well with the family and that some pilot I knew had recently decided to rejoin the Air Corps from his holiday in Europe. Somewhere in my excitement I think he said that he would keep me a surprise for you."

Steve looked over his shoulder to Howie and smiled at his friend who simply shrugged his shoulders as if to say, "Put one over on you . . . but a good one!"

Luncheon was a most enjoyable scene to view. The commander and Howie occupied the chairs at each end of the table while Steve and Maggie sat on one side with Edward and Ruth Steele sitting on the other side of the table.

The conversation was kept mostly in a light atmosphere. With the Isle of Wight military interrogation largely completed, Steve did not care to rehash his wearisome but successful escape as table conversation.

Instead, Steve used the time to become more acquainted with Maggie's parents, asking questions he was interested in hearing. For example, what was Maggie, Margaret, like as a little girl? Steve was also interested in what life was like on the Isle of Wight before the war changed everything. Howie freely joined in the conversations as well, but his interest mostly centered on the city of Cowes and the yachting world before the war.

It was almost teatime when, after looking at his wristwatch, Commander Hulbert excused himself. He told everyone to relax in his quarters while he attended to things in his office and on the base. He would be back for a cocktail before dinner, pointing out that by that time he might well need a drink.

Steve took Maggie, Ruth and Edward Steele over to the barracks so that they could meet Albert and Roger. Howie said that he would stay behind and complete his part of the transcript. In addition, Howie wanted to finish reading Steve's report.

Maggie was a hit with Roger and Albert. She spoke fluent French and had a lively conversation with the two Frenchmen. Maggie brought Steve and her parents up to date with what was said, including that Albert and Roger thought of Steve as a hero. Steve quickly countered to have Maggie state emphatically that they, in his mind, were the real heroes and that he was very proud to know them. That last part apparently went over big with Albert and Roger, and, that was exactly how Steve felt.

Steve asked Maggie to take her parents back to the commander's quarters. He would be there in a few minutes. Steve wanted to say goodbye to Roger and Albert. Not knowing when he would see them again, it was important to Steve that his companions know how grateful he was to them. The bond between the three had become quite strong.

In the meantime, Howie settled in, and after completing his part of the transcript, read the balance of what Steve had said in his report.

As often happens, when you wanted things to slow down a little, they always sped up. This was true with this day. The commander returned to his quarters, and along with Howie acting as the bartender, the cocktail hour turned into dinner and then it was 2200 hours and time to call it an evening.

While the commander waited for the car that would take Ruth, Edward and Maggie back to Sandown, Steve and Maggie took a short stroll to the pier area. It would not be very much time alone, but then neither expected to be seeing the other today. They simply held on to each other and talked quietly. Plans could now be made. The timing of those plans would be determined in a few days or so. At least they were now together again in the same country and not just on the same planet.

Just before the car arrived to take them home, the commander informed Edward and Ruth, plus Steve and Maggie, that while he wished that Steve could visit them in their Sandown home, security would not permit it at this time. He was certain that they understood the situation, which they did. Maggie would spend a couple of days in Sandown before returning to London.

Howie and Steve would spend the night at the commander's quarters again. They would be leaving early in the morning by military car and travel to the Ryde Pier. A British Naval launch would take them to Portsmouth Harbor, six miles away, where a train would take them to London's Victoria Train Station. The trip was to be made in a private compartment. The compartment on either side would be occupied by American military personnel. A military car would then take Howie and Steve to High Wycombe and the Eighth Air Force Headquarters.

With the car that would take the Steele family home arriving at the Commander's quarters, Steve said goodbye to Maggie's parents. Before Maggie climbed into the car, she and Steve held each other once again and kissed. Soon the car passed behind some buildings and was gone from sight.

"Gentlemen, I believe it is time for us to have some cognac," stated Commander Hulbert as he ushered Steve and Howie back into his quarters.

After a couple of glasses and quiet enjoyable conversation, they all decided to call it a night. Morning would come early for everyone.

The commander was already at the breakfast table going over some reports when at 0630 hours Steve and Howie came down the steps for the fresh-brewed coffee that the commander had made for them. Breakfast was once again a full English; however, they did not linger over the meal or coffee. At 0730 hours, the car pulled up that would take Steve and Howie to Ryde Pier.

"That looks like our ride," stated Howie. "Commander, thank you for your hospitality. It's been a pleasure meeting you, sir."

"I don't know how to thank you, sir," said Steve to Commander Hulbert. "Words seem so inadequate."

"The joy of being with you and seeing you with your young lady love is a great reward to me," replied Commander Hulbert. "I am so glad that you decided to drop in on the Isle of Wight. Take good care, son. I hope to meet up with you once again."

There was no salute, but there was a hearty hug. Steve and Howie then climbed into the car and they were off.

The drive that would meet the Navy launch at the Ryde Pier took less than a half hour. During the trip, little was said. Howie understood his friend and did not offer any conversation. It seemed that Steve was deep in thought and he respected the quiet time that Steve needed right now.

In fact, Steve was thinking about his friends Albert and Roger, hoping that all would work out for them. He also smiled to himself about the way Howie, straight faced, kept the secret of Maggie's being on the Isle of Wight from him until he sprung the surprise. Then too, meeting Maggie's parents was a most enjoyable experience and, could he one day be related to them? Then there was Commander Christopher Hulbert; he would never forget the kindness given him by the commander.

As their military car traveled through the main street in Ryde, Steve mentioned to Howie that they should return here one day because there seemed to be some very inviting pubs along the route.

Howie smiled, his friend seemed to be relaxing. It was a good sign. From reading the complete report, two copies were in his briefcase, Howie had more of a sense of feeling for what Steve had been through during his ordeal.

Steve would point out that in actuality; it was really through the generosity of Dutch, Belgian and French people who had placed their own lives in danger for 50 days that enabled him to evade capture by the enemy.

The military car approached the pier and came to a halt by the gate blocking the entrance to the Ryde Pier. British military personnel inspected the papers handed out by the driver, then had a peek into the back seat where Steve and Howie sat. The man, whom Steve and Howie could not tell what branch of the service he represented, smiled and said "good morning," then gave the okay to another individual to raise the gate and permit them to travel on to the end of Ryde Pier.

A British Naval launch was standing by. The car came to a stop just a few feet from the ladder they would have to climb down to board the launch. With it being low tide, Steve and Howie would have to climb down what looked to be at least eight rungs on the ladder. They thanked the driver and then proceeded down to step onto the deck of the launch. The skipper of the launch invited Steve and Howie to join him in the wheelhouse and wasting no time, they were off making their way for the six-mile trip to Portsmouth Harbor. The pace was steady, but not very fast. The sea was quite choppy and those January waters looked to be very cold.

When they arrived at the Portsmouth Harbor dock area, a British military staff car took Steve and Howie to the train that would be bound for London's Victoria Train Station.

The train had been held at the Portsmouth Train Station, waiting for its two V.I.P. passengers. As soon as Howie and Steve stepped from the train platform onto the train, it started moving. The carriage Howie and Steve occupied was the last car on the train. An American Army Military Police officer identified himself to Howie and stated that the compartments on either side of the private car was occupied by armed guards and if the two Air Corps officers needed anything to let him know. They were requested not to leave their compartment, unless a need from Mother Nature was calling. If that event occurred, they would be accompanied to the WC under protection.

Howie and Steve both had to smile at the last statement, but this was the military.

Howie thanked the second lieutenant MP officer and then said, "We would both like a cup of tea, at your convenience, of course."

After the second lieutenant left their compartment, Howie turned to Steve and asked, "Have you given some thought about your immediate future?"

"Well, I'd like to complete my 30 missions. I still have five to go," answered Steve.

"That is out of the question," said Howie. "You will not be flying combat again. If you were shot down and survived, well, you have far too much information stored in your head. The Germans, more likely the Gestapo, would interrogate you and many lives, and those who helped you, would be placed in harm's way."

"Yes, you're right," answered Steve. "The thing is, Howie, I just do not feel as though I have completed my time over here. For the sake of my crewmen who will be sitting out the war in a POW camp, not to mention the two kids that were killed, I feel that I still need to do something."

For a moment, their conversation was interrupted as the lieutenant knocked on the door of the compartment and a very young-looking private first class, with an MP emblem on his arm handed in two mugs of tea along with a dozen cookies.

"Thank you . . . much appreciated," said Steve as he took his mug and cookies from the young man.

"Pleased to meet you, sirs," said the young man as he started to leave the compartment.

Howie simply nodded to the young private first class and smiled as the he closed the compartment door behind him. Then Howie turned his attention back to Steve after taking a sip of tea.

"A year ago I would not have thought that a cup of tea tasted good . . . kind of grows on you," stated Howie. "Look, in my opinion, request to be assigned to High Wycombe. With your experience as a B-17 pilot and being an evader from capture, your value to the Eighth Air Force would be immeasurable. You sure as hell do not want to sit the rest of the war out as an instructor back in the States. Also, you'd still be over here keeping me out of trouble and, of course, you would not be very far from Maggie and London."

"You've got a point . . . makes sense," answered Steve.

"Good, because I've already put in a word for you to have that assignment," said Howie with a wide grin on his face. "A lot of high rankers are looking forward to meeting you!"

Steve looked over to Howie and had to smile at his friend. Ole Howie, New York boy, he was always thinking one step ahead; a good lawyer in the making.

"Oh, by the way, I wrote a letter to your dad," continued Howie in a matter-of-fact manner. "I told him that I was going over to the Isle of Wight to pick up his wayward son and that you would probably elect not to come home right away . . . that you would consider your tour of duty over here as not completed. I told him that in knowing you, he would surely understand."

"Thanks for breaking the ice for me," remarked Steve. "It will have my letter to him make more sense. I couldn't have said it better myself, Howie."

"When we reach Victoria Station we will leave the train station by a side door on Bridge Place," explained Howie. "A staff car will take us straight to High Wycombe. The fun and games begin there as we do the drill once again of interrogation. It will be much easier because of the transcripts . . . your one with my added part. Everyone there will be hanging on your every word. Not many have spent as many days with the Underground as you did. There will be representatives from not only the Air Force Bomber Command, what we used to call the ole Air Corps, but also the Army, Navy, plus a high-ranking officer from the British RAF will be present. They also have boys that might face what you went through."

"We have a new boss as well," continued Howie. "General Ira Eaker has been promoted and transferred to run the Mediterranean Theater of Operations. Our new commander, who may well attend the interrogation, is Lieutenant General James H. Doolittle. I know what you're thinking and you are correct . . . Jimmy Doolittle from the famous raid on Tokyo in April of 1942. All of those changes took place about three weeks ago. The general is not a big guy, about five foot six inches and maybe 150 pounds, but his presence is like that of a giant! You'll love the guy, general that is, he's very approachable and is a good listener. You can almost see and hear the wheels churning as you speak with him."

"I am assigned as your nanny for the time being . . . looking after you. I brought all of your things to my place for safe keeping. Working from High Wycombe, you and I will travel to several bases and give talks to airmen who fly combat. We will, I think, first visit the 305th in Chelveston. Be prepared not to see very many people you know, except Pappy and the ground crew. The faces in the barracks change quite often with tours finished and the lucky ones going home, others shot down . . . new faces all the time. It is war, as we know it, Stevie ole boy. From the 305th, we will visit the 306th and so on until we have made the rounds. We will be visiting two or three bases a day," stated Howie.

"Sounds like I'll be busy for a while. When do I get a chance to relax and catch up with myself?" asked Steve.

"You will have plenty of time to be with Maggie," answered Howie.

The train slowed to almost a crawl as it entered the Victoria Train Station. It came to a complete stop on the track to the far right, just a few walking steps from their carriage to the side door exit onto Bridge Place.

The Military Police who had been traveling in the adjacent compartments with Howie and Steve were standing on the train platform even before Howie reached to open their compartment door. The second lieutenant actually opened their door for Steve and Howie as they left the train and stepped onto the platform.

Because they were on the far side of Victoria, no one in particular took notice of the military contingent that left the train. The lieutenant motioned for Howie and Steve to follow him. They walked briskly toward the side door of Victoria Train Station and out onto Bridge Place where an American military vehicle was standing by. The staff car stood out among the other cars that usually traveled in and around London. It was a 1942 four-door Ford painted in the color called by the military olive drab, which was so correct! In addition, according to the "Brits," the steering wheel was located on the wrong side of the car!

The lieutenant was thanked for his service. The car doors were closed and the staff car, driven by an American Army sergeant started through London streets as they made their way to the suburban town of High Wycombe. The trip would include a drive of about 25 miles, with High Wycombe located west of London in the Chiltern Hills.

"If you'd like, I've got a copy of the completed transcript for you to review," said Howie as they settled in for the ride.

"I've looked it over a couple of times," responded Steve. "For now and during the upcoming meetings, whatever might be added will come from spontaneous recollection. I think that is best . . . anyway . . . right now I would rather just sit back, enjoy the ride and take in the view without having to duck out of sight," added Steve with a faint smile.

"Okay, no problem," answered Howie.

"How do you come to London from way out there when you do get free time?" asked Steve as they drove through Hammersmith and headed toward Hillingdon. "Do you have to travel by bus, taxi or is there train service?"

"Train service into Paddington, then an old friend of ours picks me up," answered Howie with a wide grin.

"Michael, with his old Rolls Royce limousine. Wow, I had almost forgotten. How does he?" However, Steve stopped talking as Howie held up his hand. They would go into the supply of petrol some other time.

It wasn't long before they passed through the villages of Denham, Gerrards Cross, Beaconsfield, and Loudwater, then they entered the town of High Wycombe.

The Ford staff car came to a halt at the main gate. It had been built for the military. A Military Police sergeant checked the papers handed out by the driver. The MP also looked inside the vehicle checking the photo ID of Howie. The papers explained Steve's presence. Satisfied, the MP gave a salute and they proceeded.

Just after they entered the grounds of the old Wycombe Abbey School for Girls, which had been turned into the Eighth Air Force Headquarters, Howie remarked, "We have a great bunch working here. I think there are over 100 . . . 101 with you. Oh, by the way as you can see, the grounds look like a large park and we plan to set up a baseball field. You can help with the design."

Steve smiled as the car came to a stop in front of the large, old manor house, "So, this is Pinetree!"

"That it is," answered Howie as he and Steve opened the car doors, got out and looked up at the Gothic-style three-story mansion.

"Was this an old abbey?" asked Steve as they walked up the front steps.

"Not really," answered Howie. "As I understand it, the house was designed by an architect named James Wyatt to look like an old country house that may have been a former monastery. I have done a little homework on the place, knowing you studied architecture. It is quite interesting and I'll show you what I found out another time. For now, let's see if it is showtime for you."

Both Steve and Howie returned the salute from the Military Police soldier at the front door. Another MP asked to see identification from Steve, having recognized

Howie and seeing his picture ID. Howie intervened, producing papers on Steve's behalf.

"Lieutenant, please go directly to Colonel Dawson's office," said the Sergeant at the desk in the large mansion's foyer.

Howie did not answer, but shook his head and motioned for Steve to follow him. They walked down the high-ceiling hallway to a large old oak door. A nameplate stating who was in the office was to the right of the door. Howie knocked on the door and Colonel Dawson called out to come in.

Howie went in first with Steve trailing close behind. "Sir, may I present Captain Steven Carmichael," Howie said. "You can take him off of the A.W.O.L. list. The wandering boy has come home!"

"Glad to know you, Captain," said the Colonel.

"Pleased to meet you, sir," replied Steve.

"Well, since you are no longer absent without leave, we can take you off of the Missing In Action Report. Why don't we have some lunch and get acquainted," stated the Colonel. "Later, we can review your transcripts and do a little update. When someone like you comes back to us, there is a valuable lesson that we can all learn something from." The colonel then gestured for Steve and Howie to walk with him to the dining hall.

"Thank you," answered Steve as he and Howie joined Colonel Dawson for the walk to the dining hall.

The three settled in at a table that overlooked the back part of the property after first going through the cafeteria-style food line.

"From what I've heard, you've been through quite a lot since early December," said Colonel Dawson as they started to eat lunch. "It must have been a harrowing experience."

"Through a great deal of luck and quite a few wonderful people, I'm here, sir," answered Steve as he enjoyed a sip of fresh coffee.

"We'll get into all of that later," the colonel said. "For now, let's just relax. I understand from the lieutenant that you will request to stay on over here and not return to the States. You do know that you can go stateside as a returning evadee."

"Yes, sir. I'd rather stay here and contribute in some way," responded Steve. "I know that I'm not permitted to fly combat because of the possibility of being shot down again with the information that I know, but I just would not feel right if I went home before my conscience said it was all right. I hope you understand."

"I do understand," answered Colonel Dawson. "I'm in the same boat, so to speak. They kid me about being an old retread. I flew during the First World War. Actually I shot down one German plane and one observation balloon. I left the service, completed college and became a pretty good lawyer. Quite frankly, I still loved the service and was a member of the Pennsylvania National Guard. I requested to be activated shortly after the attack on Pearl Harbor and here I am. I came over here in June of 1942."

"I'm studying to be an attorney. I was a Yale boy, you know, before joining the Air Corps," stated Howie, as he joined the conversation.

"We won't hold that against you, Howard. I studied law at Harvard," kidded the colonel, to which they all had a good laugh.

"Howie, rather Lieutenant Van Dyke, and I were talking about the history of the manor house. It certainly looks to be quite the place. I thought it was an old abbey, but the lieutenant told me that the architect James Wyatt designed it to look that way."

"The lieutenant is correct," answered Colonel Dawson, as they continued eating lunch. "James Wyatt is quite famous. He was born in 1746 and at one time, around 1776, was actually the surveyor for Westminster Abbey in London. As you can see, I also have an interest in the history of the manor. The architecture that James Wyatt liked most was medieval. He loved towers and the Gothic style . . . therein the towers and Gothic look of this manor house. You know, he died in 1813 from an accident with his carriage. It seems that while his carriage was traveling over the Marlbourgh Downs something happened and he was killed. James Wyatt is buried at Westminster Abbey."

"Very interesting history and from what I can see, quite the property," added Steve.

"There are about 160 acres . . . woods, gardens and a lake," answered the colonel.

Howie listened, but did not comment anymore. He was letting Steve make a good impression on Colonel Dawson.

The colonel continued, "High Wycombe, we are in Buckinghamshire, for your information has a most interesting city history as well. They have a market, which has been held each week since medieval times. There is another amazing thing that has also taken place since then, which is the weighing of the mayor. The town crier will call out, 'and no more or some more,' to see if the mayor gained weight at tax-payer's expense! This still occurs today in full public view. The same apparatus for weighing has been in continual use since the early 1800s. I guess that the original scale must have broken, perhaps under the weight! The main industry of this area though is furniture making, high-quality furniture. High Wycombe is a very pleasant community."

The light conversation continued throughout the luncheon. The colonel did not ask any questions that might be covered during the interrogation or, more accurately from a military viewpoint, a debriefing session. He did ask Steve about his life before joining the service and was pleased to meet a Florida cowboy! The colonel told Steve that he had vacationed in Miami and Miami Beach, plus did some fishing down in the Florida Keys before the war, but had not been in Central Florida. He was surprised that it was an important cattle-raising area.

Just as they were finishing lunch, a second lieutenant came into the dining area and handed Colonel Dawson a note. He read the note, looked at his wristwatch and said, "Thank you, Lieutenant." Then turning to Steve and Howie he held up the note and stated, "They are ready for us. Captain, there will be many questions asked by the half dozen individuals in the conference room. Each of them has a transcript of your report along with what was added by Lieutenant Van Dyke. There will also be a copy for each of you. Be relaxed because you will be among friends."

"The one problem I have, sir, is revealing individual names of those who helped me," stated Steve to the colonel as they walked toward the conference room. "You know about Albert and Roger because they are in the report and hope to join the Free French Army. However, the names of others, some of whom did not even mention names, mine or theirs on behalf of security, should be classified information. Far too many individuals and families could be placed in great danger if their identity were known."

"I agree, Captain, and if anyone were to bring up information about individuals who have helped you, I will intervene," answered Colonel Dawson. "You've taken a very strong stance in protecting those people and I know that it will be understood and respected by everyone."

The second lieutenant opened the door to the conference room and first the colonel, then Steve and finally Howie entered. The men who had been standing and talking to each other became silent.

"Gentlemen, may I present Captain Steven Carmichael, a B-17 Pilot from the 305th Bomb Group," Colonel Dawson said. "The captain has recently rejoined us after an extensive holiday in the Netherlands, Belgium and France, coupled with a sea voyage." There were smiles as the colonel lightened the atmosphere in order to have Steve feel more comfortable.

Then he continued, "The captain has provided quite an in-depth report on his experiences. Lieutenant Van Dyke, who saw the captain's plane get hit and go down, has added to the report. I am sure that you have all had time to review it and have additional questions that may well help others who might find themselves in a similar situation. The one subject that he will not address is that of individual names of those who helped keep him free from capture. I know you will all understand the importance of keeping those people anonymous for the official record. Please, be seated. Captain, the seat at the end has been reserved for you. That way everyone can see you."

Everyone took a seat. As expected, there were ranking representatives from the American Air Force, Army, and Navy. There was, in addition, a group captain from the British RAF. Each individual was introduced to Steve.

Just before the first question was asked, the conference room door opened and in walked "the Boss," wearing the three stars of a lieutenant general. Everyone stood up. Colonel Dawson, who had taken the chair at the other end of the conference room table, offered his seat to the general, but a wave of the hand from General Doolittle told the colonel to stay where he was. The general took a seat next to the RAF group captain.

The conference room door was closed and the meeting, which really turned into a meaningful lecture by Steve, began. As on the Isle of Wight, once again maps on a large easel provided a picture to go along with the printed word. Steve pointed out the basic route taken, along with specific detours that were used because of security purposes. This included the port selected to depart France. Heads were shaking as the debriefing, which lasted for more than three hours, ended.

After the last question was asked and answered, Colonel Dawson stood up and said that they had a gift for Captain Carmichael.

"Captain, this little reward has been handed out, quite frankly, not as often as we would have liked," the colonel said. "I am pleased to present you with this silver boot with wings on it. Through the wings it shows that you are an airman, but the boot states that your last mission was completed on foot," and the Colonel presented the "Winged Boot" to Steve.

Steve thanked the colonel and good naturedly accepted the "Winged Boot." It was a nice gesture and Steve was pleased with the award. He was also relieved and pleased with how the debriefing went. There were actually several questions asked that were not covered in the report. Fifty days was a lot of time to remember everything. Steve was also very impressed with "the Boss"!

After the debriefing meeting, the Colonel told Steve and Howie that he was very pleased with not only the meeting, but also how professionally each had conducted themselves. They were told to relax for the evening and to get Steve settled. Steve was also to report to Colonel Dawson's office at 0800 hours the next morning.

Howie asked Colonel Dawson if he would like to join them for dinner. The colonel thanked them, but regretted that he still had some work to do and was planning to retire early, perhaps at another time.

"Follow me. We can walk to your new quarters, then go into town for some supper," said Howie to Steve as they left the conference room.

"You live here on the grounds and don't have a room in the mansion?" questioned Steve.

"Come on . . . I'll tell you about it on the way," said Howie as they left the mansion through a back door and started walking toward some of the estate's outbuildings.

"Some live in the abbey," Howie explained, as he and Steve continued along the pathway that led to the front door. "I did for a while. However, I discovered this small, old stone hut-like building that at one time must have housed the gardener or one of those types of jobs. I found that it has everything small . . . kitchen with an ancient cook-stove, living room with a fireplace and two tiny bedrooms. There is now also a small but adequate bathroom with a shower. We broke through a wall, which was probably temporary, that had been used for storage, to get some extra space. The building was just there, not being used except to store junk, so I kind of acquired it."

"Well, it does look like part of the original building plans," said Steve as they approached the what ever you would like to call it, turned military quarters for Howie and now Steve.

"What do you think?" asked Howie as he and Steve entered the cabin-like dwelling.

"Cozy . . . inviting . . . easy to clean," answered Steve.

Howie did not answer, but walked over to a cabinet, produced two glasses and a bottle of Scotch. "Welcome to your new home Stevie ole boy!"

"Cheers," answered Steve as he and Howie touched glasses.

"It's good to be back together with you," exclaimed Howie as he took a sip of Scotch.

"How did you get the furniture . . . steal it from the mansion?" asked Steve as he settled down in a chair by the unlit fireplace.

"No . . . look, I'm a first lieutenant among big brass here," said Howie as he gave a salute with his glass to Steve before taking another sip of Scotch. "I needed to do most of the renovations kind of behind the scene. On a trip to London to see Elizabeth . . . Michael and I got into a conversation about my finding this little outbuilding and he knew exactly what I was talking about. One of the very rich people he drove for had two daughters going to the school for girls here. He would drive the rest of the family out from London for the day and while here, he walked the property, making friends with those who worked the grounds. He had actually been in this building. Well, Michael and some of his friends, some who still work the grounds, cleaned up the place, which was dirty as hell, and through some connections, the place took shape. I've kept the other bedroom with all of your things in it, just knowing that at some point you would occupy it."

"I thank you, but you certainly had more faith in my coming back than I did," said Steve. "There were many times that I figured being caught was just around the next corner."

"I have several warm blankets on hand," said Howie as he changed the subject. "It does get cool in here when the fire in the fireplace dies down. Why don't I start a fire? Then it will be warmer when we come back from town."

"What do you use the old wood-burning cook-stove for?" asked Steve as he walked around, inspecting the rooms.

"Nothing really, it just is there . . . I don't know how to operate it," answered Howie as he and Steve looked at the old kitchen cook-stove.

"I've encountered these stoves several times over the past couple of months," recalled Steve. "Those people use them for both cooking and to warm part of the house. Between the wood-burning stove and the fireplace we should be able to at the very most, just wear a sweater."

Steve then opened all of the doors and vents of the stove. In seeing that it looked clean and checking to be certain that the connection to the chimney was solid, he placed some split wood into the stove so that after they returned from supper it could be lit and provide additional warmth to their quarters.

Howie and Steve had a taxi take them to a nearby pub where they had dinner and a couple of pints of ale. They returned to their quarters at a little past 2100 hours or in non-military talk, nine o'clock. A fire was lit in both the fireplace and the kitchen cook-stove. Howie sat before the fireplace and read a book borrowed from the library that was established by the military personnel.

Meanwhile, Steve wrote a long letter to his dad. Steve had written a quick note to his dad while on the Isle of Wight telling him that he was okay and that a lengthy letter would follow, along with a new mailing address. Then for the tired young men, it was off to bed in the cozy, warm quarters.

Back in Kissimmee, Florida, at the Stardust Ranch, a joyous Ray Carmichael read and reread Howie's letter about going over to the Isle of Wight to retrieve his wayward son. Ray also had the telegram from the War Department, which stated that Captain Steven W. Carmichael was safely back in England and on active status.

Then, there was a special telegram via the Red Cross that was from Steve. It simply stated, "Hey, Dad, back from a trip to Europe . . . will write soon. Love, Steve."

At the Eighth Air Force Bomber Command Headquarters at High Wycombe, Steve reported to Colonel Dawson's office at 0800 hours on Monday, January 24th. Steve was made comfortable in the office as he sat in a large leather chair before the Colonel's desk.

"I just want to go over this one more time," said Colonel Dawson as he looked across his desk and directly into Steve's eyes. "You are entitled to go back to the States where you will be given another assignment as an airman who successfully evaded capture. Do you completely understand this, because I do not want you staying over here because of the enthusiasm of Lieutenant Van Dyke."

"I do understand, sir," answered Steve. "How I feel is exactly what I told you yesterday. I prefer to stay over here and contribute."

After a moment of silence Colonel Dawson said, "Well, I have a job for you here at High Wycombe. One of my officers will be going stateside in a few days. By the way, you and the lieutenant seem closer than most men I have encountered. I know that at one time he was your copilot, so it looks as though you two could do well working together. Is this a correct assessment?"

"Howie and I haven't cut our wrists like they do in the old cowboy and Indian movies, but we have declared ourselves as brothers," answered Steve. "We first met in flight school. When everything was on the line, if you know what I mean, we could count on each other and worked well as a team."

Colonel Dawson smiled as he said, "The Cowboy and Indian . . . that's a good one. I do understand the point you make about when things are on the line. The job will be in strategic planning. In addition, you will travel to the Eighth's air bases and give a lecture on behalf of evading capture, that is, for the lucky ones who don't fall into enemy hands right away. The way we are set up, quite frankly, you will be doing both jobs at the same time. You will have some time off, of course. London is always calling, but as you know, war is a seven-days-a-week job. I tell you that London is becoming one of the most dangerous cities in the world. With the German buzz bomb, at least you could hear it coming. These damn V-2 Rockets are silent . . . until you hear the explosion. Well, what do you think . . . want the job?"

"This sounds like a wonderful opportunity. Will I be able to have Lieutenant Van Dyke work directly with me?" asked Steve.

"Yes, he hasn't had a permanent position since he completed his combat tour and requested assignment here," Colonel Dawson responded. "He certainly knows how to get things done, like the little housekeeping set-up he has. Oh, I know all about it. Part of my job to know what is going on right under my nose," the colonel added with a broad smile on his face. "He will make one hell of a lawyer some day!"

"Howie and I do and will work well together, plus we know how to delegate duties and promote teamwork," answered Steve, who also had to smile that the colonel knew about Howie's little project and that the colonel let him get away with it.

"I'm counting on it," said Colonel Dawson. "Oh, by the way . . . the position calls for the rank of major. Your next in command will be a captain. I have this pair of gold oak leaves that I would like you to wear. They did me well and I'd like to see them on your shoulders," the colonel added as he handed Steve the gold oak leaves of a major and shook hands with him.

"Thank you so much, sir!" exclaimed Steve. "It will be a privilege to wear them. I hadn't expected a promotion. I will pass my captain's bars on to Howie. There is a lot of luck in them."

"Break the news to your partner in crime and then both of you report back to me at 1100 hours," stated Colonel Dawson. "We'll get you started in your new position. The second in command has already been reassigned. I won't go into anything else; getting you started is important."

Steve left the colonel's office and went into the men's room. Calling it the latrine in this beautiful large manor just did not sound correct. He took off his coat and replaced his captain's bars with the gold oak leaves of a major. Then he left and found Howie in the dining hall having a cup of coffee with two other officers.

Howie spotted Steve and motioned for him to join them after he got a cup of coffee. He had not seen the rank change on Steve's shoulders.

While Steve was pouring a cup of coffee and reaching for a donut, Howie got up from his table and came over to pour another cup of coffee for himself.

"We need to talk right away," said Steve.

"Duty calls," said Howie to the men whom he was sitting with.

"We both have a new assignment in strategic planning," explained Steve. "We meet at Colonel Dawson's office at 1100 hours. I asked the colonel for you to be my second in command. Are you okay with that?"

"Hell, yes! I've been just sitting on my ass looking for something to do that is more meaningful," answered Howie.

"Good . . . here, put these captain's bars on your shoulder. You've been promoted," stated Steve as he handed them to Howie.

"What are these, your railroad tracks? I just noticed you're a major!" said Howie.

"It seems as though the people we are replacing had these ranks," answered Steve as he took a sip of coffee and a bite from his donut. "It's not of importance, but I know that the captain has already been reassigned and the major will be going stateside."

"This is terrific . . . we'll give them hell!" said an excited Howie.

"Oh, by the way, the colonel knows all about our quarters and probably a lot more, but he decided to look the other way. Apparently he likes you," stated Steve.

"I didn't think Colonel Dawson really even knew that I existed," answered Howie. "I'll be darned!"

Steve and Howie sat at a separate table to continue their conversation, rather than join the individuals Howie just left. Howie had his coat off now and was replacing his first lieutenant's silver bars with the twin silver bars of a captain.

The other officers had finished having their coffee and were leaving the dining hall when one of the officers pointed to the captain's bars, smiled and gave a high sign.

"Congratulations, Captain!" stated one of the officers.

"Thank you," responded Howie and Steve at the same time.

"He was talking to me . . . you are a major now," kidded Howie as he looked at his coat before putting it back on. "I figure these captain's bars should be put on before Colonel Dawson changes his mind," added Howie.

Steve took a sip of coffee and another bite from his donut. "Actually, I didn't wear those captain's bars for very long. You'll have to break them in."

"You know, I can see my folks bragging at the country club about my making captain," laughed Howie as he finished his coffee. "Hell, the old man could not believe that I could actually fly a plane. They'll probably hold a parade in my honor when I get home . . . one or two blocks long in Glen Cove." He stood up and walked over to a large long mirror to admire himself with his new rank. With a wide grin on his face, Howie continued, "What do you think . . . how do I look?"

"Terrific! Just like a captain should look." answered Steve.

"We still have an hour to kill . . . what should we do?" asked Howie.

"Let's go into town, stop at a pub and down a few pints," kidded Steve.

"With that attitude, we won't have our job or rank very long. It's a good thing that the colonel likes me, Stevie."

"Let's take a walk on the grounds," said Steve as he got up from the table.

Howie didn't answer, but followed Steve as they walked out of the manor and toward the lake. They walked and talked, really about nothing special, just two friends enjoying each other's company.

At the 1100 hours meeting, Colonel Dawson outlined exactly what Steve and Howie's duties would entail. They would share a former small sitting room turned office and be part of a team that made up the Strategic Planning Group on behalf of developing Eighth Air Force bombing missions. In addition, since the two had come from combat groups, they would be acting as liaison to the combat bomber groups (H) and (M). The (H) means heavy or four-engine bombers (B-17 and B-24s) with the (M) meaning medium or twin-engine bombers (B-25 and B-26s).

They were perhaps 25 minutes into the meeting when a knock on the door brought Lieutenant Colonel Harold Livingston into Colonel Dawson's office. He headed up the planning group to which Steve and Howie were being assigned. Lieutenant Colonel Livingston, like Colonel Dawson, as they say, was a retread having served in the First World War. Lieutenant Colonel Livingston had served in the New Jersey National Guard since the Great War and before being recalled to active duty was a professor, teaching at Rutgers University.

After the meeting, Steve and Howie quickly settled into their new office. They prepared for the first assignment, which was to visit several air bases on behalf of evading capture if an airman was shot down on a combat flying mission over enemy territory.

The immediate schedule called for them to travel first to the 306th Bomb Group in Thurleigh, then on to the 92nd at Podington and finally to the 305th Bomb Group at Chelveston, where Steve and Howie would spend the night. The following day would be spent at the 303rd Bomb Group at Molesworth and the 91st, located in Bassinghourn.

Each of the initial visits to air bases belongs to the Eighth's First Air Division. There would be representatives from other First Air Division bases at the meetings so that important facts, plus "street-wise smarts" on evading capture, were taken back to their respective groups. The trip would start on Wednesday, January 26th. Steve and Howie would return to High Wycombe on the evening of the 27th. The transportation would be via a twin-engine C-47 Transport, as flying would make the quick trip possible.

After dinner on the 25th, Howie and Steve relaxed in their quarters. A small fire in the fireplace and a fire in the old iron kitchen cook-stove made the place quite cozy and comfortably warm on the cool evening. Howie had provided a large bag of peanuts that did not exactly go with the cognac he and Steve were sipping, but they were sure tasty!

There was a knock on the door. Steve got up from his chair to see who was there at this hour and was surprised to see Colonel Dawson standing in the doorway.

"Hello, Colonel, come in," invited Steve. "We've got a warm fire going and some decent cognac. Plus if you like them with cognac, we have some roasted peanuts."

"I've heard about this place. I had to see what you've done to the old storage shed," said Colonel Dawson as he walked in and looked around. "This is much larger than I remembered. Here, I've brought a bottle of cognac as a house-warming gift. From the looks of what you've done, I just might kick you two out and take over the place for myself. This is quite nice."

"Have a seat, Colonel. I'll fix a glass for you . . . help yourself to the peanuts," said Howie as he got another glass from the cupboard.

"How did you make this place so large . . . what . . . a couple of bedrooms and a bathroom, plus the kitchen and living room?" asked the colonel as he surveyed the quarters before taking a seat in front of the fireplace. "Did you break through the wall into the other storage area?"

"Kind of guilty, Colonel," said Howie as he handed Colonel Dawson a more than decent-sized glass of cognac. "This place and the one next to it were not being used and it seemed such a shame to see them go to waste, so through some friends we kind of reinvented the quarters to make them of use for military personnel . . . cut down on the crowded situation. It is perfect for Steve . . . the major . . . and me."

Turning toward Steve and raising his glass to both Howie and Steve, the colonel said to Steve, "Do you believe this line of bullshit?"

"It is, I admit, a fine line, sir . . . but much easier to take if you do believe it, and thank you for the house-warming present," answered Steve with a wide smile on his face.

"House warming . . . with the size of these servings, we'll go through your bottle of cognac and mine," kidded the colonel, who after a sip, continued, "well at least you liven this place up a bit. Damn war is depressing a lot of the time."

"Sir, the welcome mat is always out for you, Colonel," said Howie. "We're glad you came over for a visit and not to dump us out into the cold night."

"Better put another log on the fire . . . it's starting to die down," said Colonel Dawson as he took another sip of cognac. "I really enjoy a fireplace."

"Colonel, I know that Steve is interested and you might also want to read a letter I received from Bob Courtney, our former navigator," stated Howie as he opened an envelope. "Bob and I have continued to correspond."

"I would be interested to read it," answered the colonel.

"Read it out loud," requested Steve after he sipped a little cognac.

"Well, let's see . . . Bob is teaching navigation and doing just fine," Howie read. "He said that he is up for promotion and should make captain soon. Russ Parker started teaching at Bombardier School, but felt that most coming out of school would be just togglers, so after a visit to see family in San Francisco, he had himself reassigned to intelligence at Bolling Field in Washington, D.C. Bob goes on to say that Jim McFarland, he was our engineer and top turret gunner, visited his folks in Buffalo and is now assigned to MacDill Air Base in Tampa. Jim said that Florida is a great place to spend the winter months and that when he got some leave, would visit Steve's dad at the ranch in Kissimmee. Eddie Anderson, our radioman, went home to Tigoa, Texas, spent a wonderful 30 days leave on the family ranch and is now teaching radio. Jack Kowalski, our left waist gunner, visited family in Chicago, and Joey DeMatteo, he was initially at right waist and then became our tail gunner, spent time with family in Philadelphia and now both are teaching gunnery. Roger Earp . . . we called him Wyatt because he is related . . . a great-uncle if I remember, well he went back to visit his folks in Phoenix after getting out of the hospital. He was shot up pretty badly on one of our missions. Ole Wyatt was our first tail gunner. He is completely healed now, but instead of teaching gunnery as we advised him to do, the Arizona boy volunteered for duty in the Pacific. He is currently training in the new B-29 Superfortress bomber. He wrote to Bob that he simply had not finished his job yet. Bob also wrote that he, Russ, Jack, and Jim visited the family of Ron Lattamus in Sterling, Illinois. Ron was a replacement after Wyatt was hit and he took over at right waist with Joey going to the tail. He was the only crew member who was killed. Finally, Bob wants me to keep him informed about you, asking if there is any new news about the skipper. I think he'd appreciate a letter from you," advised Howie to Steve as he handed Bob Courtney's letter to him.

"I'll do that . . . write to Bob and the rest of the crew," said Steve as he took the letter from Howie. "When I do get back to the States, I'll also visit Ron's family."

"I'll join you on the trip to Sterling," stated Howie, who then took a sip of cognac.

"It certainly sounds like you two had a great crew. To hear that letter being read also shows the respect and leadership qualities that you both are made up of," stated Colonel Dawson. He took the last sip from his glass and set down on the small table that served as the coffee table and stood up. "Thanks for the drink and the company, boys. I'm going to call it a night."

"Goodnight, sir," said Howie and Steve almost simultaneously.

"Remember, the welcome mat is always out for you," stated Steve.

"I will remember, it's been a most pleasant, relaxing evening," said the colonel as he waved goodnight.

Steve and Howie went back into their little living room and sat down. The surprise visit from Colonel Dawson had been enjoyable. The old man was all right!

"By the way, with Maggie now back on duty at St. Thomas', we should all get together this weekend," said Howie as he took another sip from his glass.

"Good idea . . . London is calling," kidded Steve.

"Let's not make plans too quickly though," reasoned Howie. "The key is the two of us, only recently being assigned for duty here, are low men on the totem pole."

"I guess you are right," replied Steve. "When I telephone Maggie, I'll tell her that we might be able to come to London, however, it would not surprise me if we had weekend duty here in High Wycombe."

"If not this weekend, then another . . . only way to view it and at some point we can also meet the girls and take the train to York," Howie said. "Elizabeth's family has a manor just outside of York, not too far from a famous place called Castle Howard. I was up there a few weeks ago and fed a peacock! The Anderson family has a magnificent home and property. Quite frankly it makes our home in Glen Cove look like a gatehouse."

With the fire in the fireplace becoming just glowing cinders, it was time to call it a night. Steve walked into the kitchen, stoked the fire in the iron cook-stove and added two small logs. They would be enough to keep the quarters comfortable during the rest of the chilly night.

Major Carmichael and Captain Van Dyke started their assignment of visiting the First Division's air bases a couple of days later. A misty rain and heavy fog meant that the audience would be loaded with combat-ready crews since bombing missions for the day had been scrubbed.

The C-47 flight to Thurleigh was not fun. It was a little rough riding, with some stress for Steve in not piloting the plane himself, but the C-47 flight crew did an outstanding job under the weather conditions.

Steve gave about a 20-minute lecture and spent close to an hour answering questions from the airmen assembled in a large J hangar at the 306th Bomb Group. The next stop was in Podington and the 92nd Bomb Group. The last lecture also took place in a J hangar at Chelveston, Steve and Howie's former home base, the 305th Bomb Group.

While the lecture at the 305th lasted just a little over 20 minutes, the question and answer part of the program lasted much longer. The interest level was perhaps a little higher since the questions were directed to one of their own.

As Steve left the makeshift lectern and stage, he was greeted by a crusty old Sergeant Major. He did not salute, but put his arms around Steve.

"It's so good to see you, son," said Pappy.

"Thank you, Pappy. It's good to be back," said Steve to his old crew chief.

Steve, Howie, and Pappy went over to a corner of the J hangar and sat on the vacated folding chairs. No one, not even the officers who were serving as guides or the group commander, interrupted them. This short meeting went well beyond standard military protocol.

Steve and Howie also met with First Lieutenant Carl Phillips, Howie's copilot when Steve left the group to fly the Pathfinder B-17. Carl took over command of *Pappy's Pack* after Howie's tour of 30 missions was completed.

"The Kid," as Howie referred to Carl, now had 19 missions under his belt. He had just 11 more missions that are harrowing over occupied Europe before he could go home to his young wife.

Steve and Howie had dinner with their group commander and his staff. It was quite informal and both Steve and Howie felt comfortable. The conversation ranged from the time Steve, Howie, and the original crew first came to Chelveston to his escape from capture. While some at the dinner table wanted to use the word hero to describe his escape, Steve made certain that those assembled understood that he considered those who of their own accord, were in meaningful harm's way the entire time he was in their hands were the real heroes.

After dinner and before going to the Officer's Club for a drink, Steve and Howie met up once again with Pappy and Carl. They all went out to the hardstand where a well-worn but battle-ready B-17 named *Pappy's Pack* sat waiting for her next mission over enemy territory. There was still a light rain falling with poor visibility, but the ole girl stood out, almost at attention in seeing her favorite pilot.

With umbrella in hand, Steve did a pilot's walk-around, gave the ship a pat and then through the forward hatch, climbed aboard the B-17 Flying Fortress. Steve did not go directly to the pilot's seat, but instead walked through the catwalk in the bomb bay, then the radio room and into the area occupied by the ball turret gunner and two waist gunners. He then looked toward the rear of the aircraft where first Roger "Wyatt" Earp and later Joey DeMatteo as tail gunners had protected the plane's rear. With a smile and slight shake of his head, memories that seemed so long ago came to the forefront. Steve then made his way back to the front of *Pappy's Pack*. He climbed into the pilot's seat, took a long look around and quietly thanked the plane for taking care of him and those who flew in her.

Howie and Carl stayed on the ground, letting Steve be alone to reminisce in *Pappy's Pack*. When they spotted Steve sitting, in the pilot's seat, they gave a high-sign wave and he signaled for them to come aboard. After they joined Steve on the flight deck, the conversation, as Howie sat in the copilot's seat while Carl and Pappy stood behind the pilots, centered on what a great ship *Pappy's Pack* was and they spoke about the crewmen who worked so hard to protect the old war horse in the sky during battle.

Later, after they left the hardstand, Steve suggested that the four of them go to a local pub, located just off base. Pappy, however, said that he was really tired and for the young flyboys to go over to the Officer's Club and relax. A goodnight was said to Pappy. Being the crew chief, he did not have regular hours; in fact, his hours were mostly irregular.

At the Officer's Club, things looked to be much the same as when they spent many an evening here. The biggest difference was that just about all of the faces had changed. In the time Steve had been away, crews had completed their tour of missions, while others did not return from bombing raids.

Carl walked over to the officers who were sitting at the old corner table that Steve and Howie had usually occupied. He spoke quietly to the four second lieutenants and they immediately started to get up so that Steve and Howie could sit at the table.

"Please, don't move! If you don't mind, we'll get some chairs and join you," said Steve as he motioned for the young officers to stay where they were.

Two of the lieutenants brought three more chairs to the table while the others rearranged the chairs so that there was room for everyone.

"Thank you, Major," said the second lieutenant who had pilot wings on his coat. "We heard your talk this afternoon. It gave us confidence that all is not lost if you are shot down. There was that great unknown if that happened."

Steve smiled, thanked the lieutenant and asked Carl to have the four pints refilled when he placed their order. Howie, after introductions were made, started to get up to help Carl carry the pints of beer, but the lieutenant with bombardier wings motioned to Howie that he'd help Carl.

After placing the pints on the now crowded table, Carl went back to the barman and said something in a very quiet voice. The barman left for just a moment and when he returned from the storage room, he had a very large bag of peanuts.

"Well, I'll be," said a smiling Steve. "This is a real treat!"

"Nice going, Carl," said Howie.

"I just wanted you two to feel at home," said Carl to Steve and Howie.

For more than an hour, the conversation continued light and lively as everyone enjoyed a pint and happily munched away on the peanuts. Then the word came that a mission was on for tomorrow, and the Officer's Club would be closing.

Steve and Howie spent the night in somewhat of a VIP hut. The bunks were comfortable and it was warm inside, plus there was hot water for showering and shaving!

The following morning was quite a busy one with a mission under way. Steve and Howie watched the action from the elevated platform on the control tower as the B-17s of the 305th Bomb Group headed off for a mission. On this particular day, the mission was recalled because of extremely poor weather conditions over the target area, which was Frankfurt, Germany.

Before the planes landed back in Chelveston, Steve and Howie were off to the 303rd Bomb Group at Molesworth. From there they would travel to the 91st at Bassingbourn for the lecture Steve would present. The plan called for them to be back in High Wycombe before suppertime.

It was during supper that Steve and Howie learned their workweek would continue through the weekend. The trip to London and meeting up with Maggie and Beth would have to wait.

After supper, Steve managed, after several tries, to reach Maggie by telephone at St. Thomas' Hospital. While the conversation did not last very long because she was working, Steve explained that plans would have to be placed on hold.

Back at their quarters during the evening of January 27th, Steve and Howie relaxed by the fireplace. With Scotch in hand, Howie talked about long-term plans. The key was completion of law school, then what would he do with the law degree?

Howie stood up from his chair, motioned to Steve that he would refill his glass, took Steve's glass and refilled both before sitting back down.

Steve, in the meantime added two small logs to the fire, then spoke, "This Scotch is smooth . . . what is the brand?"

"Your brand," answered Howie, who reached for the bottle to show Steve. "I picked up a couple of bottles of Oban Single Malt . . . reads Clan MacDougall down on the right side of the label. It's 14 years old. Wonder why they did not keep it another year before bottling it . . . "

"Well, you're mostly right about the association with the Clan MacDougall," Steve said. "Actually, as my dad tells it, the Carmichaels were, as they say, henchmen to the MacDougalls! They would fight side by side with them . . . with some being very violent battles. The beauty is though . . . this is good smooth Scotch Whisky."

Howie took a sip, set the glass down and held his hands out to warm them before the fireplace, then said, "I hope my time here at High Wycombe will work out. Too much is at stake with those kids flying the missions and I don't want to mess up."

"Howie, you don't have to prove to anyone that you belong here, especially with what you've been through during combat these past few months," said Steve in a firm voice. "Relax and just be yourself and soon others will get the idea that you have a special experience to contribute."

"I guess you're right," answered Howie. "Yes, the more I think about it, you are right! We have been through the fire and know what hell must look like."

"We know hell . . . especially with flak burst all around you, ME-109s and FW-190s trying to shoot you down, plus ME-110s sitting off just out of our gunner's range, firing rockets at you," added Steve. "Flying a combat mission is no walk through the park." He then got up from his chair, reached for Howie's empty glass and walked into the tiny kitchen to wash the glasses. He then added a couple of small logs to the cook-stove fire so that their quarters were warm throughout the night.

"It is time to hit the sack," stated Howie.

"I've set my alarm clock. See you in the morning," answered Steve as he walked to his bedroom.

It was raining, not a heavy rain, but more than a mist as Howie and Steve walked, umbrella in hand, toward the manor at High Wycombe the next morning. There was also a low fog hanging over the area. Friday, January 28, 1944 would be another day that the Eighth Air Force did not fly a bombing mission. The weather forecasters were more optimistic on behalf of the next few days. That meant it would be a busy time for those in the planning section.

At breakfast, Howie spoke more to Steve about completing law school at Yale University. With the way things were developing between Elizabeth and him, Howie wondered aloud if he should think about joining an international law firm. His concern though, was that if he were low man, then maybe just the senior partners would do the international travel.

Steve listened and thought for a moment, then said, "Look, from what you've told me, you prefer to do corporate law. So with that in mind, between your father plus Elizabeth's father's contacts and business connections . . . start your own international business firm!"

"The U.S. and U.K. specialize, you know, that is a possibility," reasoned Howie.

"Just as long as you make time to be my attorney when I need one," kidded Steve. He then pushed his chair back and said, "Let's go to work!"

As he got up from the breakfast table and started carrying his tray toward the dining hall kitchen, Howie added, "Now all I have to do is complete law school, pass the bar and form a law firm."

"See, it's easier than you ever imagined," answered Steve as he gave his friend a pat on the back.

Both Steve and Howie fit in well with the rest of the group charged with strategic planning. Their recent experiences in combat gave the section many realistic observations on missions being planned. Their firsthand knowledge about specific target areas complemented the intelligence reports.

The following day, Saturday, January 29th, the target was Frankfurt. The mission would be led by Pathfinder B-17s because of extensive cloud cover and the smoke screen set by the Germans. The bombing raid would consist of more than 600 B-17 Flying Fortresses plus almost 200 B-24 Liberator heavy bombers. The escort called for over 600 fighters to keep the Luftwaffe at bay and protect the bomber stream. The new P-51 Mustang would accompany the P-47 Thunderbolt single-engine fighters and twin-engine P-38 Lightnings. Bombing would occur at 25,000 feet for the high group.

While no longer on combat flying status, both Steve and Howie were elated to be in on the actual planning of a mission. It gave them the feeling of still being involved.

The weather held steady enough for a mission to also be executed on January 30th. The target for the day was to be Brunswick, Germany or as the industrial city was known in Germany, Braunschweig. The city was located in lower Saxony in central Germany, slightly southeast of Hanover.

After that mission, once again the English weather brought bombing missions to a halt. The weather in England and on the Continent for Monday, January 31st, plus the first couple of days in February looked bleak, according to the weather forecasters. The bombers would be sitting on their respective hardstands.

With what looked to be a lull in the action, at least for a few days, Colonel Dawson gave permission for Steve and Howie to have a pass to London.

Steve placed a telephone call to Maggie at St. Thomas' Hospital. When they finished their short conversation, the phone was handed to Howie and Elizabeth. In no time, plans for their long anticipated trip to London were completed.

Just before Steve and Howie left for the train station on the misty Monday morning, the last day in January, Steve received and opened a letter from his dad. Reading the letter was meaningful, as his dad tried to convey his thoughts about Steve's being safe and back in England. Ray Carmichael also told his son that he understood why Steve had requested to stay in England and complete his obligation. Steve was raised that way. Ray also wrote that if Steve was getting serious with his English lady, Margaret, that he need not be concerned about Elly back home, because there was a quick wedding with the young man she had been dating at the university. It seems that his grades dropped off considerably and he was drafted into the Army. Just before the fellow was inducted, he and Elly were married.

Ray went on to say that at the Stardust Ranch, things were fine and that Lillian sends her love. She's standing over me to make certain I write that in the letter. He likewise wrote that with the price of beef and because of the demand, Steve was a rich partner. Further in the letter, Ray wrote that he had kept Mr. Briggs informed about Steve status and received a telephone call from the Tigers owner stating that the Detroit Tigers organization was very proud of Captain Carmichael. They looked forward to the time when he would change uniforms, dress the part of a Tigers catcher and have a bat in his hands!

During the train trip to Paddington Train Station in London, Steve wrote a quick V-Mail letter back to his dad. In the letter, he told Ray about his and Howie's promotions. Steve also stated that he had an interesting and meaningful non-flying job, but could not discuss it at length. He further wrote that a longer, more detailed letter would follow after he returned from the three-day pass to London.

Just outside of Paddington, Michael waited by the old Rolls Royce limousine. He spotted Howie and Steve as they exited the train station and walked over to them with an outstretched hand. The handshake became a hug as he greeted Steve.

"It's so good to see you, Major!" said Michael with a broad smile as he stepped back to take a good look at Steve.

"Thank you, Michael, it's good to see you again. It has been a while," answered Steve, nodding his head toward Howie. "According to Howie, I've been on an extended European holiday."

"You are all set for the Savoy, Captain," said Michael, noting Howie's promotion. He then placed the two officer's bags in the Rolls Royce's boot.

"Thank you, Michael, I know this was short notice," answered Howie as he and Steve climbed into the back of the limousine.

As they left Paddington Train Station, Steve quietly took in a little more of London than before. The simple drive on Park Lane past Hyde Park seemed more pleasurable. Steve smiled at the small crowd listening to a man at Speakers' Corner, probably wanting to have "the lot of them sacked!"

The rest of the drive took about 15 minutes to complete. The ride went past the Wellington Arch, Green Park, Buckingham Palace and then down the Mall with St. James Park, Steve's favorite, located on the right. As they drove past St. James Park, warm memories returned. Finally, Michael turned onto the Strand where the old limousine pulled in under the covered entrance hall of the Savoy Hotel.

While Michael helped the door attendant and porter with Steve and Howie's bags, Howie and Steve walked into the Savoy to the Reception Desk and registered. Howie had asked Michael to request rooms that would overlook the River Thames. This was fine with Reception; however, the room reserved for Major Carmichael would be on the sixth floor with Captain Van Dyke's room on the fifth floor. It seemed that rank played a part on floor selection.

Steve and Howie did not take long to settle in their rooms. Actually, they would unpack later. In a very short time, they were back down in the lobby where Michael was waiting near the hotel's lifts.

They decided to stay in the hotel for lunch rather than go somewhere else. The Savoy Restaurant would be just right for a light lunch. The conversation between Steve, Howie, and Michael was quite normal until Steve asked Michael if he knew of a good jeweler.

"I've been doing a lot of thinking about becoming engaged to Maggie," said Steve as a second round of British Bitter was requested.

"That is one giant leap, my friend," stated Howie as he finished his pint and handed the waiter his empty glass.

"I know, living in Florida, taking her away from England to start a new life far different from anything she is accustomed . . . it's a big step for us both."

"Well, I've had the same thought about Beth," commented Howie. "Beth and I have what you might call an understanding. We've already had some of the conversations you and Maggie are about to embark on."

"Any advice?" questioned Steve.

"Just talk it out from all angles," said Howie, who may have been thinking of himself as well as Steve. "This is one huge step."

Michael, in the meantime, just listened. It was something that needed to be worked out among themselves. It was a familiar story: American soldiers, far from home, falling in love with British girls. Sometimes it panned out, while other times it would turn out to be just a wartime romance, not unlike a summer fling.

Finally, Michael did speak. "If the occasion should bring about the need for a jeweler, I know of a reputable one: Sanford Brothers on Holborn." He paused for a moment, then cleared his throat and continued, "If I may . . . both of you are young gentlemen with university degrees behind you. Therefore, you aren't teenagers with a schoolboy crush. This war has made you grow up more than young people your age. The same is true with our British youth and Margaret and Elizabeth. All this said, I believe that in observing you . . . you are quite well suited for each other."

"Thank you, Michael . . . much appreciated," answered Steve.

Howie just nodded his head in approval of what Michael said. He had placed everything into proper order.

After lunch, Michael left the Savoy. He would return at six o'clock, meet with Steve and Howie, then drive over to St. Thomas' Hospital to pick up Maggie and Beth.

Having some time on their hands, Steve and Howie walked over to Covent Garden. They strolled among the shops and stalls, mostly just looking, two friends spending time together.

When they returned to the Savoy, Steve and Howie went to their respective rooms. They unpacked, showered, shaved and then dressed for the evening.

Michael was, as usual, at the Savoy promptly at six o'clock. Soon they were crossing the Westminster Bridge for St. Thomas'. Maggie and Elizabeth were waiting in the lobby when the limousine pulled up. Steve and Howie got out of the Rolls while Michael went to the rear of the limousine and placed the girl's overnight bags in the boot. Howie and Elizabeth smiled as they watched Maggie and Steve embrace. It was the first time together since their abbreviated meeting in Bembridge on the Isle of Wight. They had the look of a couple very much in love!

Once in the limousine, Michael drove back across the River Thames on the Westminster Bridge. He turned right onto Victoria Embankment, left on Northumberland Avenue and then right onto the Strand before finally pulling once again under the Savoy's covered entrance. A check of his watch showed that it was now half past six.

Steve and Howie thanked Michael, said goodnight to him, then with Maggie and Beth, they made their way to the Savoy River Restaurant. Michael, in the meantime, arranged for the small suitcases to be sent to their respective rooms.

Even though they were a little early for their reservation, the maitre d' seated them at a table overlooking the river. It was a nice gesture; however, it was dark outside and with wartime restrictions, the curtains were drawn so tight that light could not be seen from the outside.

Once seated, Howie asked if they thought that champagne was the order of the day to celebrate their reunion. It was and when the table captain came over to offer his greetings, the order was placed. In addition, hors d'oeuvres would be served when the kitchen was officially open. Maggie pointed out that in England, they may well be simply called "pickers," but at the Savoy they were "hors d'oeuvres."

The champagne was poured, toasts made and before too long, the "pickers" were served as well. It appeared to be the beginning of a special evening. The soft sounds of a piano were heard in the background.

Ordered for dinner by all four was a grilled Scottish Chateaubriand, served with pommes soufflé and Yorkshire pudding. Steve smiled when he heard the table captain state that pommes soufflé, or fancy potatoes, would accompany the Chateaubriand. He wondered if the friends he made during his escape would have thought to make a soufflé rather than just boil the potatoes.

Looking through an extensive wine list, even though the war was well underway, Steve and Howie agreed on Bordeaux that was recommended by the table captain. The wine, Château La Mission Haut Brion, was seven years old. "Grand Cru Classe 1937" was on the label that also showed a picture of the château and vineyard.

Dessert became a divided affair. Howie and Maggie ordered Peach Melba while Beth and Steve asked for the Crêpe Suzette. The sharing of dessert would take place.

Steve reminded everyone that there was dessert sharing the first time they dined at the River Restaurant. He was referring to when Elizabeth and Howie met, along with Catherine Wilks, Emily Graham, Russ Parker, and Bob Courtney. That seemed like it was so very long ago, yet only a few months had passed.

While relaxing over dessert, they listened to the four-piece band playing background music. At nine o'clock, the dancing began.

The crowded dance floor included Steve and Maggie along with Howie and Beth. They were once again dancing at the Savoy!

The following morning a taxi took Maggie and Beth to St. Thomas' Hospital for their morning shift. They would be back at the Savoy in the early evening. This also meant that Steve and Howie would have the day to relax on their own.

While the first day in February was cloudy, it was not raining. Steve and Howie lingered over breakfast in the Savoy Restaurant. They decided that a good stretch of the legs was in order. The plan, as they outlined it, would be a walk to Westminster Abbey. Steve and Howie figured that it would be lunchtime after the Abbey visit. They could then walk through St. James Park and stroll over to the Stafford Hotel on St. James Place to see who from the Eighth Air Force might be there. It was the perfect place to enjoy lunch and a pint. After lunch, Steve and Howie felt that walking down the Edwardian-style mall, passing under the famous Admiralty Arch on the way to Trafalgar Square, then the walk back to the Strand would pass for exercise of the day. Once back at the Savoy, all of that strenuous exercise would most certainly put them in the mood for some light refreshment, maybe a gin and tonic.

After returning to the Savoy, Steve and Howie said hello to some folks enjoying afternoon tea in the Thames Foyer, walked over to the lift, went up to their rooms and took a nap.

With their workday completed, Beth and Maggie went to their quarters to freshen up and change clothes. About an hour later, Michael picked them up at St. Thomas' and drove over to the Savoy to meet Howie and Steve. As the old Rolls Royce limousine pulled into the Savoy's covered entrance, Michael prepared to drive into the car park area in order to be out of the way. This was not necessary because Steve and Howie were already waiting. Michael brought the car to a halt in front of the main entrance.

Michael started to get out of the Rolls, but Howie waved for him to just settle back behind the steering wheel. He and Steve then climbed into the back with Beth and Maggie.

"We have a reservation for dinner at Rule's. The address is 34 Maiden Lane," said Howie to Michael.

"Know the place well," answered Michael as he drove onto the Strand and headed just a few blocks away toward the Covent Garden area. In only a few minutes, Michael pulled in front of the Edwardian restaurant that was well known for serving the very best of British fare.

"Here we are . . . Rule's," announced Michael.

Once in the restaurant, the maitre d' seated them almost immediately. After they sat down and ordered cocktails, Howie remarked that he had been here at Rule's in early September with Russ Parker and Bob Courtney. Howie also said that when he was just a boy, visiting England with his parents, Rule's was one of the restaurants he remembered and Simpson's-in-the-Strand was another.

It was a most enjoyable evening. Dinner, as usual when Steve, Maggie, Howie, and Beth were together, was a light and lively affair. Everyone ordered a different dish, so sharing a taste of this or that kept forks reaching across the table. Through the conversation, one could see that even in times of war, the joy of young people together brought smiles to others nearby.

The dinner concluded with the dessert of the house according to Howie, who ordered for everybody. Everyone enjoyed the English traditional dessert of steamed treacle sponge pudding. During dessert, there was no conversation. It was that delicious!

After dinner, having told Michael that they would have a taxi drive them, it was back to the Savoy for dancing and a nightcap. The four danced for about an hour and then called it a night.

On Wednesday, February 2nd, with the girls off duty for the day, it seemed as though some shopping might be in order, followed by afternoon tea and finally dinner at Simpson's-in-the-Strand. Steve also quietly mentioned to Howie that at dinner a glass should be raised for Wright Gerke. It would have been the lieutenant's 25th birthday.

Howie and Beth were going to the Burberry shop at 18 Haymarket and the Scotch House at 84 Regal Street. Howie had interest in purchasing a trench coat at Burberry. At the Scotch House he wanted to look for a tweed blazer for himself and a sweater for Beth. The war would not last forever and Howie reasoned that these were things that you could not buy in the States.

Steve and Maggie did not want to shop but would spend the day relaxing together. Maybe even a stroll through St. James Park would be pleasant, since it was a nice day.

Steve also had an additional plan. He wanted to take Maggie for a visit to Sanford Brothers, the jewelry firm that Michael had recommended. Sanford Brothers was located on Holborn in a half-timbered Elizabethan building that dated to the mid-1500s. Michael told Steve that brothers Frank and Walter Sanford founded the family business in 1923. In addition, over the years Sanford Brothers had acquired a reputation for selling quality goods at reasonable prices.

At breakfast, they agreed that the four would meet for afternoon tea at Brown's Hotel. Brown's was famous for their fine afternoon tea set before a cozy, crackling fireplace.

After breakfast and a fast trip to the room to freshen up, they were off! Howie and Beth went on their shopping expedition, while Steve and Maggie started their stroll toward St. James Park.

As Steve and Maggie walked along the Strand, almost to Trafalgar Square, Steve questioned what was in the bag she was carrying. She answered that the bread and rolls left on the breakfast table were put in the sack, as she called it, so they could feed the ducks and squirrels in St. James Park.

A walk down the path in St. James Park brought them to a bench near the lake. Ducks moved from across the lake to a spot directly in front of Maggie and Steve. Two squirrels also made their presence known. While Maggie was feeding her little friends, a few birds also flew over to join the ducks and squirrels. Looking at Maggie brought back memories as Steve thought about their first meeting, just a few months ago at the dance on the Chelveston Air Base. That was back in July on a Saturday night. So much had transpired since then! The truth was that a war can make weeks seem like months and months seem like years.

With most of the bread and rolls now consumed, actually, the waiter at the Savoy had placed much more in the bag than was on the table; Maggie gave Steve a warm smile and squeezed his hand.

"We have talked about being in each other's future," started Steve, who paused for a moment, then continued, "You realize that this would be quite different for you . . . leaving England for the United States."

"Steve, from the time I was a young girl, I dreamed that there would be a right man for me," answered Maggie as she leaned over and gave Steve a kiss. "I just never dreamed that he would be a handsome young American lieutenant, until I started dancing with you. Sometimes things workout the way you hoped they would. It seems that this 'sometimes' is right for us. Whether here in England or over in America, I want to be with you."

"Then it's okay to ask you to marry me?" asked Steve.

"I'd love to be your wife!" was Maggie's answer.

Steve stood up from the bench and reached for Maggie's hand. They embraced, kissed and strolled hand in hand up the path toward the broad avenue known to Londoners as the Mall.

Steve spotted a taxi that was coming from Marlborough Road and about to turn onto the Mall. The taxi driver saw Steve and Maggie almost at the same time and waited as they half ran across the Mall.

Maggie opened the taxi door as Steve said to the driver, "Would you please take us to number three Holborn. It's the Sanford Brothers Jewelry Shop."

"Okay, mate. I know exactly where you want to go," answered the taxi driver. "Frank and Walter Sanford's establishment."

After a relatively short drive, the taxi pulled in front of the half-timbered building that read "Sanford" above the door with the number three on each side of the sign.

The staff at Sanford Brothers welcomed Steve and Maggie. Asked how the staff could help the major, Steve said, "We'd like to see diamond engagement rings."

"Boy, you don't mess around," said Maggie in a soft voice to Steve as she held on tightly to his hand.

"Do you have an idea as to the size or setting?" questioned the clerk.

"I think a single diamond and around one carat," answered Steve without hesitation.

"Yes, an excellent choice," answered the clerk. What I'd like to do is give you a high setting to show off the diamond." Steve nodded his head in agreement.

In a small room behind the counter, a black velvet cloth was unfolded on a desktop and Steve looked at four diamonds using the jeweler's glass. The clerk pointed out particular characteristics about each diamond. With professional help from the Sanford expert, a diamond that was a little over one carat at 102 points became the choice.

The diamond ring could be set and ready for the major in an hour. Since it was nearly lunchtime, Steve and Maggie decided to eat at a nearby restaurant.

After the order was placed with the server, Steve said, "I don't know what to say about a wedding date."

"To be sure setting a date for anything is difficult nowadays," she said. "Let's not talk about specific. It can wait until the timing is right."

In precisely one hour, they were back in Sanford Brothers. The entire staff had to smile at the excitement the young couple displayed. The ring was ready.

Steve took the diamond ring from the box and placed it on Maggie's finger. The smile on her face as she showed it off spoke volumes. The fit was perfect.

After handshakes and congratulations, it was off to Brown's Hotel.

Steve did not have to explain to the taxi driver that Brown's was at 33 Albemarle in Mayfair, but the good-natured driver simply thanked the major for the exact address. The young couple was awhirl with excitement.

During the taxi ride Maggie turned to Steve, held her hand out showing her engagement ring and said, "I'm engaged to be married, you know!"

"I know, me too!" answered Steve with a smile, as Maggie moved even closer to him.

Finally, the Black London Cab came to a halt at Brown's Hotel. A doorman opened the taxi door. Maggie stepped out and waited on the sidewalk as Steve paid the fare to the driver. Then they walked hand in hand into Brown's, and were directed to the English Tea Room.

As they stood at the entrance of the wood-paneled tearoom looking for Howie and Beth, Steve thought to himself, *Now I understand what they mean by the statement when you enter Brown's Hotel, you know you've arrived somewhere very special.*

Howie and Beth were sitting at a table near the fireplace. They spotted Steve and Maggie and waved. Maggie and Steve were escorted by the maitre d'.

"The champagne is chilled and ready for you; however, a second bottle will have to be ordered since we started without you," said Howie with a big smile on his face as Steve and Maggie took their seats.

The waiter produced two champagne glasses, filled them for Steve and Maggie, then topped off Howie and Beth's glasses.

"Sorry we are a little late, but we waited for the ring to be set," said Steve matter-of-factly.

"What ring?" questioned Howie. Then Maggie showed off her engagement ring.

"Congratulations . . . this is wonderful!" said Beth as she took Maggie's hand and looked at the diamond engagement ring.

"Well, this does call for champagne . . . only the best!" stated Howie, who reached over to shake hands with Steve.

The conversation during the outstanding cream tea of finger sandwiches, scones with clotted cream and strawberry jam, homemade cakes, and patisseries, centered on what might be a future when this crazy war was finally over. Then meaningful plans could be made.

After the tea at Brown's, the four took a taxi back to the Savoy Hotel. They agreed to meet in the lobby for an eight o'clock reservation at a favorite restaurant, just a short walk down the street, Simpson's-in-the-Strand.

That evening at Simpsons, with cocktails in hand, Steve nodded to Howie and said, "Ladies, you are welcome to join Howie and me as we raise a glass to our friend, First Lieutenant Wright Ellis Gerke. Ike, as we called him, would have been 25 years old today."

The dinner itself, as always, was most enjoyable at Simpsons. The liveliness of this long-established restaurant with their meat-filled trolleys wheeled up for table-side service made for a fun evening. Not to mention dessert would be a sin. This evening, dessert was Crêpe Suzette all around.

After dinner and the stroll back to the Savoy, everyone decided it would be a short night, no dancing at the Savoy tonight. Michael would arrive very early in the morning with his limousine.

Michael was waiting as Steve, Maggie, Howie, and Beth came out of the Savoy. It was good that the Savoy had a covered entrance hall, otherwise everyone would have been quite wet from the morning rain. The limousine was loaded and they were off. Quick goodbyes were said at St. Thomas', because there was a train to catch at Paddington Station.

From the train station in High Wycombe, the taxi drove through the tree-lined roadway at the Eighth Air Force Headquarters, bringing Steve and Howie back to what now was their part in the war, strategic planning.

Both Steve and Howie had paid their dues, as they say, flying through the extremely dangerous sky over occupied Europe. While this experience was not unique in the European Theatre of War, that expertise would certainly help them in their new job. Steve and Howie would work to keep losses to a minimum. Neither Steve nor Howie could get used to the term "acceptable losses." To anyone who had flown in combat, no loss was acceptable.

While Steve and Howie were not due to report for duty until the morning, they quickly dropped off their bags at their quarters and went to work.

The weather was clearing and a mission to Wilhelmshaven was scheduled. This was the target area that Steve and Howie had bombed on November 3rd.

"Good afternoon, Colonel," said Howie and Steve looked up to see who had come into their office. They both stood up. With a wave from the colonel, they sat down.

Steve noticed that Colonel Dawson now had a single star on his shoulder in place of the full colonel's eagle. "Good afternoon, General," said Steve with a smile. "Congratulations, sir!"

"Thank you. Glad to see you boys back on the job," answered Brigadier General Dawson.

"With the weather improving, we figured that missions would be scheduled," answered Steve.

"Ah, the English weather. We managed to get the raid off to Wilhelmshaven this morning. The weather forecasters have told me that we should have decent weather for the next few days. We will have a meeting in the map room in 20 minutes. I'll see you there."

"Yes, sir," answered Steve and Howie at the same time.

As General Dawson left their office, Steve said, "Let's get a cup of coffee before the meeting starts."

The general, in overhearing Steve said, "Good idea, Major. I'll join you."

During the planning session, the weather officer told the assembled group that flying weather should hold good for February 4th, 5th and 6th.

The day's mission to Wilhelmshaven saw close to 700 B-17s and B-24s accompanied by more than 600 escort fighters attack the target with Pathfinder bombers leading the way. Bombing was through a heavy haze, clouds and German smokescreens.

Planning for the February 4th mission would call for a Friday raid on Frankfurt. It would not be an easy mission from the viewpoint of the Weather Officer. The weather over England would be better than that over the Continent. There would be a Pathfinder bomber because the forecast over the target called for heavy cloud cover. Another problem could come from flak once they were over enemy territory;

the strong head winds could make the bombers more vulnerable. They would be flying at a lower actual ground speed. Avoiding the flak batteries on the ground, especially on the way in toward the target area, was most important for the safety of the aircrews. Come to think of it, avoiding the flak batteries was always a good idea.

For February 5th, the planning group was working on bombing targets at Chateaudun and Orleans, France. On the 6th, primary targets included two destinations in France. Nancy and the fighter base near Dijon would be attacked.

The build-up of bombers and crews to fly them into battle was quite evident. The early days of the war, when 20 to 50 planes worked to make a successful bombing raid was no longer the case. Now, a minimum of 500 bombers and 300 escort fighters would fly a normal mission.

With the meeting coming to a close at 1930 hours, it was time to have some supper. The supper was one of those dinners where they were so tired that they could not remember what they ate an hour later.

Steve and Howie went back to their quarters to relax for a while before calling it a night. Steve built a fire in the small fireplace, plus one in the cook-stove. The warmth would take the chill off, on this cool February evening. In the meantime, Howie brought out a bottle of Scotch. He did the American thing of placing a couple of ice cubes in each glass. Neither he nor Steve cared to drink the Scotch "neat," or without ice.

The two, glasses in hand, sat down in the tiny living room, shoes off and feet resting on small stools that had a pillow on them for extra comfort.

"Long day," said Howie as he raised his glass in salute before he took a sip. "I know, but being here and not flying combat anymore has its rewards," answered Steve as he also took a sip from his glass. "You're right . . . by the way, have you and Maggie made wedding plans?" asked Howie. "Not an actual date. That will work itself out," answered Steve. "For now, the only real plan is to be part of each other's life." "Beth and I have also had conversations about being part of each other's life, as you put it," said Howie. Steve did not say anything right away. It seemed to him that Howie wanted to talk it out. He would just be the good listener. After a short pause, Howie took a small sip from his glass of Scotch and continued. "I've been thinking. That jeweler . . . what's the name of it?"

"Sanford Brothers Jewelry Shop. Number Three Holborn in London," was Steve's reply.

"If you don't mind, I'd like to ask them to duplicate the ring that you gave Maggie. Beth admired it and the ring certainly is beautiful. What do you think?" asked Howie.

"Well, that's great, but I see a small problem here. While it doesn't matter to us guys, I think a woman would like her ring to be different, unique and special to her alone," said Steve.

"Ah, yes, that makes sense," said Howie. "When we all visit the manor house Beth's parents own near York, I'll give her the ring. Tell me, what do you really think? I believe Beth and I could make it. I just don't want us to be caught up in something because it is popular and everyone is doing it. You know the story: the American soldier with a British girlfriend."

"Don't be silly," Steve responded. "Each individual is different. Of course, there are lonely Americans with money in their pockets who date the British ladies. However, like Maggie and me, you and Beth have found something very special. I don't believe what we have or what you two have is a thing of the times. I feel that you and I are very lucky to find what others might never find. A partner for life."

"You always hit the nail square on the head. That's solid reasoning," said Howie after he gave a little thought on what Steve just said. "Give me your glass. It's refill time," he added.

While Howie poured some more Scotch, adding a couple of additional ice cubes, Steve placed two small cut logs onto the fire and stoked it. He also added another log on the fire in the kitchen cook-stove. Their small quarters were now cozy and warm.

"Here's your glass," said Howie as he settled back into his comfortable chair.

Steve also sat back down and then sighed, "Well, it does seem as though you have joined me, old friend, with some, shall we say, solid preliminary plans!" However, before Howie could answer, Steve added, "You and Beth make a great couple and complement each other." Steve then raised his glass to Howie in salute!

"I have also thought about the suggestion you made about developing my own international corporate law firm. Beth's family and mine have New York and London business connections. After law school, this could work out. You know that with the workload and international travel, it would require a partner or two. How about this . . . you give up thoughts of becoming a catcher for the Detroit Tigers and ranching to become my law partner!" Howie blurted out with a wide smile on his face.

"I've already accepted a signing bonus from the Tigers, so I'd be your first client when the team sued me for breach of contract. Then there is the little matter of my dad and the ranch. Come to think of it . . . he would make a hell of a law partner. I would not want to go up against him in court," kidded Steve.

"No, you have got a beautiful life ahead of you," said Howie.

"My friend, from my viewpoint, we both do," said Steve. "The thing we do not know is when that future will begin. To be sure, Howie, you and I have benefited from simple luck of the draw! We are here and while both of us have had some scary, very narrow escapes, too damn many of our friends are in P.O.W. camps or were killed in battle. We need, I guess is a way to put it, to live a good productive life to honor those who will never get that chance."

"You're right. I couldn't have put it better," commented Howie. "We do owe it to those kids who wanted nothing more than the opportunity to live a life. I hope the folks at home realize what sacrifices are being made."

Steve and Howie spent another half hour, drinks in hand, before the warm fireplace. They reminisced about the early days back in the States, when everyone was naïve and seemingly so innocent about what was to come during the war.

Steve wanted to contact Commander Hulbert to let him know that all was well and also inquire about Albert and Roger. Were they all right and now with the Free French Army? Steve went on to say that he would like to once again meet with the people who had helped bring him back safely to England.

Finally, at a little past 2200 hours, Steve said, "I think it's about time.

We have an early morning meeting to plan for future targets, which may include the week of February 19th to the 27th, what they are calling, 'Plan Big Week.' I also want to start a letter to my dad. He'll be anxious for me to bring him up to date on what's happening."

"Tell your dad hello from me. I know when you include the part about your engagement that he will be pleased with your choice. Maggie will fit in quite well," said Howie as he got up from his chair, picked up the two glasses and walked into the kitchen.

Steve stoked the embers in the fireplace. He did not add another log. Then Steve walked into the kitchen and checked the fire in the cook-stove, to which he added a small log. The cook-stove actually warmed their quarters more than the fireplace.

Howie, in the meantime, had washed the glasses and put them away in the cupboard.

Suddenly, Steve said, "What's that noise? Do you hear it?" He listened intently to locate where the noise was coming from. "I hope we don't have mice running around."

"The front door? Maybe I didn't close it tight enough," reasoned Howie.

Steve walked over to the door and opened it. In walked a calico-colored cat, which started purring and seemed to make himself right at home.

"That's a cat!" exclaimed Howie.

"I know. Looks like we have a guest for the night," said Steve. "Get him a saucer of milk."

"What? A saucer of milk?" questioned Howie.

"We can't give him Scotch. Cats get a saucer of milk," said Steve as he leaned down and petted the cat.

"I don't know about a pet, Steve," stated Howie.

"He's not a pet, just a house guest, unless he decides to stay on longer," answered Steve. "Cats pick their friends and their homes."

"Here, cat, drink your milk," said Howie as he placed the small saucer of milk down on the kitchen floor. Howie then stood back as the cat walked over to the saucer and started lapping the milk. "I'll be darned," continued Howie, shaking his head.

"You've made a friend," said Steve as he watched their visitor make himself comfortable in the warm kitchen.

"Is it a boy or girl?" asked Howie.

"A boy cat," answered Steve.

"How do you know?" questioned Howie.

Steve gave Howie a look.

"Oh, yes, of course," said Howie.

"Well, I was going to write a letter to my dad. I'd better get started before I get too tired. Maybe I will start tonight and finish it tomorrow. Well, we have a long day ahead of us and there is still a war to win." Steve walked toward his bedroom. "Goodnight, Howie. Goodnight, little cat," were Steve's final words for the night.

"Goodnight, Steve. I am a little tired myself and as you said, we do have a long day before us," responded Howie. "This job of helping to win the war sure as hell isn't easy!"

As Howie walked into his bedroom, the cat followed him, nestling himself comfortably in the bed covers before Howie had climbed into bed. In no time, at all, both were sound asleep.

THE END

. . . or is this a beginning?

EPILOGUE

Steve Carmichael remained in England until June 15, 1945. He and Howie continued to work together as part of the team at Eighth Air Force Headquarters in High Wycombe, charged with strategic planning. Steve was promoted to the rank of lieutenant colonel and Howie to major by the war's end.

Steve then came home to the United States and spent his military leave at the Stardust Ranch with his dad. After enjoying time at home, Steve was assigned to nearby MacDill Air Force Base in Tampa.

Because he had enough accumulated points, Steve was discharged from the military on Wednesday, August 15th, and exchanged his military uniform for one with an Old English "D," the Detroit Tigers.

Steve became a catcher on the Tigers team and played quite impressively as the 1945 regular season concluded. With the Tigers becoming Champions of the American League, they played in the World Series against the National League Champion Chicago Cubs. The Detroit Tigers won the Series in seven games.

On the 12th of October, Steve returned to England. His dad, Ray, Lillian, several friends and, of course, his best friend, Howard Barclay Van Dyke III, also made the trip from New York City to Southampton aboard the Queen Mary. The occasion was for two weddings. In addition to the group from Florida, a meaningful contingent from Glen Cove, on New York's Long Island, likewise made the Atlantic Ocean crossing.

On October 20th, Steve and Maggie were married in Sandown, Isle of Wight at Christ Church, which was located on Broadway. Howie was Steve's best man at the wedding.

Then a week later, Howie and Elizabeth, Beth, were married in York, in the York Minster. It is the largest of the English Gothic cathedrals. Steve, of course, was Howie's best man.

Steve and Maggie built a beautiful five-bedroom home on the Stardust Ranch. They also built a three-bedroom guesthouse.

Steve was a rancher with his dad for part of the year and a baseball player for the Detroit Tigers during the summer months of the baseball season.

Flying continued to be a large part of Steve's life. In addition to the old Stinson biplane, now quite the antique, Steve flew his new twin-engine Beechcraft Model 50 Bonanza. The new plane was a six-place, all-metal, low-wing monoplane, with retractable tricycle landing gear. It had a cruising speed of 223 miles per hour and could fly a distance of over 1,000 miles without refueling.

Ray loved being the copilot on the new plane, however, to say the very least, his favorite time was spent as granddad to Steve and Maggie's three children: two girls, Jenny and Lauren, and their son named Wright.

Trips to England's Isle of Wight were an annual event. Maggie's parents and her friends had also become quite familiar with Florida. The guesthouse was usually occupied.

Howie completed Law School at Yale University in New Haven, Connecticut. Through his father and father-in-law's business connections, he started an international law firm that specialized in corporate merger and compensation law. There were four partners with offices in New York City and London.

Howie and Beth had a son and daughter. They split their time between apartments in New York City's Manhattan and the Mayfair section of London.

Howie placed his workload aside during the summer months when the Detroit Tigers came to New York to play the Yankees. He and Steve spent considerable time together, although in growing up a New York Yankee baseball fan, Howie had to be careful who he cheered for at Yankee Stadium!

There were also coordinated trips to England between the Van Dyke and Carmichael families. They spent time with relatives in a peaceful London, well, as peaceful as an exciting London permitted.

Bob Courtney, the navigator of *Image of War* and *Pappy's Pack*, returned to Bangor, Maine, after being discharged from the military. He stayed for a short visit, packed his belongings and drove across the United States to Northern California.

Bob and his former partner in the nose of the B-17, Russ Parker, the bombardier from San Francisco, pooled their money, borrowed the rest, and purchased a working vineyard in California's Napa Valley from an elderly gentleman. The vineyard was near the Napa Valley town of Yountville. The purchase included the clause, which Howie had insisted upon since he and Steve were also investors, that the old gentleman remain as an employee and tutor the young entrepreneurs. The vineyard became quite successful. It produced a variety of high-quality wine.

Top turret gunner–flight engineer Jim McFarland, "Mac," decided to make a career of the military. He became Master Sergeant McFarland, stationed at Maguire Air Force Base in Wrightstown, New Jersey.

Radioman Eddie Anderson went home to Tioga, Texas, after he was discharged from the military. Eddie ran the family ranch. He also continued to be a ham radio operator and stayed in touch with his old B-17 crew members.

Left waist gunner Jack Kowalski, operated a successful plumbing business in the Chicago area. He expanded the family business to include a wholesale warehouse where independent plumbers purchased their supplies.

Joey DeMatteo returned to Philadelphia after the war and became a supervisor of maintenance for the Philadelphia Transportation Company, PTC. He lived in South Philly. Joey was also a private pilot and owned a former military Piper-Cub.

Willie Burnett moved back home to Seymour, Indiana. He continued to work for the John C. Grub Company, Jay C Supermarkets. Willie was a warehouse supervisor. Like other members of his old B-17 crew, he stayed in touch with all of his crew members.

Roger "Wyatt" Earp flew 19 missions over Japan in a B-29 Superfortress after healing from his B-17 wounds. He decided to make a career of the military rather than return to the rodeo circuit. Roger was a master sergeant, assigned to Edwards Air Force Base in California.

Vincent Campalone completed his missions, made it through the war safely and went back to work for Mighty Bread of Camden, New Jersey. Then he opened his own bakery in the town of Cherry Hill. The bakery was an immediate hit where it specialized in fresh-baked bread, cakes and "Philadelphia Cinnamon Buns," a Sunday favorite.

Carl Phillips, Howie's copilot, became the pilot and aircraft commander of *Pappy's Pack* and held the rank of captain when he was discharged from the military. He went home to Chaska, a suburb of Minneapolis, and became a pilot for Northwest Orient Airlines.

Pappy, also known as Chief Master Sergeant Walter O. Creamer, the crew chief, saw *Pappy's Pack* through over 125 missions and several additional flight crews. The "Ole Girl," as Pappy called her, remained in England and was put on exhibition as a B-17 museum airplane. Pappy remained in the military and served in the Pentagon, in Washington, D.C.

Andre Le Cacheux, one of so many of the Dutch and French Underground individuals who was so helpful to Steve, Paul Reens at the time, lived in Orbec, France, and became a supervisor at Le Fromagerie . . . the cheese factory.

Roger LeMelland, who so skillfully navigated the small sail fishing boat from the shore of Normandy across the open water of the Channel to England's Isle of Wight, came back to France as part of General Charles De Gaulle's Free French Army. Roger was involved with the D-Day invasion force. Afterward, he worked as a fisherman and owned a store in Valognes that specialized in fresh-caught fish. Much of his catch was sold to locals; however, some of it wound up on the table of expensive Paris restaurants.

Albert Leterrier, like Roger, fought with the Free French Army and was a combatant on D-Day, June 6, 1944. Albert became a businessman who traveled between Paris and London. He arranged his business schedule to coincide with Steve's trips across the "Pond" to England. Albert also visited Steve in Florida with his family.

Steve did not forget those who, from the time he was shot down in his B-17, helped him remain free from capture. He had Howie accompany him on a month-long tour of his journey to freedom. During the trip, in which they visited all of those who had helped, Steve more properly thanked those who risked their lives for him. He also received a big bear hug and his Hamilton watch from Horst.

Before I close, if you find yourself in the Netherlands, stop by the Netherlands American Military Cemetery. The location is in the village of Margraten, six miles east of Maastricht, just off Route 278. The cemetery and memorial are most impressive. You will be moved and glad that you visited with those who paid the ultimate sacrifice during World War II. While there, stroll out toward the American flagstaff. Over to the right, in plot O, row 6, grave 6, visit for a minute with Lieutenant Wright E. Gerke.

It is important that those who served their country not be forgotten. In Savannah, Georgia, the original home of the Eighth Air Force is where just off of Interstate 95, you can visit the Mighty Eighth Air Force Museum. Take a stroll through the Memorial Garden. On the right, near the back walls, there are two black granite plaques you might like to see. One is dedicated to pilot Lieutenant Wright E. Gerke, and below, a plaque to the crew and their plane.

Finally, while we followed the activities of the 305th Bomb Group of the Eighth Air Force, which operated out of England, by the end of the Second World War there were more than 40 heavy bombardment groups flying in the Eighth Air Force. They flew the B-17 Flying Fortress and the B-24 Liberator. There were also numerous Groups that flew the B-25 and B-26 twin-engine medium bombers. Let us not forget the escort fighter Groups, the "little friends," where the pilots flew in the cramped quarters of a P-38, P-47, or the P-51. It also took a lot to "keep them flying," so an additional hats off to the ground crews!

ACKNOWLEDGMENTS

After writing my first novel, *Not Just Another Love Story*, several years ago, I didn't know if I had a second novel in me. In my 40-year business career I have written many marketing and sales plans—and I enjoy writing—but where would the next story come from?

I am an associate member of the 305th Bomb Group (H) Memorial Association on behalf of my uncle and godfather, First Lieutenant Wright E. Gerke, a B-17 bomber pilot. Through his letters home to parents, brother and sisters, and my recollection of being with him, what could become a story, not his, kept running through my mind. However, to create and write the story was another matter.

The question I asked myself was how to get started. This would be a Second World War Army Air Corps project and I needed to make certain that it was a genuine account of what really happened during that period. Each place and plane would have to be historically correct and that meant a meaningful research program would have to be undertaken. I flew as a private pilot, but to understand how to fly a four-engine B-17 bomber and have those who flew the Flying Fortress feel comfortable about those written sections was important. I also felt the responsibility for you as the reader to enjoy the story and to understand that time in history.

Several trips that included visits to Scotland, England, and Europe were necessary for additional research. For nine years I was involved with the research and writing of this story. I wanted the reader to come along with the characters in the book, view the scenes of the story as though you were there, and take part in the adventure.

To that end, encouragement and assistance was needed in order to "get it right"! The encouragement over the years came from my wife, Ruth, who would bring a cup of tea while I was at the computer transferring and editing the handwritten word to the more modern way of writing. There was always great encouragement from our daughters, Karen and Susan, checking on their dad's progress with the manuscript. In addition, folks from our St. Pete Beach, Florida, International Sister-City, England's Isle of Wight town of Sandown, Heather Humby, M.B.E., plus Isle of Wight Counsil Chairman, Ian Ward, June Hall and her brothers, David and Terry, were always there for me, plus my dear friend Morris Barton, O.B.E., was always ready to assist.

As I have said, research was of utmost importance, especially for the feel of that particular time in history. The aforementioned historian Terry Hall, Isle of Wight, England, and David Hall provided me with extremely valuable United Kingdom information. My friend of more than 35 years, Graham Parker of Birmingham, England, joined in with most appreciated support and advice.

While attending the 305th Bomb Group (H) Memorial Association yearly reunions, I listened to the stories of the heroes from long ago, and make no mistake; those who serve their country are heroes, no matter which war. My gratitude goes to the men of the 305th who so generously shared their memories.

In certain situations, you need the expertise of someone who knows an area like a native. My nephew, Gary Glading, who owns a historic home in Normandy, France, provided me with important on-the-ground information and helped with understanding particular French words and phrases.

Special thanks go to my editor, Steve Traiman, who helped bring the manuscript into the final version. Steve's support and enthusiasm, plus his correcting of my punctuation and sentence structure were most appreciated and thanks to Spencer Lucas for his creative work on the photos and map. A thank you goes to friend and attorney John R. Phillips, Jr. for his help and encouragement.

Thanks go out to Ginger Marks, Publisher, DocUmeant Publishing, who believed in this project and great appreciation also goes to DocUmeant's Vice President Philip Marks, for bringing this book to you for your reading enjoyment.

Lastly Pepper, our little black mini-poodle, who waited patiently by my side as I wrote this book, and at times she demanded that we play. After losing our beloved Coco, Pepper is a chip off the ol' block and we are blessed.

As with my first novel, I would like to pass on a fragment of my philosophy that you might share with others: "Don't permit a bad day. Maybe you will have a bad hour or two, but don't allow anyone to ruin your day!"

Wayne

ABOUT THE AUTHOR

Wayne G. MacDowell was born in Woodbury, New Jersey and raised in the greater Philadelphia area. Undergraduate studies were accomplished at Louisiana State University, where he also played football and Rutgers University. His business career began in Philadelphia in the tea industry with Lipton and after being promoted to the corporate headquarters for a marketing position, more than 30 years were spent in the New York City area. Sales and Marketing Management continues where after 20 years with Lipton, Wayne joined Chock Full O'Nuts Coffee Company as Director of Sales and Marketing for their Private Label Division. His business experience permitted extensive travel crisscrossing the USA and as Wayne would say, "Name the city and I've probably been there!" In fact, a great portion of his first book, *Not Just Another Love Story* was written in airplanes, airports and hotels. During his business career in the tea and coffee industry, Wayne was, for years, on the Board of Directors for The Tea Association of the United States of America.

He elected to take an early retirement from the business world, although he continued to consult for the tea and coffee industry, in order to spend more time with his family and to pursue his love for both domestic and international travel. "London is always calling", states Wayne! He also regularly visits England's Isle of Wight, where as Chairman of the St Pete Beach, Florida International sister-City Program, he enjoys being with their Twin-City of Sandown, on this historical island. Many of the town's sister-city committee have become . . . "family". The trips across

"The Pond" always include side trips to visit friends in France, Holland and Italy. In St Pete Beach, Wayne co-chaired the St Pete Beach 50th Anniversary . . . a year-long string of fun events and activities. His committee met for 23 months of planning on behalf of the year-long programs . . . without one argument . . . everyone pulling their oars in the same direction and the climax was a weekend of fireworks off the beach, fun and games for the children and a dinner-dance where over 650 enjoyed a most special evening.   Wayne is also on the Board of the "Friends of St Pete Beach", the "Support Our Troops Program", A Life Member of the "Friends of the St Pete Beach Library", a member of the "Tampa Bay Beaches Chamber of Commerce", the "Veterans of South Pinellas County" and for many years, Wayne has been an Associate Member of the 305th Bomb Group (H) memorial Association on behalf of his Uncle-Godfather, 1st Lt. Wright E. Gerke.

As a member of the Florida Writers Association, Wayne has given writing seminars and helps aspiring writers, telling them not to get caught up in the "cookie cutter" writing theory, but to relax, create and enjoy writing. The new book, *Not Just Another War Story* is a meaningful true to life account of the action-packed U.S. Army Air Corps during a most difficult time in our history . . . World War II. It took 9 years of research and writing in order to "Get It Right" and Wayne worked hard to place you in a front row seat! Wayne continues to enjoy life in St Pete Beach, Florida where he makes time for the pleasures of boating, tennis, volunteer work, a relaxing walk on the beach and being with family and friends.

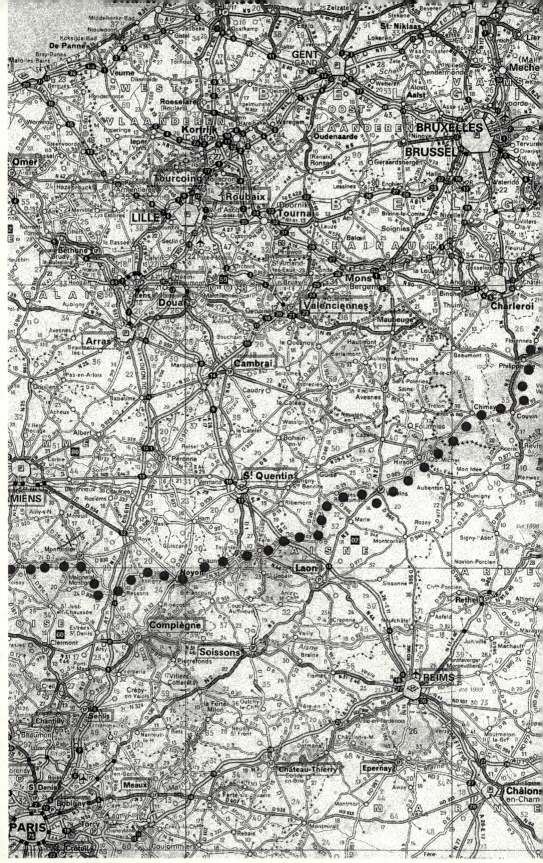

STEVE'S ESCAPE BEGINS
Margraten, Holland

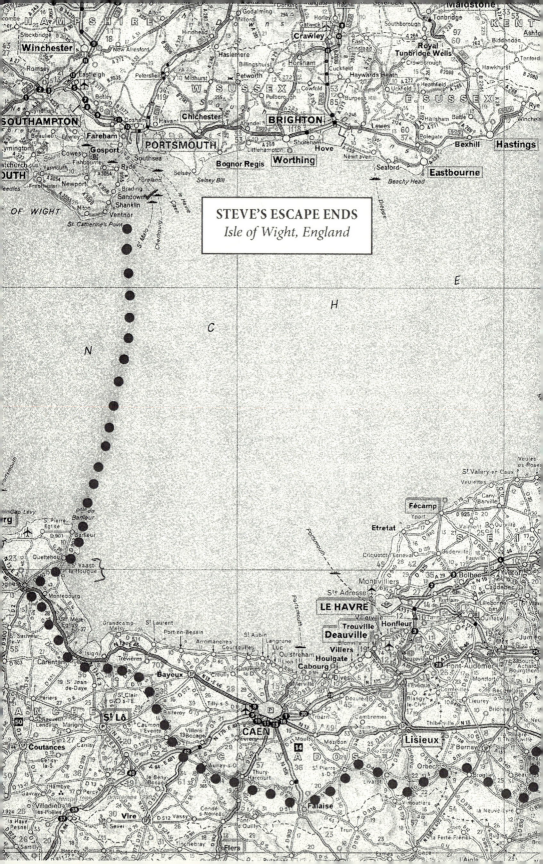

STEVE'S ESCAPE ENDS
Isle of Wight, England

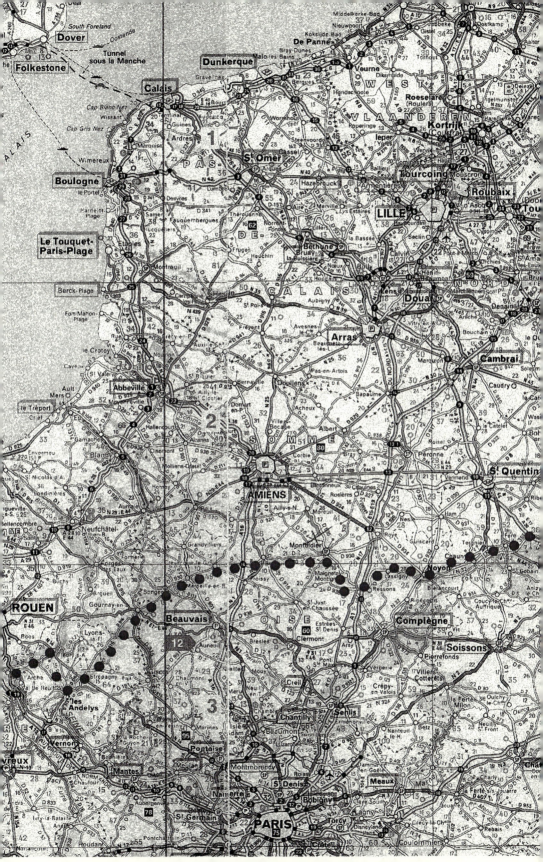

CPSIA information can be obtained at www.ICGtesting.com
Printed in the USA
LVOW07s0414040316

477767LV00001B/3/P